T0052378

RED UNICORN

BOOKS BY WESTON OCHSE

STANDALONE NOVELS

Scarecrow Gods

Blaze of Glory

Velvet Dogma

Babylon Smiles

Halfway House

Recalled to Life

Bone Chase

A Hole in the World

Aliens vs. Predators: Rift War

Red Unicorn

SEAL TEAM 666

SEAL Team 666

Border Dogs

Age of Blood

Reign of Evil

RED UNICORN

WESTON OCHSE

Red Unicorn by Weston Ochse
Copyright © 2022 by Weston Ochse
Published by arrangement with Aethon Books
Cover art by Fernando Granea.
Cover design by Steve Beaulieu

All rights reserved. This book or any portion
thereof may not be reproduced or used in any manner
whatsoever without the express written permission
of the publisher except for the use of brief quotations
in a book review.

The characters and events in this book are fictitious.
Any similarity to real persons, living or dead, is coincidental
and not intended by the author.

Printed in the United States of America

ISBN 979-8-200-95299-1
Fiction / Fantasy / General

Version 1

www.AethonBooks.com

"They had to work like Sisyphus against the constant forgetfulness of geography, because borders never remember themselves, even when you mark them down on black ink on paper."

—Paola Kaufmann, *The Lake*

INTRODUCTION

"When the Sect needs a new Invunche, the Council of the Cave orders a Member to steal a boy child from six months to a year old, if possible. The Deformer, a permanent resident of the Cave, starts work at once. He disjoints the arms and legs and the hands and feet. Then begins the delicate task of altering the position of the head. Day after day, and for hours at a stretch, he twists the head with a tourniquet until it has rotated through an angle of 180 degrees until the child can look straight down the line of its own vertebrae. There remains one last operation, for which another specialist is needed. At full moon, the child is laid on a work-bench, lashed down with its head covered in a bag. The specialist cuts a deep incision under the right shoulder blade. Into the hole he inserts the right arm and sews up the wound with thread taken from the neck of an ewe. When it has healed the Invunche is complete."

—*Testimony of Mateo Coñuecar, 1880* as written by Bruce Chatwin in *In Patagonia*

CHAPTER 1

BUENOS AIRES

MAY 1982

The blow came swift and hard and left roaring in his ears. The roaring continued, coming from above and outside the basement casements like water escaped from a collapsed dam. Hundreds of voices attached to double hundreds of feet, shuffling and tripping on the other side of the thick leaden windows as everyone tried to shove their way past the building and into the presidential square three blocks away. The laconic evening of *plein air* dinners and coffee and wine had been shattered by the rioters as one after the other shouted to everyone to join them on the way to a virtual lynching. What had begun as a hopeful campaign to reclaim the Falkland Islands from British imperialism was looking more and more like a lost cause, despite the promises of a swift victory from Generals Galtieri and Anaya.

Roaring outside.

Roaring inside.

The world was a dying lion.

At least Argentina wished it so.

Inside the bricked room of the sub-basement, the winds of war were slightly more hushed.

Eyes bored into one man at the table, face mauled, eyes blackened. Red spread in a thick pool on the wood, catching the imperfect seams between the boards and running with gravity until each rivulet was its own crimson waterfall. Both the man's hands remained gripping the wooden edge, squeezing all the harder so he wouldn't fall—so he wouldn't retaliate. He couldn't. He needed to take what they had to give or else his would be a far worse ending even than Argentina at the hands of a more sophisticated and modern British military. Still, giving the men the satisfaction of his pain was taking everything he could muster. Even now, his nose throbbed with the insult of being broken yet again.

His left arm pulsed, but not from any new grievance. What had been done derived almost back to when he was five or six; the right arm, broken in three places, twisted, and the left arm broken in two places, twisted as well, only to later have to be broken again and corrected with bolts and screws and more than a few prayers. Had the US Army known of the wound, they never would have allowed him to go to Vietnam. The success in healing was a testament to those who had spent their life attempting to do such things.

His assaulter leaned back in his chair and wiped his right fist with a handkerchief. Clearly pleased with himself. The man's diligence in removing blood from around smooth aristocratic knuckles and half a dozen gold and silver rings was infuriating.

Amboy surveyed the room through heavy-lidded eyes, careful not to move his head. Six. Five standing. One sitting. Of the five standing, he'd worked with two at a mine high up in the mountains. The other three looked like local street thugs, each dressed a little too proper, unless you looked closely at the threadbare knockoffs, probably imported instead of the classic London-made doffs Matias favored.

His adversary dropped the handkerchief on the table, stretched his hand several times to work out a kink from where he'd struck Amboy in the face, then plucked the cheroot from where it had been balanced on the edge of the table. "Your account has come due, Señor Stevens." He took a deep inhalation and stared at Amboy through the swirl of smoke.

Amboy had felt the end coming the last few years but had managed to keep his head down. With the rise and fall of the Peronists, he'd been able to blend into the background as Argentinians sought to ruin one another. He'd been just another American come down to make his fortune in the mines of South America. That he'd come straight from Vietnam was unknown to most of them. That he hadn't been back to America in all of this time was none of their business. But that he wasn't an Argentinian citizen and that he was an American was their business and it was this business that had caused him to be hauled from the bar he'd been drinking in to this basement where they'd promised to cut him if he didn't pay them what was required.

As if he could make up for Argentina's military junta's belief in their martial ability.

As if he could make up for Reagan's last-minute refusal to lend them aid.

As if he could make up for Argentina's feeling of being Europe's second class cousin.

"You know I don't have it, Matias." He kept his hands on the table, but sorely wanted to cradle his broken nose and to wipe the blood now pouring down the front of his shirt. "We had a deal. You said after my next job."

"There is no next job. Can't you hear the people outside? They are angry."

Amboy laughed, blood bubbling through his nose. "This is Argentina. People are always angry."

Matias flipped ash onto the ground and chuckled. "One might think you are Argentine. One might think you are a local. But do you know how they know you cannot be?"

"How?" Amboy asked, not really caring for the answer, but knowing that as long as they were talking, no one was hitting him.

"Because you don't care. You don't care about your friends. You don't care about the mines. You don't care about Argentina or what goes on around you. It's in your eyes. There is no fire there, *Boludo!* Every part of you lacks fire. You just live and live, but you don't live. *Che, ¡no te hagás el boludo!*"

Amboy looked down at his hands. He released the table and noticed the others in the room stand a little straighter. Even as he spoke, he could feel his words return to his Tennessee mountain roots as the words elongated and the vowels sang. "Nothing is wrong with me, Matias. This is who I am. True, I am not Argentine, but I have been a friend to Argentina for seven years."

"Then why are you not part of the revolution?" Matias countered.

Amboy laughed. "*¡Politicos este quilombo, boludo!* You are always in revolution. If there was no more politics, you'd have a revolution about tomatoes in the market."

Matias checked through a haze of smoke. "*La posta. La posta.* You speak true." He glanced at the others in the room. "*Sal de aqui.*" When they didn't move, his left hand shot towards the stairs to the main floor and pointed. "*Sal de aqui*!"

They hustled to leave, the last man, a scar across the top of his nose, paused at the bottom of the steps.

"Are you sure boss?" he asked in Spanish.

"Yes," Matias said with impatience. "Get out. I got this."

Amboy watched as the last man left them in the basement alone, then turned his attention back to Matias. He'd first met the man several years ago during a mine strike. At first, Matias had represented the owners, but then when the money ran out, he switched his allegiance and sided with the miners, fashioning himself as a more well-dressed and Oxford-educated Che Guevara. Matias was a revolutionary the same way that Ronald Reagan was a Republican—if he could make it work to his benefit, he would.

"So, what's this really about?" Amboy asked.

"Don't you feel like you need to pay me back the money you owe?"

"Money has never mattered to you. It's always been about leverage." Amboy raised a hand and scissored two fingers. Matias handed him the cigarette, Amboy took a deep drag, then returned it. He leaned back and exhaled a cloud dark enough to hide his face for a brief moment. "Money is the grease you use for the wheels of your own enterprise."

Matias clapped his hands together. "Can I steal that? *Este beuno, che*?"

Amboy flipped his hand, then cradled his nose. He scrunched his face to get everything back in place and shook his head. "Did you really have to break it?"

"Some people have a trick knee," Matias said. "As you once explained, you have a trick nose. It will break at even the slightest punch." He handed Amboy a silk handkerchief. "I made sure not to hit you hard."

"That wasn't what I meant when I said trick nose. Also, I wouldn't call that the slightest punch," Amboy said. But Matias was right. He'd had his nose broken so many times. From fights growing up on Signal Mountain, Tennessee, to fights in the Army, to fights in the mines, he'd always come away with a broken nose, regardless of whether he won the fight or not. It was as if all of his bones were those of a winner with one exception.

"*Che boludo.* Let's get down to business, *che*?"

Amboy nodded.

"There's this girl," Matias began.

"Isn't there always?" Amboy asked. He dabbed at his nostrils, trying to remove the blood.

"*La posta. Un pelo de la concha tira mas que una yunta de bueyes.* But this one is different. She's in trouble."

"You want me to save this girl? You should have led with that, Matias. We didn't need all this drama. You didn't need to use me as a punching bag."

"Not *save* exactly, *che."* Matias stared as both of his hands in a motion that Amboy recognized as being reflective. "I want you to help her, yes, but I also want to know what's going on."

"I don't get it. There's some mystery girl who needs help and you want me to help her but you also want me to let you know what's going on." Amboy rolled his eyes. "Never mind. I understand completely. Who is this girl?"

"Una Americana. She's come back from Patagonia but her mind is gone. How do you say?'

"Loca?"

Matias shook his head. "Her memory, it is—what is the word?"

"Amnesia? Does she have amnesia?"

"Some of it. Not all of it. She knows her name and remembers some things, but others are gone in the wind," Matias said, blowing across the tops of his fingers. "We'd like to know when she remembers more. What she remembers."

"Who is we?" Amboy asked.

Matias shook his head. "Too much information. I cannot tell you."

Amboy sighed in exasperation. He was so tired of politics. Why did it have to be such a part of the universe? Everywhere he went people had ideas how other people should act and what information they should have. "I still don't know what it has to do with me," Amboy said.

"Look at your hand," Matias said, his smile growing. "Look at both of your hands. What do you see?"

Amboy flexed his right hand. Knuckles bunched from punching and too much manual labor. He'd have terrible arthritis when he grew older. Both hands were ringless. Two of his nails were dirty. He cursed inwardly. If there was one thing his grandmother hated, it was a man with dirty fingernails. He'd spent days of his life at the faucet making sure that his hands were that perfect new-born pink she wanted, never mind the mine filth covering the rest of him. But whatever he was supposed to see, he didn't get what Matias wanted.

"What about them?" he asked.

"You're joking, *che.*"

"I'm not. I'm just tired. I'm hurt. I want a drink and a shower."

"*Che boludo*, do I have to explain everything? Count your fingers, Amboy."

Oh. That.

From his earliest memory his family had been different. On the mountain and in the mines, or helping with Pappy's copper still it hadn't been an issue, but then the first day in basic training he'd discovered how different he really was. His fights began in earnest then as his fellow recruits found in him a target for all of their fears, just because he had six fingers on each hand. Like it meant anything. It was just an accident of nature. Nothing more. It wasn't even a big deal. Everyone else had five digits. He had six. He did think it helped him in the mine, his ability to grab, hold, bend, but such a narrow achievement was hardly worth all of the hell he'd dealt with his entire life because of it. When he'd disappeared for six months, he'd hoped to return normal. But they only broke his arms, leaving each digit as a flip-fingered insult.

"What's that have to do with—" Amboy noticed the grin on Matias' face and knew immediately. "Her too?" Amboy breathed through his mouth as he thought about it. "You don't say." He wondered what she was like. "And you say she has amnesia? Did she get into trouble?"

"We think so. I just need to keep apprised of what's going on. There are—how you say—interested parties."

"Who are the interested parties?" Amboy asked. "I need to know what I'm up against."

"You keep asking but I keep telling you I can't tell you."

"Matias, when have you been so cryptic? You love it when you are able to show information. You enjoy being able to demonstrate how smart you are." Amboy grinned. "*Che boludo.*"

"You want to know what kind of people are interested?" Matias sighed. "The kind with three letters to their name. The American kind."

Interested parties. Three letters to their name. It didn't take a genius to figure out he was talking about the CIA. It certainly wasn't the Food and Drug Administration."

"Do you know what they want with her?" he asked.

Matias shook his head. "They just want her safe for now. They'll be in contact later."

The CIA wanted the girl?

A six-fingered girl?

Somehow, he felt that there was more going on than Matias was letting on, so he nodded, and said yes, he'd help her if they came to him.

Matias assured him they would, then left him alone in the basement with his throbbing nose and his mind filled with memories of fighting off a five-fingered world who'd somehow found insult with a poor mountain kid born with more fingers than them, as if that would make him rich or famous or someone anyone would ever want to become.

CHAPTER 2

The next morning, Amboy woke to a blood-stained pillow case. Light filtered through the curtains, catching various parts of his small single room flat in stabs of brightness. A three-drawer dresser. A small card table with a repaired leg. A single rattan chair. His narrow bed, only slightly wider and more comfortable than a military cot. The walls were once a brown wall paper whose design had disappeared over the life of too many cigarettes and cigars. The single picture on the wall had been gifted to him by the proprietress and was a poster of Uncle Sam shaking hands with Peron with the Andes in the background. Everything about the room looked as if it had been old and broken when it was made.

Amboy pushed himself out of bed, left the room, locked the door with the key around his neck, and slumped down the hall. One of his neighbors exited the single bathroom as he approached, neither man making eye contact nor sharing a grunt of acknowledgement. Inside, he appraised his nose. Not bad really for the damage that had been done. He touched it tentatively with his hands. It didn't hurt right away, so he flattened his palms, pressed his forefingers to the base of his nose and pressed vigorously and the cartilage *snicked* into place.

He blew his nose several painful times, the crust of last night's abuse filling the tissue with black bloody mucus. When his face was clean, he decided it wasn't the worst he'd ever looked. He wore his bruises racooned around his brown eyes. His forehead was scarred from an old barbed wire accident. His blond hair needed cutting and was longer than his usual high and tight flat-top that he'd worn ever since he'd joined the army back in 1971.

One thing for sure was he wasn't going to win any beauty contests. Not that he'd been hit too many times with the ugly stick growing up, just there wasn't anything special about him. He was who he was, a three-time veteran of the Vietnam War whose only real skill was to work a mine.

Just as he finished brushing his teeth, someone banged on the door.

He hollered for it to stop, but the banging continued unabated.

Grabbing his towel and his toiletries, he shouldered the door open, catching the old German from down the hall on the shoulder and almost knocking him to the ground. The man sputtered as he fumbled not to drop his own toiletries, his eyes and mouth wide as if they could help the precarious balance. Still, a comb and a metal bowl for shaving clattered to the floor at the man's feet.

The German always reminded Amboy of the guard from *Hogan's Heroes*. Only, this one wasn't as pleasant and didn't have a molecule that could have been endearing. His constant countenance was one of carefully controlled disgust bordering on rage. It was this fire Amboy liked to stoke.

"Sorry about that, Schultz. I didn't see you there," Amboy said, stepping past.

By the time he was back in his room, the door to the bathroom had slammed, diminishing the slew of German curse words being machine gunned his direction. But he ignored the results of his usual game of *Mess with the German* and all that entailed. Instead, he stared at the envelope that was now sitting in the middle of his made bed. He blinked. The bed hadn't been made. Which meant someone not only taken the time to make his bed, but they also left him a note. He didn't know which one was stranger.

Amboy rushed to the window and looked out. Plenty of folks were going to and fro, but no one looked up. It could have been anyone. A man in a tan suit and a Panama hat exited the building and glanced up at Amboy, but then looked down the street. Amboy was about to yell something, but then a woman in a dress and white hat sidled up to the man and they left, making him doubt the man was could have been the sort to make a stranger's bed and leave a note. Which meant, whoever had been in his room might still be in the building. He hurriedly went and locked the door, then checked the closet and under the bed. Other than those two places, there was nowhere to hide in his room.

He threw his toiletries and towel on top of the dresser and sat heavily in the chair, staring at the envelope as if it might be a coiled snake. Whatever was in there couldn't be good. He was sure it wasn't a love note. It didn't take a genius to realize that it was probably from Matias and had to do with the young woman he was supposed to help.

So, why then all the skullduggery?

When he finally went over and read the note, he found it was far from salacious and contained no more than an address in District 9 of the city. *Mataderos* neighborhood, where the city met country and named after the cattle market that had been there for generations. He recognized the Los Perales address and knew it for the huge public housing tract known as Bario Los Perales, which looked more like it was built in Russia or Nazi Germany than anything else.

Comprised of dozens of long three-story white buildings that looked like naval gunships placed in rows, they revolved around a communal living idea proposed by Peron. Amboy's friends at the mines had laughed at the idea when it had been promoted in the newspapers as the modern solution to Argentinian urban living, most of them from some rural upbringing where the chickens outnumbered the people at least twenty to one. Instead of Peron's arrangement of individual chalets or California bungalows built around a church in the middle, Bario Los Perales eschewed the church and was built around soccer fields, playgrounds, meeting halls, and an Olympic-sized swimming pool.

Amboy had been there once after a friend of his had died in a tunnel collapse in El Quemado. He'd brought the death letter, the one all of them were told to write by the foreman before they could even start the job. With upwards of twenty-five percent casualties in the mine, it was the idea that even in death, someone's mother or father should know how much they were loved. In Amboy's case, he wrote a letter to a fictitious mother, since his had long ago died, just to please the foreman. In the case of Santiago, Amboy had been paid an extra week's wage to deliver the letter, which he did over a howling and terribly emotional three hours with the young man's grandmother and younger brother.

He shook his head to get the memory gone.

He pulled a pair of pants and a shirt from the closet. There were two ways to dress in Buenos Aires. One way was like a tourist, wearing jeans or pants and shirts with graffiti on them, or even polos. The other was the old way and would get him more traction even though he was a gringo. When he was finally marching down the stairs, he wore brown wingtips, a tan suit with a light blue shirt open at the collar, and a wide-brimmed off-white Panama hat. He had less than six hundred pesos and twenty dollars to his name. Based on the exchange rate, he had another $145 dollars or thereabouts. He hoped that his favor to Matias wasn't going to cost more than that, or he'd be in debt all over again.

Instead of a taxi, he took a series of buses until he was overheated and ready for something cooler. It was May and the end of autumn, the seasons reversed from what he'd grown up with because of the country's location south of the equator. Normally the temperature would be hovering around sixty degrees, but today it was in the eighties, and with the press of his fellow humanity, he felt hotter than he should be. He found a bar near his destination and drank two Quilmes in as many minutes. He liked them because they tasted like the American beer he hadn't had since Vietnam.

All the way to Mataderos and outside Bario Los Perales, protestors clogged the streets, many of them holding up newspapers and shaking them with rage. Last night the English had destroyed Argentina's only warship—the *General Belgrano*—and no one knew how many of the thousand-man crew had survived. Still, the outrage didn't subside, which was one reason he dressed and acted like a local as much as he could. The last thing he needed was being mistaken for an Englishman. Being American was bad enough. Reagan had all but promised to back up the Peron Regime, but in the last minutes had pulled out, according to what Amboy read in the trades.

Sadly, he didn't really care. He didn't know whether it was his mountain upbringing and being so isolated, but he'd never really felt part of a larger institution. Being American was just that. He didn't need all the red white and blue, and Star Spangled Banner hoopla that went along with it. The same with his

Argentine friends. He could clinically understand their anger, but he never saw how it would help.

Now that he'd bolstered himself and was pretty certain he hadn't been followed, he headed to the address. It took him a moment to suss out the way the buildings were numbered, but once he did, it took almost no time to figure out where the apartment was. The place looked familiar from when he'd come several years ago to deliver Santiago's letter to his mother. The memory of it made him remember the ready smile of his friend and the heartbroken moans of his grandmother.

He'd been checking his six for most of the morning and finally noticed that the woman in the dress behind him seemed to be the same one he'd seen on the bus. She looked more German than she did Argentine, but then there were a lot of Europeans in the country. What she wanted with him, he had no idea, but he didn't have time for it. He intentionally strode by his target building and took the sidewalk to go around it. No sooner had he turned the corner, then he spied a man in a white linen suit. He was glancing at a pocket watch, but then seemed to look up as Amboy stopped in his tracks.

Their eyes met and the man's eyes widened.

Amboy ran.

He had no direction, just away from the man in the white suit. He also looked German, but his features were softened by something else—something local.

Behind was the woman and in front was the man, so Amboy took a hard right and sprinted to the nearest building. They only had doors on the side with two staircase towers on either end. He ran up one until he hit the third floor and then realized his mistake. There was no way down. While the man raced up behind him, the woman stood at the base of the building, her hand inside of her purse, undoubtedly on a pistol.

Amboy stood between the staircases feeling like a complete idiot. How had he survived Vietnam again? Oh yeah. They didn't have staircases. He spun as the man leaped out of the staircase, his hands out as if to grapple.

"Vos ist los?" Amboy asked, imitating his best German.

"Dos Madchen," the other man said breathlessly. *"Wo ist?"*

Amboy shook his head and grinned. "I'd tell you, but I don't speak German."

The door behind him rattled and an older man exited, carrying a paper bag filled with garbage. He looked like someone's abuela, deep in concentration, probably about today's news and what was happening to his country's army. He probably expected to take the garbage out and go to a local coffee house and hash it out with his fellows, each of them fist-pounding at events, promising that if they were younger the fate of their nation would be a different one indeed.

What he hadn't counted on was Amboy, who grabbed the bag, threw it in the German's face, then ran into the man's apartment. Before anyone could even utter a protest, Amboy had the door double locked and was searching through the home for another way out, hoping no one else was in the apartment. The inside smelled like cigars, coffee and something sweet. The walls were soot-layered and the furniture all had light brown doilies atop them that had once been most assuredly white.

One bedroom.

One bathroom.

One living room.

One kitchen.

One picture of an older woman above the dining room table.

One place setting at the table.

One story told every day.

Banging on the door spurred him on. He searched the ceiling. The apartment backed onto another, so there was no getting through there unless he could break through a wall. Nor could he break through the walls to the neighbors left and right. But there was a chance that some or even all of the apartments on the third floor had access to the roof. After all, how else would one get up to the top?

Then he saw it inside a utility closet.

An access panel.

But was it electric or was it to the roof?

Amboy grabbed a broom and slammed the wooden handle against the access panel three times until the haft broke. He tossed it away in disgust, but it had dislodged the wood enough for him to see daylight. He pushed through and scrambled atop the hot water heater, slipping twice as his slick-soled wingtips failed to get any grip, then heaved himself onto the roof. At the last moment, he saw his Panama hat fluttering to the ground inside the apartment like an immense dented and abused butterfly.

He didn't dally, however, and after finding his feet on the white-painted flat roof, he ran towards the other side. He saw several access panels that he might be able to pry loose. They opened upwards, so kicking them in wasn't an option. But he knew by the sounds of the German curses behind him that he had little time to figure it out. Instead, he went to the edge of the roof and without peering down, got down on his knees, grabbed the lip with white-knuckled hands, and swung his body out. He dangled for several moments until he figured out what to do, then with a kip, he propelled his body out, so it could gain momentum, and cleared the railing. He landed in the outside third-floor hallway, barely avoiding slamming his head into the wall.

He didn't dare waste a moment looking up. Instead, he chose a set of stairs and avalanched down them, his feet barely keeping up with his need for speed. With both hands on the rails, he propelled himself down to the first floor and hit the ground running, just as the woman rounded the corner. He only saw her out of the corner of his eye, but her hand was still in the purse, perhaps unwilling to identify herself with a pistol in hand in such a public space.

Two young couples walking and talking animatedly together were directly in his path. He veered only to see a mother and her baby on a blanket. He leaped over them before she could scream and went crashing to the ground. All of the air left him. His suit was stained with grass and dirt. He heaved himself to his feet and broke into a running limp around the next apartment building, and to the one on the other side. His feet seemed to know where they were going before he did, because when he arrived at a second-floor door and found himself banging on it, he wasn't even sure why, until the door opened and the face of an old woman broke into a sad smile.

He pushed himself in, apologizing profusely, then closed the door behind him, locking it, and placing his back to it.

Her wide eyes narrowed, as she moved more swiftly than her size would lead one to believe towards the window. She called into the home and a young man about sixteen came out. Amboy recognized him as Santiago's brother, Thiago. He was a few inches shorter than Amboy, but thicker in the chest and arms as if he'd spent time as a butcher's apprentice or some other hard labor demanding upper muscles. His grandmother rattled off commands. Ordering the young man to go outside and see what was going, and then, once he was out the door and it was again locked, she turned to Amboy.

"Te gustaria te o café?" she asked, her voice neutral.

Amboy grinned, offered an apologetic smile and said, *"Café, por favor, abuela."*

He sat and allowed his breathing to become normal as the abuela puttered around the kitchen, a perfect domestic salve to his recent racing terror. He kept glancing towards the door. How had they known he would be here?

And why all the interest?

He held out his six fingered hand before him and shook his head. It was just a hand. They were just digits. They didn't mean a damn thing.

Abuela provided a demitasse of coffee and pushed his hand down. "*Esconde tus dedos. De los hijos de gigantes.*"

"Hide your fingers," she said. "They are from the sons of giants."

CHAPTER 3

Thiago came in after Amboy had finished one coffee and was drinking another. All through the waiting, Santiago's abuela stared at him, her eyes pleasant, but her mouth firm. He couldn't discern whether she was mad at him for disturbing her urbane peace or for reminding her of her grandson, because although her eyes promised cakes and pastries, her mouth was a road grater he didn't want to get near.

The delicate painted demitasse cups were like tiny cherubs in her gnarled arthritic hands. He'd seen hands before like this on his fellow mine workers, most decades younger than her. But he knew it hurt. It hurt to hold things; to grab things; even to breathe. So, perhaps that was the reason for her mien. Whatever it was, when Thiago came in, Amboy stood, setting his cup down carefully in its saucer.

"What'd you find?" Amboy asked.

"Two. A man and a woman," Thiago replied, his accent just noticeable. "Looking. Asking for a gringo with white hair and black eyes," he said the last using his hands over his own eyes.

"And?"

Abuela had had enough. She chopped the conversation silent. She wanted to be told. So, Amboy listened to Thiago tell his grandmother about the man and woman who were looking for him. They offered money for any information, but he assured his grandmother that no one would say anything. Then the grandmother went over to the phone and called, clearly establishing the abuela network. Amboy listened for several moments as she rattled off orders like a military general.

Thiago took the moment to exchange greetings and they hugged one another.

"How have you been?" Amboy asked the younger man as they both sat around the kitchen table, careful to leave abuela's place free.

"We've been fine. The mine pays monthly for her son. Abuela gets a service pension from her husband as well. I've been helping out where you can."

"What about you? I thought maybe you'd be in the army?" Amboy asked.

Anger flashed in Thiago's eyes. "I wanted to join, but abuela forbid. My friends joined. Three of them were on the ship. Did you hear?"

"I heard. An English submarine said the newspaper."

Thiago spit air onto the floor. "Cowards. Afraid to fight like a man. They stabbed us in the back." He lowered his head and glared at Amboy. "Just as America stabbed us in the back. We thought you were friends."

Amboy put up both of his hands. "Whoa. I don't do politics. I am myself. You can trust me not to stab you in the back."

Thiago's expression softened. He had the lips of a woman, full and red, but beneath chiseled cheeks and a knife-blade nose; no one would ever think of him as feminine. "I'm sorry. You are a friend of the family. I become overwhelmed sometimes.

Emotion. It is both a gift and a curse for us Argentines." He paused to listen to his abuela a moment, the grinned. "The Abuela Mafia. You don't want to get on their bad side."

Amboy thought back to his time in the Tennessee mountains and knew how it could be true. The mountain grapevine was almost faster than the telephone. If someone saw you do something, there was no way that someone on the other side of the mountain wouldn't know about it before you were able to tell them. Add the imperator of an angry abuela and it made a Mafia.

"What was it you were doing here?" Thiago asked.

"A messenger of sorts. I have a friend who asked me to look in on a girl—an American—who might be in trouble."

Thiago shot a look at his abuela. "And who is this girl?"

Amboy shook his head. "I don't have a name. All I have is an address." He shuffled it out of his pocket and passed it over.

Thiago took one look, folded the paper and passed it back. "This is not your business, my friend." His voice was firm and resolute. He glanced at Amboy and added, "I know you think it is, but it isn't. Please, do not get involved."

Instead of launching into defense mode, Amboy sat back in his chair and regarded Thiago. He'd never known the boy as anything other than a petulant hero-worshipping little brother of his best friend, but now Thiago carried himself differently. Even at sixteen, he was now the notional head of the house. With no padre and no hermano, no madre and no hermana, he was in charge. Amboy could deal with that. But could he deal with the young man telling him what he could and couldn't do in the face of Matias and his threats? Given the choice of his best friend's family or Matias and his gang, he'd always choose Santiago's familia. Matias he could deal with if he needed to. Still, something bothered him and he didn't want to let it go just rest.

"Thiago," Amboy said softly.

The young man raised one scarred eyebrow.

"Why did you say what you said?"

"What was it I said?" Thiago whispered.

"You said that you know I think it's my business but it isn't. Why do you think I think it's my business?"

Thiago glanced at his abuela and Amboy followed his gaze and watched the old woman, gray shawl over her shoulders, tread carefully into the kitchen, using the walls for balance, and return with two cold unlabeled beers, probably brewed by one of the building's occupants for the luxury of the residents. Each had already been opened and she placed one in front of each of the men. Instead of joining them, she went to the cramped living room and watched the demonstrations silently on the thirteen-inch black and white television screen.

"It's pretty obvious. Are you telling me that you don't even know who you are getting?"

Amboy shrugged. "I don't know. I'm paying off a debt. All I've been told is that the girl or young woman or whoever she is has the same type of hands that I do." He held up a hand and wangled six fingers. "Something like this."

"You know what that means, yes?" Thiago asked.

Abuela asked Thiago to shush, but he ignored her.

"These fingers of yours aren't just fingers. They are a—"

Abuela cursed her grandson in a stertorous baritone.

"No, Abuela. He needs to know. He was Santiago's friend. He doesn't understand any of this." He shook his head furiously as he stood. But before he could say anything, there was a knock at the door.

Thiago's eyes went wide as he glared at the door.

"You better wait in the other room," he said without turning.

"I don't want to get you in trouble," Amboy said. "Maybe I should—"

"I'm afraid it's too late for that," Thiago said. But he reached out and squeezed Amboy's hand. "It will be alright. I will make this work." He nodded towards the bedroom. "Go. I will handle this."

Amboy slid into the other room. There was no way to look out the doorway without being seen, so he pushed himself against the wall beside it and listened.

The door opened and many feet shuffled inside. He heard subdued greetings, followed by the clink of cups. One couldn't have guests in an Argentine household without offering and accepting whatever was at hand. Voices rose for a moment, but they were so fast and on top of each other that Amboy couldn't understand. He'd learned enough Argentine Spanish to get by, certainly more than most gringos. But most people in positions he came into contact with spoke English or a smattering of German, which had become an unofficial second language in parts of Argentina after World War II with the influx of Germans, some reportedly former Nazis. *Rioplatense* dialect was the official Spanish, but many also spoke *Cuyo*, *Cordobes*, *Andean*, and *Paraguayan* dialects, depending on their geological location or origination. Even when speaking official Argentine Spanish, regionalisms slipped into conversations and Amboy often found himself not knowing what was going on in even normal situations.

He could almost feel the people through his back on the other side of the wall as they sat on the couch and the chairs surrounding the television. Maybe some were even sitting at the table. From the air he felt more exhalations than just a few people, which was a talent he'd learned in the close quarters and air-questionable mines. Down a dark thousand feet with nothing but wooden beams to keep the walls and ceilings from collapsing, one derives the ability detect people by their compression of air and their breaths, often by breathing the same rare oxygen. He felt like that now, here in the relative safety of Santiago's family's apartment in the weirdly modern Bario Los Perales.

He closed his eyes and tried to find a breath to match his. One to latch onto, so if he might become lost, he could follow. He breathed in and out. In and out. There were many. He tasted the coffee and the cream in the air. The aroma of old cooking, grease caught in the fabric of the furniture. The acrid smell of medicine from the bathroom, such things an old woman might need to sustain a life. He felt the cold chill of the old. He felt the warm wind of the young, perhaps Thiago. But there was one other. Another breath filled with warmth, but different, spiced, no, not spiced. It tasted almost alien in that it wasn't like any of the others, but then it also felt comforting, like something he knew, something he'd tasted before.

He mentally leaned into the breath and tried to discern more.

He'd done it before when in the dark of the mines, guessing who might be around him as he waited for the lift to bring them topside, each of them with their headlamps off to preserve energy in the event the worst happened. But he'd known them in advance before. He knew what they ate and drank so it was like cheating. Like Jose who always smelled of cinnamon or Santini and his onions. Then there was Tomas whose breath was already failing, his lungs dying a little more with each trip beneath the earth, rattling even as he stood in the stillness of the dark.

So, this one was definitely going to be a—

"Amboy. It's time."

He opened his eyes. Thiago stood there, frowning.

Amboy looked past him to the doorway. "Will you tell me what's going on, now?" Amboy asked.

"You'll see soon enough."

Amboy went to move, but Thiago stopped him with a hand

in his chest. He might have been a younger man, but there was an iron-strength to his arms.

"I want you to be sure," Thiago said.

"I'm sure. Let me—"

"No!" Thiago pushed him firmly back, glanced towards the door, then more softly said, "No. You need to be sure. If you start this, you must finish. *Che*. This is serious."

"Start what? I didn't start anything. It was they who chased me."

Thiago continued to stare firmly. "You won't be allowed to quit. You'll have to see it to the end regardless."

Amboy shook his head. "Listen. This is all a mistake. I just got an address and was trying to track it down."

He went to move, but Thiago held him tightly. To disengage would mean a fight and he wasn't sure if he had the stomach to fight the brother of a dead friend.

"This is bigger than an address," Thiago said. "This is bigger than any of us.'

"Why the drama, Thiago? I think too many are making something out of nothing." Then he remembered Matias mentioning that the CIA was involved and, of course, some unknown Germans. What was this thing Matias had set in motion?

Thiago shook his head. "If you go in the other room you agree to stay with it until the end. You are right in that she needs help. She's been marked by some powerful people. She's been all alone until recently when she came into the custody of one of abuela's friends."

Came into the custody? Such an odd turn of phrase. "Who is she?"

"Her name is Lettie Fennick and she was taken and held hostage until recently."

Amboy nodded and licked his lips. "Is she safe? Is she well?"

"She's safe as can be at the moment. She doesn't know all that has happened to her and we won't tell her. She's well as can be. But she is fighting us every step of the way." He grinned morosely. "It's ironic that someone like you might make her come around."

"Someone like me? I'll let that drop. What does that mean she was held hostage? Are you saying that she doesn't know what's best for her?" He remembered the mysterious alien breath and knew it was hers.

"There are powers at work that you do not understand."

"And you do?"

Thiago shook his head and smiled grimly. "I'm half your age, but in this I know more than you."

"Don't be so sure."

"I am sure. You in your American clothes from your American way of life with all of your television. I want my MTV is what everyone says. We hear it here and laugh about your fake astronaut planting the MTV sign on the moon. Your kind is spoiled. You are from a new world and we are still part of the old. You don't understand what happens in the shadows and in the dark places. Not anymore. Not in America."

Amboy had been raised near a Roman Catholic monastery which sat in one of the more civilized corners of Signal Mountain. Once a turn of the 19th century grand hotel, the mansion had been turned into a nursing home with a community of Brothers attached. When he'd been young, Amboy had conversations with many of the brothers who lived and worked there, if only to increase his understanding of the greater world. He remembered one brother named Roy, who had been more than willing to spend time with a hapless barefooted mountain kid with little schooling.

Thiago's mention of the shadows and the dark places made him remember Brother Roy's words and how he'd tried to explain to him the idea of *frontiers.*

"There are boundaries between things. Boundaries between places. When you're on one you can see the world as it truly is and recognize true evil. The woods are a frontier unto themselves. A demarcation from who we were before civilization decided that it needed to be replaced and who we are now. There are more demarcations and it's important to be able to recognize them."

Amboy had seen places like that in the American woods. He understood Thiago's meaning that so much of his own country was civilized, but there were still places with shadows. Argentina, on the other hand, especially Patagonia, had places where hardly anyone had ever been. Amboy remembered asking Brother Roy about his experiences in World War II.

The brother went silent for a time, then had said, "I saw Auschwitz. I wasn't in the camp, but I was a partisan. Part of the liberation. I was there when we freed the prisoners. That was a frontier. I saw shadows I wasn't sure were human or monster. I don't know what else happened there, but there was a reason for it besides meagre inhumanity."

Amboy considered for a moment, trying to plumb the dread in the younger man's eyes. When he finally spoke, he did so slowly, as to be completely understood.

"Thiago, what you say is right, of course. There are people in America who are like what you said. But there are others as well. I'm not from that part of America. I don't know what MTV is. I'm from the hills and in the hills we still have our old ways—we have frontiers yet to be exposed." He paused, then added, "In the hills, we still have dark places we only whisper about at night to remind our children that there are still real reasons to be afraid."

Thiago's eyes softened, as did his grip on Amboy. "Which is the reason I am counting on you. Santiago told me once that you had magic in you. I don't know what it is but you will need it to survive."

Amboy gently but firmly removed Thiago's hand from his chest. "Enough of this. I don't need any more lecturing or mysterious mummery. If I'm able to help, I will. If not, then I won't."

Thiago stared into both Amboy's eyes, moving left and right as if to see deeper inside each one. "Know this, Amboy Stevens. Greater fates than yours are at work."

Amboy sighed heavily. He needed a beer. He needed some peace of mind. He needed out of the cramped apartment. He rounded his shoulders back and forth, then he nodded. After all, what else could he do?

"The Germans who were after you . . ." Thiago began.

"What about them?"

"They are not like you. Neither of them. They are from a distinct tribe. They know about los *dedos de gigantes*. They seek them. They require them."

"Why do they want us so much? Why do they need 'the fingers of giants'? Are they trying to save her?" Amboy asked.

Thiago shook his head. "The opposite. They want to eat her alive."

CHAPTER 4

The rains came then. One moment everything was silent, the next the air was filled with the static of water beating down on the roof and shingles outside the patio. The water would be cold, carrying with it not a hint of the Pacific, instead the percolation of the frigid ice from the heights of the Andes. Amboy had stood among such showers in fifteen thousand feet at the El Quimado mine, looking down on Puente de Diablo and Highway 40 as it slid through the mountains of Salta like a mad stray bullet. Water saturating him, soaking through his clothes, him not caring as it swept the dirt of the mine and the dust from his memories away in brown rivulets. Moments like these memories would come unbidden, as if part of some internal lightning, smacking him not with voltage but a realization that he'd been here before or seen the same thing before.

This is how he felt now, standing in the doorway, staring at the odd young woman resting on the couch, a beer in her hand as she lay back against the cushions, her eyes closed, chest breathing in regular rhythm, her feet on the coffee table. He didn't know what he'd expected, but she was definitely not anything he had anticipated. Her skin was a caramel black color and her hair was dark red and cascaded from her head in six-inch curls. Her skin had freckles, something he hadn't ever really seen on a black woman before. He also wasn't sure if he had ever seen a black girl with red hair, but then he remembered that he had—the lightning had smacked a memory loose.

Once, in Chattanooga, when they'd come down from the mountain for a baseball game, he'd seen her sitting in the stands behind first base, him behind third base. The Lookouts ball field wasn't so large that he couldn't easily make her out and he'd found himself staring at her, right until she'd noticed, and flipped him off. After that, he'd tried like hell not to look at her, but he couldn't help it and sure enough, every time he'd tried to sneak a peek, he'd found her staring at him, grinning, her middle finger at attention.

Growing up, he hadn't been around black people. He'd been challenged more than once on his presumed prejudice based on being from the south, but he'd always ignored the challenges. How could he be prejudiced against something he hadn't ever known. Nary a black man lived in the hills surrounding Chattanooga. Even in the city, there were places where he'd turn one way and never see a black person, then turn another, and be in a completely black neighborhood. Whenever that would happen, he'd never once been at worry, instead treated it as normal as the air that entered and left his body, which it was.

Once driving on Highway 58, heading toward Chickamauga Damn, he'd missed a turn and went from the white Lake Hills area to East Chattanooga and Gaylon Heights. The changing of the demography hadn't been lost on him, but it was more scenic than prohibitive, so it was with an easy swagger that he pulled into a convenience store, bought a pack of Camels and a cup of coffee, then returned to his car. On the way out, he'd held the door for a young black woman carrying a baby in one arm and pulling a pouty three-year-old boy with snot surrounding his nose in the other. Amboy had nodded and smiled, and in return received a scolding glare and a single attribution: "Honkey!"

Not that he wasn't aware of the way white folks in the hills thought of black folks in the valleys. He had his share of relatives with particular attitudes. But it wasn't until after he'd left and joined the army and was sent to Vietnam that he had any real interaction with blacks and whites and the way they worked together—as often as not like oil and water. He tried to set himself outside of it, but he'd had whites who hated him for not hating blacks, and blacks hating him because they thought he was like every other white man. For the most part, he'd ignored their modalities as best he could, but he couldn't always stop others from bringing their prejudices to the soggy forests of Vietnam.

Now, back in the apartment complex created by Peron in one of his fits of Marxist ideas, he noticed that while he'd been staring, and remembering the one girl, this girl, the young woman resting on the couch, had awoken and was now turned towards him. The right side of her face as he looked at her, including the area around her left eye, was covered in a light purple port wine stain. His eyes then went to her hand holding the bottle and he instantly counted six fingers. Who was this woman and where had she come from?

"I know what you're thinking," she said, her voice soft as velvet with more than a hint of southern accent. "How did you get so lucky? A black girl with red hair, six fingers, and a map of Florida on her face." She pointed to a mole on her cheek. "This is where Miami is. I don't mind it if you stare. Miami is a fun place. I went there once with my mother on a busman's holiday."

He blinked in response, unable to form words.

She sat up and placed the beer on the table. She held out her hand. "My name is Lettie, What's yours?"

He held out his own hand and shook hers.

She counted his fingers and grinned.

"My name is Amboy. I guess I'm here to save you."

"What kind of name is that?" she asked.

He shrugged. "Family name, I suppose. You can call me Boy if you want to. All my friends used to call me that. Amboy is just my full name."

"We don't call people boy where I come from," she said.

Thiago pushed past him into the kitchen. He came back with two beers, one he took, the other he passed to Amboy.

"Who clocked you?" she asked.

Amboy's hand went to his face. "This? Turns out I owe a few debts."

She raised an eyebrow. "Is that what I am, a debt?"

"Would it matter?"

"It might."

He shrugged. "I was asked to help."

"Do you often help strangers?" she asked.

"When asked by those I care about."

"So, you care about the person who hit you? I'm not so sure you're going to make a great savior."

"Probably not, but I'm all you got." He took a swig of beer. He took a chair at the table beside Thiago. "Listen, all I know is that I was told you needed help and I should help you. This one," he gestured to Thiago with the neck of the beer bottle, "says that you also don't want help. He says you say you can take care of yourself."

"And I should let you take care of me why? With a face like that? Is that your resume?"

It was like the ballpark all over again. He felt like she was verbally flipping him off every time she spoke and it was infuriating. He downed the bottle, went and got another one, then downed half of that. He sat once again at the table, all the while, noting that Thiago and the girl—Lettie—watched him gather himself. Finally, he felt a modicum of control. He began again, but slowly as if he needed to taste each word before he let it free.

"Sorry about that. This is all new to me. Let me start over. I'm Amboy Stevens. I'm from Signal Mountain, Tennessee, by way of Vietnam. I've spent the last ten years working various mines here in Argentina mostly making some cash, living life, and enjoying myself. I know Thiago because I used to work with his brother before he was killed in a mine accident. I've been asked by two people to make sure nothing happens to you. Thiago is one, and Matias is the other. Even if they hadn't asked, I'd probably help. I'm a sucker for such things. My greatest downfall might be that I'm a joiner and a volunteer. It's why I joined the army and went to Vietnam and my family stayed up in the mountains."

"Tennessee *is* the volunteer state," she said.

He nodded. "So they say. What's your story?" he asked.

"I only know part of it. Did they tell you I have amnesia?" she asked.

He nodded. "I also heard you were loco."

She laughed, the sound of ice crackling. "Most times I feel like a cliché. I've read bad novels that started like this. I usually find them unbelievable and put them down once I discover that the protagonist has amnesia. I thought the authors were too lazy or didn't want to spend time doing a backstory, until they're able to figure out that after a hundred pages the protagonist was as boring as ever. I'm afraid my life is going to be the most boring life possible and I don't envy anyone trying to help me out."

She pulled a pack of cigarettes from her pocket.

To Thiago she asked, "Mind?"

He got up and returned with a heavy glass ashtray.

She lit one, then offered the pack to Amboy.

He accepted, lit his own, then coughed after he lit it, realizing that it was menthol. He regarded the pack. Kools. Of course. He passed it back to her.

She dropped it on the table, took a deep drag of the cigarette, leaned back and crossed her arms.

"I know my name is Leticia Fennick. I know I used to have birthmarks on both sides of my face, although it was Alabama on this side," she said, rubbing her right cheek that was now clear and unblemished. "I know because of my passport photo. I also know I came here to get rid of the port wine stains I read in article I found somewhere sometime. I figure I must have found the place because lookie lookie, Alabama's gone."

"Not a bad thing," Amboy said, grinning.

"Don't go dissing Alabama. Ever been to Birmingham? I saw *Porgy & Bess* at the theater there and I—" She sat up. "Wait a minute. Where'd that come from?"

"What?" Thiago asked.

"The memory. One moment it wasn't there, the next it was."

"I saw the same thing happen in Vietnam," Amboy said. "Guys come back from the jungle can't remember anything. It's like the brain got all tangled and has to figure out a way to rewire itself."

She tapped the cigarette in the ashtray, her face suddenly alight with a memory. She leaned forward. "I saw it as a kid. I remember cotton candy and soda. I remember the characters. Porgy, the street beggar, trying to save Bess the prostitute from Sportin' Life, her drug dealer, and—and—who was her lover?"

"Crown. Crown was her lover," Amboy said.

She napped her fingers. "Crown." Then she looked at him. "How do you know *Porgy & Bess*?"

"I'm not all cracker," he said. "We came down from the

mountains sometimes. They showed it at the Tivoli Theater in Chattanooga for a season. I had a summer job working construction because I had to get out of the mines. We built scenery for all the plays. I got to sit in back and listen and watch. I even saw Shakespeare." He spread his hands. "Not bad for a guy with most of a high school education."

She nodded appreciatively, causing the smoke around her head to fold and bend. "Not bad, Amboy. Not bad for a cracker Tennessee mountain boy."

He shrugged.

"By the way, what's most of a high school education?" she asked.

"I dropped out in tenth grade. Took a GED. I might have kept going, but the busses stopped coming and it was a fifteen mile walk to school." He stared at her for a moment and suppressed a grin. Her words were less now a finger than a friendly shove. "What else do you remember?" he asked. "I mean about why you're here in Argentina."

"Here. This is what I have." She lodged the cigarette between her lips and grabbed a faded olive-green canvas backpack from beside the couch. From it she pulled several books with rubber bands around them and began to lay them on the table. One was Bruce Chatwin's *In Patagonia*. Attached to it was a spiral notebook. Several maps. One of Argentina. One of Patagonia. Three of various sections of Tierra del Fuego. One of Torres del Paine. An Old Testament Bible. A book titled *Giants of Patagonia and the Andes*. A book called *The Lake* by Paola Kauffman. And a torn page from a magazine promising cures for skin disease and port wine stains.

Amboy leafed through them, pausing every now and then to read something aloud.

"This is something you highlighted in the Bible: From the Book of Samuel. Chapter 21. Verses 16–22. *A giant named*

Ishbibenob, who was carrying a bronze spear that weighed about 3.5 kilogrammes and who was wearing a new sword, thought he could kill David. But Abishai son of Zeruiah came to David's help, attacked the giant, and killed him. Then David's men made David promise that he would never again go out with them to battle. "You are the hope of Israel, and we don't want to lose you," they said. After this there was a battle with the Philistines at Gob, during which Sibbecai from Hushah killed a giant named Saph. There was another battle with the Philistines at Gob, and Elhanan son of Jair from Bethlehem killed Goliath from Gath, whose spear had a shaft as thick as the bar on a weaver's loom. Then there was another battle at Gath, where there was a giant who loved to fight. He had six fingers on each hand and six toes on each foot. He defied the Israelites, and Jonathan, the son of David's brother Shammah, killed him. These four were descendants of the giants of Gath, and they were killed by David and his men."

"It's well known in literature and historical documents that giants have six toes on each foot and six fingers on each hand," she said. "Not that I'm a giant. But having read all the verses of the bible that have to do with giants, I've always wondered if maybe I was a descendent." She blushed. "Or something. I know, it's silly."

"I don't have six toes," Amboy said. "Do you?"

She nodded. "No open-toed shoes for this girl. Hey, turn to Genesis 6:4 and read it."

He did and read aloud, "*There were giants on the earth in those days, and also afterward, when the sons of God came in to the daughters of men and they bore children to them. Those were the mighty men who were of old, men of renown.*"

"What does men of renown mean?" Thiago asked.

"They were men, not giants, who were well known," she said. "They were famous, probably fighters and hunters, talked about in stories. But they were already there when Adam's line began to beget and begat. Then one hundred and twenty years later, the great flood happened and destroyed them and the giants."

Amboy grinned and handed the bible back to her. "You really believe this?"

"I do. Why shouldn't I?"

"I mean. The Bible and all. Jesus. Walking on water. Giants. It's a bit much, don't you think?" Amboy noticed that she wasn't smiling like he was, so he let his slide. "Are you saying you do believe this?"

"Amboy Stevens, I'm not sure what I believe. But I am a red-haired black woman with six fingers, six toes, and a map of Florida on her face. I am not what anyone thought would come out of my momma and I still grew up to be a decent woman—I think. I know I'm college educated, but I can't tell you which college I went to yet. Eventually, I will remember. But here's what I do know. At least a billion people on the planet believe in the Bible. If you believe in it, you have to believe in all of it. It's called faith and is what the church is based on. So, the idea that someone can cherry pick things from it is ridiculous and makes the person look stupid. If you believe in Moses, then the bush burned and he spoke to it. If you believe in David, then he fought giants and won. If you believe in Noah, then there was a flood and there was an ark." She shook her head and took a deep drag, then let it out. "You can't have one without the other."

"Okay. Okay. What about this then." Amboy picked up another book. This one looked old. "*Sacred Mysteries Among The Mayas And the Quiches, 11,500 Years Ago: Their Relation To The Sacred Mysteries Of Egypt, Greece, Chaldea And India. Freemasonry In Times Anterior To The Temple Of Solomon*. Written by Augustes le Plongeon in 1886. Do you believe this? I mean, freemasonry now?"

She glanced at Thiago. "Is he always such a contrarian?" Without waiting on a response, she said, "I don't know, Amboy. It's research. I must have thought Mr. What's His Name was important so I brought it along. Thing about amnesia is you don't remember much. Why I have it I do not know." She stamped out her cigarette. "Anyone else hungry? Thiago? Amboy?"

He was about to respond, when her entire body went stiff. She began to shudder and quiver, hands locked at her sides, her feet straight. Her jaw clenched hard around the round muscles of her face. Her eyes went back inside of her head. She began to rattle off words he couldn't understand. It was almost like he knew what they were, but he couldn't figure out the context. Whatever it was she was repeating them over and over and she seemed captured by it.

Amboy had already surged to his feet. His hands out to grab onto something, anything. "What's happening?"

Thiago wasn't looking at her, but at the door. "They're coming for her?"

"Isn't it just a seizure?" Amboy asked, moving to her body, wanting to grab her, but not wanting to hurt her.

Thiago began to pack up her things. "It could be, but then why is she repeating my address over and over."

Amboy now placed the words. Sure enough. Building number and apartment number repeatedly. This wasn't just a grand mal seizure. This was something else. This was something impossible. Something crazy.

"Grab her and let's go."

She was still vibrating on the couch, stiff as a two-by-four, babbling the address.

"How?" Amboy shouted.

"Figure it out," Thiago shouted. He flung open the door and two men were waiting.

CHAPTER 5

One held a Mauser—a WWII German automatic pistol—that Amboy instantly recognized from its iconic shape and magazine. The other held what looked like a white divining rod, a version of something he'd seen his Uncle Del use when looking for waters and springs up in the hills. All that he caught in a second. He stood right behind Thiago.

"Inside, now," said the one with the pistol, thin-lipped, German.

They both wore dark suits with white shirts and Pratt-knotted ties. Neither of them wore hats, which should have set them apart. Both had military cut blonde hair. Outside the rain had stopped. Heavy droplets still dripped from the edge of roof as the day began to die into dusk. Somewhere nearby, birds called to each other, the only other sound other than the hum of traffic from the highway a quarter of a mile away.

Thiago began to back inside and bumped squarely into Amboy.

Instead of backing away, Amboy shoved Thiago as hard as he could into the man with the divining rod.

Both were momentarily stunned and the man with the pistol turned partially to react to what was happening. That was all the edge Amboy needed. He leaped forward and performed a Superman punch, something he'd seen a Thai boxer once do, jumping into the air and kipping both legs behind to draw more power as his fist came down on his opponent's cheek.

The man crumpled, and before he could hit the ground, Amboy had the pistol in one hand and the man's collar in the other. He pulled him inside, then motioned for the other man to follow his unconscious accomplice, the pistol now in Amboy's possession. The other man looked stunned, so Thiago grabbed him and threw him into the room, scattering chairs and slamming the table against the wall. He glanced outside and checked left and right in the outdoor hallway, then slammed the door.

Amboy handed the pistol to Thiago and returned his attention to Lettie, who was no longer vibrating, now just undulating like an exhausted fish might, trying not to die as it gasped air on a wooden dock. He shoved aside the living room table and sat beside her on the couch. He grabbed her and placed a hand on her forehead. "Shhh. It's okay, Lettie. It's okay. Whatever happened is going away now."

Her breathing slowed and her eyes rolled back into her head, but she was still out of it. She'd be okay. At least he was pretty sure of it.

He went around and grabbed a length of curtain, ripped it from the window, then ripped it into smaller strips.

"My abuela is going to kill you," Thiago said.

"Not if she kills you first," Amboy said, grinning maliciously. "I'll tell her this was your idea."

"The hell it was."

"Don't you want to tie these guys up?"

Thiago glared at the two, then nodded furiously. "Of

course." He glanced at the man who had the divining rod, who seemed to be ready to get up, and hammered him across the face with the pistol.

"Then was it my fault I just happened to think of it before you? You would have thought of it soon enough, which means it was your idea."

"I'm not sure that's how this works." Thiago accepted several strips and tied up the man he'd just hit who was now moaning, trying to staunch the blood from flowing over his face. Then he tied the other one. By the time he was done, Amboy stood beside him, holding the weird divining rod.

"Feels like it's made of ivory," Amboy said. "And look at these inscriptions. They look religious. And this one is repeated. *OA9*. Have you seen this before?"

The rod was Y-shaped, as divining rods normally were. Two smaller handles met to form one long rod. Along the entire length were various markings and etchings, many showing a great age. He recognized a few variants of a cross and what looked like Stars of David, but the others he didn't understand, especially the OA9, which had been etched all over as if by different hands.

Thiago shook his head. "I've never seen that before, but we're going to need to leave. There's going to be more after these two."

"Why do you say that?" Amboy asked, still examining the rod.

"These were the dogs. We still don't know who unleashed them." When he saw Amboy's confusion. "Do you think she just had a seizure by accident, one in which she gives up my address? There's a *hechicero* out there somewhere." Still seeing confusion, he added, "*El hechicero. El Brujo. El hechizidor.*" Finally, he shook his head. "A witch. That was *nigromancia* plain and simple. There's going to be more."

Amboy held up the Y-shaped divining rod. "You saying this is black magic?"

"*Como no!* Of course. Grab Lettie and let's go."

Amboy shoved the divining rod into his pants behind his back and draped his jacket over it. He spied her bag, shoved the books and papers back inside, and grabbed it. He hooked the bag around his neck and arm, then picked her up. She wasn't as heavy as he suspected. Thiago was already at the door. When he saw that Amboy was ready, he opened it and glanced left, then right.

"Follow me," he said, and was off, the pistol at his side, but ready.

Amboy struggled to keep up, carrying both the bag and the young woman.

They made it down the first set of stairs and across the courtyard to the Olympic swimming pool, before Amboy almost slipped and fell on the wet grass. Had it not been for the concrete lip surrounding the pool, he would have crashed into the water. Regaining his balance, he was able to turn and follow Thiago as he ran straight, then right, leaving the barrio. He beelined to a telephone booth where the phone was already ringing.

By the time Amboy caught up to him, breathing heavily and almost out of gas, Thiago was responding to someone on the other end of the phone, nodding his head and repeating, "*Si. Si. Subterraneo. Como llegamos*?"

Thiago hung up the phone and shoved the pistol in his waistband.

"How did they know it was you?" he asked, gesturing to the phone.

"Abuela," was all he said. Then he ran down the street, forcing Amboy to follow him.

Five minutes later, a flatbed truck pulled up, burlap sacks covered by canvas in the bed. The front was a dark blue with enough dents to wonder if it hadn't been recently resurrected from a junk yard. The man behind the wheel gave them no heed, merely stared straight forward.

Thiago climbed into the bed and beckoned Amboy hand him the girl. Soon, all three of them were under the canvas as the truck bumped and shimmied down the road. The sacks smelled of wheat and had all the comfort of bales of hay. The canvas was another matter. It had covered innumerable objects bound for market. Amboy detected a mélange of scents both pleasant and gory, including the entrails of pigs and offal from cattle. Only he would be able to identify such aromas, mixed as they were amidst the mélange of fruits and vegetables coating the inside, while the toxic fumes of vehicles and the city continually tried to permeate the pores of the canvas top. Amidst it all, he could smell his two companions. The balmy aftershave worn by Thiago with hints of saddle leather and spruce trees, and then Lettie, who was all menthol, cinnamon, and the sweat only a woman can own.

Amboy had always had an encyclopedic relationship with scent. He'd known people who could read a page and remember it forever. He had an uncle who could hear a song and replay it error free, or almost. And Amboy? His most useless tool had been to remember every smell he'd ever smelled. He remembered all the way back to his grandfather's smoking jacket that smelled of vanilla tobacco and the sassafras tea that he steeped and drank from the weeds in the back yard. The old man would hold him after his mother fed him, and the aroma of the old man had been so comforting, that when he'd died when Amboy had been ten months old, the baby had cried for a full week until they'd figured out the reason and then wrapped in him in one of his grandfather's smoking jackets.

It didn't take long for the jerking rumbling ride to awaken Lettie, whose first impulse was to sit up, only to be propelled back by the canvas that had been pulled tight and cinched to the corners by the driver.

"What the—where—what happened?"

"How are you feeling?" Amboy asked.

She began to rub her muscles as if taking inventory. She groaned and winced as she touched various parts. "Like I was hit by a bus, run over by a train, and drop-kicked down a flight of stairs. What did y'all do to me?"

"You had a seizure," Amboy said.

A bump shoved them all into the canvas then gravity gripped them back down to the bed of the truck, sending zings of pain through Amboy's spine. Any more of those and he wouldn't be able to walk.

"We're in a truck? How'd we get here? Where are we going?" she asked

Amboy shook his head. "You know as much as I do. Thiago here arranged for transportation with his grandmother." He turned to the younger man, "How did she know where we were and what happened to her when they brought Lettie to the apartment?"

"I told you," the Argentinian said. "Abuela Mafia. They were preparing. They knew something would happen."

"And you didn't tell me?" Amboy asked.

"What would you have done?" Thiago asked. "Sometimes there no reason to change the progress of things. *No da.*"

Amboy shook his head. "Of course, I want to know the progress. I need to prepare for what comes next."

Thiago shrugged, but said nothing.

"Can someone please—" BUMP "—tell me what kind of—" BUMP "—seizure I had?" she asked, fighting against the undulations of the truck.

Amboy gritted his teeth and found a grip on one of the

floorboards beneath him. What was the driver doing, trying to hit every bump? "You went stiff. We thought you had a grand mal seizure. Then you started repeating the address where we were and then there were two Germans. One had a gun the other had a divining rod. They wanted you. We saved you and got you out of there."

"I had a seizure all the way into the back of a truck?"

"I carried you," Amboy said. "One of the Germans had a gun. The other had a divining rod."

She went stiff so fast that Amboy thought she might be having another seizure.

She whispered. "Did you say divining rod?"

"Yes. Do you remember something?"

"There were men in dresses—no—robes; one had a white divining rod. It was dark outside. The wind—it howled like something alive. I remember being cold. So cold. And there was chanting in a language I didn't understand. Low and guttural. But something I had heard before. Now I think it might have been German. It was like a landslide of hard syllables."

"That's pretty much what German is," Amboy said. "What else do you remember?"

"There was wind. So much of it. Like the entire world was shrieking. Or was it the sound of seals." She shook her head. "So much noise. Then, I remember feeling—"

Her scream was so sudden and fierce and loud that the driver slammed on the brakes.

Had the bags of grain been at their feet, Thiago, Amboy and Lettie would have slammed into them, most likely crushing them. Since they were lying on top of them, they slammed into the bags, spines compacting, necks popping, heads banging. They did little damage to the bags, but their bodies had painfully accordioned. All the way through, she continued screaming.

Amboy slammed a hand over her mouth.

Thiago, after a moment of confusion, slammed the rear of the truck cab and screamed, "*Vaminos. Vaminos*!"

The truck started up again, but not after several people tried to lift up the canvas.

"Lettie. What's going on? Lettie. You have to stop screaming," Amboy said, all but climbing on top of her to keep his hand in place. She fought him all the way and finally socked him in the stomach, sending him crashing back to the truck bed.

"I can't breathe!" she said, coughing through the words.

More hands grabbed at the canvas.

People shouted for the truck to stop.

Thiago slammed his hand against the cab.

The truck driver sped up, just as Lettie broke into tears.

The sound of the crowd turned animal, now a new beast, strength collected by the many.

All Amboy could do was stare up at the canvas, try to recover his breath, and smell the deaths of hundreds of swine.

CHAPTER 6

At one time or another a case of wine had been spilled on the ground, becoming forever part of the dirt and dust filling in the spaces between the stones that made up the floor. So, although they didn't have any wine or beer with the cheese and bread that had been left for them, their brains were heady with the tang of deep red Argentinian alcohol. Such was the state of things in the underground beneath San Telmo Market in downtown Buenos Aires.

The underground had first been built in the 16th century by the Jesuits who'd come to the New World to convert the indigenous tribes of Argentina. The conversion wasn't popular, so the Spanish priests needed a way to hide and escape. Over time, they built what soon became an entire underground city, including a hostel for wayward priests. Decades turned to centuries and Buenos Aires grew into a major industrial European city in South America. When the rains came, lacking a cohesive sewer system, the water and sewage was diverted to the underground, which had been expanded, so that the streets would be free of such offal. But by the 20th century, sewage systems had been promulgated throughout the city, allowing once again a city beneath the city to be reborn.

The three of them had their own room under St. Telmo Market. Although there was no electricity, they had candles for light, and various cast-off furniture to use. This room, they were told by Thiago, was one of dozens spread out under Buenos Aires used as safe rooms, to protect members of the *Asociación Madres de Plaza de Mayo* from assassination by the military and the government. The association was established in 1977 by Azucena Villaflor de De Vincenti to provide notice to the government that they knew their adult children were being taken and killed. The association asserted that between 1970 and 1980 more than 30,000 men had been 'disappeared.' So, the association of mothers held vigils in the Plaza de Mayo in front of the Presidential Palace, to bring attention to the injustice and outrage. The safe rooms were developed after the founder, Madre Villaflor, was kidnapped from her home by armed men, taken to an ESMA torture center, then put on a death flight from where her body was dumped into the ocean. Whether she was dead before or after she was thrown from the plane was speculation, but it had been known from several witnesses that many of the young men were hurled screaming into the night.

All this Thiago explained as he arranged the furniture and checked the integrity of the door. Then he left them to get supplies and evidently guidance from the Abuela Mafia, which was ostensibly a subset of the *Asociación Madres de Plaza de Mayo.*

Amboy was famished, but he was more concerned about Lettie. The young woman looked as if she'd been broadsided with someone else's reality, her eyes wide and staring as she sat slumped on an old half wine barrel, her back against the rough gritty stone wall. He remembered the last moments of the truck ride himself, and how tumultuous and terrible it had been. No one really knew who they were beneath the canvas, in fact, as a group, the bystanders near the truck tried to free them. So many had already been disappeared by the government it was as if the crowd had surged forth as one rough beast, surrounded the truck, flipped it on its side, then, judging by his screams, torn the driver limb from limb. They'd been pulled free from their ill-perceived safety beneath the canvas, and shoved to the rear and almost forgotten. The mob had been so set on delivering justice that they seemed to immediately forget for whom the justice was to be served.

"Do you remember anything else?" he asked, breaking the tense silence.

Her head swung as if on a pendulum towards him, her eyes ablaze. "They killed him," she said, no question at all.

"I think they did," Amboy said.

"Why would they do such a thing?"

"I don't pretend to know," he began, his voice low and humble. "But with the disappearances of all the men, the night raids by the government, and now the loss of the Falkland Islands, I can't help but feel that this might be a transitional moment for the country. The people—the people don't know who they are. They're angry. They're disturbed. They don't have any cohesive targets for their anger, at least none that won't come back at them, take them to ESMA, then on a one-way flight over the ocean." He shook his head. "I don't know, Lettie.

"I heard his screams," she said.

Amboy remembered hearing similar screams. A young Vietnamese guerilla caught in the wire, skin ripped and twisted, unable to move, the bunker commander disallowing them to shoot the man and put him out of his misery. "His cries will do more harm to the enemy than they will us," the man had said. Amboy had disagreed, but soon learned the truth of it. The next night, five VC came to rescue him and all five were gunned down, tracer bullets from the M2 and M60 threshing through them. When the young sapper finally died on the fourth night, more than twenty VC had died trying to rescue their own, the entire time the young man screaming and screaming as if he'd invented the sound. But the memory still tortured Amboy. The screams of one who knew there was no saving, calling not for help, but for death—anything to make the pain go away, anything to make the living stop.

"I heard them as well. I also heard you scream. What was that about?"

She glanced at him, then stood. She pulled up her shirt and turned around. "On my back, what is it you see?"

He looked then stood, a hand going to his forehead. "Jesus. What have they done to you?"

"There's something there. I feel it now." She looked imploringly over her shoulder. "Tell me, Amboy. What is it?"

"You didn't know it was there? You didn't feel it?"

Tears came to her eyes. "I can't explain it. One moment, I didn't know it was there, the next I knew it was. The divining rod. There was a ceremony and the pain was—" She lowered her voice until it became a hiss. "Amboy, tell me what it is."

"It's—it's not nice. It looks evil. Like a mantis or something. Here." He went to the table and rifled through her bag until he came up with a notebook and a pencil. Then he sat at the table and drew a picture.

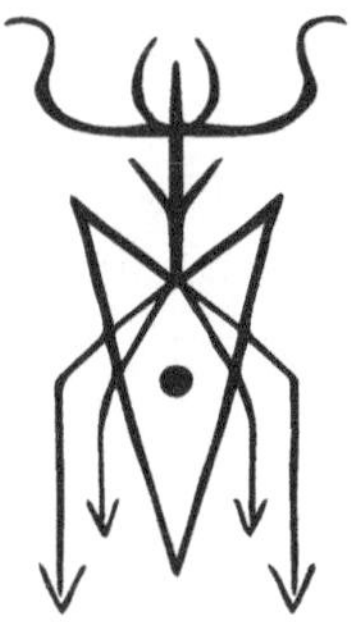

The tattoo on her back was still swollen as if it had been made in the last few days. Aligned with her spine, the image ran from her tailbone to the center of her back. And although nothing more than lines, it emanated an evil—a promised violence—the eye drawn to the circle in the center of the depiction.

He showed her the image.

She lowered her shirt and came over, staring at what he'd drawn. "It looks like it might be a face with horns. Or a mantis as you say, something climbing up my back." Her shoulders jerked and twitched. "Oh, Amboy. I want it off. I want it gone."

He shook his head. "It's not so simple. You said there was a ceremony. Do you remember where you were?"

"Only that it was cold." Her head jerked up. "And there were people around. They wore red cloaks. Even over their heads."

"But you don't remember anything else." He said back in the old wooden chair. "Why did you come to South America? Why do you have maps of Argentina, Patagonia, Tierra del Fuego? We need to start at the beginning but we have no beginning."

She sat once again on the half cask and hung her head, arms dangling over her knees. "I just don't know. This is beyond stupid." She held up a hand. "I feel as if I wanted to find out about these. To see if there might be some where I could go where there's be others."

"I can totally see that. The question is always out there, right? Are they just a mutation or do they mean something."

"Exactly," she said, backing away from the image. "One day we'll be able to figure out why some people have this unusual formation. We'll have the medical answers for it. But is there also a spiritual answer? Why did all the Greek scholars leave the notation of six fingers and their relation to giants in the Bible? Why didn't they excise them with so many other translation mistakes?"

"Wait? What? Do you mean that it was a concerted effort to leave them in?" Amboy asked.

"Of course. Here's what we know. During the Hellenistic Period, most Jews began to speak an early version of Greek, replacing their Hebrew. There were so many versions of the Bible, each written from different points of view, each capturing different ideas, but all of them in different Hebrew dialect. In an attempt to consolidate these points of view, seventy Greek scholars came together and they were called the Septuaginta, which means seventy in old Greek. These scholars edited all the versions of the Bible and created one unifying text. The first version of the Septuaginta Bible was only the first five books, which constitute the Torah. They eventually translated and consolidated all the books of the Bible. Now, get this. According to legend, the seventy scholars worked separately and met seventy days later and all seventy of the new versions of the Bible were exactly the same."

"That seems a little far-fetched," Amboy said.

"Perhaps it was. But they were trying to instill the idea of divine rightness in their work so that it wouldn't be disregarded out of hand. Which goes back to the point: why did they leave mentions of six fingers throughout the Bible? Why was it so important to them?"

"Perhaps one or more of the scholars were six-fingered," Amboy said. "Never underestimate self-interest."

She stared at him for a moment like a bird trying to fathom how to land on a tree drawn on a flat surface. "Don't you believe there's a reason for you having six-fingers?"

"You mean, does it make me special? I'll tell you what it did. It made me tough. Even in the hills, the kids could be mean. Then they saw how strong I was with six fingers rather than five and most of them wanted to be like me. These fingers," he said, holding them up, "are just fingers. I could lose one or two or all of them tomorrow and it wouldn't change who I am."

She blinked several times, then stared at the ground. "Well, you don't have six-toed feet either."

He nodded. "No. I don't at that. There's also a lot in the Bible that I don't really believe. I mean, the Ten Commandments. Those are solid. I get them. Good ways for anyone to live. But parting the Red Sea? Talking with a burning bush? It's really hard to believe in that stuff. Remember, now. I come from the hills and in hill country the belief is fierce. Genesis 19 and all the fire and brimstone and the Wrath of God is the God I was raised on. Angels destroying buildings and Lot's wife turned into a pillar of salt for disobeying. Yeah. That's what I was brought up on, so the idea that anything in the Bible is true doesn't really sit well with me, even though it was so much a part of my heritage. I guess I think that any creator would be a better shepherd to his or her flock."

"Then what does the Bible mean to you?" she asked, clearly flustered.

"It's a book written by a bunch of old men several thousands of years ago trying to explain the unexplainable. A campfire tale."

She frowned and turned away from him.

The tension in the room grew and grew until he could feel it like a violin string about to snap and kill them all. Instead of letting it, he said one final thing for a while.

"When I was in Vietnam, I looked for evidence of six fingers. I spent three tours there. I'd walk up and down the battlefields. I'd check the body bags of our dead. I saw more dead men than any three morticians in America. If there was one thing we were good at, it was killing. For every fifteen of them we killed, one of us died."

"Then why did we lose the war?" she asked.

"She speaks." Then seeing her frown, he apologized then said, "Why did we lose? That's a bigger question than we probably have time for, but let me simplify it by saying that they were fighting for something. They had an idea. They had a purpose. Us? We were just there fighting because we had to. We'd won other wars because we'd fought for something. We'd been on the right side before. The problem with Vietnam was we ended up on the wrong side.

"Back to my story. I searched high and low for evidence of six-fingered Vietnamese and you know how many I found? None. Not a single one. I must have personally seen five thousand dead and not a single six-fingered enemy. What does that tell you?"

"That the Vietnamese weren't in the Bible?" she offered.

He grinned savagely. "That could be it. I was never sure. But then again, how many red-haired caramel-skinned black girls with a map of Florida on their face are there in the Bible?"

She stared at him for a long moment, once again the girl behind first base, flipping him off. Then she got up and found a space in one of the corners with a bunch of hay and lay down, turning her back on him.

He did the same, opposite her and as far away as he could get. In no time, he was asleep, dreaming of the man screaming in the wire, over and over, non-stop, and then realizing that it was him, unable to live, unable to die, stuck in a purgatory of razor wire and pain, his six-fingered hand in the air to stop the universe from forever beating him down.

CHAPTER 7

The door creaked open, heavily in the darkness as if it weighed fifty tons. Sometime in the night the candles had gone out. Amboy felt warmth next to him and realized that Lettie had come to join him—the necessity of heat outweighing her need to be right. She still slept, snoring lightly. A sliver of light carried by the intruder showed him to be squat and square. Amboy moved to get up and woke Lettie. Her eyes snapped open, but he tapped her on her hand and made a *no* gesture by waggling a finger. He then crept onto two feet and padded to the wall next to the door. As the door continued to open, he grabbed the intruder and propelled him towards the table, until he hit back first, bending backwards until he could bend no more, Amboy's face in his.

"Who are you? What do you want?" he snarled.

"Easy. Please. Thiago and his mother sent me," said the voice, rough from ten thousand cigarettes. His accent was Oxford English. "I have something for you."

Although pressed to the table, the man didn't seem in fear at all. What sort of man was he? Amboy wondered.

He stepped back and let the man stand. "Careful. No sudden moves."

Even with his feet adjusted under him, the man still only came to Amboy's shoulders. He had a bag in one hand and a large flashlight with a handle in the other. He wasn't as stout as he'd seemed in the door. He'd just been carrying a large bag.

"Who are you?" Amboy asked.

"I am Father Paz. A friend of the family. We are here to help." He held out a bag. "Here. I brought food and drink. Thiago sends his apologies. You must be hungry."

"How did you know where we were?"

"As I said, I am a friend of the family. Not only does the *Asociación Madres de Plaza de Mayo* use these safe rooms, but so does *Movimiento de Sacerdotes para el Tercer Mundo*. The Movement for Priests in the Third World. I am one of the members. The underground, I know it well. It has saved us on many occasions."

"You sound English?" Lettie asked, going to the table and checking the contents. She came out with a bag of chips, which she opened right away and began chomping.

"My father was English. I went to and then taught at Stonyhurst College in England for a time, before I followed my mother back to Argentina."

"What happened to her?" Lettie asked, pieces of chips falling from her mouth. She tried to catch them and ended up covering her face.

"My brother was 'disappeared' and my mother became one of the Mothers of the Plaza. Then she was disappeared as well. I never saw either one of them again. They were the only family I ever had except for the church." He pulled a screw top bottle of wine from one of the bags, opened it, and took a large slug. "It's why I do what I do now."

"And what is it you do?" Amboy asked.

The priest turned to him, his face made of stone. "I'm a priest. I do what it takes."

Then the priest removed his overcoat. Beneath, he wore a black shirt and white priest's collar, and black pants over black workman's shoes—the sort of shoes one might see a deliveryman or a street worker wear, definitely designed more for comfort than for looks. They spoke of a certain practicality the priest had. The only piece of flash was the white belt he wore, like a second priest's collar around his waist.

His face bore a self-mocking expression that seemed to be a more-or-less permanent fixture on his face. His hair was beginning to recede and he seemed to be about fifty. He had fine Latin features and stark blue eyes.

For the next ten minutes, Amboy and Lettie ate bread and hardboiled eggs and more cheese. They found places around the corner and outside to use to relieve themselves. Paz, as he'd asked to be referred to, had brought one bottle of juice and three bottles of wine. The juice was gone fast, which meant that if they wanted something to drink, it would have to be the thick, red Argentinian wine, which one could only drink straight from the bottle.

Paz finished one bottle and started on another. "You'll need to excuse me. Vino rojo and I have a peculiar relationship."

"Communion, eh, father?" Amboy said, laughing.

"Please call me Paz. I'm no longer officially a father."

"Then why the outfit?" Amboy asked. "Didn't you introduce yourself as a priest?"

"I did so to try and eliminate confusion. These are the only clothes I own. Plus, I am used to them. They give me a certain amount of invisibility when I need it."

"Were you defrocked?" Lettie asked. "Was it a woman?"

"That's not a real thing—defrocking. And no, it wasn't a woman. Bishop Bergoglio and I had a misunderstanding. I'm what you call, on probation."

"But you said you aren't a father?"

"Alas, the Bishop doesn't want me give mass for a while until I come to terms with certain things, but he has not laicized me. He found out what happens when he does." He took a deep drought, then held the bottle in the crook of his arm as he stared into the corner of the room. "Last time he did such a thing to two young priests who disagreed with his strategy, the military came in and disappeared them, because they assumed that they were left wing propagandists released by the church. The bishop was distraught and never wants that to happen again, so we have a gentleman's agreement, the Bishop and I." He took another draught. "I can still help where I am needed. Whenever Thiago's mother needs me, I am there."

"How do you know them?" Amboy asked.

"She and my mother were best friends. When my mother . . . when she left—it was Francesca who took me in and took care of me."

"Then you know Santiago?" Amboy mentioned.

"And how you came to let her know about his death. Yes, my son. I know it all. He was like a nephew to me."

Amboy regarded the man a moment, then said, "Then you know why she's going out of her way to help a stranger named Lettie whose only claim to fame happens to be that she has six fingers on each hand."

"Hey," Lettie said, eyes narrowing.

"Oh yeah, and a map of Florida on her face. If you look real close, you can see the mole that designates Miami."

Lettie gave Amboy a look that could boil a potato.

Paz lifted the bottle, but thought better of taking a drag.

Instead, he hugged it a moment as he considered Amboy. Then he said, "The world is filled with various organizations. Besides *Las Madres* and *Los Sacerdotes,* there organizations with more worldly views. *La Asociación de David* is one of them. Have you ever heard of them?"

Amboy shook his head. He remembered Matias saying that it was the CIA who was interested in Lettie, but nothing about the Council of David.

Lettie shook her head as well.

Pas turned to her. "Ms. Leticia Fennick. Can you guess why an organization interested in giants would keep track of six fingered persons?"

She considered a moment, then said, "It's because you want to find giants. David after King David, right? The killer of giants." Her eyes narrowed. "Do you kill giants? Is that the purpose?"

"Not I. And no, they don't. At least, not as they have shown me. They are just seeking physical proof that many of the miracles of the Bible are true. It's hard to capture a burning bush, but discovering if there are still beings that are thirty feet tall, that is a true undertaking."

Lettie smacked the table with her right hand. "Aha. I knew the truth of six fingers and no one would listen to me." She gave Amboy a look and all he could do was roll his eyes.

"Did you say thirty feet tall?" Amboy asked, trying to keep his jaw off the floor. "And you've seen these beings?"

"No. No. No." Paz took a drink. He seemed impervious to the wine. "We've just been asked to protect pilgrims who come to South American in search of answers."

Now it made sense to Amboy. The idea that the Central Intelligence Agency might want to keep track of a person who was also being watched by an organization that believed in giants made a sort of sense if one believed in all the world domination conspiracy theories that seemed to be everywhere.

"How did you know I'd come?" Lettie asked.

Paz grinned. "Magellan."

Amboy's eyes narrowed. "Who?"

"He's talking about the explorer, Ferdinand Magellan," Lettie said. "He was a controversial Portuguese explorer who was the first person to circumnavigate the Earth. While he was down around Cape Horn in South America, he and his mapmakers made an interesting notation on the map. It showed two giants and a normal-sized person with the words *Tierra de Pattagones* above them and the words *Gigantum Regio* beneath, because he and his men recorded they saw red-haired giants of considerable proportions. They reportedly brought several aboard and were going to take them back to Europe, but they died on the voyage and had to be dumped overboard. So, when, Father Paz—I mean Paz says Magellan, this is what he means."

Paz nodded. "You were on a list. When you got your passport, your name was flagged."

A thought came to Amboy. "What about me? Am I on a list?"

"What do you think?" Paz asked, good-naturedly.

"If she's on the list, then you must have been keeping track of me for some time."

"Not me, son. Other organizations."

"Like the CIA?"

Paz's eyes twinkled. "Looks like little birdies have been talking. So, you want to know if you were on the list. I cannot confirm or deny, but I do know that one Amboy Stevens from Signal Mountain Tennessee. Son of Conroy and Ava Stevens. You were assigned to Delta Company, 3rd Battalion, 21st Infantry Division and partook in the last ground combat operations by US Army troops in Vietnam. Your unit was deactivated and returned to the United States, but you and a few others were kept behind and assigned to OPERATION ENHANCE PLUS, where the US turned over most of its military equipment to ARVN. You didn't leave Vietnam until the spring of 1974."

"They needed someone to make sure they didn't break the equipment we were giving them," Amboy offered. "Thing was, we just didn't want to have to transport it all back. Plus, the war was already done by then."

"After the war, instead of returning home, you spent three months in Thailand, then moved to El Quemado Mine in northwest Argentina, where you met Santiago Flores and became friends of the Flores family. Did I leave anything out?"

"That I love chocolate, cold beer, and long walks on the beach?"

Paz grinned. "If only we could all have the needs of a *Playboy* Playmate." He sipped his wine. "Yes, Amboy. You were on a list. You still are. My guess is there are many sorts of lists in the world and it's decent chances that each of us is on at least one at the same time."

"I suppose I am lucky I wasn't picked up."

"You were always with the right people."

Lettie sighed. "And I ended up with the wrong people."

Amboy took a deep draught of wine himself now, but he wasn't contemplating the existence of giants, or that the CIA kept tabs on him along with the Vatican and a Council of David, but rather the disappearing happening all around him. The priests, Paz's mother, and Santiago's own abuela, Francesca, involved in an organization to protest the government. As an outsider, he'd felt sort of impervious to the happenings of the government. But had he really been? He could have been disappeared just as easily as anyone—more easily, because he had no history in Argentina.

No family. No trail of tears where people would mourn him. He could be given a one-way-all-expenses-paid flight over the Pacific Ocean and the world would still go on without him.

The idea of dying had never really bothered him. But the idea of dying for nothing certainly did. In Vietnam, he would have died for his friends, all the smelly, unruly, godless bunch of them. But here in Buenos Aires? If they took him, who was he dying for except for the whim of an idea from a corpulent government official who just happened to come across his name on a list?

"Father—er—Paz, do you know what this is?" Lettie asked, showing him the drawing of the tattoo on her back.

He grabbed it, slamming it face first into the table to hide the image.

"Where did you see this?" he said, setting the wine bottle down and pulling up a chair. "Was it in here?" He glanced fearfully at the walls.

The complete change in the man's demeanor was startling.

Seeing his response, Lettie's face all but collapsed on itself as she began to cry.

"I didn't mean to scare you," Paz said hastily. "This thing—I dare not name it—but it is—"

Lettie was in full-blown sobs now. She couldn't speak. Her head was hunched into her shoulders as her whole body was wracked with terror. She clawed at her shirt, trying to rip it from her back.

Amboy rushed forward and grabbed her arms to keep her from doing damage to herself.

"I don't understand," Paz said. "What did I say?"

"The image," Amboy said, struggling with Lettie even to get words out. "They put it on her back."

"Oh, dear God, Madre de Dios." He crossed himself, then

grabbed the wine bottle and swept everything off the table until it was clear. "Remove her shirt. I must see what they have done."

"Lettie. Lettie . . ." Amboy began, but she was still in a frenzy to remove it herself. He stood back as she ripped it off at the collar, exposing breasts, her flat stomach and as she twisted in his grip, the ugly evil thing that had been carved into her.

Paz touched her on the shoulder. She shrugged it off at first, then when he touched her again, he said, "Easy now, child. We will fix you. Be careful so that we may all go with God."

She stopped struggling, but trembled nonetheless as she lay on the rough wood, her left arm covering and protecting her breasts, her right hand gripping the table.

Paz took a swig of wine, then with a sad face, drank no more. Instead, he blessed himself and the wine, saying, "Blessed are you, Lord, all-powerful God, who in Christ, the living water of salvation, blessed and transformed us. Grant that when we are sprinkled with this water or make use of it, we will be refreshed inwardly by the power of the Holy Spirit and continue to walk in the new life we received at Baptism."

He poured the wine onto the scarification, red rivulets of wine following the grooves of the scarring. The image seemed to waver and lose shape a moment.

Lettie hissed with pain.

Paz poured more wine onto the image and it seemed to lose shape again, but returned.

He shook his head in frustration. "It's too deep. Been there too long."

"Can you remove it?" Amboy asked.

"Given time, I can. Until then, we're going to have to be careful." He grabbed Lettie's ripped shirt and patted the area dry. Turning to Amboy, he said, "Give me your jacket for the girl."

Amboy immediately stripped off the jacket.

Paz put it around her shoulders as he helped her stand. He led her to the chair and handed her the bottle of blessed wine. "Drink the rest of this. It's important. Every last drop, now."

She nodded blindly and holding the jacket together with her left hand, necked the bottle with the other.

"What's going on?" Amboy asked. He felt as if something were staring at him from behind, He couldn't help but turn-about, searching for what seemed to be just out of the corner of his eyes. An itchy feeling scratched at the back of his neck.

"You're feeling the *lilin.* It is a creature of old, made from the fears of those around it. To be afraid of it gives it strength."

"Why was it put on me?" Lettie asked.

Paz hesitated, then said, "To keep track of you. This is like a homing beacon. Given the right tool, one can always find it."

Amboy pulled the divining rod out of the back of his pants where he'd forgotten it. "Do you mean something like this?" The symbols were now glowing where they hadn't before. He felt a heat in his hand as it grew hotter and hotter. Amboy couldn't help but stare as the rod seemed to come alive.

Paz smacked it out of his hand.

When the white rod touched the ground, it became a snake, hissing along the ground.

Amboy chuffed, "What the hell?"

The rod-become-snake hissed once more, then slithered out the door.

Pas whirled on Amboy and Lettie. "Children! You all are children. And you had that the whole time?"

"I took it from some Germans who came to take her away."

"And you didn't think it was important?"

"I did. I just forgot about it." He stared towards the door-way. "Did it just turn into a snake?"

"What if I told you that it had always been a snake and that its appearance was a glamour?" Paz asked.

"A glamour?"

"As in not real. Something you were meant to see but wasn't really what it was."

"Are you saying that it wasn't a divining rod? I saw all of the symbols on it. They looked pretty real."

"Let me guess. *O9A*. Order of Nine Angels. A Gnostic Satan group whose efforts are well known by the Vatican." Seeing the surprise in Amboy's eyes, Paz said, "What? You thought I was just a drunken out of work priest? I told you that the Bishop keeps me around to do certain things. These are the certain things I become involved in. *Que quilombo!*"

Everyone turned to the knocking at the door.

A policeman stood, looking in.

Amboy felt the fight coming to him. He clenched his fists and shifted on his heels. They'd come too far to be stopped now. He edged towards the policeman. "What do you want?" he growled.

Paz put a hand on his shoulder.

"Easy now. Padron is with me." He moved to the door. "*Che boludo. Como andes*?"

The policeman whispered in his ear for half a moment, then left, but not before glancing at Amboy and Lettie.

When Paz turned around, his face was a dark aspect of what it had been.

"What did he say?" Amboy asked.

"It's not good." From somewhere he produced wine and took a deep drink. He shook his head and cursed under his breath.

"What is it, you old drunk?" Amboy asked, gripping the priest's shoulder.

Paz glanced at him with sad eyes. "Thiago. They have him. He's been sent to ESMA."

The words landed like grenades.

Amboy backed away to stay away from the mental shrapnel, but couldn't get far enough. He was hit in a dozen places, each one a painful memory of Santiago and the promise he'd made his friend to take care of his family.

Paz stood, his mouth open, his eyes showing the sadness of someone who knew death was coming.

ESMA, or *Escuela Superior de Mecánica de la Armada*, was the Higher School for Navy Mechanics, once a place where actual teaching went on, but for the last dozen years or so a place of torture and the last stop before being disappeared on a plane over the Pacific.

Thiago was there now, improbably waiting on his one-way ticket to oblivion.

CHAPTER 8

The police officer waited to escort Amboy safely out of the underground. Although Amboy checked as they were leaving the warren of brick and mortar tunnels, there was no sign of the divining rod turned snake. Just the usual detritus of an underground—trash, roots from above ground plants, and moss from the humid air. The entire place had an odd smell, something old, something new, but nothing like a wedding dress. The police officer told Amboy that a plan was already in motion to rescue Thiago. Matias was waiting for him. Amboy couldn't imagine why Matias would even care about the younger brother of his dead friend and was as eager to discover the truth of that as he was to rescue the young man.

Matias was poring over a map on the wall when Amboy strode in. Back in the basement where this had all started, Amboy no longer was seated in the chair being punched in the face. Instead, he went straight to the table and chose the weapon he wanted from those laid out. He went for a M1911 Colt 45 because he'd fired one before in 'Nam. Besides him and Matias, five other men were in the room, the usual suspects from the previous evening. Instead of fancy gangster apparel, they now wore the blue uniforms of the Naval Police, replete with leather belt, pistols in holsters, and batons.

"You found the girl?" Matias asked.

"I did."

"No worse for wear, I presume," Matias said.

Amboy thought of her seizures and the crowd overturning the truck. "No worse."

Matias grinned and gave him a hoary eye as if he knew exactly what had happened, but he let it go.

"What I don't understand is why you're involved in this," Amboy said.

Matias shrugged and turned back to the map. "I'm involved with a lot of things."

Amboy grabbed the man who'd so recently broke his nose and spun him around. "Listen, I get that you want to seem aloof and cosmopolitan. Not only do I get it, I admire it. But I need answers. I need to know why you are even involved. I owe this family a debt and I want to make sure that we aren't frivolous with our time."

"Did you think you'd save Thiago by yourself?" Matias asked, shrugging angrily out of the grasp.

Amboy was forced to take a step back. "I didn't think—"

"That's right. You didn't think. Americans never do. They expect others to think for them." Seeing the argument about to arise in Amboy's eyes, he added, "Questions. It's all about questions. Why this? Why that? Why everything? Why don't you just do things? Can't you just see what needs to be done and do it without asking the world why it should be so?"

Amboy was more than a little stunned. Not only had he not thought he'd be breaking into one of the most secure facilities in Argentina, but he never once believed that Matias would have his skin in the game. The man normally eschewed chance, which was why he aligned himself based on the winds of war and the murmurs of gossip. Amboy would have to be secure in the fact that Matias knew what he was doing and that there was a plan afoot to obtain Thiago without the lot of them becoming food for the fishes.

"I take it we're not going to break in," Amboy said, nodding at the thugs in uniform.

"I've never found a frontal assault to be the best choice," Matias said, relaxing and stepping away. "Subterfuge will get us where greater numbers won't."

"Do you know the layout of the building? Do we know where they are holding Thiago?" Amboy asked, realizing that he'd just asked two questions in a row.

"Yes and no." Matias grinned, acknowledging the obvious. "We know the layout. The basement is where they have interrogation and torture cells. The main floor is where they have their operations, planning their kidnappings, tortures, and interrogations. Second floor is where the officers sleep and live. The third and fourth floor, however, is where they do the worst things."

"There's something worse than torture?" Amboy asked. He was trying to suppress the anger of being drawn into the drama that was Argentina. He'd thought himself separate from it. He'd thought himself different enough that he wouldn't have needed to participate in the grand charade of a country that would disappear men and their mothers.

But then came Santiago—and then his family—and now Lettie.

"It's where they keep the prisoners. They call it *capucha* or the hood. It's always dark. The windows are blacked out."

Amboy picked up a canvas pack and pulled free a futuristic-looking scope. "That's what this is for. AN-PVS-4s. US STARLIGHT technology. This is state of the art. It wasn't even made until after I'd left Vietnam. I only saw one in El

Quemado because of a mine collapse. It allowed us to find bodies in the dark when we had no other way to see."

"Our three-letter friends are sponsoring this raid."

Amboy considered this a moment. It was the second time the CIA had been mentioned. What was their interest in Thiago? What was their interest in Lettie? He needed to have that conversation, but it could wait. Instead of broaching the subject, he said, "We're not just going after Thiago." It was a statement, not a question.

"We have several targets on our agenda."

"That explains the uniforms. They can't be easy to get." He looked around. "Speaking of, where's mine?"

Matias put a hand on his shoulder. "Compadre. We can't have you in the background. You're a star. You and me are going to be prisoners. Everyone knows me and are amazed I haven't already been picked up, even though I pay an exorbitant amount of money to be left alone. And there's no way once you open your mouth that anyone is going to believe that you are a native Argentinian, no matter how good your vocabulary is. So, we both get a starring role in this—how do you say—off Broadway production."

"I feel honored," Amboy said, frowning. He held up the pistol he'd chosen. "And this?"

"You'll need to leave it."

"Where will I get a weapon?"

"When you need one, you'll have one. I promise."

As it turned out, Amboy's role was less of a starring role and more of a supporting actor. A new man in a suit who spoke American-Spanish so poorly that he had to be translated laid out the plan of attack. They'd arrive by sea in a replica naval police boat made just for the purpose. They were currently in Montserrat District and ESMA was all the way north in Belgrano. On a good day, one could get there by car in twenty-five minutes. But with the rioting and the influx of Argentinians protesting the dire results of the Falkland War, it might take hours to crawl through traffic; each minute a chance they might be captured. On the water, they could arrive in thirty minutes and keep anyone interested in their behavior or destination at bay.

After the briefing, everyone suited up according to their roles.

Amboy and Matias wore handcuffs on their wrists, hands in front. A key rested inside each front pocket to release them when they needed. They also wore blindfolds, required to cement their roles as anarchists arrested by the government and bound for interrogation and perhaps a one way trip to the Atlantic Ocean.

Once on the boat, they were placed on seats out of the wind. Amboy wanted to see, but it was out of the question. They didn't know who was watching and their behavior had to be perfect, so he was forced to play the role of a prisoner.

To pass the time, Matias asked, "What did you think of Father Paz?"

Amboy thought of the old man and his last words before Amboy had left with the policeman. The priest had been concerned, not only for Thiago, but for Amboy as well. He wasn't used to people caring about him in such a way, so when posed with the question, he sloughed it off.

"That old drunk?" Amboy asked. "He seems harmless enough."

"Do you think so? And don't let the drunk act fool you."

"I did see him do something, but it's something I can't talk about here." The rod. The snake. The holy wine.

"Did he tell you about his past?" Matias asked.

Amboy glanced at the other man. What was he getting at? This didn't seem to be just a conversation to pass the time. "Only that he and the Bishop were at odds," he said.

"Did you hear about the San Patricio Church Massacre?"

"That was before my time, I believe," Amboy said. "I do remember hearing something about it though. When was it?"

"1976."

"Okay. I was working in the mine by then." The boat hit a wake and bumped hard. He grabbed ahold of his seat between his legs to keep from flying. When he was completely drenched and sure that he wasn't going to flip overboard, he added, "We didn't get much news in the mountains."

"The short version was that two priests and three seminarians of the Pallottine Order were killed by unknown gunmen in their church while they slept. The murders were in retaliation to a bombing that happened two days previous. The problem was that the Pallottine Order wasn't involved in the bombing. It's been assumed that the killers knew that because they left a message for MSTM, who they believed did the bombing."

"*Movimiento de Sacerdotes para el Tercer Mundo*. Yes. I have heard of them. Father Paz mentioned them."

"Do you know what he did?" Matias asked.

"Was he involved in the bombing?"

"He organized it and set it in motion. The *Movimiento Peronista Montonero* did the actual bombing of the Argentinian Federal Police Headquarters."

"Wait? I thought the government was Peronista?"

Matias laughed. "You Americans with your Democrats and Republicans are so simple in your politics. When Peron returned from his eighteen-year exile in 1973, his organizers split into two groups. One right wing, which he embraced, and the other left wing, which he kicked out of the party a year later. They're the ones who planted the bomb."

"And Paz organized it. Why?"

"Can you guess?"

Amboy saw in his mind's eye Paz sitting in the underground room. *My brother was 'disappeared' and my mother became one of the Mothers of the Plaza. Then she was disappeared as well. I never saw either of them again. They were the only family I had except for the church.* Then after the divining rod turned into a snake. *What? You thought I was just a drunken out of work priest? I told you that the Bishop keeps me around to do certain things. These are the things I become involved in. Que quilombo!* Yes. The man was definitely more than projected.

"I suppose that's why he drinks so," Amboy said.

"I'm surprised you don't drink as much with all the men you've seen die . . . the ones you've killed."

"That was different. I was in a war."

Matias laughed. "What do you think we are in? A game? This is as dirty a war as there ever was. Mothers are on vigil because their sons are stolen in the middle of night. Groups combat the government and disappear. Then we are attacked by England and, instead of protecting the little guy, America sides with the one country that tried to force it into a subservient rule. How many did you lose in Vietnam? Sixty-five thousand? Argentines have lost half that already and haven't been able to even raise enough weapons for our own Buenos Aires Tea Party. This Dirty War of ours will probably be forgotten by history because, after all, we are a second-class European city in a third-class world, but for us it is terribly real. And for you, my friend, it is about to become even more real."

Shouts could be heard from ahead.

"Why are you telling me this?" Amboy asked.

"Because you need to be careful about getting involved. If you get too close, Argentina will grab you and never let you go."

Amboy hated being lectured to. "I can take care of myself."

The sound the men in the boat shouting greetings.

Matias leaned over next to Amboy's ear and whispered, "Of course you can, my friend. That's what everyone says. But for now, let me be the first to welcome you to ESMA. Welcome to Torture City."

CHAPTER 9

They went from open air with the petrol and dead fish odor of Rio de la Plata to the claustrophobic oppression of a tunnel with a single light and too many shadows. Even not being able to see, Amboy could feel the tightness of the quarters. The aroma of rock and water and the algae-covered dirt beneath their feet didn't hide the fear sweat that sprouted on the backs of everyone's necks. Unlike normal sweat, the stench of fear was a vile cocktail of vinegar and hopelessness. Somewhere a man wore cologne. It was soon evident he was the one giving the orders. As they passed from the maritime tunnel into a basement, the smell exploded into a fragrance of human waste, blood, vomit, and rotting human tissue. Somewhere near was an abattoir where men and probably women were relieved of body parts, possibly as an inducement to talk, but more probably as entertainment for their captors.

Amboy had seen his share of torture in Vietnam. After most of the Americans had left and he'd been assigned to various South Vietnamese units. Their sport was the capture and manipulation of hapless North Vietnamese soldiers. These would most certainly die a slow death as the South Vietnamese took out the demise of their own capitalistic dreams upon the malleable and supple flesh of the young men under their care whose only crimes were to be poor, from the north, and believe in the communist ideal. Amboy had seen it all, from dismemberment, to burning, to freezing, to electrocution, to even flaying. What one man could do to another would never surprise him ever again.

So, when he was presented with the same ripeness of prolonged death in the basement of ESMA that he'd smelled in the basements and boarding houses of Saigon, he set his jaw and prepared for the moment when he would own his own action. The moment when he would have a weapon and be able to punish those who needed punishing. Back in Vietnam, he'd been unable to reprove, but here, he was James Bond and had a license to kill.

The sound of a power tool and a scream shattered the relative silence of the booted footsteps of Matias' naval police officers and his own shuffling gait. A woman by the sound of it. Or it could have been a man, his vocal cords cracking octaves even for which a soprano might not aspire. Based on his limited knowledge of the map, Amboy believed they were being taken to the operations center on the first floor through the basement. Matias's men would be on the lookout for all three of their targets. If they saw one, they were to mark the location, but not do anything until they got to the operations center where the weapons locker and ammunition supply were. They needed to secure those at all costs.

Oddly, one thing that they'd been able to discern was that the building was almost empty during the day. It was as if the officers of ESMA knew how terrible their work was and required it to transpire under the cover of darkness. Meanwhile, outside there was to be a staged accident, created for the sole purpose of garnering the attention of those within.

He stumbled on the stairs going up. He was moving too fast to find them. His foot caught the lip of the stair again and he went down, pain erupting from his shin. His hands kept his face from slamming into the stairs, but just barely. Were they trying to make it more difficult? A thought went through him. What if this wasn't a ruse? What if he was actually being taken to ESMA for processing and torture? Would he even know the difference? When would he stop pretending—when they began the power tools on him? Would he recognize he'd been tricked at first blood? First scream? Was this all Matias's idea? Had Amboy run afoul of the CIA or the government and was now persona non grata?

They made it up the stairs and he felt himself pushed.

"*Hijo de puta!* Move faster," someone said.

He stumbled forward as he was shoved in the back and slammed face first into an unyielding surface. He felt his teeth loosen. Blood welled from a cut. He pushed away and managed to stand unsteadily, his head spinning.

Was this still a game?

He was still pretending, right?

When were they supposed to start fighting?

The room shook with the impact of a crash like a great sledgehammer on the street outside.

Men ran to the windows and looked out.

Much cursing was followed by the sound of a dozen pairs of feet running past and out the front door.

Was it now?

Why was it taking so long?

The sound of flesh on flesh.

Blood iron smell.

Blood.

And now, vomit.

Fuck it.

He reached up and removed his blindfold.

Three of the guards had their pistols to the sides of ESMA officers' heads.

A fourth was on the floor, wrestling with an ESMA officer.

Two other ESMA officers were dead, abdomens sliced open from knives.

He took three steps and kicked the wrestling ESMA officer in the jaw, sending him into a somnolent stupor. Amboy shoved his hands in his front pocket, and after a moment trying to retrieve it, pinched the key between his thumb and forefinger and unlocked his cuffs. He reached down and cuffed the unconscious man to a chair using the handcuffs that had so recently bound him.

Matias stood at the front door, locking it, and barring it from the inside.

"Come on," he said, handing Amboy a .38 caliber revolver. "We don't have much time."

With all the ESMA officers on this level subdued, they left one of Matias's men downstairs and ran up the stairs.

An ESMA officer in his underwear, carrying a pistol in his right hand, shuffled to the top of the stairs yawning. When he saw what was happening, he raised his pistol and fired.

Amboy felt the heat of the round sear past his check.

A body fell behind him.

Amboy raised his own weapon and fired twice, catching the man in the stomach and chest.

The man fell forward, his head splitting as it bounced off the marble stairs on his way to the bottom.

Amboy stepped out of the way as the body tumbled past. He glanced behind him and saw one of Matias' men had fallen forward. Blood had already begun to pool on the white marble stairs. Amboy reached down and grabbed the lock and chain he'd been holding. Now that guns had been fired, the reports still echoing up the staircase, the idea of silence was a joke. On cue, he and one of Matias' men ran up to the second-floor landing.

Doors opened to either side.

A man tried to exit, but Amboy put the still smoking pistol barrel to the man's head and he backed away. Amboy could have shot him outright, but the guilty and the innocent were ambiguous in the building and unless they offered any sort of danger, he was reluctant to turn himself into the killer he'd once been. He quickly affixed the chain and locked to the door, keeping the ESMA officers inside. A glance across the landing told him that the other man had done the same.

Amboy followed him and the remaining three men up the stairs.

Matias was the first to find the light switch.

The idea was that there was no way that there would be a completely dark room all the time. There had to be lights for those who cleaned and took care of the prisoners. They were right. Matias found the master switch behind a metal cage. But they were wrong about the place being cleaned regularly, something Amboy could have told them before the light even went on. Still, his nose could never have invented what his eyes beheld.

Everyone was strapped to a metal bed. Once white mattresses were the color of dried blood and body fluids. Five rows of beds with all the warmth and cleanliness of a field hospital during the Crusades.

A man whose eyes had been burned away moaned in the bed nearest. Amboy could still smell the vestiges of singed skin and lashes, each hypodermic of aroma a reminder that screams had accompanied the wounds in real time.

Another man whose face had been so beaten that the bones had rearranged into the topography of a lost continent.

Another man who'd died in his own vomit, a bolus still in

his mouth and hardening on the mattress, his manhood roughly removed, gaping wound filled with piss, puss, and dried blood.

Still another, chained only by the arms, chains not necessary elsewhere because he had no more legs.

Amboy stood unable to move, stunned at the sight of bed after bed of the ravaged and ruined. The atrocity humans could reap on each other could not be overstated. Where was the Golden Rule? In this land of Christians, where was mercy? Then he reminded himself that it certainly hadn't been imported from Spain. When the Old World met the New, it was all about subjugation and exploitation. During the height of the Inquisition, when the Holy Roman Church refined their own torturing techniques, they traded gold for humanity, importing one, only to export the other, turning captured people into slaves to do their own bidding. No. This was nothing new. It was just new in this manner to Amboy, whose upbringing in the backwards hills of East Tennessee was a paradise many of the peoples of Argentina would have loved to have been born into.

A shout made him spin.

He squatted as he turned, so the bullet passed above him. He fired from his knees catching his adversary in the chest. As the man fell, his pistol clattered to the ground and slid under a nearby bed.

Amboy dove for it, knowing that he only had a few rounds left in the pistol he held. He came up with it in his left hand, now doubly armed.

Back on his feet, he remembered the mission.

Find Thiago.

By the looks of it, they'd already found one of the others they were looking for and were helping him to his feet.

Amboy ran past them, head on a swivel as he searched for the brother of his best friend. But soon they'd cleared the floor and he was nowhere to be found. As they left, the screams of those who remained became a background static so like the room-filling cheers at a baseball game if there was but an opposite.

If anything, the fourth floor was worse than the third. The light only lit half the place and the floor was littered with old garments and ripped bed clothes.

Matias shot two women who had been sitting at one of the tables, playing a game of checkers. They were dressed in nurses' outfits if nurses' clothing came with gun belts. The first took it in the back of the head. The second took it in a surprised face that was about to exclaim something.

They found the second man they were looking for on the fourth floor. He'd been truncated as well, missing both of his legs, the incisions still raw and red, staples that looked like they'd been made for attaching boards puckering free of the skin.

Matias grabbed Amboy. "*Che boludo.* We have to go."

"We can't." He tore his arm out of Matias's grip. "We need to find Thiago."

"He's not here."

"Then we need to look again."

"I'm telling you. He's not here."

Amboy wanted to scream bullshit. Had they convinced him that Thiago was here to get his help? Had the boy never been here in the first place?

Machine gun fire erupted from below.

It was answered from outside.

Matias shook his head and ran for the stairs.

Amboy stared after him a moment, then ran back through the beds. He couldn't leave. Not yet. He had to be certain. His entire reason for coming was to find the boy, save him, for as God was his witness, Santiago would demand a reckoning once Amboy died.

He called for Thiago, running from bed to bed, shaking the dead and unconscious until he could make out each face. He was just about to give up, when he saw a man in a fetal position he hadn't checked. He called again, but there was no answer. He tried to get the man to turn around, but he wouldn't. The man fought Amboy's efforts. With herculean strength, Amboy turned the man over and saw the face of Thiago.

Or what had been Thiago.

One of his eyes had been removed, the space where it had been still a red and raw indentation. His face had been re-arranged. Both cheekbones, things that had made him handsome and had accentuated his smile were now crushed, sharp edges stabbing through his skin. His front teeth had been shattered and were now broken shards, parodies of what they once had been. His lips were swollen and cracked in seven places, still bleeding because of the depth of the wounds.

"Oh, Thiago."

"*Leabf* me," he whispered, the pain of merely speaking making him wince. Tears came from his remaining eye. "*Leabf* me alone."

"I'm not going to leave you."

Amboy went to help the young man up, but Thiago fought him.

Angry arguing voices came from the stairwell.

Amboy fell to his knees and peered over the bed.

Two ESMA officers came into the room in tactical formation, ready to be fired on. They scanned the room. When they saw the nurses, both of them cursed. One pulled a walkie-talkie from his utility belt and spoke into it. Then they both began to move into the room, spreading out.

Amboy aimed his pistol at one and then the other, but they were too far away. He couldn't really hit anything with a handgun over ten meters and both of his targets were dispersed and twice that distance away.

More machine gun fire erupted from downstairs.

The men glanced at each other, back into the room, then ran back towards the stairs and were soon rattling down them.

If this was them clearing the floor beneath, he might have a few more minutes to get Thiago out of there. But where? How? Then he remembered the stammered briefing given by the embassy suit. What does every government building on the planet have? Fire exits!

Amboy turned and noted that he was at the far east end of the fourth floor. Sure enough, not fifteen feet from them was a sign that read SALIDA.

He grabbed Thiago, but he still fought.

"Listen, your abuela has already lost one grandson. Do you think she wants to lose another?"

Thiago shook his head, tears and blood merging pink on his face.

"Your good looks can be fixed. Hell, with an eyepatch you'd look like a pirate and girls dig pirates."

He didn't get the smile he'd hoped for, but Thiago stopped struggling.

"Run," he said, the word clear as a bell. "Run," he said again.

Amboy patted him on the shoulder. "Don't worry about me. I'm not going anywhere."

Thiago gave him an odd look that went beyond pain. "Don't—d—d—don't—"

"Don't what?"

Thiago grabbed him by the collar and pulled him so Amboy's ear was mere inches from Thiago's mouth. "T—T—Trust them."

"Trust who?" Amboy asked, glancing over his shoulder to the door. He needed to get moving.

Thiago shook his head. "D—Don't trust," he managed to say, then he sagged back on the bed, all of the energy out of him.

Amboy grabbed the sheet from the bed and ripped it in two. He crossed both pieces around Thiago's back, looped them under his arms, then grabbed and slung them over his shoulders. He tied the lower two pieces around his waist. He tied the upper two pieces across his chest. Then, with bent back, he stood, hefting Thiago onto his back.

The young man didn't scream, but a moan of such suffering escaped it came almost as a gasp. If Amboy had the choice and the ability, he'd kill every one of the officers that comprised ESMA. The one he'd allowed to live had been lucky. Had he seen him after witness to their vile inhumanity, his forehead would still be smoking.

Amboy managed to carry Thiago to the emergency exit door, then fought to get it open. It had a handle. Who puts handles on emergency doors? Weren't they supposed to open easily? A voice in his head reminded him to complain to the management when this was all over. After thirty seconds of what felt like a bad Benny Hill sketch, he finally managed to open it and found himself on a metal balcony.

He could see the polluted waters of Rio de la Plata off to his left across Avenue Leopolde Lugones. If he could find a way to get there, they might actually make it. To his right was the front of ESMA, which was probably the last place he should go. With the machine gun fire he'd heard and the accident that had been staged, he had no idea what sort of chaos he might descend into.

Of course, there was always up. He could chance the roof and maybe wait until nightfall, then scurry down one of the fire escapes.

Who was he kidding?

It was now or never.

He began to descend, gripping tightly the sheets holding Thiago in place. They had one television with three channels in a house of nine people growing up. His grandmother kept it on most of the time. The only shows he ever really watched were *The Andy Griffith Show*, *The Brady Bunch*, *Gilligan's Island*, and *Star Trek* when he could see them—usually at night when she'd fallen asleep in her chair. *The Andy Griffith Show* was closer to reality than *The Brady Bunch*. Their California lifestyle was about as foreign as living on a desert island or in outer space. But what stuck with him, and what he was strangely reminded of at that very moment was the voiceover that Captain Kirk did at the beginning of every episode of *Star Trek*. Why it came to him, he didn't know, just as he hadn't known he'd once whistled the theme song to *The Andy Griffith Show* while on patrol in Vietnam.

"Space: the final frontier. These are the voyages of the starship Enterprise. Its five-year mission: to explore strange new worlds, to seek out new life and new civilizations, to boldly go where no man has gone before."

Was it his brain trying to reset itself after the insanity of the ESMA torture house? And to think Paz's mother and brother had been taken there before they were killed. For the love of God, what had happened to them prior to them being thrown out of an airplane.

He made it to the bottom of the fire escape unnoticed. He was out of breath. Sweat had soaked through his shirt and he was constantly adjusting his load which seemed about to fall off at any time.

"Easy, Thiago. We only have a little ways to go."

His load was getting heavier, but he'd be damned if he'd let Thiago fall to the ground. He'd heard of a staff sergeant back in Vietnam who'd carried his best friend who'd had his legs blasted off more than thirty miles through snake-infested, triple canopy, hostile enemy territory. Both of the men had survived and yearly they toasted each other. He'd like the same thing to happen with him and Thiago. He didn't have thirty miles to go and there were no snakes, but he did have a good hundred meters and there were serving Argentine Naval Officers between him and freedom who had long ago lost their moral compasses.

He met the first one when he turned the corner.

"*Parar! ¿Quién eres tú?*"

"I'm Captain Kirk of the USS *Enterprise*," Amboy said, pushing past, giving it all or nothing. He saw the entrance to the compound. ESMA officers were keeping people out, but no one seemed to be keeping people in.

The officer behind him grabbed for him and Amboy brought the pistol up and aimed for the man's eyes. Instead of standing, the man ducked, held up his hands, then turned and ran.

With nothing else to do, Amboy began to sing one of the only songs he knew front to back. "*Just sit right back and you'll hear a tale, A tale of a fateful trip, that started from this tropic port, aboard this tiny ship.*" By the time he got to the final chord, "*Here on Gilligan's Isle*," he was at the gate and pushing past. "*Excusa, por favor. Pronto. Excusa. Che boludo. Excusa.*"

He pushed his way through with less effort than he believed he would need. He deposited the pistol in an open handbag. The other was still in the small of his back, hidden by Thiago. Amboy made it to Avenue del Libertador and saw a string of taxis. He headed to the nearest one, but instead, found his route changing as a knife was placed in his ribcage enough to make him want to comply.

"Just follow me, asshole," said a voice in his ear. "You have got to be the stupidest man on the planet or the luckiest."

A van skidded to a stop.

The door opened and two masked men were on either side.

Amboy was pushed towards them and they grabbed him and Thiago and pulled them into the van.

The door slammed shut.

A rag went over his mouth.

It smelled of acid, chemicals, and a hundred thousand pounds of pillows.

And all went black.

CHAPTER 10

The room was ten by ten with wooden floors, walls and ceilings. A droplight hung from the ceiling above his cot just out of reach. He awoke with a mouth so dry, it was as if all the liquid had been sucked out of him. He moved his lips, dry snapping like a turtle left too long out of the pond. The room smelled of pine and wood glue, the tell-tale aroma of plywood. He'd been in enough of these cells to know what they were used for. He just wanted to know why he was in one.

Then he remembered.

Thiago.

Where was he?

ESMA?

Amboy reached to the small of his back. The weapon was gone. He noticed his shoes were gone as well as his belt. His shirt had been ripped open and hung buttonless and filthy. Was this a prison? Were they afraid he might commit suicide? What a ridiculous notion. Or were they afraid he might use them as weapons?

He stood and checked the door. The hinges were on the outside and there wasn't any handle. Still, he pushed against it and felt a little give. He decided what the hell, and began to bang on it.

"Hey! Let me out of here."

He waited.

Nothing.

After several minutes of banging and yelling someone banged on the door from the other side.

Amboy stepped back.

The door opened to two men. Both had their lower faces covered with red bandanas. One bade him follow, the other dropped in behind, carrying a machete. They looked like campesinos, deeply tanned, fit, sinewy muscles, and barefoot.

Amboy glanced back and noted that there were five more square wooden cells in addition to the one he'd so recently occupied. Birdcalls and the rustle of trees made him realize that they were in the jungle and nowhere near the city. Gone were the sounds of traffic, the hum of conversation, and the ever-present pollution, to be replaced by the buzz of insects, the hush of light wind through the trees, lush green foliage, and the tinkle of laughter from somewhere nearby.

They left a copse of jacaranda trees on a dirt path that opened up onto a lawn that was so tightly mowed it could have been a golf course. Up ahead stood a white-washed mansion on a raised hill. He could see a line of royal palms rising from the back, but in the front and on the side were classic Argentinian palo borracho trees. Also known as drunken stick trees, their fat bases hugged the ground like swollen sacks, rising to a luxurious canopy of twisted branches with red and white flowers. A sidewalk ran from the front to the left where several sports cars and a Range Rover were parked on a paved driveway. A red door was set into a gabled front porch, but they weren't going in the front door.

He was escorted around the side.

A collie ran towards him, tail wagging, barking friendly, sniffing at his dirty tan suit pants.

A pool came into view, its indigo blue waters sliced by the lithe figure of a young girl diving into it. Marching around a luscious deep red Bougainvillea, he spied two men sitting at a white metal glass-topped table on a stone patio, both drinking from tall glasses. Each of them wore white linen suits, collars open to the neck. The older of the two with a five-day old graying beard wore sandals. The younger with the smooth features of a Hollywood leading man wore brown leather huaraches. They'd been laughing about something, but paused when Amboy entered stage left.

The younger one beckoned.

"Come. Come. Join us, Señor Stevens," he said in perfect English.

Amboy allowed himself to be led to a chair between them. As he sat, he was acutely aware of how dirty and unkempt he must appear in comparison to the two men. Still, he squeezed his toes in the grass and relished the earthen feel. He closed his eyes for a moment and let the wind brush his skin.

A young female servant in a brown and white uniform presented him with a tall glass of liquid that looked like the ones his new best friends were drinking. He took a deep draught, fighting not to down it, and discovered that it was gin and tonic, with a lot more gin than tonic. It did little to assuage his cottonmouth, but gave him a heady rush with the taste of a juniper forest in the morning dew under a sky of vomit.

"I take it you slept well, Señor Stevens?" the younger man said, his Argentine accent slight, but apparent.

"What did you give me?" he rasped, managing not to stumble around the consonants.

"We were in a hurry to get you out and in our excitement, we probably gave you a little too much chloroform. Just know that everything is now under control. There's nothing to worry about."

"There was nothing to worry about until your people grabbed me—us," he amended.

"Extenuating circumstances, I'm afraid."

The man spoke in the smooth tones of a bureaucrat used to mollifying other people's feelings. He had a surety of voice and delivered everything with a pleasant grin that just begged to be knocked askew.

Amboy set his jaw. Took another sip, swallowed, then set the glass down. "Where's Thiago?"

"Straight to the point. I like that."

"Straight to the point would be me asking who and what the fuck do you think you're doing? What happened to my shoes and belt? Where are we? Why did you decide to get involved with my doings? And where the fuck is Thiago? That's to the fucking point."

"I told you he wasn't going to be happy, Nolan," said the older man. His voice and drawl pure Texas. "Why don't you get this boy some shoes?" He raised his glass and it was replaced by another.

"Hey Daddy," came the voice of the girl. "Watch me!"

"I see you, honey. You go on now," said the Texan, beaming as his daughter climbed back onto the diving board and sliced deftly into the water. Now closer, Amboy thought she might be somewhere between eight and ten. Then a thought occurred to him. Was this really her daddy? Or was it—

"Wallace is right, of course," the man named Nolan said. "Your friend is going to be fine, or as fine as the best doctors can make him. I had him flown to Montevideo where I am assured that he's being treated well. As soon as I get more information, I will provide it, of course."

"Who are you?" Amboy asked, softer, less stressed.

"Our name or letters aren't so important," he said with an apologetic smile. "Just know that we are on your side and were concerned for your safety. That you were able to enter ESMA and return with your friend is beyond amazing. Your compatriots did not fare as well. As you know, the place is a black hole of information and humanity. Later, if possible, we'd like to debrief you and ask you about what you saw inside. Perhaps, provide us with an updated layout?"

Amboy nodded. By the mention of letters, it left little doubt that the man in front was a CIA functionary of some sort. If what Nolan said was true, then he was the muscle. He needed to deal with the brain, so, he affixed his attention to the Texan.

Amboy sipped at his G&T and stared at the older man beneath lidded eyes.

Nolan glanced from him to the Texan.

The older man guffawed. "Did you see what he just did, Nolan? Our boy here just dismissed you as a target and switched to me. Careful, son. Nolan is a lot more than the effeminate fool he shines on. As for me, I'm afraid that I'm the reason you are here."

"Is this your place?" Amboy asked, not taking his eyes off the man.

"This? Hell, no. It's something that the—something Nolan uses every now and then when he wants to get away from the city. And while I do appreciate the European charm of Buenos Aires, I must say, the current state of affairs isn't conducive to good business or behavior."

"They probably don't like it that Reagan decided not to back them against England."

"That Hollywood phony gets us into more trouble than he's worth. But what did they really expect? Good or bad, we have history with England. Most of Americans are from good English stock. If they'd been smarter, they would have set about courting the Spanish. There hasn't been a good Anglo-Spanish war for four hundred years." He took a grand sip of G&T, his eyes twinkling. "I'd pay to be involved in such a war if no more than to watch both sides deplete their resources so I could come in a the eleventh hour and resupply."

"Which side?" Amboy asked.

"Does it matter?"

Amboy stared at the man for a moment, calculating the response, then asked, "What is it you do?"

"Some people call me daddy. Some people call me late for dinner. Some people call me Senator. Titles don't matter." He stuck out a thick hand that had seen its share of ranch work. "Wallace Thompson from Waco, Texas."

They shook hands.

"I read your file, boy. You have a solid if not outstanding military record. What made you come to Argentina?"

How could he explain it? So much water under the bridge. He'd followed his friend Oteil Stanislas from Vietnam. The son of a former SS commander had been his best friend in Vietnam and they'd made sure that each other would survive their multiple tours, promising to have each other's back. In exchange, Oteil introduced Amboy to the mining community. He openened the door for him and allowed him to stay in a place where he didn't have a history like—as a child, disappearing in the night only to return months later with broken arms. Losing contact with Otiel was something Amboy regretted the most.

So, he kept his response as simple as he could. "The mines. I like working in mines. It's an old family business. Doesn't matter what's in the earth, we bring it out. My family can trace its way back to Cornwall where my ancestors worked in the tin mines."

"*Doesn't matter what's in the earth, we bring it out,*" Thompson repeated. "I like that. Hopefully, you'll help us out. We're going to need some of your help after all. We need something brought out."

"Why me? I'm sure you have a lot of assets."

"The thing about a game board is that the edges are a known quantity. So are the game pieces. You are already in play. To put someone else in play might spoil our advantage."

"So, you have an advantage, now?"

Thompson gulped his drink. "In that no one knows you are working for us, yes?"

"I never said I was working for you." Amboy held up his glass. The servant came and he said in perfect Argentinian Spanish, "Can I have a pitcher of water, please?"

She looked to Nolan. Once he nodded, she went away.

"What do you expect me to do?" Amboy asked, licking his lips and watching the girl out of the corner of his eye. She wore a pink two-piece bathing suit and was smelling flowers.

"Where you're going, we need some eyes."

"Where is it I'm going?" Amboy asked, his eyebrow raised. How they knew about the future was of sudden intense interest to him.

"We can't be sure. But the board is set and you are all we have."

The servant returned with the pitcher and a clean glass. Amboy thanked her and poured himself water. Drank it. Poured himself another.

He looked from one to the other and sighed heavily. "I hate cryptic conversations. I feel like I'm in a Humphry Bogart movie."

"Now you're talking *The Maltese Falcon*," Nolan said. "The highlight of all detective movies."

"I could have been talking about *The African Queen* or *Casablanca*," Amboy said. "Or even *Key Largo*. That's a good one. Just an honest man against gangsters."

Nolan laughed. "I like that. An honest man. But what makes you think we're gangsters?"

Amboy merely stared at him.

Wallace shook his head. "You're talking movies now. If you had our Hollywood president, he could talk with you. He sure read enough scripts in his day—still does. I don't know movies."

"Oh, but I do," Nolan said. "Gangsters. That's a good one, Stevens. What was it the Bogart character said in *Key Largo*?" He snapped his fingers. "*When your head says one thing and your whole life says another, your head always loses.* I think that's appropriate."

"Are you saying that even though I say I won't help you, I'm going to end up helping you?"

"Is that what your head says?" Nolan asked playfully.

"My head is still a little fuzzy from the chloroform you gave me."

"Here's one you'll recognize from *The Maltese Falcon*. Sam Spade said it when they wanted to know why he was investigating. *When a man's partner is killed, he's supposed to do something about it. It doesn't make any difference what you thought of him. He was your partner and you're supposed to do something about it. And it happens we're in the detective business. Well, when one of your organization gets killed, it's . . . it's bad business to let the killer get away with it, bad all around, bad for every detective everywhere.*"

"Jesus, Nolan," Wallace drawled. "You're a walking movie dictionary."

Nolan grinned. "It's not that. I'm an auditory learner. I'm hyperthymesiac. I remember everything I hear."

"You're talking revenge," Amboy said. "You want me to go back to ESMA. For Thiago."

Nolan held out his hand.

"But really for your own reasons," Amboy added.

Wallace deposited a hundred-dollar bill into it.

"I told you he'd understand without us telling him. He feels it. He wants it. He literarily needs to do it."

"Your ninth-grade math teacher?" Amboy asked. Then added, "Your first-year philosophy professor?"

Nolan grinned. "Ooh. A challenge. Ms. Hardaway taught math—geometry really—and I still remember my proofs and theorems. I didn't take philosophy, but I did take Poly Sci and can recite Machiavelli in original Italian, although I don't know what it means. It does work well at parties, though."

"You also probably majored in underwater basket weaving," Wallace said.

"Close enough, I suppose. English Literature." Nolan's face turned serious as he leaned across the table. He poured himself some water, drank half, and sat back. "We have a party tonight. You're invited of course. I'll make sure you have the opportunity to clean up and send some clothes your way. We seem to be about the same size. Later, we should be able to get together and make plans. Then tomorrow, we'll go back inside the beast."

"We?" Amboy asked. "Are you coming?"

Nolan's Cheshire cat grin returned. "Figure of speech, my new friend. Figure of speech."

CHAPTER 11

A servant led him to a room in the main house on the second floor and in the back. There seemed to be a row of similar rooms, tiny apartments that shared a common bathroom. With the high ceilings and impeccable taste in period furniture it seemed more like an upscale hotel. Even after he'd showered, shaved and stood in front of the gold filigreed mirror of his room, he reminded himself that however gilded his cage was that it was still a cage.

They'd laid out a suit and other clothes while he'd been in the shower. Pressed white linen. Pressed blue shirt. Brown leather huaraches—Mexican close-toed sandals. Everything fit well if not a little loose. Nolan was maybe one size larger. At least he wasn't smaller. In the heat and humidity of South America he'd much rather wear loose clothes than tight. They'd even provided him a watch with a light leather band. He checked the time as he put it on. 5PM. If there was to be a party, guests would be arriving soon.

Once he'd finished dressing, he sat on the edge of the bed, regarding the immediate future. That they wanted him to go back into ESMA was clear. He felt it was a suicide mission, however. Matias and his crew had gotten lucky. They'd done something no one had ever tried before and that was to break into a torture house. Now that it had been done, ESMA would be ready. Nothing would come as easy as it had previously, so he didn't know what value he added to the mission. All he could hope for was that whoever was to lead the clusterfuck had more sense than him. Who was he kidding? If he had more sense he'd be gone from here. He'd seen enough second lieutenants show up to Vietnam with all the education and military training a brave nation had to offer, only to stare wide-eyed and wonderous at how absolutely fucking backwards everything could possibly be.

A knock came at the door.

He opened it to a servant who informed him that it was time for cocktail hour.

Cocktail hour. How definitely civilized.

He straightened the collar of his blue shirt, swiped some of the wrinkles out of the jacket, and followed the servant down the stairs.

People were already beginning to gather in the two hours he'd been alone.

A sizable group stood outside on the patio served drinks and canapés by passing servants.

Another group stood in the library on the first floor, chatting in front of a large painting.

He headed for this because it was nearer, his hands at his side, not really wanting to connect with anyone, but aware that he needed to at least make an effort if he didn't want to become the perennial outsider. Plus, he was curious. He wanted to know the reason for this sophisticated shindig.

A servant slid by, passing him a flute of champagne.

He automatically took a sip, the bubbles juxtaposing on an image of the man at ESMA who'd had both eyes burned away.

He felt sick to his stomach but couldn't find a vase or anything to pour away the champagne. So, he held the flute in a clenched fist, ignoring the contents.

Five people stood in front of a painting—or maybe it was a photograph. The image was almost hyper-focused. Nolan, and two couples. One young. One old. The painting or the photograph was the center of attention. The lines seemed too perfect and sharp for it to be a painting. It seemed to have been drawn in a fog, the background a ghostly misshapen image, pieces of the central figures obscured by wisps of weather swirling off green and granite earth, withered and twisted trees around it.

A full moment passed before he understand what he was seeing. A man riding a great beast, a single horn coming from the beast's forehead. If it was to have been a unicorn, then the features were all wrong. It wasn't a horse. It wasn't even recognizably any animal that he'd ever seen. The face was monstrous while the eyes looked world-weary, as if it had seen eons come and go and was ready to go itself. Hair hung from its body in waterfalls of white. The man on its back sat straight, head high, chin elevated, eyes staring out from the picture—or photo.

Amboy shook his head. It couldn't possibly be a photo. Yet . . .

"Ah. Mr. Stevens. Welcome," Nolan said, noticing him for the first time. "We hope you found your room and the service to be pleasing."

Amboy nodded, offered a smile, but it felt more like a queasy frown, then pointed at the object of his attention. "What is this?"

"This?" Nolan laughed. The younger two of his group departed, leaving him and two others, an older man and a woman, each wearing formal attire, just as Nolan was. It appeared that Amboy was the only one wearing a linen suit. Was it an oversight or was there a reason for it? Maybe to put him in his place. Wouldn't Nolan be surprised when he discovered that Amboy just didn't care.

As if presenting a fifteen-year-old for her quinceañera, Nolan stepped aside and swept his arm. "This is the Red Unicorn of Tierra del Fuego."

"Not what I expected a unicorn to look like," Amboy said.

"What does a unicorn look like, Mr. Stevens? If your idea was informed by Walt Disney then it might be a horse with sparkles and a filigreed horn." He chuckled. "The truth is far from that reality, let me promise you."

"Why do you call it red?"

"I've never seen one in person, mind you, but I am told that when it feeds, it guts its prey with that great horn of his, and the blood then flows down and across its face all the way to its flank."

"Never seen one in person?" Amboy smiled, brought the champagne to his lips, then lowered it, reminding himself of the men he'd seen in the *Hood.* "You're joking, for certain."

Nolan grinned. "Am I?"

"You doubt the existence?" the woman asked, her accent definitely German.

"I don't doubt much. I just find it hard to believe that there are unicorns."

"The same could be said about elephants, until one actually sees one," said the man, also German. "If it wasn't for circuses and zoos, no one would believe that such a creature could exist, based on the description."

"Don't forget the giraffe," she said.

"Of course. And the giraffe." The man sniffed his nose at the picture.

Amboy was already tired of the party. He wanted to go back to his room, but decided to play along for a moment. "Then why aren't unicorns in zoos?" he asked.

"Why take something out of its habitat when you can go and visit it?" Nolan asked.

"The same could be said about the elephant," Amboy said, remembering Wallace earlier talking about board pieces and wondering of this wasn't a continuation of the conversation.

"But there are far more elephants than unicorns," the man said. "Plus, knowing where to find it is exclusive." He glanced at his wife. "We don't want just anyone snooping around and taking pictures. Anyway, what good is a secret if everyone knows?"

His wife nodded sagely and the two wandered off together.

Amboy watched them leave, eyes raised, trying not to frown. Nolan caught his expression, so he asked, "Who are they?"

"Forgive me. That's Otto and Giselle Hess. He's the counsel at the German embassy. They're not bad folk. A little stiff, but then again, who isn't these days with internal strife and the war and all."

Amboy turned and glanced around the room where pockets of people stood together chatting.

"What's the occasion?" he asked.

Nolan shrugged. "We come together several times a year. Interested parties. Governments come and go as do international alliances. We try and make sure there's something to fall back on when and if everything goes. This current mess notwithstanding, we have efforts in place that need to be seen to finish." He raised his glass. "Enjoy dinner. Make sure you pay attention to the festivities afterwards. I'm sure you will find them fascinating."

Amboy turned back to the painting and regarded it once more. He realized then that they never did discuss who was riding it. And why *would* someone ride such a beast? Then he saw something in the foreground that disturbed him. It looked to be a crowd of people, but it couldn't be right. The proportions were all off. The size differential made it look as if the people were in miniature. Yes. It was definitely a painting. And not that good a one it turned out.

He headed outside, looking for fresh air. He was still thinking about the painting, when he almost knocked over a miniature human. As it turned out, it was the girl he'd seen swimming earlier.

"Sorry about that," he said.

"I saw you earlier talking with my dad," she said.

"Guilty as charged. What's your name?" he asked.

"Meagan," she said proudly, her shoulders going back. "Have you ever known someone with that name?"

"I haven't. What sort of name is that?" he asked.

"It was my grandmother's. She was a hell of a woman," she said in all seriousness.

He laughed throatily. "I bet she was. You should be proud."

"What's your name?" she asked.

"Amboy Stevens," he said, glancing past her where he saw an argument unfolding between a young Argentinian and Nolan. Both men seemed ready to come to blows.

He felt a tug at his jacket.

"Didn't you hear me?" she asked.

"No, I'm sorry, Meagan."

"Why did they name you Amboy? Is there an Amgirl?"

He laughed again. He glanced over her shoulder again, but the two men had moved on. "My mother chose the name. She said it was an old family name, but I don't know of anyone else with it."

"Did you get made fun of?" she asked.

"I did until I let people know that wasn't acceptable behavior."

"My daddy gets mad at me for fighting too. But sometimes you just have to."

He nodded. "Sometimes you do. You were quite the mermaid earlier," Amboy said. "You must love the water."

She blushed. "My daddy says I was born to swim."

"Well, not everyone likes the water," he said, imagining all of those being hurled from aircraft into the Pacific Ocean by ESMA. The Disappeared.

"Why wouldn't someone like water?" she asked, eyes wide.

He dismissed destroying her childhood and instead said, "Everyone is different. Some people are afraid they might rust."

"Well, that's just silly," she said. "They think they are made of metal. No one is made of metal."

"How can you be so sure? There's that picture of the unicorn in the other room. Isn't that silly?"

"Oh. No. Uncle Nolan says I can go see it this year." She made a pouty face. "He wouldn't let me go last year. He said I was the only one so it wasn't safe." She heard someone calling her name, flashed Amboy a grin, then took off, moving her limbs in gyrations only a gangly little girl could manage.

Amboy watched her go, wondering why she was there and had free range. He also wondered if there were any other children at the festivities.

He kept his eye out for Wallace, but didn't see him before dinner. Amboy ended up being seated by the Japanese oil minister and his wife, neither of whom spoke a lick of English or Spanish. It was all nodding and smiling and gesturing throughout dinner, which was some sort of fish wrapped in banana leaves paired with steak. If there was one thing he didn't mind was the Argentinians' love of beef. They'd have it at every meal if they could. He'd seen their cowboys too and would put them up against the best America had to offer.

Dessert was key lime pie and a stiff coffee. The coffee was the best part and even though he knew it was likely to keep him up tonight, he had three cups. Visions of the men and women of ESMA kept creeping into his mind, much like the images he'd succeeded in warding off from Vietnam. With those, he had several tricks of immediately moving his thoughts to something else when it strayed towards certain memories. The problem with ESMA was it had been too recent and he had yet to determine the tricks.

Just as he was finishing his third cup of coffee, Nolan stopped by, touched his elbow and asked him how dinner was.

"How is Thiago doing in the hospital?" Amboy asked. "Is he out yet?"

Nolan paused, but didn't lose his smile. "I haven't checked but I will do so first thing in the morning."

Amboy grinned. It was exactly the response he'd expected. "When you do, I want to join the conversation. I want to speak to Thiago's abuela and ask her how things are going."

Nolan's smile hitched but never fell. He paused a moment, then nodded. "I'll make sure you are notified."

"I'd appreciate it." Amboy began to turn away, but turned back. "Oh, and Nolan? If I don't talk to abuela, then we might as well take my token off the board."

Nolan didn't miss a beat. "Of course, Señor Stevens. I wouldn't have it any other way."

Amboy found it hard to be angry with the man. He definitely had the agreeable quality that organizations needed. Nolan could sell water to a drowning man and walk away with a year's subscription as well. He was that good. The thing about confidence men, though, was as long as you knew it and you trusted the fact that you knew it, you'd be okay. You just couldn't fall for the man's or woman's spiel.

Eventually, everyone began to migrate down the front lawn, past the six small buildings, to an open amphitheater he hadn't noticed before. Seating had been arranged in a semi-circle around a raised mound of grass. People sat in white chairs and were waited on by the staff from the house. Some gentlemen stood at the full bar, but others merely waited for a passing steward carrying a tray of either champagne or after dinner bite-sized desserts.

Amboy spied the Japanese couple bowing and conversing with Wallace. Past them, he saw a group where the Hesses were holding court. Amboy could have sworn he recognized some of them. All German, he surmised, they did look familiar. Nolan was also making the rounds, shaking hands like he was at a reception.

Amboy regarded the stage. An elevated grass hill, it stood about a body's length higher than the rest of the ground. The grass was cut short. Behind it stood more drunken trees, their limbs skeletally intertwining until they represented a scenic backdrop for the events that were about to transpire. Off to the left, he noted were eight young girls, each dressed in a white dress, barefoot, with a crown of dandelions. The girls were of every nationality. Asian, Western European, Slavic, Latina, and one African American.

He had a notion and turned, surveying the crowd. Sure enough, he saw them. A regal African American couple, tall and impeccably dressed, shaking hands with some others he didn't know, but at ease and not at all feeling in distress. Who were they? And was this their daughter? And if this was their daughter, then that meant that many of the couples present had daughters about to be a part of a ceremony. Maybe it was like a quinceañera, but with younger girls. Curious. They all did look the same age. Eight, perhaps? The event had a carnival buzz and soon, people began to take their seats. Amboy was too ripped on caffeine to sit, so he was satisfied to watch the events from behind the back row.

Once everyone had been seated, he heard the sound of a single violin, playing a song he'd never heard, but at the same time, it felt familiar. Part eerie. Part hymnal. Part something that made him pay attention and the hairs stand up on his arms and the back of his neck. He searched until he found the locus of the sound. A woman dressed in black, small and twisted like the trees—ugly really, but producing beautiful music much like the drunken trees produced beautiful flowers. Then the girls began to move. Eight of them, each dressed the same way, each young and gangly and barely containing the energy they encompassed. Each of them wore smiles one might want to capture for eternity. Once onstage, they formed a semi-circle facing the gathered ensemble, not a single one of them able to stand still.

Amboy watched with interest.

What could be next?

Whatever he thought it could be, it wasn't what they rolled out on a wheeled crucifix.

After Amboy got over the shock of the man's nakedness, he realized that he recognized him. The man from ESMA. The man he'd let go; someone he could have killed but didn't, now hung from ropes on a portable elevated crucifix. His feet were nailed to boards, forming an X rather than directly beneath him. His hands were likewise nailed to boards.

Murmurs rose from the crowd. Not from shock or repulsion, but from excitement.

Amboy got the definite impression that this was a version of something that they'd seen before. What then? What could possibly be next?

The man began to wail when he saw the audience.

Several members bade him to be quiet, not at all interested in his well-being, but rather the continuation of the ceremony. They treated him as if he were a member of the audience making noise enough to disturb their viewing experience, rather than the apparent centerpiece of a terrible theater.

The violin became louder and worked from major chords through to minor ones, using the same melody, but with less pleasant material. Finally, its noise was so much more a shriek than music and people soon found their very hearing at risk, hands going to the ears. Then it stopped abruptly in mid-note.

A white stag strode onto the grassy stage, tossing its head left and right, regarding everyone and no one as a stag is wont to do. Snuffling from its nose, it occasionally paused to paw the ground. Amboy was struck by the intense whiteness of the creature. It wasn't so much the pureness of the hue, but rather the absence of any other color. Other than its obsidian eyes and red nose and lips, it appeared to be a spirit, some ghost of some natural being who'd suddenly stumbled onto a South American Passion Play where eight-year-old girls were the Greek chorus.

The stag's rack of antlers was so immense it seemed from a larger creature which was why its neck was so thick and covered with white fur. The stag began to sniff around the man. It inspected him, thoroughly, then moved onto the girls.

The prisoner released himself on the grass below him, which served to enrage the stag.

It kicked him in the stomach with its hind legs, drawing blood.

The audience gasped, met with some tittering as some made comments to their partners.

The young girls were of more interest, the stag striding stately to the right end of the line. It moved to each one as if inspecting them, sniffing and occasionally prodding. It passed Meagan, prodding her like the rest, then moved on. She could barely keep her excitement, giggling to the audience, her face preternaturally charming. Amboy couldn't help but share her smile. What a wonder to be near such a beast. He'd seen brown stags half that size in the mountains of Tennessee, but never seen any human to deer interaction. He could only imagine what it might feel like to be near something so immense, natural, and special.

Once the stag was done with the girls, it began to circle the man. It twitched its tail several times, something Amboy knew from hunting that meant that it wasn't happy. For any other deer, he might say that it felt nervous, but he couldn't imagine this particular stag ever feeling nervous. It sniffed at the captive and shook its head when it came near the offal the man had left in the grass. He almost felt sorry for the man, but he was ESMA. He was a torturer and by definition the worst sort of human—one who relished in the fear and terror of others.

Then the stag stood on its hind legs. He'd never heard a deer make a sound like this before, but it screamed and as it rose into the air, the violinist began again, matching it in tone and intensity. The instrument came alive, just as the stag attacked. The twisted woman sawed the bow furiously across the strings. The stag came down on the already bloody abdomen of the man with both front feet, gauging great pieces of meat free. It backed away, then rammed its antlers into the man's torso, twisting and tearing, the man screaming for a moment, then dying just as suddenly as the twisting of the antlers obliterated his heart. Gouts of blood covered the grass in waterfalls of the man's insides.

A movement to the right caught Amboy's eyes.

Meagan, delighted and clapping.

The Japanese girl next to her had her eyes downcast.

Every one of the other girls seemed sickened by the scene.

Back to Meagan, he wondered what she was seeing and thinking.

Then he noticed her hands.

The wooden structure holding the man began to buckle because the antlers had already gone through the man's stomach and back, shattering the spine, and had been working on the wood. At the last moment, the beast backed away, its pure white coat now soaked in blood much the way Nolan had described the unicorn and the reason it had been called red.

The stag pawed at the ground. It turned to regard the crowd and shook its antlers. Blood and pieces of meat rained down on the audience. Instead of being disgusted, they reveled in the display, each one grinning at their partner, sharing the blood by making marks on each other's cheeks. Laughter joined animated conversation until someone hushed the ensemble.

The stag was now moving towards the girls.

Amboy noticed all of their hands.

He straightened. He'd seen what it had done to the man. Were the girls next? Was that what this was? Some sort of pre-pubescent South American slaughter? Why was he even here? He searched out the crowd for Nolan only to discover that the man was staring directly at him. He raised a drink, then gestured to the stage. Amboy turned back to watch.

The stag's maw dripped; blood had run down from the antlers to coat the mouth as if it were some savage vampiric beast. Everywhere it went, it left a trail of the man's insides. Again, it moved to the right side of the line, examining and inspecting the girls. The violin had calmed a bit and was no longer in minor keys, keeping to the majors and creating an almost baroque-like church atmosphere.

The stag stepped from girl to girl, sniffing and investigating until it reached the end. It moved back up the line, doing the same.

Men and women began to stand up in the crowd, cheering in their own languages. What had been horrible was now sport.

In English, Amboy heard, "Choose her. Choose her, damn you."

Followed by a "You cursed it. Now it's ruined."

As it turned out, the couple he thought were African-American were Jamaican, their singsong calls for the beast to choose their daughter as loud as anyone's.

The sounds of the crowd grew louder and louder.

He could no longer hear the violin.

The stag seemed to take energy from everyone and galloped back and forth, sometimes kicking with its hind legs, sometimes rearing back.

Finally, it began to settle, snuffing and puffing, until it eventually stopped in front of Meagan.

No, not her he thought. He didn't know what it meant, but he knew it couldn't be good. *Please not her.* His grip tightened on the back of the seat he had been gripping.

The stag leaned forward and poked her in the forehead, then backed away, revealing a blood-red mark.

Cheers came up from a corner of the crowd.

Amboy recognized Wallace and several others. They inexpertly high-fived each other, faces radiant with joy.

Then the crowd moaned.

The stag also poked the Japanese girl in the head, leaving the same mark.

Some cheered, some booed.

The stag turned and glared at the crowd.

Everyone went silent.

Each girl, whether chosen or not, looked for their parents. Some brought their hands above their eyes to shield it from the light, but he didn't need to see them to know. Six fingers. All of them.

The stag stood still, chin up, surveying everything, as if taking note, or taking names. It was eerie the way it gazed upon everyone, including Amboy who felt the heat of the gaze when it washed over him.

A man ran onto the stage to wrangle the beast, which seemed

as if it wanted to stay, but then acquiesced, no longer a god, now merely a male deer, something living and hardly deadly.

Meanwhile, the reverent silence had turned into the cacophony of post-sports match, one side happy, the other not, and everyone yelling at everyone else.

Amboy didn't need this shit.

He bailed, found a G&T, and headed back to his room.

CHAPTER 12

They came for him the next morning.

He'd already washed. He'd dressed in last night's clothes, wiping them down and smoothing them as best he could. Room service had provided coffee and toast, which he'd inhaled until there was nary a crumb left. Afterward, he'd stood at the window, staring at the blue reflection off the pool and the trees beyond, remembering the previous night and the crazy sporting event involving the stag and the eight young girls with six-fingered hands.

Nolan arrived with another man, this one looking like he'd stepped out of an issue of *Soldier of Fortune*. "This is Frank. That's his only name. Don't ask him for any other. He'll be leading your endeavor."

Endeavor.

Like climbing a mountain.

Jumping out of an airplane.

Spelunking into a cave.

Any one of which was dangerous on its own, but neither one having armed men waiting for them on the other end in a place known for being one of the world's worst active torture chambers.

Yea.

Endeavor.

"Greetings, Frank." He didn't offer to shake the man's hand. Frank smelled of gunpowder and cheese, the latter unexpected and unexplained.

"Stevens. I understand you know your way around combat."

"Three tours in Vietnam and forty-five minutes inside ESMA."

That earned him a solid look. "That will do it."

Nolan stepped aside so Frank could lead Amboy down the stairs and out of the house. They went to the outbuildings, one of which Amboy had awoken in just yesterday. Four of them were filled with angry-looking Argentinians. As it turned out, they'd been Argentine Special Forces and had been drummed out of the army for various reasons, which made them available for service with the organization for which Frank worked. They seemed more than eager to assault ESMA, which Amboy guessed probably had more to do with their anger at not being able to play ESMA's terrible games instead of any real animosity towards them. Alternatively, perhaps that was Amboy's own discrimination. He couldn't be sure.

Regardless, by seven in the evening they were in place, two blocks from ESMA HQ, prepared for assault.

By ten at night, they were finished, half their number, bloody, stabbed, and shot, unbelieving at the amount of carnage he'd been capable of when pushed over the edge.

Before they'd left that morning, Nolan had been as good as his word. Amboy had already changed into the tactical gear they'd wanted to wear and felt as if he was more a prop in a movie than a soldier in a campaign. Still, he knew how serious the business was to be and that the equipment might be necessary to survive. He doubted he'd have the same luxury of luck that he'd had last time he'd been in the torture capital of the universe. He might actually have to work in concert with someone, use tactics, act military, rather than flying by the seat of his pants and hoping for the blessings that had always seemed to be there for him.

Nolan had greeted him with the same smile he'd greet a landed potentate. He'd dialed a number, handed Amboy the phone, and soon he was speaking with Abuela. She was profuse in her appreciation and let him know that the doctors in the hospital in Montevideo indicated that Thiago would recover. There was no mention of the way his face would look afterward, nor would there be. To an abuela, her grandson was and would always be beautiful.

Amboy remembered Thiago's last words to him. "Don't trust them." Who had he been referring to? Was it Carson? Nolan? Was it Paz?

The abuela bade Amboy make sure he would be safe and to ensure the safety of Lettie. He had to admit, she'd been the last thing on his mind lately. He'd needed the reminder. They had a connection and he was suddenly as worried about her as he was Meagan, most recently chosen for something yet to be determined by a mysterious white stag.

No, it couldn't be Paz. The old priest had his own horrible history and they were just two lost souls intersecting on the avenue of best intentions. If they could only keep straight and ignore the lures from the alcoves and sideways. In fact, Amboy wanted to go to Paz, tell him what had happened—ESMA, the unicorn, the stag, all of it. The three of them, Paz, Lettie, and Amboy, they could get away from the craziness, go anywhere. If Lettie insisted on going to Patagonia, then they'd go. Instead of a place in Tierra del Fuego, they'd find another, somewhere they could fish and hunt and drink and talk and be a weird little family and live out their days without three-letter agencies and mothers and fathers promising their six-fingered children to some erstwhile nature god.

Amboy wasn't used to the feelings that were coursing through him. He'd grown up in a large extended mountain family, but it hadn't been the same kind of family he'd seen his friends have when he'd gone to Vietnam. His family was one to push you outside as fast as they could, let you find a way to survive. They didn't have the money or the time to take care of the children they kept having. The elderly were revered but the children were forgotten. His brothers and sisters were more like cousins, and even then, it was as if everyone knew they were related but it hadn't mattered how.

He'd encountered fellow soldiers who had one or maybe two siblings and their relationships were close enough that they cared about holidays and they cared about how the other ones felt. Amboy felt himself at odds with the idea that he might care about his brothers' birthdays or buy his sisters something for Christmas. Surviving had always been the gift. Living had always been the bow on the invisible box. All Amboy had been raised with was the idea that everyone needed to be fed and that no one outside of the family should ever do anything untoward to a family member. As long as those two algorithms were followed the math of the family was precise.

So, then why was the idea of Lettie as a sister to him so important? Why was he so concerned with the immediate future of Meagan? And Paz—good old Paz: right or wrong he seemed like an older brother or a favorite uncle with whom he wanted to spend time. Had the man bombed those he'd felt were guilty of killing his mother and brother? So, what if he did? If this was true, and the rules of war were in play, why was it wrong? Paz was even more a lost soul than Amboy—an old man who'd lost something, who was trying to regain something, be someone again. Was it so bad?

The feelings of warmth when Amboy considered them and played memories in his mind's eye were feelings he wasn't used to experiencing, except on the rare occasions he'd allowed himself to be real friends with someone in Vietnam or his very real friendship with Santiago in the El Quemado mine. He felt the pull of belonging and it was strong enough that he despised Nolan and Frank Just Frank for forcing himself away from it. For as much as he hated ESMA, his affection for his new friends was greater.

While Matias had been able to successfully save the two men they'd gone after earlier, their debriefing of those men had revealed that a man once thought dead was still alive. This time they weren't going in after a victim, but rather one of the torturers. Frank and Nolan and the rest of the people who worked at their three-letter agency wanted this man for interrogation. He knew things no one else knew and they wanted to know them.

Then they debriefed Amboy using architectural renderings of the insides of ESMA. He pointed out what he'd seen of the second and third floors, as well as what he'd heard in the basement when they'd arrived by boat through the canal. Frank was thorough in his questions and the debriefing took several hours.

Once they were finished, they had a plan. But like the cliché said, no plan survived contact with the enemy. So, it was after all six of them infiltrated that evening under the cover of darkness wearing their 3rd Gen AN/PVS-7 Night Vision Goggles that they were able to make it into the basement through the canal, but no further, because the enemy was waiting for them.

The initial firefight was furious.

Amboy and the attackers wore ballistic masks on their faces and ballistic armor on their forearms and thighs. Although it was meant to deflect incoming rounds, it wasn't thick enough to guarantee such results. They wore Level IV body armor in their chests. Two rounds slugged Amboy in the torso, knocking him down. He wasn't injured beyond bruising, but the bruising was like being hit by a baseball bat slung by a Babe Ruth lookalike.

Two of the others weren't as lucky.

One went down with bullets through his faceplate.

The other was spun like a top when three bullets flashed through an unprotected shoulder after his weapon jammed.

They each carried French-made MAS FAMAS machine guns. They were bullpup by design which meant that the trigger housing was forward of the 30-round magazine and feed. The problem with the weapons was that they were known to jam. But Frank and his team couldn't use anything American. They had to stay with what the Argentines used and this was one of their primary weapons. The irony, of course, was that the ESMA officers were using state-of-the-art American weapons and could get away with it.

Frank was also not one to be kept from his target. He didn't care about the torture victims who were in the act of being disappeared. To him, they were already dead. So, he threw several fragmentation grenades behind the enemy, creating a carnage of both pressure and pain for both friendly and foe alike.

Amboy kept his head down as they traversed the basement, alternately firing and helping the wounded man on their team. The dead one they left behind, as they would him if he caught a bullet. He went through two hundred rounds before his own rifle jammed so then he used it as a hammer, hitting his opponents across the face.

The entire time he was inside he thought of Thiago and what they'd done to the young handsome boy.

He thought of Paz and his brother and how he'd probably been likewise tortured and then disappeared.

He also thought of Paz's mother and how she'd stood vigil on countless nights, showing ESMA that the light would find their darkness, only to fall victim to that same darkness.

He thought of the ARVN torturers he'd seen in Saigon right before the fall, knowing that it was too late for the information, but not caring because all they wanted was to take their twenty pounds of flesh before they had to assimilate and pretend to be Ho Chi Min-loving communists.

He closed his heart and he closed his mind for a time and made the men of *Escuela Superior de Mecánica de la Armada* the nail and he the hammer. He became an architect of an MC Escher structure where up and down was like good and evil and no one knew which track to tread. For him it didn't matter, because what he was building would soon be torn down, towers of pain, splintering as they fell, rooms of sorrow crashing into basements of despair. So, he hammered forward, creating as he went, building cities on the bodies of the dead, each one encasing memories of a man turned evil who'd once played ball with a mother or a father or a sister before life lured him into the clammy darkness of the immoral soul. Even his companions stood aside as they watched his fevered construction, their fascination accompanied by equal amounts of envy and terror at his ability to so quickly create something so deadly that to see it made one fall victim to it. Past the first floor. Up the second floor. Onto the third floor he went, erecting himself and the creation until the up and down and the left and the right confused his quarry and all it had to do was beg, which he allowed it to do after he rearranged its limbs into something more resembling a human and less a torturer. But the problem with reassembling was that what once was could never be again and a man so rearranged could never do things a man should be able to do, including communicating the dark secrets that had been the engine for this terrible machine.

Ten PM that evening when they were in a safehouse, recovering, he allowed Frank to slap him one time, only to reassure himself that he was still alive. Somewhere inside ESMA he'd failed to feel anything. Any emotion. Any feeling. Anything. Instead, he'd gone somewhere else while his body did what it had do to.

When Frank reared back to slap him again, Amboy caught the wrist with his hand.

They argued.

He'd killed their target.

So fucking what.

They agreed they'd never exchange presents at Christmas.

Amboy was left weaponless on a street corner, no money, no prospects, but alive and angry and tired and needing of a thousand hours of sleep where he could dream of a life where his friends didn't have demons carved into their backs and they weren't cold-blooded bombmakers who drank too much and smiled so sweetly.

CHAPTER 13

The rain washed away most of the blood and brain matter coating his clothes. Twice military police vehicles had pulled up next to him to see what he was doing and both times they'd pulled away without stopping. He didn't know if it had been the blood or the fury that still lived in his eyes, but he'd kept on walking, thoroughly soaked, ankle deep in sludge. He circled part of the city for a time, still fighting, still battling. His hands were jammed in his pockets, but his right forefinger was pulled into his palm, forever firing weapons he'd long since thrown aside. His vision was filled with the blood of those who deserved it, but in their receiving, he couldn't help but feel that he'd become what he most despised. He saw them not as attackers, but victims of his own inability to handle emotions that had been held in check until they'd been forced to the surface by the actions of a capricious government and a questionable three-letter agency.

An abuela found him sitting past midnight on a curb, cars rushing by, splattering water on him without him even moving. She brought him coffee and sat with him until he drank some. They both were wet by the time he stood and they both stumbled to the front of a botanica that had long since been closed. The abuela rapped on the metal that covered the door and another abuela behind it lifted it open. Soon, they were inside, and clothes were being stripped from Amboy. He was sitting on a chair naked, his head hanging low, being washed with warm water, the women silent, their expressions intent.

When they finished, they provided fresh bread and soup. He didn't taste any of it, but accepted it nonetheless, allowing them to minister to him. Then it was as if a switch clicked in his mind and he was once again himself. Gone was the architect and back was the man who'd once been a boy running the trails on Signal Mountain Tennessee never having known that men across the world would one day try to kill him, and he'd have to kill them instead. He sobbed, allowing the grandmothers to console him, drawing from them unconditional love, filling the empty space that had so recently been filled with the violence only a dedicated man could ken.

Then after a time, he wiped his face and cleaned himself. When he returned, he was almost Amboy again. He asked for someone to take him to the underground. It was as if they knew exactly what he needed and where he had to be. The one who'd found him escorted him into the back of a bar that was still open. They slipped past undulating dancers, ignorant of their passing. Behind the rows of bottles and into the back they went, finally stopping at a door in the floor. A bouncer opened it for the abuela and they descended the stairs to a cold storage unit. In the back, behind several cases of vodka, was another door, this one much older. She gestured for Amboy to open it and when he did, it revealed a murky barely lit corridor behind. She turned on a flashlight and bade him follow.

They walked in silence for what seemed like an hour, turning left, then right, then left again. Amboy tried to keep track of the journey through the underbelly of Buenos Aires, but it was no use. Without the abuela whose fast-sure feet propelled her small frame forever forward he'd be hopelessly lost. Suddenly they were at their destination. The door had been broken open, cracked around the hinges.

He rushed inside.

The table and chairs were shattered as if a battle had transpired.

A broken bottle of wine told a novel of a tale.

He searched, twisting around, looking for any indication of where his friends might have been. But he couldn't see anything that appeared relevant. He was about to kick the remains of the wine when he felt a hand on his arm.

The abuela pushed him firmly aside, then knelt near the wine. She moved glass away from the mess the broken bottle had made one piece at a time. He didn't know what she was doing, but she eventually revealed a Rorschach-like stain which seemed to please her.

She glanced back at him, crossed herself and said, "*Madre de Dios. Lo ves*?" She pointed back at the stain. "*La Rosa. Lo ves*?"

He looked and for sure the stain looked much like a rose. But then it could also have been just a blotch, much like wine would do whenever it hit a stone floor. He looked at her wide trusting eyes. She definitely believed. But what did it mean?

"*Padre y la nina. Se donde estan ellas.*"

"Where are they? *Donde estan ellos*?"

"*Santa Rosa. Ves la rosa*?" She stood. "*Vamonos. Sígueme.*"

She seemed to know where she was going. All Amboy could do was follow.

She left in a hurry, grabbing her jacket and pulling it around her. They didn't go back the way they'd come, but rather continued in a different direction. Had he been outside, he could have known where they were headed, but underground he was as twisted and turned around as if he were in a mine, his sense of direction useless without the sun or a geographic fixture to mark himself by.

A memory of a sign post at El Quemado mine with wooden arrows pointing to various locations with their mileage. Down a Coronado Shaft 2,012 meters stood a signpost. New York City 7,333 km. Paris 10,573 km. Mexico City 6,118 km. Beijing 18,313 km. Baghdad 13,241 km. Hell 2 km. He'd always loved that last one, and sometimes absolutely believed it.

They'd been gone five minutes when he began to smell something out of place. It took a second, but then he recognized it as caraway. He knew it as a pickling spice. His grandma and aunts would use it on many of the root vegetables. As long as he'd been in Argentina, he didn't remember smelling it more than on a few occasions. With all the fresh vegetables, he'd never known them to need to pickle a lot of things to last through a harsh winter.

So then why was he smelling it?

Then he smelled something else.

Sulphur.

That couldn't be good.

Just as he was reaching out to warn the abuela, they stepped into a wall of complete blackness. She dropped the flashlight, leaving them both in darkness. He felt weak and tried not to fall to his knees. The absence of light was so complete that he couldn't see through it. Sickness grew from the inside out. Soon, his entire body was shaking. Sweat seeped from his pores.

The abuela moaned on the ground a few feet to his left.

He wanted to go to her, but he had to be ready for what came next. Now that it was completely dark, he knew he didn't need his eyes, so he closed them. Ignoring his chattering teeth and his shaking body, he concentrated on three other senses.

He called on his ability earned in the mines. He forced himself to listen more closely, then opened his mouth to elevate his sense of smell, knowing that any lingering taste in the air, no matter how microscopic, would improve his ability to detect scents. The sickness continued to grow inside of him. He knew he needed to find a way free of the darkness.

He managed to roll to his right until he came up against the wall. He was aware of how out of synch his body felt. He'd so recently been a master of it, creating from his all too fragile human limbs a creature of destruction whose ability to invent havoc had been profound. But now his limbs felt those of a baby, lengths of bone and muscle unused to control much less movement. He sluggishly stood, using the wall as both a guide and as a crutch. He tried to be careful not to make any new sound, but he felt lucky to stand, even doing so, aware of his knees shaking to holed him upright.

He smelled the caraway again—mixed with sulfur.

A diabolical heady cocktail of evil.

The abuela moaned several times, then screamed something nonsensical and the darkness evaporated.

A beam of light pinned him to the wall like a bug to felt.

A beam of light from a large flashlight held by one man.

Beside him stood a woman bent over and furiously scratching a symbol in the floor. She wore a black leather skirt and a leather bikini top, showing a midriff scarred from child-bearing stretching and her ample cleavage. She wore high-heeled black boots and black fishnet stockings on her legs. Her long black hair seemed to be alive as it flowed around her head. Her face was both pleasant and mean. Her age could have been anywhere from thirty to fifty.

The man beside her wore a black turtleneck shirt tucked into black pants with black shoes. His blonde hair was cut short like Amboy's, but his face seemed to be chiseled from stone. He held two things in his hands. One was a large flashlight. The other was a pistol.

"What the hell is going on?" Amboy demanded. He stood straighter. Now that the darkness had evaporated, he felt strong again. Almost hale.

The woman continued scratching on the ground, the scent of sulfur becoming stronger and stronger.

"We're looking for your friends," the man said, German-accented.

Go figure.

Which told him two things. They knew who he was but they didn't know where they were.

"You can pound sand," Amboy said, showing his teeth.

"You will tell us," the man said.

"I'm not telling you nothing," Amboy said.

"Anything," the German corrected with a tight smirk.

"Is this what this is about? You came to correct my English? If so, it's going to be awhile."

"Where is Ms. Fennick?" the man demanded.

"How am I supposed to know?"

"You were going somewhere. Where was it?"

"Nowhere unless your hooker friend will get out of the way." He pushed away from the wall now that all of his energy had returned. "What's she doing anyway? I thought you might be too old for hopscotch."

As if on cue, the woman straightened and backed away, gesturing for the man to follow.

The German glanced at what she'd done and fear rode his eyes. He blanched and backed with her, clearly not wanting to be last in the room.

Amboy didn't know why they weren't attacking. They had a gun and he didn't. Retreating made no sense. This worried him more than anything else. If they attacked, he'd know what to do, but by leaving him, it created a vacuum of answers to a myriad of questions. Then he remembered what she'd been doing—scratching on the ground.

Diabolical hopscotch.

He stepped towards the alien marks when he heard a hiss from his left.

The abuela was scratching on the ground herself, furiously making some kind of symbol as the light from the others dissipated down the hallway.

Just before the light died completely, Amboy saw where their flashlight had landed and ran to it, falling on his knees as he searched for it. He finally came up with it in his hands, but it wouldn't turn on. He hit it with the side of his hand and the light sputtered. He hit again and then nothing. He felt his breathing increase as the tension of the moment spiked. He forced himself to be calm.

A scraping noise came from where the couple had just been.

The abuela cursed under her breath as if she might be casting a spell.

He ignored both noises and unscrewed the cap of the flashlight.

The scraping noise became louder and more insistent. Whatever it was, it might be getting closer.

He tried to move faster, but dropped the cover to the flashlight. He closed his eyes and grimaced, ready to be attacked by whatever it was making the noise, all the while searching blindly with one hand for the dropped cap. Suddenly, he had it. He tugged on the spring that was meant to provide the contact circuit to the batteries, then reseated the batteries. He screwed the cap back on the flashlight then thumbed the ON button. He was immediately blinded, the light shining directly into his eyes.

He shook his head to clear the spots that had invaded his sight and swept the beam to where the abuela was furiously working.

Her head was bowing over and over as she murmured just below his understanding. The drawing she'd been working on had a multitude of crosses, including arrows of all shapes and sizes, intertwining and across the width of the passage. It hurt his head just to look at the markings, his stomach freefalling the more he stared. All he could do was glance and that was almost too much.

The scratching became more insistent.

He swept the beam towards the sound.

Where the black leather harlot had been marking on the ground, now a figure pulled itself from the floor. But that was impossible. The floor was made of stone and couldn't be permeated unless somehow the black-clad woman had created a hole in the world.

And the figure.

It was made of nothing.

Or something.

Sticks, it seemed, arms so thin as to be almost absent.

No muscle.

No bone.

Just sticks.

He couldn't stop watching as it pulled itself completely from the hole, standing on two legs bent like the hind legs of an animal instead of a human. The thing topping its body if you could call it a body and you could call it a head was merely three sticks molded together into an upside-down triangle.

When it moved, Amboy backed away, his entire body fighting not to convulse with fear.

There was nothing fluid about it. The creature was all stops and starts. Even as the triangle, empty of any facial features, turned his way, he felt the power of the creature's empty gaze. He felt its hunger. Its need. Its . . . requirement to consume Amboy.

Someone grabbed him. He began to fight it, but then realized that it was the abuela. Blood trickled from her nose and the side of her face was already bruising, where he'd elbowed her in an effort to get away, but she remained strong enough to fight through his terror. He allowed her to propel him towards her and stumbled to the line of symbols she'd crudely drawn upon the floor. Out of the corner of his eye, the creature began to stalk towards them—fits and starts—moving as though on an old movie that had been poorly spliced together.

The abuela's hair had fallen from where it had been captured atop her head and now flowed around her face, wisps of gray and brown and white, matted with sweat and soot and blood.

"*Madre de Dios. Reza por mí. Sálvame.*" She breathed heavily. "*Sálvame.*"

The miasma of white-chalked writing was no longer static and instead swirled in a dizzying spin in his vision.

The creature came on, three stick-like fingers on each hand, reaching towards him on arms twice as long as they should have been. It began to reach towards him, but then stopped, as if it could feel the invisible barrier the abuela had made. It traversed awkwardly from left to right, then back again, but couldn't find a way past.

Rearing back, the creature brought a fist against the invisible wall and the hand shattered, fragments flying in all directions, only to disappear before they hit the floor.

The abuela's head rebounded as if she'd been struck, but she straightened, then pointed a gnarled finger at the creature and shouted, "*Anda tu. Demonio se fue*! *Anda tu. Demonio se fue*!"

The creature towered over her and seemed to want to attack,

but her words were like bullets, each enunciation forcing it backwards as if it'd been machine gunned by some crazy grandmother magic.

She continued pointing towards it, her words lost in a continuous cackle that now sizzled around her.

More fits and starts. Finally, it stepped back into its circle and when it did so, it lost balance, teetering. It seemed to reach out with its handless arm, then fell back inside the hole, disappearing through the floor with the sounds of sizzling and then a great *ZIP*.

Only then did the abuela fall to the floor, her hair and face drenched with sweat. "*Demonio se fue*!" she whispered.

Amboy slumped to the ground beside the old woman. Instead of grabbing her, his intuition told him to join her. *Demonio se fue*!" he said.

She repeated the words again.

As did he.

"*Demonio se fue*!"

They remained that way until the circle was the size of a basketball, then an orange, then a quarter, then a penny, and then . . . gone in a powerful suction of darkness that left them gasping and grinning and laughing.

CHAPTER 14

The Basilica Santa Rosa de Lima rested in the San Cristobel neighborhood of Buenos Aires just west of San Telmo. It wasn't exactly a hop, skip, and a jump to the relative safety of the center of the Roman Catholic presence in Argentina, but after a short cab ride in the early hours of the morning, Amboy and the abuela found themselves deposited on the front steps of the basilica, the Byzantine copper dome gleaming green in the morning dawn.

Waiting for them were Father Paz, two young acolytes, and a nun standing by his side, all dressed in floor-length black cassocks. The nun also wore a folded white head covering.

She and an acolyte helped the abuela up the stairs, the old woman's feet barely functional.

The other acolyte gripped Amboy firmly by his elbows and helped him from the cab.

Without a word, Paz turned and headed inside the vestibule.

Everyone followed at a respectful distance.

Amboy barely had a glimpse at the impressive inside before they were out a side door and into a courtyard. The abuela was taken one direction and he the other. He wanted to thank her, to say something, but the moment had passed too soon. All he could do was hope and pray that one day their paths might cross again and he could thank your properly.

He soon found himself inside a long hall. The acolyte gently but firmly guided him into a room near the end and left him at the door.

Amboy opened the door to a room with a single bed, an end table, a dresser, a small desk with a light and a chair. It was like the negative of one he'd been living in most recently. Instead of faded paint and pictures, the walls were whitewashed and immaculate with a single wooden cross hung above the bed. He noted a pitcher of water and several glasses atop the dresser. It reminded him how thirsty he was. He closed the door behind him and sat on the bed. He'd just rest a moment, maybe catch his breath, then he'd get a drink, perhaps even get cleaned up.

He was glad to see Paz.

That meant that Lettie was around somewhere as well.

He glanced at the window, which had been covered by a lowered shade.

Gosh, he was exhausted.

He lay back on the pillow and . . .

. . . fell into the bottom of a mine.

The smell of urine and vomit was as heavy as the stench of sulfur. His body was compressed on all sides except for his head which seemed to hang in space. It was impossible to breathe, his chest so constricted by weight. From somewhere below he heard a moan. The air was filled with the distinct taint of fresh copper. Although not unknown in an iron mine, Amboy knew it to be blood and it probably was coming from his brother.

Mining in Tennessee came in three types. The easiest way was to scrape away pieces of the mountains and sift through the dirt until miners found the ore they needed. Any old ore really. Just something to sell—something that would get them through a week or so before they found another piece to sell. Many of the digs were hidden beneath the trees, no one wanting either the USGS or the tax man to take notice of their comings and goings.

The other way usually involved them finding a cave, then spelunking a way inside and down. If a vein was found, then they'd begin digging and blasting, tunneling as far down as possible, following the vein of ore until it zig or zagged to where it could no longer be reached. The problem with this method was that cave systems were notoriously unstable and miners often found themselves buried alive and lost forever.

Then there was shaft drilling, which was just what it said. Drills go down, ore comes up, and people don't need to be put into danger. Unless, of course, one comes across an old played out shaft mine, decides to widen it, then dig perpendicular tunnels into the dolomite surrounding the shaft. Such was the case of the Whitmire Mine.

This was such a mine.

They'd been chasing bauxite—pisolitic cream, pink, and deep red. Amboy had been in tunnel three when it collapsed three hundred and seven meters below the surface. He'd been nearest the shaft, while his friends Tim Whitmire and Billy Picket had been further in. There hadn't been any real reason for the collapse. No one had bumped a joist. There hadn't been any movement or warning. One moment they were enlarging the tunnel and the next it was on top of them.

The memory he most remembered was the feeling of complete comfort. Wrapped on all sides, with the mountain pressing equally across every surface of his skin, it was as if the land was caressing him in a deep embrace. Unable to move even his toes, he soon began to fall in and out of consciousness, the earth speaking to him. Calling out to him. Saying his name over and over until he told it to shut up.

Then he realized it wasn't the earth calling to him.

It was the foreman who was trying to save him.

He tried to call back, but he couldn't make a sound. His lungs were constricted. Then it dawned on him. If he couldn't speak, then he couldn't breathe. He began to gasp for air, like a fish out of water, his mouth an oval as it tried—

Then the earth started to shake and he—

Awoke to Lettie straddling him, shaking him with both hands, tears coming out of her eyes.

He blinked several times.

Where was he?

Then he remembered.

Everything.

The murders.

The blood on his hands.

The abuela.

The thing beneath the city.

"Amboy! You weren't breathing," she said, pinning him to the bed.

He stared at her for a moment, unbreathing, caught in the last webs of the dream. Then he inhaled sharply. Oxygen flooded his system. He felt alive—revived.

He tried to get up, but she wouldn't move.

"Okay. Okay. Let me stand."

"Are you sure? You were wailing, Amboy, and I didn't know what to do."

Vestiges of being crushed remained, her hands like the weights of mountains.

"I—can you—please move."

She stared at him, motionless.

"Let me up!" He pushed her to the side, knocking her onto the bed. She had to grab the sheets to keep from flying onto the floor. "Jesus. Doesn't anyone listen?" he said to everyone and no one as he stood, rubbing first his shoulders then his thighs as if to brush aside the dreamslide that had buried him alive. Then he remembered Tim and Billy, further down the shaft. If only he could—

"Hey! Don't be an asshole," she said, managing a sitting position in the bed.

Amboy shook his head, not in disagreement, but to clear it. "I'm sorry. I was feeling—closed in—tight." He lurched to the window and slung it open. He leaned out and took a deep breath, shuddering.

"Are you okay?" Lettie said, making her way up. "You looked like you were dying?"

He wiped his face with a hand and scrubbed the top of his head with his knuckles. "Memory, was all. Memory and a dream. Twisting what really happened." He glanced at her, then remembered the broken door and the spilled wine in the subterranean room. His entire demeanor changed as he was slung back into the present. "Are you okay?"

She shot him a sideways smile. "Take more than that to hurt me, chum."

"I s'pose so." He glanced over to the chair by the desk and noted the blanket beside it on the floor. "Were you watching me sleep?"

"I couldn't sleep myself, so I thought I'd watch over you."

The smell of blood and urine and rock. The claustrophobia of the dream still lingered. "Maybe good you did."

"Where were you? What was happening?"

"Inside a mine. We had a cave-in. My friends were crushed

and never recovered. It's a miracle they were able to get to me, all told."

"Cave-in as in the ground fell on you?"

"As in almost half a mile of dirt entombed me when a tunnel collapsed." He wiped at his shoulders and chest again. "It's the inability to move that's the worst. It's why I want to be cremated. No way do I ever want to even chance waking up in a coffin. Having no control of my body, having to have it locked in a position forever would be the rudest hell I could fathom."

He flashed to a false memory of himself inside of a cave, the darkness as weighty as any rock, his arms locked awkwardly so he couldn't move them properly. No longer the master of his own limbs or even his head, he couldn't turn, he couldn't see; all he could smell was his own naked fear, like vinegar and rotten vegetables.

She cocked her head as she pulled her leg into an Indian sitting position. "I thought you worked in mines. How does that work if you you're claustrophobic?"

"A lot of us have claustrophobia. It's just a matter of reminding yourself when you get there that everyone has done the best they can to protect us. Back in Tennessee we were wildcatting anyway. There weren't a lot of safety measures we followed."

"Wildcatting? Sounds like fun."

He laughed already beginning to feel a little better. "If you call working at night, no safety standards, long hours, shitty pay, hiding from the taxman and every other government entity fun, then I suppose it is."

"It's like you're making moonshine."

He laughed again. "Making moonshine would have been more fun, probably." Then he added, "And less dangerous."

"Then why did you do it?" she asked.

He shrugged. "It's what we do. Mining has been in the

family for hundreds of years. Instead of asking me why we did it, ask me why we didn't. Frankly, I don't know if I even had a choice in the matter. You worked and you got to eat. There never was a time when you chose what you were doing. You just did what you were told to."

"Is that why you left Tennessee?"

"Vietnam is why I left Tennessee."

"Why you and not your brothers or cousins? I've been thinking about that and do you know what I figured out?"

"What?"

"I bet they didn't even know you were born. I bet you had to get a birth certificate to prove you even existed. You had to work at leaving is what I think, so there had to be a reason."

He stared at her long and hard. "You're pretty smart for a girl with Florida on her face."

"And you're pretty fly for a white guy." She grinned despite herself. "So?"

He gave her a half nod. "You're right. I had to get out. I had to leave. After the cave-in, I didn't want to be around those people anymore. I wanted something new, something different, something that wasn't that damned mountain. I felt like I was destined for something I had no control over and I didn't want anywhere near that destiny. It took some doing. My people hated me for it—for drawing attention—but I had to leave."

She knotted his sheet in her hands and blew a strand of hair out of her eyes. "And the safest place you could think of was Vietnam?" she asked incredulously.

"You know? I wasn't as scared as a lot of people over there. I think it's in the way you value life. Where I came from life wasn't valued a lot, so if something happened—something bad—it was expected and the loss wasn't that big a deal. I mean, the mountain people—my family included—had kids like rabbits.

We were everywhere and I doubt any family survived ten years without one or two of the kids dying from something or some other. Snake bite. Fall from a cliff. Broken leg that went septic."

"It sounds just awful."

He shrugged. "Maybe it was but it was all I knew." He flashed a grin, picked up the blanket from the floor, and sat in the chair. "What about you? What was your family like?"

She laughed. "You don't want to hear about my brothers and my mother, they—" She inhaled, eyes wide. "I have brothers and a mother." She scrambled across the bed and then leaped into his arms. "Amboy. I have a mother. Her name is Agnes. I have three brothers and their names are James, JJ, and Jerome. Did you hear that? They all start with J." She kissed him on the cheek, stood, and twirled, clapping. "James teaches at Shaw in Raleigh. Is that where I'm from? My brother JJ—oh he's a bad man—he's been to jail for heisting cars, but he's a good man at heart. And Jerome. Jerome?" She paused, then put a hand over her mouth. "Wait? Jerome?"

She turned to Amboy her eyes so wide and worried that he wanted to reach out and hug her, but something held him back—something was always holding him back.

Her frown curved into a private smile. "Jerome is now Jerri. Jerry with an I not a Y. Jerri moved to Atlanta." She clapped and twirled again. "Oh my god! I have a sister!"

He laughed, incapable of keeping a straight face. She stretched the reality of cuteness and he had to remind himself that she had to remain like a sister. He couldn't look at her in the way he was increasingly looking at her. He needed to refrain from doing anything that would bring her harm and he seemed to be nothing but bad luck. But damned if she didn't have some of the best freckles and the way her red hair twisted down to cover her forehead; it was just too—

"Why are you frowning?" she asked, staring pointedly at him.

"Wha-what?"

"You were staring at me and frowning. I know when people stare at me. I've spent a lifetime with people looking at me and judging me."

He stuttered, "I w—wasn't judging. I think you look great. I was just wondering what happened to you after I left to rescue Thiago. I returned to the room we were in and saw how trashed it was. I was just worried, is all."

She frowned for a moment, then set her jaw and strode towards him.

He stood, not wanting to be hit in the face sitting down.

She closed her fist and punched him in the chest. "That is for making me worry about you."

He barely felt the blow and blinked at her, his entire soul grinning.

Then she threw her arms around his neck and kissed him deeply. "And that's for calling me great."

He started to fight, then realized that was the last thing he wanted to do. But as soon he began kissing her back, the door opened.

It was Father Paz.

"If you two monkeys are finished fornicating, I need you. Come join me once you get some clothes on."

The old priest gave them a bored look, then closed the door.

Amboy glanced down and noticed that he was wearing nothing but boxers and his T-shirt. Worse yet, the bulge he was showing was worse than Pinocchio's nose on its fifth lie. He pinned Lettie back with a glare. "What happened to my clothes?"

"You fell asleep in your pants and shoes. I took them off for you." She smiled and blinked brilliantly.

"How long has it been?"

"Nine hours."

"Nine hours?"

"Yes."

"I slept nine hours?"

"Yes."

"And how long have you been watching over me?"

She grinned and headed for the door. Once there, she glanced over her shoulder, gave Pinocchio a glance, then grinned. "About the same amount of time." Then she opened the door and closed it.

He stared at the door for a long hot moment, then grabbed the blanket she had been using and brought it up to his nose. He inhaled and marked her scent for eternity.

CHAPTER 15

The coffee in the sanctuary was worse than in the military. Then again, the priests and nuns of Buenos Aires were on the front lines of protecting the souls of the people of the city, which was not much different than his experience in the army. So, he sat and drank it, letting the aroma of burned coffee beans gather around his face. As bad as it was it felt like home. He was safe and surrounded by people who authentically cared for him.

Lettie had buttered thick homemade farmer's bread for everyone. She slid a plate with a piece on it in front of him.

Father Paz was drinking coffee as well, unusual in that this was the first time Amboy had seen him without a glass or bottle of wine.

They each ate their bread in silence, the only sound their own mastication. When they were done, they stacked the plates in the center of the table and both Lettie and Paz turned to him.

"I heard you were busy the last two days," Paz said.

Lettie raised an eyebrow, clearly interested in what he'd been doing.

Amboy gave them a summary version of the first trip to

ESMA, then the party at the house in the country, then the last trip to ESMA, which he glossed over. When he was done, Lettie stared at him with narrowed eyes.

"What? What did I say?"

"It's not what you said. It's what you did." She paused. "Did you really kill all of those people?"

He thought about it and tried to figure out a way to explain how he felt and what he'd done, but the best he could do was four words. "I was at war."

"Vietnam was ten years ago," she said.

"Not every war has a name," he said.

She stared at him; her mouth open.

He wondered where her previous look had gone and why it had abandoned her. He'd like it better when she was dancing and hugging him, rather than sitting with her arms protectively around her knees, staring at him as if he were something alien.

"What is it?" he asked, knowing the answer before he even said the words.

"When you told me that you didn't value life the same way as I did, I didn't know it was because you had become a—a—"

"A murderer?"

"I was going to say killer."

He couldn't look at her. "I did what I did. I did what I had to do." He let that sink in a moment, then added, "I'm never happy to kill people. But I went to finishing school in Vietnam. I learned more there than I cared to."

"I'm not one to say that people should be killed," Paz said, adding a lightness to the conversation that had been missing, "But if you're going to do it, the officers of ESMA aren't a bad choice."

"I heard a story about you," Amboy said to Paz, glancing at Lettie out of the corner of his eye.

"The world is full of stories."

"This one ended with a bombing," Amboy said.

"Nothing ever ends with a bombing. That's something that usually causes a lot of other things to happen."

"Were you involved?" Amboy asked.

Paz shoved his coffee aside and folded his hands together on the table. "Are you serious? Do you really want to have this conversation now?"

"If not now, then when? We are either in this together or we aren't."

Lettie had been following the cryptic dialogue enough. "What are you two talking about?"

"Do you want to tell her or should I?" Amboy asked.

"You know so much about it, why don't you tell her?" Paz said, gravel and glass in each word, any previous attempt at levity like the rattle of grenade pins on a concrete floor.

Amboy stared at Paz for a long moment, then shook his head. "No, this is a story for you to tell when you are ready. If we are truly confederates, you will need to talk about it one day. Soon." To Lettie, he said, "I'm not sure if it even matters, but I don't enjoy killing," knowing it was a lie and how much he'd enjoyed mowing down those who'd tortured Thiago and ruined his face forever. No, not a lie. He didn't enjoy killing. He enjoyed revenging—if that was even a word.

She looked at him as if to judge, to see into him. Finally, she nodded and said simply, "It matters."

"I'm more interested about the house in the country," Paz said. "Contrary to what you said, it doesn't belong to the United States Embassy, but rather a private company."

"Is it the Council of David?" Amboy asked, knowing that it had to be with all the six fingered girls.

Paz shook his head. "The home is registered to the Misión de Investigación y Descubrimiento de la Patagonia."

Amboy sat back. Another organization? "Patagonia Research and Discovery Mission. Sounds innocuous enough."

"The man you described as Nolan is CIA, so we now know that the United States government is involved somehow. For what reason, we can only speculate, but nothing I can think of has a good ending."

"I don't want anything to happen to that girl, Meagan. I know I don't know her, but—shit. Why can't people just leave everything alone? Why do they have to go and do crazy shit like parade eight-year-old girls in white dresses in front of a crowd so they can be selected by a giant white stag for God knows what? I mean, if this was a pedophilia ring, we'd take it down, wouldn't we?"

"I think it's more than that," Paz said. "The Bishop made some inquiries. He discovered that the Mission has billions in various stocks and bank notes, but no tangible assets or properties, other than the compound they took you to. Then he was politely asked to cease and desist his interest by a Cardinal in Rome."

"Wait. One of the higher ups told him to stop investigating?" Lettie asked.

"Exactly. A Cardinal definitely rates as a higher up," Paz said, flashing a smile. "What the Mission is doing is of deep concern. Especially since you said there was a heavy German presence. The church has been trying to keep track of groups of them who fled Germany in the wake of World War II."

"I thought I recognized several of them but I didn't know from where." He glanced at Lettie. "The ones we took out at Thiago's apartment. Did they come back for you? What happened in the underground?"

"We'd planned on laying low," Paz began. "I wasn't even allowed back at the Basilica because of some of the things I'd done and have been involved in. But when they came and I rescued Lettie—or rather we rescued each other—the Bishop took official interest. There are plenty of fine German folk in Argentina, but then there are some trying to revive things best left forgotten. Have you ever heard of the Ahnenerbe?"

Both Lettie and Amboy shook their heads.

Paz nodded and stared into his empty cup. "It's better that you hadn't. Most of it was rife with conspiracies and ideas that were so far from the truth as to be Martian in origin. I'm talking death rays and little people. But then there are a select few programs that actually dovetailed into things we've been trying to keep restricted."

"By we, you mean the church?" Lettie asked.

Paz nodded.

"By restricted you mean—" Amboy thought of the stick figure creature.

Paz gave him a look that said a thousand words even if his mouth said none.

"What is the Ahnenerbe, though? Is it an organization? A club? A cult?" Amboy asked.

"Yes, yes, and more yes," Paz said. "Think of it as an organization created by the Nazis to find ways to prove the superiority of the ancient Aryan race from which they believed that the Germans descended, even if the proof might be occult in origin."

Lettie snorted. "What you're saying is a bunch of German white supremacists started a club to help prove how superior they were to everyone else."

"We'd call that a self-licking ice cream cone in the army," Amboy said.

Paz ignored them. "Not only that, but they sent people to the far ends of the Earth looking for artifacts, like the Spear of Destiny—the spear that Casca Longinus used to stab Jesus in the side—just to bring back so that they might have proof of magic and then determine a way to wield it."

"We're straight into Indiana Jones now," Amboy said.

"Indiana Jones y Los Cazadores del Arca Perdida. Yes." Paz clapped. "Great movie. And yes, the movie was about that. Did you know that Hitler began employing dowsers as early as 1934? He called it radiesthesia and inadvertently tapped into a kind of magic that is real. But it was Himmler we worried about the most. He ran the SS and established a witch division that searched for evidence of magic, sorcerers, magicians, etc. In fact, he's the one who discovered the power of the runes. He used the Armanen Futharkh which were a set of runes from ancient Aryan priest kings. Even the two SS symbols are two sun runes making a double sun, which is an early description of the eclipse and a time where the Earth exudes immense power."

"You're saying there are Nazi occultists in Argentina doing God knows what," Amboy clarified.

"That's exactly what I'm saying. You've seen what the dowsers can do. You've seen what the runes are capable of . . . of inviting into our universe. We can't have foreign agents running around Buenos Aires using magic without the church knowing for what and for why. Hell, it's one of the reasons we're here in the first place."

"Even though I saw it with my own eyes, it seems so far-fetched. Magic? Something from nothing? Can it really be?" Amboy asked.

Paz stared at him for a moment, then stood. "There's never something from nothing." He gathered the plates and the cups of coffee and took them to a sideboard. He returned with three glasses and a bottle of wine. He poured for each of them from the bottle, drank his glass, and then poured himself another.

Finally, he spread his hands on the table so that each finger was spread wide. "Are you asking the church if magic exists? Did Christ not change water into wine?"

"Somehow I knew your answer would have something to do with wine." Acknowledging the irony, Amboy drank a sip of heady red wine, enjoying the burn as it slid down his throat. "I'm being serious."

Paz cocked his head. "I am as well. What do you think a church is about? Why do you think we are here? To collect pennies from the poor and turn them into bricks of gold? I will gladly acknowledge that over the course of two thousand years the church has accumulated the sort of wealth that might make one disgusted with the amount, but that was a mere side effect of trying to civilize a world where magic was but a turn of the head or a blink of the eye away. We've spent thousands of years trying to make sure children don't burn down the world with a match."

"The Catholic Church," Amboy began in a sotto-radio voice. "Keeping the world safe one soul at a time."

"Is that so bad? You who don't go to church and who might not even believe can stay safe in your beds. George Orwell said *we sleep safe in our beds because rough men stand ready in the night to visit violence on those who would do us harm.* Many attribute this to soldiers, but he said it in reference to the clergy."

"I call foul there," Lettie said. "It's well known that Orwell saw Catholicism and Communism as much bosom buddies as Romulus and Remus. He ridiculed the church at every opportunity he had."

Amboy only knew Orwell from a book where animals talked to each other. He'd thought the man a children's author, never having read any of the man's prose. Then he realized what Lettie had said.

"Hey? You're smart."

"And sexy. Quite the catch," she said, fingering Miami like a mime. She continued, grinning. "Evidently I went to college because I clearly know that Orwell quoted Karl Marx who not only said that *Religion is the opium of the people*, but also that it was *the sigh of the soul in a soulless world*."

"Acknowledging that we all have souls," Pax said, his face joyous with the chance to argue. "Don't you see? Even Marx thought there was a soul? The father of communism himself believed in something that couldn't be tasted, felt, or proven, but lived within all of us. Why is that do you think? Because he saw things. He'd been witness to things.

"As far as Orwell, he did spend a career castigating the church," Lettie said. "Don't forget that he was Church of England which is no friend to Catholicism, so to make fun of Catholics was a literary sport for him."

"He believed in God but not religion," Amboy said, earning him an approving glance from Lettie.

Paz held his right hand up. "Exactly. He believed in God. He believed in the need for people to be good. He just thought that organized belief was problematic." He laughed. "Since when has that not been an issue? I'll bet even when Christ was a corporal his followers had problems with the way he organized them."

Lettie's eyebrows narrowed until they met Frida-style in the middle. "He was a corporal?"

Paz laughed again. "No. But I heard that once from a British officer from Sandhurst and always wanted to use that in a sentence." He took a drink. "One more for the bucket list."

"Can't you be serious?" she said, not happy at being laughed at.

"This is me being serious. Now you know why I'm always in hot water with the Bishop." He addressed Amboy. "What you saw was the use of symbology. Some call it Runes. Some call it cuneiform. Others call it hieroglyphs. Knowledge of that sort of magic has been around for ten thousand years. Only in the last thousand or so years have we been able to control their use."

He tapped the table with his fingers. "Hmm, perhaps control is too optimistic a word. Let's call it limit—we are able to *limit* their use. It's why the church spent so many hundreds of years going into the deepest darkest places. We had to discover their magic so that we could develop ways to learn it—to limit it. My Jesuit brethren have special courses they take before disembarking that allows them to prepare for such things."

Amboy glanced at Lettie, who met his eyes, then back to Paz. "Everyone knows this?"

"It's not common knowledge. Most of the clergy are dedicated to the well-being of the people which is perhaps even more important. I mean, why save a society that is cancerous. Why not let it just implode?"

"The fall of the Roman Empire," Lettie mused.

"We'd like to take credit for that, but they earned all the credit themselves. It wasn't magic that brought them down. They spent centuries doing the same thing, trying to destroy other magics so that they might continue their domination. No, the empire's decline was due specifically to their inability to take care of themselves, the disparagement between those with and those without, and the withdrawing of those who could do greater good from the society at large."

"I don't see much difference in the way the world is running now," she said.

"Well, we do spend our time trying. But look outside," Pas pointed to the window. "You have two decades of Peronism in Argentina. You have a war that is about to be lost because all of Argentina's friends have turned their backs on her. You have poverty and displaced indigenous peoples whose livelihood has forever changed because of the continued sprawl of humans."

"Yet God will fix it all," Lettie said.

"It's all a matter of faith, Lettie," Paz said. "Do you have faith?

"Do I have faith that I will be saved? Oh, that's right. You have to acknowledge God before he'll let you into Heaven. Just ask St. Augustine, who determined that babies carry the taint of original sin until they get a few tablespoons of holy water on their heads."

Paz clenched his mouth in frustration. "Where's this anger coming from?"

"Wait? Are you remembering all this?" Amboy asked. "How do you know so much about Augustus?"

"Augustine," she corrected, tossing him a shallow grin. "An Algerian Bishop who was elevated to Saint because he stole ideas from Plato and promoted them as his own."

Amboy and Paz exchanged glances.

He couldn't help but see her anger, but he didn't know where it came from. It was as if there were two different Letties.

She continued. "The Bible says that God made man in his own image, right?"

"In so many words," Paz said.

"Pretty much those words," she said. "So, if man is in his image, then which man? Your God is white even though he came from the Middle East. Or possibly even North Africa, like Augustine."

Paz laughed. "Okay. Okay. Clearly you have issues. I'll ask you again, why are you mad?"

She took a moment then shook her head and bit her lip. "I don't know. And I know it doesn't make sense. I just can't help but feel super angry when we talk theology."

"Essentially, you're talking Genesis 1:27: 'So God created man in his own image, in the image of God he created him; male and female he created them.' We take those words from Genesis to mean so much more than just physical appearance. The term image is an imperfect term which came from the translation . . ."

"Imperfect is right."

Paz cocked his head. "Is that it, Lettie? Do you feel imperfect?"

"I can tell you that there's no way I was made in God's image. I mean, come on. A map of Florida on my face? I should rent myself out at rest areas so the elderly won't get lost."

"I don't think you fold so good," Amboy said.

She rolled her eyes. "You're hilarious."

"Why'd you choose?" Amboy asked.

"Choose what, Vague Boy?"

"Alabama over Florida?"

She brought her hand up to her cheek, baby soft with what looked like new and perfect skin. "The size. It had nothing to do with the people. Alabama took up more space and I wanted it gone."

"Are you worried that the reason you lost your memory has to do with how you changed your face?" he asked.

"Do you mean by losing a port wine stain of Alabama now I can't remember my Christmas from when I was seven?"

Amboy nodded. "Well, can you?"

"No."

"Then it's possible."

"A meteor falling to Earth is possible. Father Paz being a cross dresser is possible."

Father Paz shook his head. "Not possible."

She ignored it. "Anything is possible, Amboy. That's why me and you have six fingers on each hand. We are the impossible made possible."

"I hear what you're saying," he said.

She rolled her eyes. It was something she was good at.

Amboy pressed. "Think about it. I mean, we can't be sure because you can't remember, but you went down almost to Tierra del Fuego for a procedure on your face and came back without a memory. Ever wonder if they didn't intentionally take more than they said they were going to?"

"But why would they do such a thing?" she asked.

"Why ask why?" He downed his wine, then pushed the glass aside. "We can't know unless we go there and find out."

"Well, I'm fresh out of money, so unless someone comes up with another five thousand dollars."

"Was that how much it cost? Five grand?"

She banged the side of her head with the palm of her hand and grimacing "Evidently. Either I'm remembering or I'm making this up as I'm going along."

Trying to save Lettie any more aggravation, Amboy tried to turn the conversation back to where it started. "We were talking about magic—symbology, is that what you called it?"

"We still are, my son. We've never changed. What you saw in the underground were doorways between worlds."

"Other worlds? Like Heaven and Hell?"

"That's too simplistic. The problem with boundaries is that they don't know they exist for a reason. Just as there are administrative lines on a map to demark where one country starts and another ends, there are lines where one world can start and the other world ends. All one has to do is find them and they can produce what we are colloquially calling magic."

Amboy remembered the frontiers mentioned by Brother Roy and said as much.

"Yes. I know Brother Roy," Paz said. "I forgot how close he was to where you grew up. I should have made the connection." Paz made a brief concerned face, then let it go. "And I know others like him. They are out there to watch the frontier. The borders and boundaries between the light and the dark. They are border guards of the soul, so to speak."

Amboy thought of the circles that had been drawn on the

ground by the hooker and the symbols drawn on line by the abuela. "I saw this woman all in black drawing something that allowed the evil thing to come in and then the abuela drew something else that seemed to protect and give us power."

Paz nodded. "Both of them knew how to obfuscate the boundaries. In the case of Señora Silva she tapped into an energy source that was powerful enough to save you. In the case of the other woman, she opened a hole in our universe and let in a lilin."

Lettie inhaled sharply. "Like the thing on my back," she said, leaning back so the chair would cover her back.

Paz gave her a sad smile. "Many of the same markings. Just as you have been marked by the symbol, variances of the same symbol can be used to summon one, opening doors so it may enter."

"What would it have done to me if the abuela—Señora Silva—hadn't been there?"

"It would have taken your life force," Paz said, simply.

Amboy just realized what Paz had said. "What about the Señora? How is she? Where is she? I need to thank her."

"She's moved on, my son."

"You mean she left?" he asked, hoping that was what he meant.

"This world. Yes. Her sacrifice did not go without notice, however. The church will take care of her and her family."

"Wait." Amboy felt his face crack wide open. "She's dead?"

Paz put a hand on his shoulder. "I'm afraid so."

"She—She died for me?"

"She died for her. You were but a reason for her to live, not to die. Just as keeping the boundaries sacrosanct is a reason."

"Why'd she do it?" He wiped tears from his eyes that had sprouted unbidden. This was getting to be too much. He didn't like this game they were playing. The quiet stoic old woman had done for him what he hadn't done for her. "Why did she choose me?"

"You needed help. She could provide it. Is that so bad? Listen. Don't make this about you. This is about her. She decided to channel the energy knowing that it would kill her. She decided to fight rather than die alone and tired and old. You need to respect that."

"Is there going to be a ceremony?" he asked.

"A private one. This evening. After compline. In the crypt. The Bishop is going to give her rites. Until then, we need to find a place to talk a lot more private than this. Walls have ears. Even those in the church. For one, I want to find out why Lettie was down in Patagonia."

She started to speak, but he held up a hand.

"I know. To get rid of Alabama. But I want to know why and how. The answer could be the most important information we have."

CHAPTER 16

Father Paz had gone off with a meeting with the Bishop, leaving the pair to their own musings. They had lunch, then found themselves in the courtyard sitting at a bench under a palo borracha tree, its arms spread wide enough to dim the high sun that had the grass and flowers sparkling with its brilliance.

Lettie wore jeans over white canvas shoes and a simple aqua-colored blouse, with a pastel flowered jacket over it. She'd turned her face up to absorb the sunlight, soak in some of the precious heat from the moderate weather. Her port wine stain accentuated her locks of red curly hair. The mark was as much a part of her as anything and Amboy didn't want it to go. Sure, he understood why she might not want it, seeing it as it probably was, a blemish on what otherwise might be a perfect beauty. But there were many beauties in the world, but only one who looked like Lettie.

Amboy had found clothes waiting for him in his room when he'd woken. They were far from the normal attire he enjoyed wearing. He now wore jeans over huaraches. He'd been left a well-worn Led Zeppelin concert T-shirt which seemed so out of the norm as to make him feel uncomfortable. But no hat. He felt almost bald without one.

"Know what I think?" Lettie said, rather than asked.

He looked at her and his eyes hopscotched her freckles.

"I think you wear old man's clothes so people won't notice you."

"What do you mean, old man's clothes?"

"I see the way you feel," she said. "You're like a cat in a dog's skin."

"I'm just not used to wearing these things. They are worn by—"

"Almost everyone? Jeez, Amboy. This is 1982. We're the MTV generation. T-shirts and jeans are our uniform."

He rolled his eyes. "I've never seen MTV."

"Okay, old timer. You want to dress like someone's grandfather, you just do that, but know this. Maybe the reason you dress that way is so people won't notice your beautiful six fingers."

He began to argue, but then found he couldn't. He was wrapped around her use of the word beautiful and the idea that she was right. Maybe his almost pathological desire to fit in was because he didn't want anyone to notice the differences. And here he was with Lettie. It didn't matter what she wore, unless it was a veil in a country where people wore veils, she'd never fit in. Who was the braver of the two? It didn't take a genius to figure that one out.

"Let's talk about Chatwin," Amboy said, trying to steer the subject away.

She'd lit a cigarette, and pinched it between her lips as she pulled her copy of *In Patagonia* out of her canvas bag. "There's a lot of marginalia inside this one," she said as she flipped through. "I copied some of them and they are clearly mine. But there are others. It's like I inherited this book or it was given to me."

"Do you remember why you thought the book was important?"

She flipped it until she showed a picture of handprints on a wall. "This picture was taken at the Cueva de los Manos."

"The Cave of Hands."

"Right. Count the fingers."

He already had. Many of the fingers had six digits. "Where is this?"

"Santa Cruz Province. Down south."

He looked at her. "Have you been there?"

She shrugged. "Your guess is as good as mine. I don't think so, but I'd like to."

"Long way to travel. Probably have to do it by bus."

"I have a memory of taking a bus once," she said, her eyes closing as she took another long take at her cigarette. "I was alone and young and had a backpack in my lap. I remember being scared."

He waited to see if she would say anything else, then asked. "Where were you going?

She shook her head. "I don't know. It's just a skeleton of a memory. I do remember the ocean and the smell of fresh mangoes. Isn't that weird? I wish I knew where I was going and why I was so scared."

"Perhaps you were a little girl traveling alone. That would scare anyone," he said.

She nodded and took another puff.

"I've been meaning to ask, what happened down there? Did they come for you?" he asked.

"I felt them first." She opened her eyes and looked at him. "The dowsers. They were nearby. I knew they were coming for me. I could barely keep my body from vibrating. The damn tattoo itched like mad."

"I saw the door had been broken in."

"I guess it could have been them. When I mentioned my feelings, Father Paz started wrecking the room. He left a hidden message, then we left. He locked the door behind us."

"You didn't see anything? The lilin?"

"Nothing." She shuddered. "The way you described it. I'm glad not to have seen it. And to think I have a mark on me that's like a homing signal."

The last thing he wanted was for the lilin to get her—take her—do whatever it was going to do to her. He looked around, seeing no one, he said in a low voice, "Then let's go. Let's just go. We'll take a Chevalier and get out of here."

She laughed. "Kind of impetuous, isn't it?"

He shook his head. "I'm tired of waiting around. I'm tired of talking. I'm more of a doer, you know? I started this adventure because I was strong-armed into watching over you. Then I was asked to by a friend. Now, I feel as if we're on the same journey, you and me. The only thing that separates us is Florida," he said, nodding at her cheek and offering her a slow grin.

"And the fact that I'm black and you're white. And I have red hair and you have blonde."

"And I'm a man and you're a woman. Blah. Blah. Blah. So what?" He pointed at her satchel. "All we need to figure it out is in there, I'm sure of it."

She reached in, pulled out the article and passed it to him.

He translated and basically it said. *Miracles Do Happen. Have Port Wine Stain? We Remove Them. 100% Guaranteed.* Then it provided an address in Rio Gallegos, Argentina.

"This is it? It's why you came?"

She twisted her lips thoughtfully, then took a drag from her cigarette. "I think I was here before, maybe doing research on these." She wiggled her fingers. "And I came across this in a magazine. I've looked up Rio Gallegos. It's a long way south. Almost all the way south."

He stared at her and thought of the underground and all the hiding they'd done and then the Germans who had come after her, then him later. He had an idea that might be considered rash. Hell, it was rash, but he didn't care. For some reason he wanted to maximize his time with her and this was the only way he knew for certain he could do it. Plus, no one would expect them to make the move.

"We could take a Chevalier there as well. Hell, we'll make it a road trip."

She looked at him as if considering, then shook her head. "That might not be such a good idea. Chatwin details a whole chapter about what's down south. Take a look at Chapter 52."

He took the book and turned it to the proper section. He saw the word *Brujeria*, which he knew had to do with witches, then Council of the Cave. The supposed council was located in two places. One place was unknown and the other in Buenos Aires. He read about raising the dead and flaying the skin and then wearing it. About how some members could change into animals, influence thoughts and dreams, open doors—he wondered if the German woman was a member of the council—then some creature known as The Deformer.

He closed the book at that point, but kept his thumb in place. "I thought this was a travel book," he said, looking up.

"That's it. It is just a travel book. Right up until it's not. Why would Chatwin do that? What came over him to want to add all the sordid details at the end with no foreshadowing?"

Amboy closed the book. "This doesn't change my mind. We need to go to the hotel Chatwin stayed at. What did he call it, a *poisonous green colored* hotel? There can't be that many. Maybe you stayed there, do you remember?"

She shook her head again.

He loved when she shook her head and the way her red curls swayed.

"I bet you stayed there. If we can find someone who saw you there, perhaps they can help answer some questions."

"We don't have any way to protect us? We also don't have any money?"

"What if I can take care of both of those problems? Will you come? Are you game?" He desperately wanted to get out of Buenos Aires. He wanted to leave the politics and the hatred behind. Like the country around the mine, once one got out of the cities, Argentina was a heaven on earth.

She seemed to consider, then nodded. "But we have to clear it with Father Paz first."

"No. Let's go now."

"What about the funeral?"

He paused and nodded slowly. "I'm devastated that the abuela died. I'm also pissed. She was killed as certain as they tried to kill me with that—that creature. Her death is even more reason to leave. How many more people are going to have to die? How many more people am I going to be forced to . . . to kill." He lowered his head.

She moved to his side and put her hand on the back of his neck. "I know you're a good man, Amboy Stevens."

He turned to her and grabbed her other hand. "Let's go. Right now."

"Are you serious?"

He nodded sharply.

The next thing they knew, they were walking side-by-side into the church, then out the front door. They caught a bus to his rooming house. He'd thought about leaving his things, but he had some money squirreled away as well as some items that he felt he might need. They got off the bus two blocks from his rooming house and then checked for surveillance before climbing up the fire escape to the third floor. The window was always open. They slipped inside and soon, they were in his room, the doorjamb busted and his things tossed like a hurricane had localized itself on his meager four hundred square feet of existence. He'd half expected it.

He grabbed a wrinkled but clean tan suit jacket off the floor, slung it on and felt immediately better for it. He checked the back of several drawers, cursing each time.

Lettie stood just inside the doorway, looking around.

"Did they take everything?"

"Not everything," he said. "Just the obvious."

He went over to the bed and shoved it aside. Using a pocket knife he found on the floor, he began to pry at a board. It took several tries, then suddenly the board popped free. Inside was a metal ammo box with a handle. He pulled it out and opened it. Inside was a .45 Cal pistol, which he dropped in his pocket, along with four magazines of ammunition. His passport was also inside, as was a roll of money. He shoved these in his other pocket.

At least they had a stake now. They could afford to travel south without any fear of running out of cash. He'd been saving it for years, thinking that maybe he might one day return to Signal Mountain and buy a home outright. But the longer he'd stayed in Argentina, the more he thought of himself a citizen of the world, rather than a citizen of Tennessee. He stood, believing that this was a great way to spend his life savings.

"Don't turn around," came Matias' voice.

His heart twisted, but he didn't move.

"If you so much as reach for that pistol, your girlfriend is going to wish you hadn't."

Amboy raised his hands. “Now, isn’t that ironic. Wasn’t it you who told me I needed to take care of her in the first place?”

“Game pieces change,” Matias said. “The board changes. A queen becomes a pawn.”

Amboy grinned. “I didn’t know you were a queen. Sounds like you’ve been talking to Wallace.” He turned around slowly. Sure enough, Matias held a Mauser to Lettie’s side. She looked like she might be about to cry. He needed to take care of this. “And here I thought we were friends.”

Matias grinned. “We’re still friends, Amboy. I appreciate what you did for Thiago. He’s good people, as you Americans are fond of saying. This . . .” He shoved the pistol deep enough into Lettie’s side to make her squeak. “This is business.”

“No, this is bullshit. I had your back, Matias. We went to war together. Doesn’t that mean something to you?”

The other man paused, his eyes drifted to the poster on the wall with the picture of Uncle Sam shaking hands with Perone, then back to Amboy. He lowered his voice and said, “Of course it matters. You are a brother to me. It’s just that the game has changed.”

“You don’t have to play the game, Matias. You can choose to stop playing anytime you want.”

“*Vos ist los*?” came a deep voice from the hallway.

“*Nicht ist los, alles kaput*,” Matias said.

“*Vos ist kaput*?”

The lumbering figure of Schultz came into view. But unlike his namesake from *Hogan’s Heroes*, this one was all business. As broad as the doorway, his eyes were pure steel. The frown of his mouth revealed several brown teeth surrounded by stainless steel replacements.

“*Meine Freundschaft ist kaput*,” Matias said.

“*Wen interessiert das*,” said Schultz.

"Schultzy. How goes it? Long time no smell," Amboy said. "So, you're the one pulling Matias' strings. I suppose you answer to Wallace as well.

The German gave him a single glare, then turned away.

"Seriously, Matias? You going to take that shit from this guy?" Amboy asked.

"Easy, my friend. This isn't as simple as you think it is. There are a lot of moving parts."

"Amboy. I'm scared," Lettie whispered, her eyes pinned to the pistol poking into her side.

"Everything's going to be okay," he said to her.

"How can you say that?" Matias asked.

"Because I trust you," Amboy said.

"Then stop it."

The German snarled, "*Wir müssen gehen*."

"Why shouldn't I?" Matias asked, ignoring the German.

"Because I know you," Amboy said. "Matias. Money talks. Bullshit walks. You could either share twenty thousand dollars with him or you could have it all to yourself."

His eyes narrowed. "What twenty thousand dollars?"

"Carefully, I'm reaching into my pocket. The pistol is in the other." Ever so slowly, he pulled free the roll of money and held it in a hand. "This five thousand dollars. The rest is in the hiding space. How badly do you want to share?"

The German began to shove his way into the room, but Matias and Lettie were solidly in the doorway. Matias made no effort to move, so the German smacked him on the back of his head. "*Aus dem Weg*!"

Matias rolled his eyes and growled.

The German smacked him again.

Matias, turned, placed the pistol between the German's eyes and pulled the trigger.

The explosion stunned everyone.

Blood splattered Matias's face and the side of Lettie's, creating a fictitious state where angry Germans died.

She staggered forward into Amboy's arms.

He caught her, then began to wipe blood away from her face with the sleeve of his jacket.

"I was getting sick of being part of their organization anyway," Matias said, his words filled with equal parts of regret and disgust. "I mean, if you're going to take over the world, you might as well have fun doing it. With them it was all anger and arguments. Bullshit sentiments about what they should have had. Now, about that twenty thousand."

Amboy reached into the space and pulled out six more rolls. He grabbed four of them and tossed them to Matias. "Here. Take it."

He caught the money, eyed it eagerly, and then pocketed it. With the gun still in his hand, he asked, "What about the rest?"

"You agreed to twenty thousand."

"But you still owe me money," Matias said with a grin, his hand out.

"Are you really going to stand there and play that game? I'm here because of you. I had our back at ESMA. We're even, got it?"

Matias seemed to consider for a moment, then nodded and shoved the pistol into a holster under his shoulder. "You're right, of course."

But as he turned to go, Amboy asked him a question.

"Where are you going to go?"

Without turning around, he answered, "I'll think of somewhere. Argentina is getting a little crazy. Maybe Colombia," he said. "Or someplace even more crazy, like Hawaii." He shrugged. "I don't know, but something tells me we'll see each other again."

Amboy nodded. A flash of a dark place lit only by fire. Pain in his shoulders. His neck a spike of fire. He wasn't at all sure that Matias was right.

Once Matias left, Amboy grabbed another jacket and Lettie's hand and was out the door and down the fire escape before the police skidded to a stop before the rooming house. The dead German was going to be a problem. They just didn't know how big of an issue, but they were going to find out.

CHAPTER 17

Spaces between places in Argentina were sometimes larger than American states. Planes were too expensive for everyone to use and the trains were constrained to specific routes. So, everyone traveled by Chevalier when they went out of town, unless they were fortunate enough to have their own vehicle. Even if one did have one's own means of transportation, the comfort and ease of the Argentinian bus system made the American Greyhound bus system seem archaic, cheap, and something that should have gone extinct long ago. Chevalier was the opposite, featuring seats for the rich and elderly as well as the farmer and his chickens. Amboy and Lettie found themselves on an overnight trip heading south in the lower suite class section of a two-tiered Chevalier bus.

They'd purchased some of the things they needed at the Buenos Aires bus station. He'd bought a leather valise and she'd bought a cotton knapsack with flowers that almost matched her jacket. Then they'd filled them with cheap clothes and some toiletries. They hoped to grab some more on the way to the cave, but didn't have the time for actual shopping before their bus left.

They had a space separated by curtains from the other suite customers. Ultra-wide side-by-side seats laid down flat and allowed them some respite. After a dinner of sandwiches and several beers bought from a vendor in the aisle, they removed their shoes and jackets and, to the hum of the wheels on the road and the murmurs of the other suite customers, spoke in hushed tones. They lay facing each other, Amboy on the aisle, holding each other's hands in front of them.

She shuddered for a moment, then closed her eyes.

"Was that the first time anyone has ever held a gun to you?" he asked.

"I think so. It was so real and so terrible at the same time."

"And the first time you've seen someone killed?"

She opened her eyes. "I never saw it, but I felt it." She took her hand and wiped the spot where the blood had been. He could still see the mirage of the stain so much like the state of New Jersey. "It felt so hot. So sudden."

They lay together for a time, then she asked, "Can I ask you something?"

"By asking you just asked."

She grinned sadly. "I know. But this might make you uncomfortable."

"That describes half my life."

She looked at him until he looked back at her. "I want to ask you about Vietnam."

He closed his eyes for a moment and let the gunfire play out. He didn't open them until it subsided. "I know what you're going to ask. Most of the time that's the worst question to ever ask a veteran. But under the circumstances, I know you're trying to reach some kind of internal understanding."

"How can some backwoods mountain boy understand so much about the inner workings of a girl's mind?"

"I don't know. I think I've talked more with you than pretty much anyone else. I'm usually the silent one." He held up a hand and added, "Just be careful. You can ask anything, but be careful that you really want to know the answer."

"Maybe that's it. Maybe you spend more time listening than you do talking. I've known enough men in my life who seemed to just want to be heard, as if in the process of speaking, they were becoming smart."

"I've never been really smart. I've read a few things and seen a few things, but never had much of a formal education. I barely even went to high school."

"I'm still blown away you know *Porgy & Bess*. I mean, how many white boys have seen that black opera."

"I used to sing *Summertime* all the time when I was working. It's such a great tune to work to. It reminds me of summer days when there's nothing much to do, except I'd rather be doing that *nothing* much more than working."

"That's sweet, but that's not what the song's about. The second verse nails it. *Summertime* is about losing one's innocence. Talks about one of these days you gonna fly, but until then momma will take care of you. Don't you see, when you are finally able to fly, there's nothing momma can do. You're on your own and the whole bad world can do what it pleases to you."

He stared at her for a long minute. "I guess we're back to the Vietnam question then. You know, when I decided to fly and go where my family couldn't protect me."

She frowned sadly. "I should have never asked."

"You didn't."

"But I was going to."

"Still." He closed his eyes and let the gunfire surge and die again. By the time he opened them, his ears were still ringing with the explosion of the rounds. "By now you know I've killed plenty of people. I think they all deserved it and I'm hoping they did, but I know in the war that some of the Vietnamese I killed were like me—young and scared and half the time firing with their eyes closed. You don't get used to it. You just endure it.

"I didn't get to Vietnam until the end of the war. Most of the fighting was already over. We'd all but left the country. I was assigned to a small unit helping out ARVN," he said, pronouncing the letters as one word like to rhyme with Marvin. "That's the Army of the Republic of Vietnam. It was my first week in country and we were south of Saigon doing a sweep when we came under fire. I remember hitting the ground and forgetting absolutely everything I'd learned in boot camp and infantry school. I wanted nothing more than to cover my head with my rifle and scream until I couldn't scream no more. But something inside of me took charge. I found myself switching my rifle off safe and aiming through the elephant grass at where I thought the enemy's rounds were coming from. I fired three and four round bursts until my magazine went dry and my bolt carrier locked to the rear. Then I loaded another magazine and pressed the bolt receiver forward. I fired again and again and again until I was the only one firing."

He stopped, gasping, the memory of it leaving him out of breath.

She waited, staring at him, her mouth slightly open, a red curl covering her left eye.

"We finally got to our feet. I was shaking like a leaf and tried to keep it under wraps, but some of the old timers—and when I say old timers I mean folks who have been there a few months—just looked at me and grinned, but they didn't say a word. We swept the enemy position and we found three bodies. One was a man. The other was a girl. And the third was a water buffalo that was still breathing, even though it had too many holes in it to survive. My friend Mario went over and shot it in the head, but I wasn't paying attention. I was just staring at the two bodies. A man and a girl. She could have been his daughter."

"Did she have a weapon?" Lettie asked.

Amboy stared at her a moment, then nodded. "Both she and her dad did."

"Was it you who shot her?"

"I'll never know. As far as I know, none of my rounds made it. Then again, all of them might have hit her. I think I shot one of them. So, when I think of the first time I killed someone I always think of them."

"How old was she? Do you know?"

"She couldn't have been more than twelve or thirteen. Asian girls have a way of defying figuring out their age." He glanced at her. "That's probably just me." He wiped an asshole tear from his eyes. "The thing is, we were a unit of twenty and they were only two. Why did they fire at us? Why'd they even do it? It's like they wanted to die."

"Maybe they did," Lettie said. "Maybe they were tired of it. At thirteen she'd seen nothing but war. God knows what happened to her or her mother. Sometimes it's better to be dead in a bad world than alive in a bad one."

He gave her a weak smile. "I suppose."

She rolled over, lit a cigarette, then rolled back. Her eyes were hidden behind roils of smoke. After several thoughtful inhales she asked, "Do you ever consider yourself a murderer?"

He blinked several times, then took the cigarette from her mouth, inhaled, exhaled, then put it back. "No. Murderer is what someone calls someone. It's a point of view. Do some of the relatives of the people I killed think I'm a murderer? Probably. But I always killed for purpose. I always killed for a reason. It's like—it's like we all signed up for a game where winners and losers were chosen by who survived."

"Do you think that girl signed up for your game?" she asked.

"By the time she was old enough to walk the game was already going. She didn't have a choice."

"But you had a choice to fight," she said.

"You mean, go to Canada?" He shrugged. "To tell you the truth, it never even occurred to me. Maybe if it had, I would have gone. All I knew, was I wanted to get out and the war was the best reason of all to leave."

"It's terrible that to leave you had to kill."

"I hope that I always killed from a position of superior morale code."

"Was your code superior to the girl's?" she asked.

He side-eyed her. "You keep bringing up the girl."

"She was your first," she said.

He nodded. "She was." He remained silent for a few miles as memories played out in his mind. Then, "We had this game in school I liked to play."

"I take it we're not talking jump rope."

"Hardly," he said, grinning. "It was called Kill the Man with the Ball. Ever heard of it?"

"No. And it sounds like a terrible game."

"No one really died, silly."

"But you called it Kill the Man. Pretty violent for a child."

"You're telling me. I saw more lacerations and broken bones than most places. My guess is that it's a pretty old game to gauge a person's heroism potential. Might even go back to medieval times."

"What was the game?"

"Simple, really. There was a ball and a bunch of guys and whoever grabbed the ball got tackled."

"Then why would someone grab the ball?"

"Exactly what I wondered right up until the moment I

grabbed the ball. When it's sitting on the ground in front of you and you have the ability to grab it, you do. I can't explain it."

"Like the girl. She picked up the rifle."

"And became part of the game."

"So, because she had a gun it was okay to kill her," she asked.

"Jesus, but you are being judgmental. If I say yes, am I a killer? If I say no, will you believe me?"

She shrugged. "I don't know. I do know that you are not like Matias," she said.

"No, not like Matias. He'd sell his mother if he had one."

"He didn't have to kill that man. Why did he? And don't say because he'd picked up a gun."

"Loose ends. Matias likes to solve pretty much every problem with violence."

"Matias is a murderer," she said.

Amboy nodded. "I agree."

"He'd kill anyone to remain free."

"I agree to that as well."

"What would have happened if he left the German alive?"

"The German and his organization—if it's the Mission—would track him down and probably kill him."

"This *Mission*—what are they going to do now?"

"Probably the same. Track him down."

"And us?"

"Us too. They'll be looking for us everywhere."

"So, we're on the run."

He grinned, took a smoke from her again, then returned it. "We always have been kiddo. The irony is that at the same time we're running away from something that might hurt us, we're also running toward something that might hurt us."

"Makes us look like geniuses," she said, matching his grin.

"Kill the Man with the Ball," he said.

She put out the cigarette and they kissed long and hard. He tasted the menthol and the tar from the cigarette, but he also tasted her, juicy, slightly cinnamon, and wonderful.

Then they slept and he dreamed of the dead Vietnamese girl laughing with her father, playing in the rice paddies, the water buffalo tied nearby, ready to take the harvest on its back. Then the scene disrupted by a group of ARVN and US soldiers, sauntering out of the elephant grass as if they were on a Sunday stroll. The girl screaming as she's grabbed by two Vietnamese soldiers. The old man shouting until Mario stabs him through the neck with his bayonet, then the man's more worried about staunching the blood flow, even when his eyes never left the men ravaging his little girl's body, his eyes and heart more wounded than his own wound which quickly takes him until he stares through silent eyes at how life can flip in a second. Then everyone took turns, the ARVN, one after the other, proving once and for all that rape was never about sex but about hatred and rage and a total fucking lack of empathy. Then it was the Americans' turns and everyone declined except for Mario who laughed as he fucked the girl, then laughed again as the ARVN killed her, then the water buffalo, then cooking the buffalo and eating the flesh with the rice, the dead girl lying to the side, her legs splayed, her eyes staring at the sky wondering why it couldn't have been Summertime when the living was easy. Then two days later, when he and Mario were in the bush together and he put his rifle to Mario's head and pulled the trigger, faking an ambush, returning with Mario's dog tags, but remembering the girl and the dad and the water buffalo and knowing that he really was a murderer because of the way he'd killed his friend in the coldest of blood, even if was for a reason that would almost let him sleep at night.

Almost.

CHAPTER 18

The distance between Buenos Aires and Cuevas de los Manos was more than twenty-three hundred kilometers. Twenty-nine hours by bus if it went straight through, but nothing ever goes straight through. They stopped a few times in the night, but it wasn't until they reached Bahia Blanca that they had to disembark and find their next bus.

The San Francisco de Asis Bus Terminal had an impressive array of services. The buffet was already crowded by the time they arrived. Still, they were able to grab a tray full of fruit and eggs and then order coffee and juice to drink. They inhaled their food in silence, all the while watching over each other's shoulders. They'd spoken about surveillance and the need to watch each other's back. They weren't looking for anything specific, but rather anyone who was giving them undo notice.

Not that people weren't taken with Lettie's appearance. Amboy noticed that she had a way of moving through crowds that didn't allow someone too long a view of her face. Just enough to wonder what they'd seen and by the time they turned around, she was gone. It must have been a knack she'd developed over the years. He noticed that she liked to keep her cigarette in her mouth when she smoked as well. Where a lot of folks would hold the cigarette in their hands, she welcomed the added veil of smoke and what it did to obscure her appearance.

So, he wasn't surprised when a man or a woman passed by, saw Lettie and whispered to their companion. To them, Lettie was a unicorn—a one of a kind with red hair, black skin, and a map of Florida on her face. No nursery rhyme or children's song ever prepared them for such a thing as Lettie. She was rarer then Puff the Magic Dragon living by the sea and more special than a black sheep with extra wool. She was herself, an original, an idea made flesh, and more unicorn than anything he'd probably encounter in his entire life.

And she liked him.

She glanced up as she was eating and tossed him one of her grins. He'd thought they were only for him and they might have been, but he'd only been in her life for a short while. So, when she gave it to him, he felt jealous of all the years he'd not been the object of its radiance.

She was his unicorn.

And he'd lied to her.

He knew it and hated himself for it, but he couldn't tell her the truth. She wasn't prepared for it. She wouldn't understand. One had to go through things, experience violent occurrences, and develop an impervious mental skin before such words could ever be uttered with understanding. He'd created the version of the story about the father and his daughter and the water buffalo that best suited the person he wanted to be. He'd said it so many times, he'd almost believed it. But he knew the truth and the truth wasn't something everyone was prepared for. Perhaps one day he'd tell her, but he hoped he'd never have to, because if he did, it meant that she'd been through a hell he'd never want for anyone.

"You eat something bad?" she asked.

He slipped back to the present. "What?"

"You look like you've eaten something bad? Can I get you some water or something?"

He took a sip of coffee and sat back. "Just ulcers, I guess. All the stress."

"Not like we don't have any. How long until the next bus?"

"They don't even open the doors for two hours." He bummed a cigarette. After lighting it, he said, "We should find some place to hole up."

She gestured with her fork. "Does it look like anyone is looking for us?"

He appraised her for a moment, then said, "Don't forget that thing on your back."

She paused eating, then tossed her fork on her tray and pushed away from the table. She lit her own cigarette and took a few drags, then crossed her arms. "I haven't forgotten." Her smile was nowhere to be found.

"We just need to remember."

She gave him a look like he didn't know what he was talking about. "Don't you think I don't know? I have this thing indelibly marked on me. I remember for a split second being under someone's control and the next thing you were carrying me like a sack." She gestured with her cigarette. "You don't think I remember?"

Couples next to them glanced over, aware of their anger.

He caught a glance from a man in a suite who merely shook his head and grinned as if Amboy should know better than to argue with his woman. Happy life is happy wife.

"Keep it down, Lettie," he said, scooting in and leaning over the food so he could lower his voice and be heard. "Shit. You're drawing attention."

She stood and in a voice much too loud to go unnoticed

said, "Do you want to see me draw attention? I can show you some damn attention." She grabbed her bag, put out her cigarette in the middle of his plate, and stalked away, head high, Florida leading the way.

Amboy gave it a few moments, then shook his head as he grabbed his own backpack and followed her. He heard murmurs of *Americanos* and *Recién casadas*. All he could do was ignore the others and follow after.

She'd left the restaurant and had both of her bags over her right shoulder as she window-shopped. Not only were there several stores that sold newspapers and magazines and cigarettes, there were also places one could buy tourist knickknacks celebrating Bahai Blanca as the gateway to Patagonia. He watched as she picked up various snow globes and shook them, then put them back. The problem with her shopping was that she didn't have any money. Not that he didn't care to give her any, he just hadn't thought of it because they'd been together all of this time.

He saw the shopkeeper watching her. Then she did something spectacularly opposite of what one wanted to do when they didn't want to draw attention. She took one of the snow globes, shook it dramatically, momentarily watched the snow fall, and then dropped it into her new knapsack. Then she walked nonchalantly out.

The shopkeeper grabbed a short length of stick, the grip wrapped in tape, and launched himself after her. The stick's working end looked as if it had shared itself with plenty of folk, dented and chipped in places. It even had a dark brown stain which had to have been blood. The shopkeeper seemed intent on using it.

Amboy intercepted him, shoved a few bills in his pocket, and gave the man a sad smile. "*Lo siento. Mi esposa esta loca.*"

The shopkeeper's mouth fell open, then he turned to Amboy and grinned. When Amboy pulled the cash from his pocket, the man was even happier. Of course he was. No one spends fifty bucks for a snow globe.

Amboy hurried to catch up to his false bride. Why did he need to worry about her tattoo or Germans with divining rods? She was making herself known quite exceptionally.

She'd found a store that sold decent clothes. Not the tacky *Amo a Bahai Blanc*a shirts, but honest to god clothes ranging from denim to silk to alpaca wool. She was sizing a blouse in a floor to ceiling mirror when he passed her and said, "Smooth move."

She stuck out her tongue and continued modeling for the mirror.

He walked past her, dropped his valise on the ground next to him, and began to check the sizes on a line of men's shirts. All he had was the Led Zeppelin shirt and as much as he appreciated the artwork, he needed something that would help him blend in. And in the countryside, the locals were far more conservative than in the cities, so seeing someone in a comfortable T-shirt would be more memorable than if they were wearing what everyone else wore.

He selected two long sleeve button downs. One in tan and the other in navy blue. Then he moved over to the pants and chose two pairs of chinos. Finally, he saw and decided to get a new pair of shoes. His Mexican sandals were okay, but he needed something sturdier in case they had to do a lot of hiking or trekking.

When he went to the counter, a pile of clothes was already waiting for him to pay for. He merely glanced at the woman behind the counter, gave her a brief smile, and then counted out the dollars as he did the rate conversion in his head. It might have been easier to use Argentinian pesos, but everyone loved the dollar and businesses made more money from the resale.

Then he looked around for Lettie. He'd assumed that she would have been waiting somewhere outside the store or perusing another store. It was clear that her anger had softened a little and he was eager to get back in the good with her. But try as he might, he couldn't find her. It seemed that everywhere he looked, she wasn't there. He even went back to the buffet restaurant. Nothing.

She was gone.

Disappeared.

A pit opened up inside of him as he stood and wondered where she had gone. He spun around at once angry and despondent. If someone had taken her—a snapshot of him shooting Mario in the back of the head. But what if she'd decided she'd had enough? What if she wanted something better?

Then his mind went into overdrive.

He ran into the nearest store and handed his valise.

"I'll be back," he said, not caring even if the shopkeeper kept the things or even resold them, as long as he found Lettie.

He was now in fifth gear. His attention was heightened. He noticed everyone's movement in his range of vision, noting those who looked away, those who watched, and those who appeared oblivious. He headed outside first, gently checking the positioning of the .45 he'd stuffed in the small of his back. He knew it was there, but needed the comfort of actually feeling it.

He saw more young men than women. All seemed to be in various stages of waiting. Some reading their papers. Some in conversation. Some smoking and staring at the ground, either contemplating where they were going or where they came from. But there was no Lettie—not that he could miss her in her red hair and caramel-colored skin.

He swept through the waiting area around the curb, then entered the terminal from the far side and began to go through the shops. People saw him coming and got out of his way. He ignored them, his eyes only seeking Lettie. He was focused on the finding or the destruction, his stiff-legged purposeful march telegraphing his intent. Then he saw a policeman coming his way. Amboy's Fuck-Me-Running Meter spiked and he forced himself to slow and to present as passive an image as possible. Being questioned was one thing, but if the policeman found his pistol, they'd throw him in a hole and forget about him.

And of course, it was in a regional version of Argentine Spanish. Either he could try to speak capital Spanish, or be the unfortunate and not too smart American. Since he was an expert at being the latter, that's what he did.

"Can I help you officer?"

"You. Americano. Papers, por favor."

Amboy pulled out his passport and his mineworkers union pass, which showed he was allowed to be in the country for work and not merely a tourist. He pointed to it and said, "El Quemado." Then he made a motion like he was hammering a small rock. "Mine. Miner." He pointed to himself. "I'm a miner."

The police officer's eyebrow raised. He glanced at the workers pass, then flipped through the various stamps in the passport then closed it. But instead of returning it, he held onto it.

"You work in Salta. Why so far south?" he asked in semi-perfect English.

Embarrassment and thanks washed over Amboy.

"My girlfriend and I are being tourists. I have some weeks off and we wanted to see the south. Maybe Patagonia."

The police officer made a face. "Everyone wants to see Patagonia. Why not here? Why not greater Argentina?"

Amboy offered a sympathetic smile. "I agree. But she is new to Argentina and doesn't understand her beauty."

He spied commotion over the policeman's shoulder. Two men and a woman arguing in an alcove behind a baggage area. An after-image of a woman with red hair blossomed in his vision.

His eyes returned to the policeman's just as he looked down at the papers one last time. After a moment, he handed them back.

"Be careful. Be smart."

He tipped his hat and walked away.

Be careful. Be smart. Yup.

As soon as the cop turned a corner, Amboy fast-walked towards where he'd seen the argument. He heard her before he saw her, voice quavering, anger and fear mixed in equal proportions. When he saw what was happening, his heart leaped into his throat and he full stopped.

She stood with her back to the wall, a German Mauser pistol in her hand, pointing at the men. The barrel shook. The men edged closer.

"Get back," she whispered. "Stay back. Leave me alone."

She hadn't seen him yet. He glanced behind him. Seeing nothing, he turned back, pulled his own pistol and shoved it into the back of the nearest man like it was a knife and he wanted to separate the man's spine.

"What the fuck do you think you are doing?" he said in English then Spanish.

The man stiffened.

The other turned to look, revealing hungry eyes and broken rotting teeth from addiction to cocoa leaves. His skin was gray with dirt. He smelled as if he hadn't showered since the last monsoon.

These two were nothing but beggars. For one hot instant, he considered killing them. No one would miss them. They were already lost to society and probably themselves. Their subsistence was entirely dependent on the misfortune of others. Would they really be missed? Then he wondered who he was becoming. He'd once been the Amboy who'd gladly killed his friend because it had been the right thing to do. It was a happy murder that he didn't often worry about. But he also knew he couldn't be that version of himself. He'd escaped that when he'd gone to Argentina. No one knew what he'd done with ARVN. To everyone he was an American miner who wanted to live the Argentinian good life rather than return to his backwards existence in the mountains of East Tennessee. So, just as quickly as the urge to kill surfaced, he beat it down. Still, the fact that the idea lurked in the recesses of his humanity told him how close he was to becoming that which he most reviled.

"*Vaminos,*" he said with a rough voice. Then he repeated it and shoved the barrel into the man's spine twice as hard, making him twist and cry out. *"Sal de aqui!"*

The one whose face he'd seen grabbed the other by the arm and they were soon running in the direction of where the policeman went. He wasn't afraid they'd go to him. What would they say? 'We tried to rob a woman and she stopped us with a pistol'? This was 1982. So many people had weapons for protection seeing theirs wouldn't be so much a surprise. As foreigners they weren't supposed to own one, but they could still be explained away. In the end, they were tourists, protecting themselves. What judge would disallow them that?

He watched them run, glancing fearfully back once at him, then spinning around the corner like twin dust devils. Then he went to her, first taking the pistol from her shaking hand, then putting it in his side pocket, along with his own. He put both arms around her and made soothing noises. Her entire body shook from fear and pent up action, her endorphins firing and filling her system with no way to release it.

Finally, she said, "I wanted to shoot them. I wanted to kill them."

Kill the Man with the Ball.

He understood the feeling. It was addictive. Cathartic.

"But you didn't," he said.

"Only because you came along."

"I think you know better than that. You were just defending yourself. You were scared."

"But that doesn't mean I should kill a person."

"No. No it doesn't at all," he said, not believing it for a second—knowing he was just moments away from killing the pair if they'd so much as put up a fight. Not because he wanted to kill and not because he enjoyed the killing, but because they'd threatened Lettie and no one gets away with threatening someone he—

The word came but he let it go.

He couldn't deal with it now and didn't even want to recognize it.

Instead, he kissed her tears dry on her cheeks and hugged her furiously.

CHAPTER 19

They managed to just make their connection after gathering their purchases and running for the bus. They had a suite again. They'd forgotten to buy food, though, so they'd have to get off and grab something at the next stop which was in six hours when they arrived at Neuquén. It turned out neither of them was hungry. Lettie had been so disturbed by what had happened that she'd immediately grabbed a blanket, wrapped herself inside of it and turned towards the windows so she could watch the land roar by. Which had left Amboy to sit and wonder what the hell they were doing.

He admitted to being rash. They'd left with little to no plan, deciding to go to the Cave of Hands merely because there were six-fingered handprints there. But what really were they thinking they'd find? Would there be a welcome party for those tourists who had six fingers? The idea was pretty ludicrous. They were just going to see something, but upon seeing it, would it change them?

Much of his ability to plan had been colored by his intense desire to be near Lettie. He'd never really felt anything like that before. Sure, he'd been infatuated with women because of their beauty or a smile or the way they walked across the room, but with Lettie it was so much more and he couldn't find the pulse of it.

He knew he needed to have a better plan than just going somewhere. Right now, they had two locations. One was the Cave of Hands. The other was Rio Gallegos. The latter was not only the capital of Santa Cruz County, but the city's airport was also being used for Argentina's Air Force to provide for the defense of Las Malvinas, so the city might be in a sort of crisis. From what he'd seen in the various newspapers, the war was almost over for Argentina. They'd lost their major naval ship with the sinking of the *General Belgrano* and were also losing the air war. The Argentine military was bracing for some sort of attack on the airfield by British Special Forces. Amboy didn't know if it was going to be such a great idea to insert themselves into the situation. He'd been the meat in a shit sandwich before and it was never a pleasant situation to be chewed up and spit out.

Still, their single solid lead was where Lettie had had Alabama removed from her face and that was in Rio Gallegos. If they could find the place and if he could interrogate the people who worked there, then perhaps they could also discover what had happened to her memory and who exactly she was. It made more sense to go there so then why were they going to the cave first?

While Lettie slept or internally dealt with her brush with mortality, he needed to use his military training to come up with a cogent plan. Something that was proactive instead of reactive. He was tired of doing things because he had to or as a result of someone else's actions. That was the reason he'd been so brash back at the basilica. If he removed himself from that section of the board—as Wallace would have said—no one could play him or move him. He could finally move himself.

He remembered something from the Chatwin book, *In*

Patagonia. Gently, he relieved her of her canvas work bag and pulled the well-thumbed paperback from inside of it. He flipped to chapter 52, where it mentioned the Witches of Rio Gallegos. It mentioned that there were two branches of the witches. One in Rio Gallegos, the other in Isla Chiloe, Chile. He grabbed a map and found the island far west of Rio Gallegos and on the other side of the continent, off the southern coast of Chile. He noted that they were currently geographically closer to Chiloe than they were to Rio Gallegos.

Grabbing one of Lettie's notebooks, he flipped through until he saw her writing about the witches, specifically looking for the word 'deformer.' When he found it, he began reading:

> *Also known as the invunche, the deformer is a monster created specifically for assisting the warlocks (or witches) in their work. The deformer is created using the first-born son of a foreign family. The procedure is unknown, but the deformer is first baptized by the warlock, then its left leg is broken and wrapped around the subject's back. His tongue becomes forked. He is fed only the milk from a black cat and goat meat. A magic cream is applied to the deformer's back that soon creates rough black hair and scales to form. The purpose of the deformer is to guard the cave for its lifetime. It can also be used as a mechanism for revenge or curses by warlocks.*

Amboy looked up from his reading and tried to imagine such a cursed creature. He shook his head and continued reading. He flipped a page and noted that the Incas referred to the area of Isla Chiloe as the Place of Seagulls. How many seagulls would there have to be for it to be referred to as such. And why were there so many seagulls? He shook his head and continued reading.

Chatwin's description of the deformer has some additions that talk about a tourniquet being placed around the head of the deformer and it incrementally being twisted until the deformer can see down its own spine. Chatwin also states that an incision is made in the right shoulder through which the right hand and arm are twisted through and then sewn in place.

The very idea of such a thing was so far-fetched that Amboy struggled not to roll his eyes. But then he remembered the lilin he'd seen in the underground and the tattoo carved on Lettie's back. That there was some sort of magic going on was clear. But how much—and did they really want to rush their way into the lion's den? For a brief moment, he wished that Paz was with them. The priest seemed to know more than his fair share of the magic and organizations going on in Argentina. What did he say? Discovering and managing magic had been and still was the reason for the Catholic Church to have a presence all over the world.

Amboy found himself flipping through Lettie's notes as he thought. He paused when he came to a page headed "List of Monsters in Patagonia":

Cuero. Possibly a freshwater stingray of some sort. Natives believed it could fly, but all other references of it are aquatic in nature.

Succarath. According to a Franciscan Priest and Cosmographer Andres Thevet—Towards the Patagones, a very fierce animal can be found. It is called a Sú or according to others Succarath and it is usually found on the riverbanks. It has a hideous figure, at first sight it seems to have the face of a lion or even that of a man, because from its ears grows a beard with hair that is not too long;

its body narrows towards the rear, its front end is very large; its tail is long and very hairy, and with it, it hides its pups that it places on its back. This does not prevent it from running swiftly away. (Also reported to have been seen by Father Guevera in 1764—what is it with all the priests having all the fun?)

Unicorn. Chatwin mentioned one at Cerros de los Indios. Signs also present at Lake Posadas which his vicinity of the Cave of Hands. Also, interspersed on walls with hands are pictures of unicorns being hunted. Is the unicorn real? Or was it? What if there were still unicorns?

Included was a copy of a picture that looked as if it had been painted on rock. Something out of an encyclopedia or something. It didn't look much like a unicorn. Then, neither had the unicorn on the walls of Nolan's place. What had he called it? The Red Unicorn of Tierra del Fuego.

Using the map again, Amboy saw that it was a full day's ride and nearly fifteen hundred kilometers from the Cave of Hands and the pictures of the unicorns to Tierra del Fuego. Perhaps the unicorns had been in the area of Lake Posadas thousands of years ago. Considering the remoteness of the area in pre-history, it was possible that such beasts could have lived and survived there. But the Cave of Hands was now a certified tourist site and probably heavily inhabited, or at least as inhabited as Salta which was pretty inhabited for being in the middle of Nowhere, Argentina. If the unicorns ever existed, the reality was that the unicorns had to have either become extinct or driven to a place where they could still exist in peace.

Amboy grabbed a small travel book about Tierra del Fuego. Ironically, there was no fire. The area was a cold, wind-swept and desolate place that to this day was sparsely populated. He read that the reason it was called the Land of Fire was because of all the fires from all the various indigenous groups that were seen from the European ships sailing by during the night. Still, the Land of Fire seemed just the sort of place to make it a good candidate for a creature that was not supposed to exist remain undiscovered by the greater world. Perhaps Nolan's *Misión de Investigación y Descubrimiento de la Patagonia* had it kept secret somewhere on one of the many islands that make up the region.

He further read that the name Patagonia was derived from when the Portuguese explorer Ferdinand Magellan first met the giants of the region in 1520. He and his men stood only as high as the waists of the indigenous men they interacted with and their feet were of incredible proportions—*pata*—being the Portuguese word for feet. The place became known as the Land of Big Feet or Patagonia.

Amboy read further.

In 1579, Francis Fletcher, ship chaplain for Sir Francis Drake, recorded meetings with gigantic Patagonians.

In the 1590s, one-time pirate and illegitimate son of Sir Henry Knyvet, Anthony Knivet claimed to have observed dead bodies ranging from twelve to fifteen feet in length.

Also, in the 1590s, William Adams, an Englishman aboard a Dutch ship rounding Tierra del Fuego, reported a violent encounter between his ship's crew and unnaturally tall natives.

In 1766, the crew of HMS *Dolphin*, captained by Commodore John Byron, witnessed a tribe of nine-foot-tall natives.

All of these reports had since been debunked, but the debunking lacked any proof other than the application of common sense. Amboy wondered what common sense would make of the creature he saw in the Buenos Aires underground. He could just see a scientist surmising that nothing like that could exist because he'd never seen evidence of it before. Well, if Amboy had the capability, he'd take that non-existence scientist into the bowels of the city and let him see the demon creature for himself.

He sighed.

He'd always hated those who didn't believe in something just because they couldn't be persuaded to.

He glanced over and noted that Lettie was staring at him. Her hand held up the side of her face, elbow on the armrest. Her placid countenance was unreadable.

He looked down at her books scattered over his lap and grinned.

He grinned haphazardly. "You took me to school," he said. "There are so many interesting facts here."

She adjusted her position until both of her hands were clasped beneath the side of her head. Her knees were drawn up beneath the blanket. She'd turned towards him. Her back rested against the side of the bus.

"Those all aren't facts. They're witness accounts. They're only as reliable as the witness."

"Aren't eyewitness accounts supposed to be the best?" he asked. "I know in court a witness is worth a thousand words."

She smiled grimly. "That's only because it gives the judge and jury something physical to focus on. In real life a witness is subject to bias and memory distortion and memory reconsolidation. Plus, it's been proven that the questions asked can cause someone to remember something that never happened."

"You're doing it again. Remembering something. And this isn't just an eyewitness account."

"I know," she said. "I don't know how I know this, I just do. For instance, Psychologist Robert Buckout was able to demonstrate that eyewitness can be mistaken. In his study, over two thousand test subjects watched a thirteen-second clip of a robbery from a local news broadcast. In the video, viewers watched a man in a hat run up behind a woman, knock her over, and take her purse. The man's face was only visible for about 3.5 seconds. The clip was followed by Buckout asking participants for help in identifying the man who stole the purse. He provided a lineup of six men, each holding a number associated with their position in line. He asked the participants to identify which number corresponded to the man who robbed the woman. The perpetrator was suspect number 2. About the same percentage of participants chose suspects 1, 2, and 5, while the largest group of participants, about 25 percent, said they believed the perpetrator was not in the lineup. And this was after they had just seen it occur."

Amboy had seen his share of people forget things that had seemed obvious, but he was surprised at the number of people who had failed to identify the perpetrator. Still, he said, "But don't you think seeing giants is different? I mean, I'd remember if I saw a giant. It's not the same as seeing someone rob someone."

"You'd like to think so," she said, smiling. She sat up in an Indian position, drew her blanket to her lap, and lit a cigarette. "Many people make the mistake of looking at the amount of evidence and believing that increases the likelihood of something being true or not. But if all the evidence is wrong then 0 + 0 + 0 + 0 still equals 0. In order to consider any evidence-based ideas, one must first develop a way to grade the quality of the evidence with appropriate modifiers."

"Er . . . modifiers?"

"Yeah. Like, what was the physical condition of the observer? What was the geography like? What was the weather like?"

"So, the sworn testimony of a drunken sailor on a boat on high seas in a storm has less value than a man standing on a ship in still waters staring across the ocean on a clear sunny day? Is that it?"

Her eyes widened. "That's absolutely correct. Just because historians disbelieved the witness accounts doesn't make then untrue. The problem is that we have too many missing variables to ascertain what modifiers would be necessary to process the evidence and obtain an empirical truth."

Amboy grinned and almost laughed.

"What?" she asked.

"You sound like a professor—'missing variables to ascertain what modifiers would be necessary to process the evidence and obtain an empirical truth'."

"I know I have the information in me, I just don't know why, but the more I listen to myself and the more I begin to think, the more I wonder if I wasn't some sort of scientist."

He nodded. "You do have that way of looking at situations. Whereas I like to act on impulse."

Her smile turned into a frown as she stubbed out her cigarette. "Speaking of impulse, I owe you an apology."

"For what?" he asked.

She stared at him for a good thirty seconds before she sighed and looked down at her knees. "For being an ass. I shouldn't have gotten mad and stormed out on you like that."

He considered her for a moment, then said, "I know it's not popular conversation, but we need to continually remember we're being chased not only by regular people but also by what probably is a group of witches."

"More likely a Congeries of Warlocks."

"Congeries? What the heck is that?"

"Sure. Like a coven of witches or a congress of apes or a murder of crows. The collective noun for warlocks is congeries."

"First of all, how do you even know that?" he asked, shaking his head. Then he added, "I know, you don't know. Second of all, since when can't we just say a bunch of something?"

"You can use bunch for all I care," she said. "I just happen to know the collectives for a lot of things. Go ahead, test me."

He put his hand on his chin. "Okay, what about dentists?"

She laughed. "You'll like this. They are called a wince of dentists."

"Oh stop."

"Serious," she said crossing her heart.

"What about Texans?"

"A spread."

"Midgets?"

"A shortage."

He laughed. "No way. What is this? A Laurel and Hardy sketch?"

"It's called venery, which comes from an old game of hunting words. It's a play on tautology or using two words to convey the same meaning. Most languages have various words for collectives. Chinese uses shapes and has different plurals for the different shape of the noun such as long or flat or tall." She lit another cigarette. "I was just being silly. You can say a bunch of Texans and the meaning comes just as well."

He stared at the books on his lap and nodded.

"What?" she asked. "What were you thinking?"

"I was thinking about unicorns. I wonder what the plural is."

"For things that don't have a plural you can make them up. The rule is that it can either be an onomatopoeia, which is a sound associated with the word. Or it's characteristic or habitat or even something delivering commentary, like when you see a murder of crows. They use the venereal term *murder* because when the crows are together, their beaks almost touching, it's like they are planning to murder someone. It's merely a commentary on what they look like when they appear together in groups of three or more."

He thought for a moment, then said, "So a Patagonia of Unicorns wouldn't be all that wrong then, would it."

She nodded, then shook her head. "Nope. It wouldn't be wrong at all." She leaned back down and put the cigarette in her mouth, the smoke curling up to the ceiling. "It even sounds good," she said around the cigarette. "A Patagonia of Unicorns."

If he only knew then what they would eventually encounter, he might have just turned around at the next stop, left the Chevalier, and pulled the sidewalk over their heads.

CHAPTER 20

By the time they reached Neuquén they were starving. The bus driver announced a forty-minute layover and they both rushed out to get supplies. The bus station was a microscopic edifice of capitalism and only offered a grill and a cart where an old woman made tortillas, empanadas, and choripan. It might have to do, but Amboy went in search for a suitable meal, while she went in search of wine that might elevate whatever they had.

They split up.

Eyeing the setting sun, he rushed down one street, then another. Neuquén had few restaurants and the ones they had sat only a few people. Everywhere he went, the place was either full, or closed. Many looked promising with checkered table clothes and candles, somewhere he'd love to sit and have a formal dinner with Lettie. Others were holes-in-the-wall, which weren't very romantic, but promised some incredible food. Still, nothing was available to them. It was as if the universe had decided for them that if they were to eat it would be at the hands of the abuelas cooking at the train station.

He decided that if they were going to eat, it was going to

have to submit to the universe's desires. Choripanes were one of his favorites anyway. He'd come to love the grilled sausage sandwiches with chimichurri sauce when they broke for lunch in the mine. But by the time he returned to station, the line for food was ten feet deep.

He sighed, realizing that had he only stayed he could have been one of the first. But it was an amiable crowd. Most of the passengers were Argentinian or Chilean, either out for a holiday, or heading home. He found himself joking around with several of them as they waited. He found people were eager to talk to him when he spoke to them in their own language, his American accent slight but present. A pair of newlyweds made one distinct being as they stood, attached at the hip, like a two-headed, multi-armed amore beast, forever kissing and staring soulfully into each other's eyes. He couldn't help but smile as the crowd watched the innocence among the pair, each one probably remembering a time when they had their own inseparable moments of love.

Suddenly, an old man shouted, "Get a room," and the crowd erupted in laughter.

The bride blushed but the groom raised a fist in the air and pointed to the bus. "That is our room!"

And the crowd erupted again.

Amboy was halfway to being served when a man next to him tipped his hat.

"You're American?"

"Si, soy Americano."

"Your accent is almost perfect," he replied in English.

Amboy glanced at his new best friend. About forty with a pockmarked face and close-cropped black hair. He wore a thin tan summer suit with an open collared white shirt and a cream-colored Panama hat. Not much different from the way most men were dressed, although the quality of the material of the man's clothes was better than Amboy was used to seeing.

"I've been in country for a while. I work at the mine up in Salta."

"You on holiday?"

Amboy noticed a stiffness about the man. Not that he was uptight, but more a rigidity—the way he kept his spine straight and his head up, eyes always moving, albeit casually. Probably military or former military.

"My girlfriend and I are. Going to the Cave of Hands." As he said it, he slid his own into the front pockets of his pants. "Have you been there?"

The man nodded. "Many hands and many guanaco. Rock art made by cave peoples. Very old."

Amboy edged forward a little in line.

The man followed.

Instead of filling the silence that followed, Amboy reveled in it. Although he'd chatted with some of the others, this particular gentleman set his worry senses flaring. Like he was back on the mountain and a stranger arrives. They're either terribly lost or a government man and one couldn't trust either one of them.

Out of the corner of his eye he saw Lettie. She held up two bottles and fired a thousand-watt grin.

The newlyweds cheered and so did the rest of the crowd.

Lettie began to blush, but then rolled with it, spinning a few times, then bowing to the crowd. She winked his direction, then made a motion that she was going back to the bus. He nodded and she scampered back inside.

He felt a lightness of being that could have continued except—

"That's your girlfriend?" the man asked.

Amboy was pretty sure the man already knew, but there was a game being played. The question was, was this man working for the government and did he know of his attacks on ESMA. Or was he working for . . . Amboy closed his eyes and shook his head slightly. It could be the Council of David or the Mission or the Catholic Church or any one of a number of organizations they'd probably ran afoul of without even knowing it.

"She's not your girlfriend?"

He looked up. "What? Oh, yes. She is. I was just thinking." He flashed a devil-may-care grin and shrugged his shoulders.

"She's very pretty."

"Yes, she is."

Amboy realized that he'd been calling her his girlfriend before out of convenience, but now it was true. The idea of it thrilled him and he almost gasped as a hundred thousand phantom butterflies snapped their wings at once.

"One should be careful with such beauty. One wouldn't want to lose it."

Amboy stilled. He tried to maintain the façade of a fun-loving American on holiday, but he hadn't missed the implied threat. "Beauty is always transient," he said. "Nothing lasts forever."

"Shame for that," the man said. "One would hope that it would."

Amboy was next. Just as soon as the man and his grandchildren finished their order, then he could make his. He couldn't wait to get back on the bus. Not only because it would put him nearer to Lettie, but it would get him away from this man, whatever his agenda was. He decided to go on the offensive.

"Why are you on the bus?" Amboy asked.

The man smiled. "I'm not."

Amboy turned to him. "What do you mean? Do you live here?"

"No, I'm in a car. We just happened to arrive at the same time as you."

"You're traveling by car to the cave?

"We're not going so far as that. We just stopped because we were hungry. Like you."

The man had gestured behind the bus. Amboy saw what looked like a black late-seventies Lincoln Town Car. A driver sat in the front seat and another figure almost hidden in shadow was in the back.

"Where you coming from?" Amboy asked.

"Buenos Aires."

"That's a long drive in a car. Not much between here and there."

"That's one of the things about this great country. There isn't much in between, but when you get someplace there's suddenly enough." The man gestured forward. "Looks like it's your turn."

Amboy looked. Sure enough, it was. He proceeded to order and got them both several empanadas—jalapenos y pupeserio e jamon and queso. He grabbed a pair of choripanes and stood for a moment considering some lomito. A fast food staple, the lomito was a steak sandwich with the works—tomatoes, lettuce, onion, chimichurri, mayonnaise, fried egg, ham and melted cheese—but it just seemed too much. So instead, he settled for some torta frita with fig jam for dessert. Once he had everything packaged and already greasing the inside of the paper bags, he turned to hurry back to the bus.

He noticed that the man wasn't there any longer.

The bus driver honked his horn. Five-minute warning.

Passengers began to jostle back to the immense two-story vehicle. Somehow he'd gotten behind the newlyweds and everyone began laughing again because they were trying to walk and kiss at the same time and not doing well at either. He found a way past them, then stumbled up the stairs into the Chevalier. Three suites down on the left, he pulled aside the curtain and deposited the food on a pull-out table. The two bottles of wine were present, as were two wine glasses, but Lettie was nowhere to be seen.

He stuck his head outside of the curtains and glanced up and down the aisle. Then he went to the window and looked out. Maybe she'd gotten tired of waiting and went to look for him. Still, no Lettie. The bus driver gave one final honk, then began to pull away. Amboy ran to the back of the bus. He checked the bathroom, but the door was locked. He knocked several times and called her name, but there was no reply except for something bumping against the door. He peered out the back window. Sure enough, the town car was there and he could see several figures in the back, but was one Lettie? Panic set in as he rushed back up the bus to the driver. He had to make him stop. He had to—

Lettie popped her head out of the compartment. "There you are." She was eating an empanada. "Stop goofing around. I'm starving."

Amboy felt everything snap painfully back in place and allowed him to be pulled into their compartment.

She handed him an empanada.

"These are to die for," she said around a mouthful. "I need something to wash this down. Get me some wine," she said in a regal voice.

He grinned and did as told. "Where were you?" he asked.

"In the bathroom."

"But I was in back and—"

"Were you checking on me? Were you worried I'd be left off the bus?" She tousled his hair. "How sweet."

"I didn't see you back there?"

"I had to use the one on the top deck. I think there are newlyweds on board."

"There are. I saw them."

"I did too. They didn't lock the bathroom door at first. I frankly didn't know a woman's legs could wrap that high," she said, she grinned at him. "But then again, I haven't tried."

He blushed as he handed her a glass.

Soon, they were seated side-by-side, rolling comfortably back and forth as the bus began to ascend into the foothills of the Andes, air shocks keeping the bumps to a minimum. The empanadas were incredible as were the sausage sandwiches. He hadn't realized how hungry he was until he started eating. They finished with the fried dough, smearing it with the fig jam and chasing it with the last of the first bottle of wine.

They agreed that the food was as good as any fine restaurant they'd ever been to and laughed over their belches. They opened the other bottle after they'd cleaned up their mess of papers and bags, and sat back and drank more casually.

"Tell me about your family," she said.

"I already have. We had a big family, just not much of a family life."

"I never heard you mention your mother, though."

"She died when I was five."

"How'd she die?" she asked.

"Emphysema. She had lungs blacker than any coal miner. It was her fault really. Smoked three packs a day. She just couldn't stop."

"Must have been hard growing up without a mom," she said.

He shrugged. "I didn't know the difference. Not having one and not having any friends who had one, I really didn't know much what they did. I had three brothers and four sisters. I was the oldest."

"Wait? If your mom died when you were five, how can there be seven of you?"

"Oh yeah, my dad remarried. She was a distant cousin and she had kids and didn't have a way to take care of them. Marriage of convenience, really. My mom had me and a brother and a sister. When new mom came, she brought the rest and one of my new sisters was older. Between the two of them, they made sure that I didn't die and tried to feed me when we had food."

She smiled wistfully as she stared out into space. "That's pretty much what mothers do, except they also hold your hand when you're hurting, read you stories to teach you about the world, be your confidante when you need one and your harasser when you don't need one. Mothers can be so much."

"Are you remembering your mother?"

"No, just imagining how she would be."

"Well. I never had that."

Night had fallen and they both stared out the window at the occasional well-lit building or home they passed. She offered him a cigarette, he declined.

"Why didn't you start smoking?" she asked. "I mean besides the occasional cig."

"You know. I smoke every now and then. Probably because I never had a mom to hold my hand and tell me what was wrong."

"She did die from smoking, though. That's a pretty good example."

He shrugged again. "People die all the time. If someone gets hit by a car, I don't stop crossing the street."

"That's sophistry if I ever heard," she said, shaking her head. "You know what I mean."

He sighed. "Yes. I know what you mean. I know I shouldn't smoke. I probably shouldn't cross the street either. But when your job has a higher death rate than being in Vietnam, then you tend not to sweat the small things."

"I guess the answer is obvious," she said. Then she looked at him, a twinkle in her eyes. "Did your dad really marry his cousin?"

He rolled his eyes. "Here we go."

"No, seriously," she said. "We joke about you people, but never really thought it was true."

"You people?"

"Yeah. Mountain folk. Rednecks. You know. You people."

If her grin was any wider it would have eaten her face.

He put his wine down and took her into his arms. "Let me tell you about us people," he said, but then he said no more. He kissed her deep and long, moans coming from the depths of them and merging in their mouths. They kissed for what seemed like hours but was just a few moments and they might have continued if it wasn't for the moans coming from the back of the bus.

They separated and glanced towards the closed curtains.

"Are you serious?" they both said at once.

Then they cracked up, each one lightly punching the other in the chest. He poured them more wine and they sat drinking slowly.

"What are you thinking about?" he asked.

"My mother. I'm trying to picture her, but I can't. All I know is her name. Same with my brothers. I'm trying to picture them, but the only one I can see is Jerri because he's dressed in a Japanese mumu. I'm also trying to remember who my father is. He's a blank spot in my memory. Can you describe your father for me?"

"I always thought he was made of stone. He'd been a miner since he was six years old. His hands were so hard they hurt you when he grabbed you. I don't think he meant to, but the calluses were so tough. He had hair like mine, but his face was a chiseled square. He had a dent in his nose and a clef in his chin like Kirk Douglas."

"Did you like him?"

Amboy made a thoughtful face. "I loved him for sure. I also admired him. But you know how it is. You don't always like who you love."

She smiled wistfully. "I wished I knew that. Maybe soon my memories will come back."

He grinned. "I hope they do." Seeing her expression, he added, "No, really I do."

"But what if we learn things we don't want to know?"

"Like what? What could we possibly learn that we wouldn't want to know? You have amnesia. We'd love to know everything about you, right?"

She sighed. "What if I'm a bad person?"

"You won't be."

"What if I have a ton of kids?"

"You'd remember. You'd know."

"What if I am married?"

He stared at her for a moment, then turned away. What if she was? Could they go on? Should they go on? They were surely becoming a thing, but what if that was only the result of her just not remembering who she was? What if she was married and had a family to go back to? That means everything they were doing here was terribly wrong.

She gave him a steady look. "I asked, what if I was married."

"Then we'd deal with that appropriately," he managed to say without his voice cracking.

She seemed to consider his response. After a while she said, "You love me, don't you?"

She breathed cinnamon and sweated flowers.

"I'm not sure what that is," he said.

"Does your heart ache for me?"

Like it might break in two.

"Do you miss me when I'm not around?"

Like a face misses its eyes.

"Do you long to hear my voice?"

Like the body misses its ears.

She punched him lightly in the front of his shoulder.

"Come on, Amboy. Tell a girl what she wants to hear."

He wanted to, but he didn't deserve her. He didn't want her to have to settle for him. He knew he was in a unique position of power. He could love her with every piece of him and revel in the idea of her, but if he was to tell her, if he was to let her know how special and unique she was in the life of a simple man named Amboy Stevens, then he'd put her in a position where she'd have to either feel the same way or not. And it was his fear that she did love him and if she did it was the worst decision she could possibly make because he was so unworthy of even being in the same room with her. He was a murderer. He was just not the right person for a woman who presented herself to the world with a beaming smile, perfect eyes, and Florida indelibly etched into her soul.

CHAPTER 21

The bus stopped again at midnight. They'd slept for an hour and both awoken fully charged. It was as if they didn't want to spend the time together sleeping, they'd rather be awake so that they could get to know each other even more. The newlyweds had thankfully finally finished and they'd each gone to the bathroom by the time the bus stopped and pulled over. It was only a gas stop, but the inside was well lit and they both decided to stretch their legs.

The driver promised them a half hour with the usual honk of the horn as warning.

They were higher in elevation and no longer in the low pampas of Argentina but in an Alpine forest. The smell of the air was cool, clear and clean, nothing like the exhaust- and noise-filled streets of Buenos Aires. They'd stopped in the town of El Bolson. A river ran behind the gas station. She grabbed his hand and pulled him to the sound. Soon, they came to the water. Grass reached its edge. Trees overhung on the other side, causing deeper shadows in the half-moon light. If they didn't have a bus waiting to take them away, it was the sort of place they would want to stay.

An owl screeched from somewhere deep in the woods bringing him memories of his own mountains with its own forests. He'd loved the trees since he could remember, running beneath the leafy branches, in and out of the dappled shade. Back home they had both kinds of trees—the ones that shed their leaves every fall and the different variations of pines. Here they had pines and the heady smell of it took him back.

"Hey, about me getting all serious back there . . ." Lettie began, but left it off there.

"What about it?" he put his arm around her.

"You've been nothing but help for me."

He noted how platonic she'd become and didn't want her regretting how open she'd been to him. He needed to step up, he knew it, so he took a deep breath and said, "It's because I want to help you, Lettie. I know you might have this great and mysterious past, but we have what we have now and I'm just happy to be in the moment with you."

"Is happy all you want?" she asked.

"Happy is a start, don't you think?"

She turned and kissed him square on the lips. She lingered for a moment, her eyes searching his for the truth of it, then they parted. She turned to the water and sighed.

The owl screeched again.

The way the light winked over the tips of the water as it rushed over rocks and submerged trees reminded him of the refrains of the song *Easy From Now On* from an album by Emmylou Harris called *Quarter Moon in a Ten Cent Town*, which told how for everyone there's a time to lay one's heartaches down. Perhaps now was the time. She wanted him to tell her that he loved her. Even in the short whirlwind romance they had, he felt everything she'd said and wanted to tell her how he really did feel.

She spoke. "I just wanted you to know . . ."

She began to shudder a little as if she'd just gotten cold.

"I just wanted you to know . . ." she said again, this time her entire body began to vibrate.

He turned to her and a hand on either shoulder.

"I just wa-want you to-to know—"

Her entire body went stiff and despite trying to catch her, she fell on the ground. The last time he'd seen her this way was in Thiago's apartment and he remember what came next. He found a piece of wood on the ground and forced it into her mouth so she wouldn't bite off her tongue. She was in the middle of a grand mal seizure, only this one wasn't induced by epilepsy. This was caused by something far worse.

He jerked free his .45 cal pistol and swept the landscape. What had once been a pleasant memory of home—what had so recently been a place where they professed their feelings for one another—was now a scene of danger. He didn't see anything at first, just the back of the store and the river and the trees, but then movement came from a bush at the edge of the river. He focused in on that and screamed for it to show itself.

Nightmares have a way of casting an afterimage when one wakes from a particular savage one. Sleeping through the night, only to have your mind create something so terrifying that one awakes with a start, the evil still imprinted on the backs of one's eyelids, as if it had just been there and was real, is something that makes many people afraid of their dreams. What if they come true? What if the evil one imagined somehow is able to escape?

Amboy's thoughts were filled with this for one microcosmic moment as a figure made completely of sticks stepped forth from the thickness of the brush—a figure he'd seen before beneath the earth, beneath Buenos Aires. The knees on the legs were articulated backwards making it more insectile or like those of a goat. Arms, as apparently skinny and fragile as the legs, ended in three long talons. The body supported a triangular head with eyes that glowed red in the night. It seemed to peer at him through the darkness, some unholy intelligence shining from the eyes. Its desire was palpable and projected the feeling of unstoppability.

As the creature herky-jerked towards him, he felt the fear rise, his body screaming to flee. But he couldn't leave Lettie behind. He had to stay with her. He knew that if he left her for even a second, she'd be gone—taken. He backed up to where she was shaking and straddled her body. Still, one glance at her told him she wasn't going anywhere by herself. Whatever this thing was, its proximity triggered the magic in her tattoo.

"You can't stop it, you know?" said the man from the roadside food vendor. "It's inevitable. It won't be stopped."

Amboy swung his pistol at the sound.

The man stood beside a woman who carried a white dowsing rod similar to the one he'd seen being carried by the German in the doorway of Thiago's apartment. He could see its glow and how the women held it as if it were electric.

Amboy's mind was afire with the need to both confront the evil creature and these interlopers. "What are you doing here?"

"To make sure the lilin feeds as it should."

"Feeds. The hell it will." Amboy spun, took aim and fired at it. His shot took out one of the creature's legs. But even as it fell, the leg reattached itself and the creature rose on it as if nothing had ever happened. Fine. If he couldn't kill the creature, he'd kill the creature's owners.

He turned back to the man. "Make it stop. Make it stop or I will kill you."

"I told you. It's inevitable. It won't be stopped."

Amboy shot him in the leg.

The grotto exploded with sound.

The man went down, cursing. His eyes folded into the back

of his head. Unlike the creature, he didn't stand back up. His hands went to staunch the blood. He said through gritted teeth, "You can kill all of us but you can't stop the lilin."

Amboy ignored the man. "And you," Amboy shouted at the woman. "Put that down!"

She looked at him and grinned, her teeth filed to points. She raised the dowsing rod and aimed it at Lettie making her shake even more.

He shot the woman as well, aiming for her stomach but not really caring.

She fell forward, dropping the dowsing rod.

As it hit the ground, it turned into a snake and began to slither away.

Amboy ran over and grabbed the tail. The snake tried to simultaneously wrap itself around his arm and bite him. Amboy didn't care if he was bit. Screaming into the night, he began to bash it against the ground over and over until the head exploded. Then he threw it at the man and the women. "Here. Fucking douse with this."

Lettie screamed.

He spun and saw the stick creature on top of Lettie. Her shirt had been pulled up and the tattoo on her back was pulsing a bright harsh light. Amboy fired his pistol into the creature, somehow missing with every round. He took a running start and lunged, falling into it, taking it down in a football tackle. Touching it made him nauseous and he felt the empanadas and the choripanes and the red wine surge toward the surface, but he clamped his mouth shut. He jerked at the creature's neck and brought his hand around for a punch, but was suddenly in the air, hurled a dozen feet.

He slammed to the earth and as he did, he let loose vomit. Everything he'd eaten and everything he'd drunk shot from his body in a series of convulsive heaves. He found himself on all fours, his back arching, his insides trying desperately to crawl to the outsides, all because he'd touched the lilin. He tried to clear his throat and his mind and finally managed to stand, albeit unsteadily.

He turned to where Lettie was and saw that she was trying to stand as well.

The lilin was nowhere to be seen.

Maybe he'd scared it away.

He ran tremulously towards her and helped her get the rest of the way to her feet, both of them almost falling in the process.

"Are you okay?" he asked.

Her eyes were blank.

He checked her back and the tattoo was gone. Completely. Not even a trace of it. Her back now as unblemished as the cheek that had once had a port wine stain of Alabama on it.

"How do you feel?" he asked.

She blinked several times. "I—I feel fine. Groggy. What—What happened? Did I sleep?"

"I'm not sure. I think the lilin was here."

That made him wonder about the man and the woman. He saw where they'd been shot and strode over. Blood glistened on the grass and a broken white walking stick lay nearby, but nothing else. Had they really been here? Who did he shoot? Where had they gone? For a moment, he wondered if any of it had happened. He picked up the pieces of the stick and saw faint indentations in the dark that could have been religious markings. He tossed the pieces into the water and watched them submerge, then bob to the surface, carried downstream and out of sight.

Then the bus driver and another man came running around the corner of the building.

Amboy held the gun to the side of his leg and turned so they wouldn't see it.

"What happened? We heard gunshots?" the driver said.

Amboy pointed towards the water with his free hand. "Thieves. They came for us. They tried to rob us."

Both men stared at the water, but there was nothing to see.

The owl screeched again, this time closer, then it descended, flying across the water, its great wingspan a moving darkness in the darker night.

The bus driver said, "Come on. There's sometimes trouble in the provinces. They probably heard you were American and thought you an easy mark." Then he gestured to Amboy's side. "And put that away. Some people might not like it."

He frowned and for a moment thought to argue. But seeing the look of concern and worry on the driver's face he shoved the pistol into his side pocket. If he needed it, he could jerk it quickly free.

Lettie had dirt and leaves on her back and the back of her head. "Come one. Let's get you cleaned up before we get back on the bus." He plucked some of the bigger offenders from the back of her jacket and her hair.

They went inside to the bathroom in the store. It was well lit and an older woman sat on a stool behind the counter, reading a magazine. A soccer game was on the black and white television. She smoked a cigarette without ever taking it out of her mouth.

Lettie went into the bathroom, still shaking and confused.

Amboy waited for her, grabbing a pair of cokes and a candy bar, and paying for them by dropping cash on the counter. They'd had enough wine for one evening. He sure didn't need anything else to cloud his memory. He went over what had just happened and still couldn't figure out what had happened to the people or the stick creature—the lilin.

And the people, where were they?

The bus coughed once, then started up.

Amboy hammered on the door for her to hurry. He heard the air suspension engage on the Chevalier and banged on the door again. Was it going to leave them? He ran outside and banged on the door.

The driver glanced at him or through him it seemed, then returned his gaze to the road.

Amboy banged on all the windows as he passed, trying to get the attention of those in the lower suites. Surely, they would recognize him and tell the driver to stop. He had to jump to reach each window, and soon found himself breathing hard. But when he reached his own window, he saw something that left his blood cold. Lettie, sitting in the seat, staring straight ahead, then turning to someone he couldn't see and laughing. He banged on the window, and she glanced his way, but saw nothing.

He tripped over a curb and fell, watching helplessly as the bus pulled away.

He climbed to his feet and screamed for it to stop, but it kept on going.

He collected the bag he'd dropped and limped back to the store.

He asked the woman behind the counter, "What happened to my friend? Did you see her leave?"

She didn't reply. She continued reading her magazine, glancing occasionally at the television.

He went to the bathroom and found it unlocked.

And empty.

Bars blocked the windows.

He'd never seen her leave.

But then he saw a single leaf on the ground of the bathroom. Like one that had been on Lettie's back. One she'd gotten from having a seizure on the ground because of the proximity of a monster.

He reached down to pick it up and watched it crumble to dust between his fingers.

CHAPTER 22

He felt invisible. He couldn't get anyone to notice him, even the woman behind the counter. He picked up a bag of chips and dropped it on the floor, but she just looked away. He even jumped up and down on them and scattered the remains across the store, but she didn't say anything. She merely sat where she sat, spat on the ground, crossed herself, and continued smoking. He was at a loss for what to do. Something had happened he didn't understand.

ESMA officers he could deal with.

German religious fanatics he could deal with.

He even thought he could deal with the lilin, but the more he thought about it, the less he thought the creature had simply gone away. The more he considered, the more he worried that it might have taken Lettie over and she didn't even know it. He remembered how she'd laughed as if there'd been a person next to her on the bus. Wait! What if there had been someone next to her? But then who could it have been? She'd been suspecting him. Could it have been him—a version of him? Or something worse?

He glanced at his watch.

She'd been gone for three minutes but it felt like three hours.

The sound of a motorcycle engine coughing to a stop brought him back to reality. He ran out the door, almost knocking down the driver who'd come into to prepay for a tank of gas. He passed without even noticing Amboy.

Outside was a new Moto Guzzi V50 Monza motorcycle in white with black accents.

Amboy had ridden motorcycles before. He preferred the highway to the city because of all of the stops and starts. Now was his moment. He stood beside the motorcycle. When the driver came back out, he waved at him but the man made no notice.

"Hello. Can you hear me?" he asked.

The man ignored him.

"I'm going to borrow your motorcycle," he said.

Still, the man ignored him.

"It's going to suck for you, but I need this."

The man began to whistle as he stared up into the pin-pricked night sky.

Amboy stood to the side, tapping his foot impatiently as the man gassed the motorcycle to full, then when he was hanging up the hose, Amboy climbed on, started the machine and took off. He looked in his rearview mirror as the man ran a few steps, then stopped and removed his helmet and stared at the motorcycle as if he couldn't understand what was happening—how it could be driving away without him.

But it had.

Once again Amboy appeared to be invisible.

And this time he didn't care.

He tore down the road, flipping through second, third, and fourth gears. He had the motorcycle up to ninety kilometers per hour. He hadn't been on a motorcycle in a few years and hugged the center line, fearful of getting caught in the gravel dribbling off the shoulder. The road continued to climb upwards, the turns becoming more and more frequent. He took one of the turns a little sharp and was forced to slow down as his rear tire almost skidded out from under him.

He pounded the handlebars in frustration. But then hit a straightway. He hammered the clutch, roaring up to one hundred and ten kilometers per hour. He tried to go faster, but the machine had a limit and that seemed to be it. Still, he held it for as long as he could. Then finally, he spied a double set of taillights which had to be the Chevalier.

The bus seemed to be slowing. Was that because Lettie had finally figured out that he wasn't onboard? Was all of his effort going to pay off? He concentrated on the road in front of him gaining ground with every kilometer. The trees began to get thicker as they rose and the air cooler. His eyes were almost closed and already shedding wet tears from the effort to stay open against the wind.

His concentration was so focused that he failed to see the herd of deer on the side of the road, hesitating and eager to cross, until it was too late. One, two, three dark figures crossed in front of him, blocking his view of the bus. Then a large doe stopped in the middle of the road and turned to stare at him. With almost no time to react, he tapped his back brake and then his front and swerved at the same time shooting past the deer, close enough that her tail rubbed against his right leg. He turned to see the rest of the herd cross, then returned his attention to the road in front of him.

Now with his heart firmly in his throat after the potential disaster, he did the only thing he could. He accelerated, shouting at the motorcycle, cursing it, heaping love upon it, anything to cajole one more kilometer per hour from it. The road became steeper and he saw the bus getting closer. He could see figures in the back windows now, both on the upper and lower levels. Both sides of the road were illuminated by the lights coming from the suites and the uncurtained windows on the upper decks. He was near enough he could make out the writing on the back of the bus.

Then the road leveled off and the bus shot forward.

But he matched it, with the motorcycle getting even closer.

He swung wide to get beside the bus, hoping to somehow surge in front of it. He began gaining on it. Incrementally, but gaining, nonetheless. Meter by meter he got closer. He began looking for things to grab onto as if he were Steve McQueen. Such was his desperation that he'd try anything. But the outside of the bus was as smooth as the side of a 1968 Ford Mustang GT.

He leaned forward until his forehead was almost touching the handlebars, hoping that the reduction in drag might give him the tiniest edge.

And it did.

He gained more. He could almost reach out and touch the tail light.

Then they hit a curve and he had to decelerate, lest he be hip-checked by the bus and launched over the edge. He glanced down and saw the drop—easily a hundred feet. Nothing he'd ever survive. He could decelerate now. He could quit. Maybe call ahead. He could stop all the car chase nonsense and take his stolen motorcycle to the next town and just call the police and tell them that his girlfriend had been kidnapped by a—demon—no that wouldn't work. Shoot, he could figure out something.

They hit another straightaway.

Once again, he was in touching distance of the bus.

He wondered what the bus driver saw in his side mirrors.

Amboy had somehow become invisible, but the motorcycle wasn't. It was still a quarter ton of Italian metal and rubber, now to the side of the bus with apparently no driver. He'd most certainly stop and investigate, right? Or would his superstition take over. Like the headless horseman of Patagonia, he was chasing them, and to catch them might risk their very souls.

The bus shivered towards the edge of the road, forcing him onto the shoulder. He held the handlebars tight, but as he did, his wheels hit the gravel on the side of the road and he immediately knew his mistake. The machine wobbled from front to back like Lettie in the middle of a seizure. He tried to control it by man-handling the handlebars, but they were wobbling too powerfully and all he could do was hold on, lest his arms de-socket from his shoulders. Then the front wheel bit into the road but the back continued a slide to oblivion. Amboy saw it happening all at once and he knew he had two choices—either bail and pray he wouldn't die, or ride the bike into the crash that was most assuredly coming.

He bailed, kicking out with his foot as he pushed the handlebars away. He knew he was going to be in pain yet he screamed in advance, not because he knew what was coming, but because what was going, the bus disappearing around the corner, Lettie inside of it, god knows who she was with or what she was with, his only concern for her well—

He hit the ground harder than he thought possible and—

Bounced and—

Rolled—

And rolled—

Then, tree—

CHAPTER 23

His face was wet when he came to. Blood ran cold down his cheeks as he awoke to a light rain. His head throbbed and his side felt staved in. The pain began in his toenail and made a straight line towards his forehead. Everything in between was agony. He tested both legs and his arms and was thankful to have movement in them.

It was still night. A quarter moon peaked through tree branches. A chill in the air invaded his lungs with every hitching breath.

He heard two voices speaking Spanish.

"Front is shattered, but I know a guy who can fix it."

"Are you sure you didn't see anyone?"

"No one that I could see. My guess is they already got help."

"Well, if we get to Epuyén and they aren't there, then I'm claiming this as salvage."

"As long as I get half."

"Then grab the back and I'll get the front."

Amboy realized what was happening and grabbed a sapling to help him stand. It broke and he fell with it, shots of pain machine gunning his ribs. They had to be broken. He could already feel his breathing subscripted. He just hoped he hadn't collapsed a lung.

Still, he found a larger tree and managed to get to his feet. When he knew he wasn't going to fall, he looked up and saw two men staring at him.

"Did you hear that?"

"Sounded like a branch breaking."

"Think it might be the driver?"

"I think it could be a bear. Come on. Hurry."

He fell again, this time dragging his legs behind him until he found a tree to pull himself to a standing position.

Glancing fearfully behind them, they each grabbed an end of his wrecked Moto Guzzi and heaved it into the back of a blue and rust-colored old pickup that was missing a tailgate. They glanced back again, eyes worried at what might be in the woods, neither of them even fathoming the idea that there may be an injured invisible man standing and staring at them. They got in and the driver started up the truck.

Too late, Amboy realized his ride was leaving. He tried to run, but almost fell as the pain soon overwhelmed him.

The truck coughed, lurched forward, and then stalled.

Amboy picked himself up from his knees, leaned forward and let momentum carry him. On two stiff legs, he stumbled until he hit the back of the pickup. The driver's head jerked as he glanced into the rearview mirror. Amboy grabbed the rear wheel of the motorcycle and used that to pull himself into the bed of the truck. The moment his feet left the ground, the truck coughed back to life and he was soon trundling down the road. He held onto the motorcycle, using its weight to keep him from falling out.

He was in and out of consciousness. Had it not been for the constant shifting of the load and the effects on his ribs, he would have fallen into a dead sleep. But as it was, the rumbling bumping journey to the small town of Epuyén was a torture that he welcomed. As incremental as it was, he was still going in the direction that Lettie had taken. Even as far away as she was, anywhere near her was a benison to a life without her.

The truck pulled to a creaky stop at a bar called Punto 40, its neon sign a light in the darkness, inviting those who might need sustenance an oasis in the middle of the northern Patagonian forest. He pulled himself up as the two passengers got out. They made a beeline for the door and were soon inside. He could use a beer or a bottle or something to blot out some of the pain. Then he heard bells—church bells. He turned his head towards them and saw through the trees a lit white façade of a building. It had to be a church. If anyone knew what to do it would be the church—or Father Paz.

He pulled himself out of the bed of the truck and fell face first onto the dirt parking space next to the truck. He felt blood pump from his trick nose and knew he'd broken it again. He lay there for a time as pain blossomed and subsided over and over like a volcano undecided whether or not it wanted to erupt.

Another pickup truck pulled in from the road, forcing him to roll until he was up against the tires, lest he be run over. A pair of men, wearing cowboy boots and jeans climbed out of their truck and trundled into the bar.

Using both pickups, he managed to get to his feet. Then began a forty-minute journey of falling and rolling and standing and falling and cursing and standing and moving forward until he came to the steps of the church. The door was unlocked and he stumbled inside. The cool calmness of the place immediately soothed him and mad him worry a little less.

He glanced around. The inside of the chapel was well-lit, but no one was in attendance. He needed to draw someone's attention. He needed to figure out a way to get help. Using the wall, he made his way to the old carved wooden confessional. Red cotton curtains covered each open window on each door. He climbed into the penitent's space and pulled a rope which in turn engaged a bell. He only had to pull it twice before a man entered the other side of the confessional.

He formed the Spanish words in his head before he said them, just to make sure he had them right. "Forgive me Father, for I have sinned. It has been ten years since my last confession." Which was a lie. He'd never been in a confessional. But he'd seen movies and he'd heard others and he'd talked to Santiago about going, because he'd gone several times a week.

"Why so long and what have you done such that it means you feel you need a confession?"

"I know this will sound strange, but I need to speak with Father Paz."

"There is no Father by that name here, my son. I am Father Santos and you may speak with me."

Amboy took a breath. How much should he disclose? He didn't want all hell breaking loose.

"Father Paz is at the Basilica Santa Rosa de Lima in Buenos Aires. I am working for him. I need to speak with him."

There was a pause as the father considered the request. Then, after a few moments, "You are in a confessional, my son. It is a place where you may converse with God through me. This is not a telephone booth where you can call a priest in Buenos Aires."

The response wasn't as bad as it could have been, but not enough to his liking to be beneficial. The pain blossomed in his side and he almost passed out. Did he have internal injuries? He must have.

"Tell me your trouble, my son."

I'm invisible, Father. No one can see me. My girlfriend was taken by a stick demon and thinks that I am still on the bus to the Cave of Hands with her. Other than that, I'm really perfectly okay. "You wouldn't understand. I really need to speak with Father Paz."

"Even if we were to contact this Father Paz, I'd need to know a reason. I am but a simple country friar and it is not good for me to contact the archdiocese without a particular reason."

"Tell him that Amboy Stevens has lost Lettie and needs help."

"Are you this Amboy Stevens? Did you lose someone? Lettie? Is that your dog?"

"Lettie is my girlfriend."

"I'm not so sure that the archdiocese is concerned with the love life of a young man."

Amboy felt his anger surge. He wanted to reach through the delicate lattice separating them and yank Father Santos through. But he lacked the energy. In fact, the whole time he sat he felt it ebbing away. His body seemed to be vibrating with a low-level of electricity, even the effort to turn his head seemed to be too much.

"Father Paz. He will understand. He—he wants to know."

Amboy was done. He felt as if he might be dying. If this was what dying felt like it wasn't half bad. He remembered the feeling when the mine collapsed and his body was pressed upon on all sides by tons of stone. This was similar. His skin had no feeling. He could feel his insides and the mess they were. The pain had gone somewhere in the back of his mind. He leaned against the inside of the confessional and closed his eyes.

He heard the father but not the words.

Eventually, the door to the penitent's side opened.

From slitted eyes, Amboy watched the father lean in and look around.

He breathed. "I am here, Father."

The priest jerked back, his head smashing into the upper part of the door.

"*Madre de dios*," he said, crossing himself.

"I am here and I am not a demon," he said with his remaining effort, wondering if that was in fact true. He had no way of knowing. Perhaps that's what he really was. Maybe he'd become the stick creature. Perhaps they'd changed places. Wouldn't that be something?

"*El demonio. El diablo.*" The priest began to back away.

"Call—Father—Paz."

And then everything went dark.

CHAPTER 24

The air in Hell was colder than he thought it would be. A breeze caused him to shiver. His wrists felt raw and bloody. His ribs felt constricted as if he'd been wrapped too tightly in his funeral garb. His legs and feet by comparison felt warm, even comfortable. Which circle of Hell, he wondered, had such a dichotomy? Would the furnaces of damnation be turned on soon and would he experience a searing heat soon that would make him wish to be cold again? What sort of devious demonology was he going to experience for eternity? And why was everything dark?

He opened his eyes to a white universe.

Then he closed them again if only to return to the dark comfort of Hell.

But it was different now. He could hear things that almost made sense. He could sense things. He smelled someone familiar—the scent of leather and body odor and red wine.

"I was wondering when the Amboy Demon was going to awake," came a familiar voice.

He opened his eyes to the white again.

"Demon?" He wiped his eyes with the side of his hand and

his vision became clearer. The white universe was the ceiling as were the walls. He turned his head and saw Father Paz sitting in a chair in the corner. He wore his usual black suit with a white shirt and priest's collar. A glass of wine rested in his hand and a half empty bottle sat on the side table.

"The local diocese thought for sure they'd captured a demon. I'm afraid you were tied up when I finally arrived. You must have struggled to be free because the skin was completely rubbed away."

Amboy noticed the places on his wrists that had been worn raw by rope. He felt them beneath the bandages and they were still tender to the touch. "They had me tied up?"

"Well, you were raving with fever and you were invisible."

"Then how did they know to tie me up?"

"Evidently they threw a sheet over you."

Amboy jerked his head back to look at Paz. "You can see me?"

"Of course, I can, son."

"But I was invisible."

Paz took a sip of his wine. "An imperfect term for an imperfect condition. You were never invisible. People just couldn't see you. I promise, had you walked into a lion's den, you wouldn't have walked out."

The very idea of invisibility was ludicrous even in the face of the evidence. "But how can that be, Father? How can I not be seen? It just seems so impossible."

"We call it a taint. When you come into contact with something powerful and demonic it can affect you in such a way that normal people don't want to acknowledge your presence. It's as if their eyes could see you but their minds couldn't decipher what it was seeing. You are not invisible. Evil people can see you. The truly evil. But there aren't many of those out there, thankfully.

So, to say you were invisible is basically true." He took another sip. "But as I said, imperfect. The proper term would be tainted."

Amboy tried to sit up, but found the constriction around his side too tight, making him unable to make the necessary bending.

"How can you see me now?"

"Baptismals are good for a great many things. We keep them around for more than just babies. It's just that most don't know the breadth and scope of the reasons behind their placement." He took a sip of wine. "Tell me what happened, son."

Amboy ran through the entire story from when he'd rashly decided to just up and leave to when they encountered the demon on the side of the river, to when he'd stolen the motorcycle and tried to run down the bus. He included the interlude with the German and their town car in Neuquén. When he finished, he realized two things—how naïve they'd been and how lucky he was to be alive.

"Did you see the town car when you stopped and the demon was present?" Paz asked.

Amboy shook his head and in doing so felt a twinge of past pain. "No. I didn't see them at all."

"But it doesn't mean they weren't there," Paz said.

"Are you saying that they were invisible as well?"

"They might have been, but the town car would have been visible."

Amboy repeated, "But it doesn't mean they weren't there. Do you think they might have been controlling the demon?"

"One doesn't control a demon," Paz said, "but they can influence it. In many ways, demons are like children. For the most part they are primordial in nature and only desire specific things, most commonly the ability to own the life force of a person. One has to bind a demon to something, then they can influence it. Otherwise, it is free to roam naturally and as invisible as it is primordial."

"Is that what it did to Lettie? Does it have her lifeforce?"

Paz's face turned to stone. "If it is in her, there is a battle taking place. It will try and fool her and it will try and win her over. If it succeeds, she will lose access to her body and become a passenger in herself."

Despite the pain, Amboy managed to sit up. He discovered that his ribs were wrapped in bandages which meant he definitely had broken ribs. He glared at Paz. What the old priest was talking about was possession. He'd seen the movie a few years ago of the girl who'd been possessed and the priests who'd tried to free her. One of the priests had eventually nose-dived out the window and down a steep flight of stairs. But the young girl. The things that the demon had done to the girl. If just part of what was in that movie reflected reality then Lettie was even now being terribly abused.

"We have to save her," he implored.

"Of course we do, my son."

"We have to get to her and free her from this thing. We need to go now."

"It's not that easy," Paz said.

"I don't care. We have to go."

Paz slung back his wine and stood. He strode over until he was hovering over Amboy.

"Do you not think that maybe this is what you deserve? You took your fate by the tail and it bit you. All I asked you to do was to stay in place until I could gather the necessary forces to protect you. But no. You are Amboy Stevens. In your universe you are king and so you brought her into your universe. The problem is that your universe lives within the rest of ours and follows by other rules."

Amboy felt a flush of heat in his face. "This is my fault? How is it my fault?" he asked, even as he said the words, realizing their folly. "I never chose this. I never asked to be here. I was compelled to join this enterprise."

Paz stared at him through heavy lidded eyes for a good thirty seconds, then said, "Please don't give me the old 'I was just minding my own business' bullshit, Amboy. If there's one thing that's clear it was that you and Ms. Fennick were destined to meet. That it took a thug to make it happen doesn't matter. You did it. You became a part of it. And you led her to a demon who probably is fighting for her soul if she hasn't already lost."

Amboy raised a fist.

"Go ahead if it makes you feel any better." Father Paz raised his chin. "Hit me. Punch me. Take out your frustrations on an old man. Because we both know who it is you really want to punch."

Amboy felt his fist begin to shake and all at once understood the truth of what Father Paz was saying. The priest was right but that didn't give him the right to bully him into understanding. He could at least . . . Amboy caught himself. No. He'd caused this to happen. He'd been the one to leave the security of the Basilica and go on a wild goose chase. He'd been the one to lure Lettie out of a place of safety and put her in harm's way. Images of ARVN and some of the American soldiers doing bad things to the girl filled his mind, one image stacking on top of the other until a mountain of terrible crashed through his mind. Knowing that this could be Lettie and he'd been the cause of it made his heart hitch.

He dropped his hand and hung his head. He couldn't go back. All he could do was go forward. They could still rescue her, couldn't they?" He opened his eyes and stared through a prism of tears at Father Paz who was retaking his seat and pouring himself another glass of wine. He peered through the redness a moment, then took a sip.

"The thing about the provinces is they grown their own grapes. This one is from high in the mountains and has the effervescence of an American pinot noir from the Russian River Valley."

"We need to save her," Amboy said, voice hoarse with emotion.

"Of course, we do, my boy. That's why I am here."

"Do—Do you have a plan?"

"We're trying to find where she went. When we do, then we can formulate a plan."

"We don't even know where she is?" Amboy asked.

"We know that a bus arrived at the Cave of Hands and that a woman matching her description—which is rather unique as we both know—was seen getting off the bus. But after that, we have nothing."

"But that's good news. We knew she was there. She could be nearby, even at Lake Posadas. Do you have people looking?"

"We do. The problem is that others are looking for her as well. I can say with a certain amount of belief that the *Misión de Investigación y Descubrimiento de la Patagonia* isn't involved."

"Then whom?"

"We might have to go back to the beginning. We might have to determine why she was lured to Rio Gallegos in the first place. Perhaps there's another group at work here."

"The sorcerers? But I thought they had disbanded a hundred years ago."

"All the best organizations make people believe they have disbanded. I wouldn't believe it for a second, Amboy. Something like that who'd tapped into an old magic running through the region wouldn't give it up unless they absolutely had to. I've been reviewing some of the reports from the Jesuits during the warlock trial. They make for interesting reading. Most interesting is that many of the members of the coven could not be found."

"A congeries."

"What?"

"The name for a group of warlocks is a congeries. I think it's the same thing is for a male sorcerer. A congeries of sorcerers."

Paz glared at him with a single eye, then said, "Whatever the term, many of them went missing during the trial and although many were hung, the rest escaped. My intuition tells me that the answer to the problem lies somewhere around Rio Gallegos."

"So, we go there." Amboy began to get out of bed. "I'm feeling better than I thought I would. I mean, after the crash, I thought it might take me a few days or a week to get back on my feet. I'm really glad I'm a fast healer." He swung his feet out of bed and took his weight on the floor. He felt an ache, but the mind-numbing pain was gone.

Father Paz looked on in concern. "You should still watch yourself. You broke two ribs and bruised several others. They were worried about a collapsed lung for days, but everything began to heal."

Amboy raised his arms slowly above his head until he felt the tension along the sides of his chest, then froze. "Wait. Did you say days?" Amboy searched around for his watch, but didn't see it. "What day is it? How much time has passed?"

"Eight days."

A pit opened inside Amboy.

Eight. Days?

So long?

He sat back down hard on the bed as the feeling that he'd now lost everything struck him plumb between the eyes.

CHAPTER 25

The mountains of Patagonia and Tennessee had more in common than he would have anticipated. The lush scenery was comprised of more hues of green than he would have thought possible, ranging from the brightest at the tops of the trees to the darkness hugging their bottoms. The lake besides Epuyén could have been transported from the Smokey Mountains, the arctic blue of the water like the solitary blue eye of a trapped leviathan. But what made the difference was the Andes rising like a white wall above it all. White frosted peaks that brushed the clouds were an impenetrable wall for transit unless one were able to fly over or knew the secret trails to get one through.

The air felt crisp and clean. Much different from the cloying humidity of Buenos Aires and the constant confused energy of the capital city that filled the air with a chaotic electricity. Here, on the eastern edge of the country where it bumped against the great mountains, living was entirely different. Simpler. Cleaner. It was as if he were back in Tennessee.

Part of him wondered why he'd ever left.

The simplicity of existence in the Tennessee Mountains was a comfortable way to live. Sure, they had their invisible boundaries, be it familial or because of certain social morays, but they were few and to break them didn't mean death or incarceration, but rather remonstration and/or servitude. There was a life of sustenance. Be it nuts or berries or birds or coons, each of the mountain children had to hunt for the greater good. Those who didn't hunt worked the land or the stills or even worse—the mines.

Amboy rubbed at his right arm and let his fingers linger on the place on the upper and lower arms when each had been snapped in half when he'd been a child. They said it had been from a fall, but no one would tell him where it happened. And it hadn't occurred on their mountain, but over on the Stegnars' mountain—a place he'd never gone before, nor had he ever needed to go there. Not that they were in feud, but they had their own spaces and the silent rule was that every family kept to themselves.

Even now the arm ached, as did his other.

No one ever told him how they'd become broken either. The adults said it had been an accident. But everyone had treated him differently after that. The other kids, with rare exception, stayed away from him. Aunts and uncles who used to offer him ready smiles shifted their gazes when he came by and answered his questions with an economy of words. It was as if the young five-year-old boy with casts on both arms was a creature returned from the dead rather than a poor child who'd been in the wrong place at the wrong time.

They told him he'd fallen down an old unmarked vertical mining shaft. They hadn't found him for days, until they'd final brought in Uncle Jackson's Carolina Dogs, their barking all but covering his cries for help. He had no memory of the shaft. No memory of his arms being broken. One moment he was sleeping, the next he was broken and days had gone by.

But there were nights, especially while on patrol in Vietnam, when he remembered several things that had to be invention rather than actual memories. The first was an eye, singular and not really human, always gazing upon him. The weight of the looks keeping him cowed and afraid to move. The other was the smell, like something from a zoo—a paddock from some great unwashed beast who lived and slept and shit in the same few feet.

He'd smelled that stench once outside of a zoo and that had been in a hillside near Saigon. The NVA had a tunnel system they'd had in place for years. Instead of going into it, ARVN had flooded it with gas, flushing out several North Vietnamese who exited coughing, snot erupting from their faces, sweat and blisters across their skin. They'd waited three days to go inside and he'd been with the first team. By then the riot gas had dissipated, but the scent of occupation had remained, the walls and the odds-and-end furniture inside the maze like a second skin for those who so recently had occupied the place.

Rather a place of animals than one where humans had existed.

The sound of a plane drew his attention and he turned to watch it. Unaware of an airport in the neat slot the town made between the mountains, he understood how the craft would land once he noted the pontoons. He paused to watch it fly over the water, then make a laconic turn, slow enough that it seemed as if it might stall and fall from the sky, then straighten and come in for landing, skipping several times across the top of the water until eventually settling its weight and allowing the friction to stop it, the propeller barely moving.

He turned back to the church—Capilla Ntra Sra de Lourdes or Our Lady of Lourdes Chapel. He wasn't an expert in Catholicism, but anyone who spent any time in Buenos Aires couldn't help but earn a PhD in church knowledge. Named after the original chapel in Lourdes, France where an apparition of the Virgin

Mary was seen on three occasions by a shy fourteen-year-old girl, this chapel was also a place of pilgrimage. Many came seeking the healing waters of the lake, just as they went to Lourdes to seek the healing waters of the spring dug by the witness to Mary's appearance.

There'd been a time when he'd have scoffed at such an idea—the appearance of the mother of Christ and the presence of water that could heal. But that was before he experienced the lilin . . . before he'd become invisible.

He shuddered and hugged his arms to his body.

A week ago, he'd been making a living doing this and that. Living was easy in Buenos Aires if one knew the tricks. But then came Lettie and everything had changed. An image of her talking animatedly to someone on the bus as it pulled away pulsed through his mind.

He held out a hand, all six fingers, the last one, what he called his double pinky, small, extraneous and apparently the reason for all of the interest. What was it about six fingers that made people so excited? He remembered the girls all dressed in white at the crazy party he'd attended, each one eager to do what? Become what? Provide what? Their parents seemingly more than willing to serve their child up on a platter and super proud that they'd born a bairn with extra digits.

A young man in a black frock came running towards him.

"Mr. Stevens. Father La Paz would like to see you," said the man who was barely past boyhood. His head had been shaved and he had the look of a penitent. A true believer.

Amboy nodded. "Let him know I am on my way."

The man ran back the way he'd come and Amboy returned his attention to the scenery. He'd been walking the Chapel's lawn, not really wanting to stray too far away from it without someone with him or a weapon of some sort. Which brought him to the greater problem. His pistol had little effect on the lilin. Holy water might be the answer, but what was he to do, carry with him a bucket?

An image of the old black-clad abuela came to him shouting in her ancient voice, *"Demonio se fue!"*

"Demonio se fue!"

She'd been able to banish the demon, but she'd died in the aftermath. Was that his destiny? Was he to save Lettie and die doing it? He rubbed at his arms again. The idea didn't really bother him. She had a certain sadness about her he'd love to find a way to dismiss. He didn't want to die, but he'd die for a cause, if he had to.

What was it his friend Otiel had said that one day in the jungles of Vietnam? *"Sure, I'd die for you. Why not? Life has to have a meaning, no?"*

What meaning did life have then?

Was he supposed to sacrifice himself for someone else's greater good?

How was he supposed to know? And who decided who it was who would be the ones being saved and who the ones were who saved? Part of him—that petulant child he'd once been on the mountain—wanted nothing more than to grab his passport, board a plane and return to Tennessee where the problems of the world were in microcosm. But he knew better than that. Just a single flash of Lettie's smile buckled all of his determination to ignore everything and redoubled his desire to help.

Was it love?

He wasn't really sure what that was, but just thinking about her made him feel a little sickness in the center of his stomach, an uneasiness that he couldn't just ignore. It was unimaginable that he'd allow some Germans or the Wallace Thompsons of the world grab her for some crazy ceremony meant to make themselves into a super race.

And the abuela.

He couldn't allow her death to be for nothing. The whole *lilin* creature pissed him off. It shouldn't exist. It shouldn't be doing to Lettie anything and when he found it, he'd find a way to destroy it once and for all.

CHAPTER 26

As it turned out the sea plane was for them. The trip to the Cave of Hands was normally ten hours nonstop, but there was never such a thing in Argentina as nonstop. But by sea plane it was a different story. The geography was too mountainous and filled with forests for many planes, but there was never going to be a shortage of lakes along the Andes wall, which meant each one was its own organic airport.

The plane was an Ansett Brothers Sandringham and was first made in 1943. Inside were six individual leather captain's seats and two leather sofas. Paz mentioned that it had once been used for mail delivery but was now privately owned. With not much to carry, they boarded and were soon headed south. The plane had no stewards or attendants, so they helped themselves to the sandwiches and cold beer provided. Once the plane hit sixteen thousand feet, the pilot announced that he was putting the plane on auto and came back to join Paz and Amboy.

The pilot wore jeans and a collared shirt with mother of pearl buttons. He had white leather cowboy boots on his feet and a slicked back head of blonde hair. He seemed to be about thirty and was clearly American. He grabbed a sandwich and sat down roughly on one of the sofas.

"Tough times in the country, ain't it?"

Amboy glanced toward the pilot's cabin. "Are we safe?"

"This old bird's been around as long as I've been alive," he said. "Hasn't had a hitch in her gittyup yet."

"If that's supposed to make me feel better, you might want to work on your delivery," Amboy said.

The pilot laughed and held out a hand, then seeing crumbs on it, wiped it on his pants, then offered it again. "Name is Tod Clark. Friends call me Todo. And don't worry about any of this. I logged over a thousand combat hours in Vietnam and now just move people back and forth."

Amboy admired the teak wood interior of the plane and all the added touches. Whoever owned the plane sure had money to burn. He wouldn't be surprised if the bathroom had fixtures made of gold.

"Any word on the weather?" Paz asked. He'd found a bottle of wine and had already poured himself a large glass.

"Nothing to speak of. We'll be at our destination in a little over two hours, so whatever's going to sweep off the mountains will miss us."

"Where do you come from?" Amboy asked.

Todo stood and rolled his shoulders back and forth. "Buenos Aires is where she normally parks. Me, I'm from El Paso. Grew up on the border and no one around here seems to understand my version of Spanish." He tossed out a sentence as an example and Amboy found it hard to cut through the gutter words and the pidgin terms.

"What's a guy from El Paso doing flying around a priest and a nobody?" Amboy asked.

Todo glanced at Paz, but Paz didn't give him any indication

he noticed. Finally, the pilot shrugged. "I go where I'm told and do what I'm told."

"Is that your motto?" Amboy asked, not happy with the answer. "Go where you are told?"

Todo seemed to consider the question, then frowned. He grabbed a cold beer and opened it and rested his elbows on his knees as he leaned forward. "If I had my druthers, I'd be working with the Argentine Air Force. Fellas down in Rio Gallegos are badly outnumbered and outclassed."

"What would you do? Turn this into a gunship?"

Todo laughed. "Hell no. This has the aerobatics of a drunken hippo. I flew the A4 and A6 in 'Nam and was one of the few to never be shot down. If they'd let me, I'd be in a Skyhawk and showing the Tories that they can't still be in charge of the world."

Amboy narrowed his eyes. He hadn't heard that term used ever in real life, just in old books.

Seeing the look on Amboy's face, the pilot said, "Not to worry. I know General Haig has his marching orders, it's just that the people of Argentina counted on us. They depended on America to bail them out and to keep La Thatcher at arm's length. But in the end, we folded, and isn't that our way?"

"We've been allies with England for centuries now."

"Have you looked out the window?" Todo asked, nodding towards a porthole. "You're not in England any more. You are in Argentina. It's Europe in South America and much different than all the other Third World shitholes."

"In the universe of haves and have nots, being a shithole is hardly the fault of the country," Amboy said.

"Oh no?" Todo laughed. "Tell that to the workers and the farmers who make no money because it all goes to the government. The leaders countries choose too often become the poster child for how fucked up a country is."

"You're talking about communism," Amboy said, the roots of the conversation beginning to dawn on him. "Giving the people the power."

"How is it, though, that when the people finally get the power they decide that their first act of independence is to destroy those who have been in power before them?"

Amboy took a draw at his beer and decided he didn't want any more. He sat it down. "Maybe the people of these countries are like wolf packs. There can only be one alpha. If another comes along, then they have to challenge or get rid of the other."

"So, you're saying that people are like wolves," Todo said.

"And you're not?"

Todo laughed again. "My boss said you were an original." He shook his head. "I have to say, it was grand meeting you." And then he headed back to the cockpit.

Amboy wondered for a moment who his boss might have been and then it came to him. Wallace Thompson, US Senator from Waco, Texas. He turned to Paz, who was sipping his ever-present glass of wine and staring out the window.

"Why are we on a plane owned by Senator Thompson?" he asked.

Paz turned to him, then sighed heavily. "We needed to move fast. It's not as if the archdiocese has a fleet of planes. Even if they did, helping me is at the end of their itinerary."

"But Wallace Thompson. Do you know how involved he is with the Red Unicorn and the six-fingered girls?"

Paz blinked several times, the worry lines gaining shadow, he wrinkles growing deeper. Then he shook his head and spread his free hand. "What would you have me do? Vet everyone to see who they are before I accept their assistance?"

"Vet everyone?" Amboy narrowed his eyes as he fought back a spike of anger. What kind of rube did Paz take him for?

"How would you even know to call on Wallace? How is he even on your radar?"

"A lot of American and Europeans are involved with Argentinian politics. Like Todo inexpertly said, we are a new Europe but without the baggage of thousands of years of king and queen trading. We've been primarily a stable country and have experienced unimaginable growth since World War II."

Amboy flashed to Oteil and his SS parentage.

"How much of that success comes from Nazis?"

Paz shoved back the remnants of his glass, swallowed, then set the glass down. He leaned forward and tried to put a hand on Amboy's knee, but the other shifted in his seat so he couldn't do it. "Don't be so harsh. We don't deal with Nazis. We are the oldest church in the world. We have our own problems, but we try and do what's best."

"Something is going on here I'm not sure about. But let me share something with you, Father. Here's something I learned in Vietnam. America went there to support the South Vietnamese because they were what we knew—more like us. But was that a good thing? How many of the Vietnamese elite learned from the French to embrace the idea of bourgeois—a solid upwardly mobile middle class—and to disassociate with those who worked the land? Just like the French, when we go there, we imported elitism. We were told we were at war with the North Vietnamese, but were we really?"

"They murdered priests and nuns, my son."

"Which is terrible, but weren't they the pawns of the elite on the bourgeois chessboard? They were the front line soldiers who tried to get the poor to understand that their place was necessary and that they might have a better place in another life if only they'd peacefully embrace this one?"

"That's a little simplistic," Paz said.

"Is it? Is it too simplistic? It seems pretty on point to me."

"I never saw you as a communist sympathizer," Paz said, his voice gravel and on the road to anger.

"I sympathize with anyone who is put down. I feel bad for anyone who had a thumb on their head."

Paz sighed. "It's true that the Germans have had an influence on Argentina, just as the Russians had when they fled the murders of the Romanoffs. They have opened their arms to those who feel they need a place to flee."

"To include the Nazis."

Paz shook his head. "I'm not in a position to speak for Argentina. All I can say is that this has always been a place of new beginnings. Don't you believe in second chances, Amboy Stevens?"

"Of course, I do but—"

"Then how can you suffer the idea that there are those who shouldn't receive a second chance. After all, the Catholic Church is built around the idea of second chances. Confess and you shall be cleansed. Humans are far from being those perfect beings we try and make ourselves out to be."

"That's an age-old question. Do rapists get a reprieve? Do pedophiles get a second chance? A book came out in 1978 called *Atrocity at Auschwitz*. Did you hear of it? It was an inside tale of what happened in one of the Nazis' concentration camps. What the book described was horrible. As well as the ovens where people were sent to perish, there were the living standards which made it clear that the Nazis did not believe that the Jews and other peoples inside the camp were human. And these are the ones you feel can be redeemed?"

"Amboy, my son . . ."

"I'm not your son."

Paz paused, then restated, "Amboy, my son, I can feel your anger. A lot of it has to deal with the idea that we don't know where Lettie is right now. You are scared and worried and angry. I get that. Know that I have no love for any Nazi. But we have to have space in our hearts for people to repent. You see, we have the idea of original sin. Babies are born with it. Therefore to make it into heaven they need to be redeemed."

"How can a child have sin?"

"It's complicated."

"Isn't it always? It sounds like a money-making scheme to me."

Paz sighed. "Original sin derives from the actions of Adam and Eve. Every child of them is born with the sin they created and thus needs to be redeemed. There are those from Russia and Germany and even America who are from oppressive regimes and horrible families who are guilty by affiliation. Are they to be condemned as well?"

"Maybe their sin was that they didn't stop the terrible things from happening?" Amboy said.

"Then they have sin and guilt. I'd think such a people might have need of the Catholic Church."

"Talking to you is like having a conversation with a record player. You keep saying the same things."

"Perhaps that's because the existence of sin and of redemption is a common theme among us humans."

Amboy jerked his attention to the priest. Not because of what he said, but because of what he implied. "Among us humans?" he said. "You say it as if there are other points of view."

Todo's voice came over the intercom. "Strap in, folks. We have some rough air ahead."

Just as Amboy managed to snap a strap into place he felt the plane shudder. He gripped the handrails hard enough to turn his knuckles white. He felt the plane pitch and turn, the force slamming him into the side of his seat. The bottles they'd been drinking flew off the table and smashed against the bulkhead.

He closed his eyes and tried to settle himself, but his mind went to combat, back when he was in a Bell 212 and taking fire above a Vietnamese jungle, the chopper juking and junking like a Shriner driving a tiny car home after a night of partying. He slammed shut his eyes and allowed his mind to wander through memories of ARVN torture, *lilins*, and six-fingered girls who seemed destined for an uncertain fate.

CHAPTER 27

The moment they hit the water and taxied to a ramp, two frocked priests stood, visibly vibrating with the excitement that Paz seemed to be bringing to them. Once the plane pulled to a stop and the door was opened, they entered and began telling Paz that they'd located Lettie. Evidently, she hadn't gotten far. The workers in the Cave of Hands had seen her walking around and having an animated conversation with herself. At first, they'd wondered if she might be crazy, but then when they saw her hands they called the local diocese. Out here on the edge of the world it seemed as if they were more eager to believe in possession than any possible chemical imbalance in the brain. Regardless, they had no healthcare workers, so it was him or nobody.

"Do we have his contact information?" Amboy asked.

They'd landed in an immense pristine blue glacier lake, split right down the middle by the spine of South American and the countries of Chili and Argentina. On the Argentina side the lake was known as Lake Buenos Aires. On the Chilean side it was known as General Carrera Lake. That side of the lake was their destination—a huge rock rising out of the water with a warren of marble caves beneath. Known far and wide as an incredibly picturesque tourist destination, what wasn't known was there had long ago been a hermitage atop the rock that couldn't be seen from below. According to Father Paz, the diocese had boarded up the Virgin del Buen Viaje ten years ago. But according to the two young priests, even boarded and no longer part of the official church, the old priest who'd been working The Rock, as it came to be known, refused to leave his assignment.

Amboy could almost see this rock when pointed out to him, a black speck on the horizon. But they weren't going to get there that evening. Not only were there no boats available, but ominous clouds had already formed and had begun tumbling down the side of the Andes. A storm was about to hit and no one wanted to volunteer for the trip.

They bundled up and headed south in a van provided by the diocese. Paz, Amboy, and Father Godoy rode in back while Father Rivas drove. They'd been driving about thirty minutes when Amboy looked out the window and noted how afar they were getting away from the lake—away from Lettie.

"Where are we going?"

"Cuevas de los Manos," said Godoy. He had red hair and was clearly of mixed German-Spanish ancestry. Folly for him that it wasn't the best mixture. His nose was almost the size of his jaw.

"Do you really think it's time to play tourist, Paz?" Amboy asked.

"We have the time and I want you to see first-hand what the cave is about."

Amboy didn't want to get any farther away from Lettie than he already was. He felt that each yard away would be a mile of effort returning. But he wasn't in charge of the moment and he doubted that the young Father Rivas would listen to him over someone from the Archdiocese of Argentina.

"It's a cave. It has handprints on the walls," Amboy said in frustration. He stared out the side window of the van as the first thick drops of rain began to hammer down.

Two hours later, he stood inside the cave, lights highlighting thousands of hands, many of which had six fingers. It might have been just a cave, but he was suitably awestruck by what he was seeing. The cave was a UNESCO World Heritage site with handprints dating back as far as 13,000 years.

He tried to imagine being a hunter-gatherer back then and joining a celebration or a ceremony to place his hand on the wall. The print of it there meant he existed. Not just as a person as part of a tribe, but now as part of the planet. Before industry, before technology, man was much closer to the earth. Each plant and leaf, catalogued and known by its taste and characteristics

Likewise, man also knew the animals he encountered and kept records of them much in the same manner he recorded the handprints. Here and there were depictions of guanacos—a member of the camel family, but smaller and found in abundance on the grassy hills. But there were also other creatures—creatures with single horns that many believe to be unicorns. And all of them, no matter where they were on the walls, they were colored in red.

Why make unicorns red? Was the color of significance? One would think that they would be of various colors, much like the imprints of the hands, but those who had chosen to recreate the image of the unicorn 13,000 years ago chose a color who's only known bodily comparison came from the blood within them.

As he stared at a hunting scene showing stick-figured men with spears chasing after a unicorn, he couldn't help but think of Lettie. She was a red unicorn of a sort. Red hair, red marks on her face, she was as rare a beast as anything in mythology with a single horn. She was also hunted. They wanted her. A mysterious they, somehow connected with a shadowy group of Germans, wanted her for some diabolical purpose—so diabolical that they'd sent a version of a stick demon after her.

Suddenly, the stick men on the wall before him began to move. He could hear their cries, both savage and victorious. The whisk of legs through the tall grass and the pounding of feet became his own. He looked down and his feet were covered with leather, straps wrapping around his legs. A joy filled the hollow of his chest. Looking left and right he saw different versions of himself, all eager and up for the wild chase. He felt the surge of adrenaline and the need to be first. His hands began to throb as he tightened his grip on his spear.

He called out.

He yawped!

The world was his own.

Then the unicorn turned. No longer merely the size of a guanaco, it was now a horse, then larger, then larger still, until it achieved monstrous proportions. Its skin was more a hide than skin, lacking in the smooth hairs of a horse. Its feet were cloven with spikes protruding from the heel of each. A black mane ran from the center of its head down the entire body until it became the tail, waterfalling off the back in whispers of darkness.

The first of him reached the unicorn, but before it could spear the dread beast, the mouth came down on his head, ripping it away and chewing. This was not a sparkly plush unicorn meant for little girls. This was the real thing, a beast with a horn and teeth who had been chased almost to extinction until it became mythological. Yet another of him launched himself into the air, the spear in two hands ready to come down between the creature's eyes. He was met by the horn, piercing his chest and skewering him as if he were a piece of meat ready for a fire.

A hundred versions of him surrounded the unicorn. They

all looked like Amboy but with slight variations. Shape of the eye here. Curl of the ear there. Frown of the mouth. But what they all had in common were his narrowed eyes, the head of blonde hair, and the pair of six-fingered hands.

One after the other they approached the unicorn and one after the other they were defeated.

Then it was his turn. He ran at the beast, shrieking from his very soul, the sound wound from his ankles and propelling upwards through his entire body until his words became weapon and even the unicorn was taken aback.

It tossed him away with its horn.

Then squatted pressing its front down, eyes closed.

Submission.

Amboy felt himself slowing.

He let the spear slip through his fingers.

His arms began to burn and twist and he found himself walking backwards towards the unicorn, yet his vision was still perfect and uninhibited. He was just about to lay his hands on the unicorn when he was jerked back.

Anger fused through him.

How dare they even touch him in this moment of—

He stood before the wall. He'd ripped off his clothes. His hands were bloody and scraped from where he'd been banging against the rock wall. His cock was hard. His breath came fast. His chest heaved. His eyes bulged. His skin was covered in a sheen of sweat.

He turned and saw Father's Godoy and Rivas staring at him, horror on their faces.

The other tourists had fled, leaving him alone with the priests.

Paz came to him with a robe and placed it gently around his shoulders.

Even so, it felt electrified and Amboy wanted to twist it away. But then the feeling subsided. The heat of the hunt evaporated. He felt the chill of the cave and grasped the edges of the collar and pulled them around him. He noticed his clothes on the ground, ripped to shreds. How had he the strength for such a thing? To be able to rip through cloth so easily?

"Wha—What happened?"

Paz stood somberly in front of him. "What happened to you is what happens to everyone who views this who was born with six fingers on each hand. The rest of us have no idea what you experience. This cave, this room, this vision, is not meant for us. It is like a message across the millennia to those of you who still exist."

"Still exist? Were there more of us?"

"Too many. God created the Great Flood to get rid of your kind."

"Does he hate us that much?"

"God never hates, but he was afraid of what you might do."

"Doesn't he . . . Didn't he have the power to change things?"

"God creates then allows his servants to live as they desire. Rarely does he intervene."

"So, God is a him?" Amboy asked.

Paz shook his head. "Just a pronoun of convenience."

"Why is it that God would target us?"

"Because you were here before him. Your kind, the six-fingered kind were the originals. How well do you know your Bible?"

"Enough to get me in trouble."

Paz laughed softly. "Like most people then. Genesis 6:4 *The Nephilim were on the earth in those days, and also afterward, when the sons of God came in to the daughters of men, and they bore children to them. Those were the mighty men who were of old, men of renown*. In the King James version, popularized by the protestant reformation, the Nephilim are named giants."

"Are you saying I'm Nephilim?" Amboy asked.

"That's an unevaluated term. We really don't know what it means. Breaking down the passage is that there were beings on Earth before God created man. Were these beings created as a result of the creation of the world or were they here before is up for debate. But then man came. And they had children with those who came before and their offspring were men of renown."

"Men of renown. Like knights or something?"

"Or something. There's a belief that David and many other heroes of the bible were offspring of the original people and those made by God."

"Wait a moment," Amboy said, hitching the robe over his shoulders better. "Then what am I?"

Paz grinned and placed a hand on Amboy's shoulder. "You are a man of renown. You can trace your lineage beyond the first man. You were of the original cast. Your fingers tell us that."

Amboy held his hand up in the wan light of the cave and examined them. Bloody and scraped, there was still no denying that they had six fingers on each of them. He'd always thought of himself as a freak when outside the mountain. But to listen to Paz, he was from a special breed of person. Was that why the images had so affected him? Had the same thing happened to Lettie?

He was eager to answer those questions and ready to get to the bottom of things, except it seemed as if the universe had its own ideas.

"Mr. Stevens. Please drop the robe and come with us," said a voice from behind him with a distinct German accent.

CHAPTER 28

Amboy turned and noted two men standing between him and the priests. Both were dressed in the white linen suits and hats popular in Buenos Aires. For some reason he noticed that their shoes had been recently shined. As absurd as they were, they seemed perfectly in sync with what the men were wearing. He wondered at the mindset—they were about to go capture someone at gunpoint so they needed to shine their shoes first.

Paz was the first to react. He slid Amboy's .45 caliber pistol out of his deep pocket and held it to his side.

Amboy noted the move, but didn't make any indication that he'd seen it. He'd been in tighter situations. The idea was to speak softly and not make too many moves. By the way the pair's eyes twitched, they were new at this and seemed super nervous.

"I'd rather not drop the robe if that's okay with you."

"We're not messing around," the one on the right said.

"What do you want?" Amboy asked.

"You. We need to speak with you," said the one on the right, who seemed to be in charge. He glanced at Paz. "We need to do it alone."

Amboy regarded the pair, then looked over their shoulders at Paz whose eyes were steady and unblinking. Amboy bit his lower lip. "I don't think so."

"You don't understand. I have a weapon," said the left hand man.

Amboy laughed. "If you think you are the first person to ever point a weapon at me, then you couldn't be more wrong."

"Come with us," said the other one.

"I don't think so."

"You don't understand."

"Oh, but I do."

They glanced at each other as if they couldn't understand his responses. Just as they were about to open their mouths to repeat the order, he held out a hand to stop them. Their mouths shut.

"You keep saying that," he said, "and I keep saying fuck you."

The pair shuffled nervously.

"Now what? Are you going to shoot me?" Amboy asked, taking a step forward.

They took a step back and the one on the left stepped right into the raised barrel of Paz's pistol. He stopped cold, then shivered as he glanced back at the length of metal pressing hard into his back. The he saw the look in the priest's eyes and he lowered his weapon by forty-five degrees.

"Perhaps both of you should put down your weapons," Paz said.

The one on the right had a pained look on his face as if all of his careful plans had just been dashed. "You don't understand, Mr. Stevens. We are here to help you. Do you remember Vietnam? Do you remember our uncle, Otiel—Otiel Stanislas?"

"Oty! I remember him. But how do you know him?"

"He's the one who sent us. Things are not as they seem, Mr. Stevens. You are in grave danger."

"The only danger comes from you," Paz said. "Godoy, check outside and see if there are any more."

Godoy didn't move, instead he shot a worried look at the two young Germans.

"I said, go and check outside, Father Godoy," Paz said, fire heating his words.

Godoy sighed, then pulled a small Mauser from the pocket of his clergy pants. "I'm not going outside. Please drop your weapon, Father."

Paz gave Godoy a disgusted look. "You too? Are all of you traitors?"

"I'm not a traitor," Rivas said, his fingers to his chest, his eyes raking across all of them as if searching for a safe place to be.

"Then take the gun away from your partner," Paz ordered.

Godoy now pointed his pistol at Rivas.

Rivas' eyes popped wide. "How am I supposed to do that, sir?"

"Good enough, I suppose." Father Paz brought the pistol around and shot Godoy in the chest.

The sound rocked the cave, stunning everyone for a moment. Pieces of dust and debris fell from the ceiling. Amboy's ears rang.

The docent ran out of his office and down the corridor waving his hands.

"No shots. Not here. Please, take it outside."

"Father Rivas, get the pistol," Paz said calmly, now training the .45 on the two Germans.

Rivas glanced at the body of his friend but didn't move, his face a mask of fear.

"Rivas! I said get the pistol."

The slim Argentinian priest jumped forward, leaned down, grabbed the pistol by the barrel and then backed away.

"And you," Paz said to the docent. "Go back inside. This is church business. Let me handle this."

The docent's mouth had been hanging open and he snapped it shut, swallowing hard. He nodded once, then twice, then backed away, his gaze dragging across the body of the dead priest.

"What do you mean Oty sent you?" Amboy pressed.

The more he looked at the pair of Germans, the more they seemed nothing more than a couple of scared kids. Their suits were too large. Their hats fell too low over their brows. They claimed to be Otiel's nephews. Amboy had lost track of his friend shortly after they'd arrived in Argentina. Once he'd been hooked up with a mining job, Oty had gone his own way. Amboy figured they'd meet somewhere down the road, but the more time had passed, the more uncertain that future had become.

And now he was sending two men to supposedly warn him of a danger to his life?

How did that even make sense?

"How do I know you're Oty's nephews?" Amboy asked.

"We don't have time for this," Paz said, glancing disgustedly at Godoy, then back at the entrance to the cave.

Amboy held out his hand. "Give me a moment. If this is true, I want to get to the bottom of it."

"This is a ruse and nothing more," Paz said.

Amboy eyed Paz, but didn't respond. Instead, he strode over to Rivas and plucked the pistol from his hand. He let the robe fall until it was around his waist and cinched it there with his left hand, while holding the pistol in his right. He turned so his back was to the wall and everyone was to his front. Not that he was worried about Paz. The old drunken priest had already proven his loyalty and friendship. But he didn't understand why he'd so quickly pulled the trigger on Godoy. That was totally out of character, or at least the character to which he was aware.

"You. Nephew," he said pointing with the pistol. "What is your name?"

"Uwe. This is Gunter."

"Uwe. If what you say is true, your uncle would have said something to you only he would know. Isn't that right?"

The young man nodded.

"Then give." Seeing the confusion over the word he added, "Tell me what he said."

"He said to say this. Remember the night you and Marvin went into the tunnels right before the fall of Saigon. Do you remember what you found?"

"Who's Marvin?" Paz asked.

"He means ARVN," Amboy said, pronouncing the letters like a word. "The Army of the Republic of Vietnam. Yeah. I remember." The irony was that he'd recently remembered the events in the tunnel, especially the smell.

"What did you do to Marvin and what nickname did you give him?" Uwe asked.

Amboy remembered the moment well. Unbeknownst to the rest of them, the NVA had captured several Saigon street girls. After they'd been interrogated and tortured for their information about the comings and goings of GIs, they'd become objects of sexual perversity. An entire room had been found with cages upon cages of these women, living a special horror that should have been reserved for the dead. But for all intents and purposes, these women were dead. No one knew of their existence and no one expected them to return. Their lives were at the whim of their persecutors.

All but one had perished. Several looked as if they'd died days before, while a few others looked as if they'd died due to asphyxiation because of the gas. Unable to move and find clean air to breathe, they'd gagged and suffocated, their bulging eyes and clawed hands evidence of their horrible demise.

The single survivor was anywhere from twenty to forty, her body smeared with dirt and filth. The only part of her that was clean was the space between her legs, rubbed raw and red from overuse, but cleaned continually with a rag from a bucket of filthy water. Amboy had been the second into the tunnels and had stumbled upon the room just as their compadre was pulling down his pants. Marvin, as they'd called him, had been their friend. They'd spent hours drinking and eating and talking and bonding.

They all hated the North Vietnamese.

The NVA was evil.

They were not to be trusted.

But on this day ARVN was evil.

Amboy could still remember the look on Marvin's face when he'd entered the room. His friend had turned, paused as he'd unfurled his already hard member, and grinned, a wink and a promise that his turn would be next.

Amboy remembered feeling sick to his soul.

What he'd done had been reflex.

Five steps and he'd stuck the K-bar through the man's neck.

ARVN the Martian they'd come to calling him, because whatever he'd been doing, it couldn't have been human. The girl had lain sobbing as Amboy's dead friend fell atop her, pulsing blood, drenching her in the hot mess of yet another attacker, another abuser.

The image remained for several long seconds and then melted away.

Amboy sighed and wiped the hand holding the pistol over his face as if to wipe away the memory. "Yeah. I remember. Who was it, then?"

"Marvin the Martian, whatever that means," the young man said. "And you stuck him like a pig." He nodded. "Stuck him like a pig, yep. That's what my uncle said to tell you."

Amboy nodded. "That's about right."

"What is it exactly that your uncle wants?"

"He said to tell you two things."

"I've really had enough of this," Paz said, bringing his pistol in their direction without really aiming it at them. "We need to leave before the authorities arrive or we might miss getting to speak with Lettie."

Amboy felt like he was being pushed and he hated being pushed. "Paz, since when did you become Wyatt Earp?" he asked, not expecting an answer. "Let the boys talk." He turned back to the young man. "Uwe. Speak to me. What is it Oty wanted to tell me?"

"He said to tell you first that he was sorry."

"Sorry for what?"

"He didn't say, only that he was sorry. I get the impression that he let you down on something big," Uwe said.

"I have no idea what that might be," Amboy said. "Your uncle had always been straight with me. He saved my life on more than one occasion and me his. We were great friends who just drifted apart."

The sound of sirens in the distance caused everyone to glance towards the exit.

"We have got to go," Paz said.

"My uncle also said he would make you safe," Uwe said, sparing a look at Paz.

Amboy either didn't notice nor did he care. He shook his head and said, "Tell your uncle that I'll catch up with him later. I have business to attend to. Something only I can do."

"But he said—"

Paz cut him off. "The man has spoken. Now leave him alone, please."

The two German young men seemed ready to argue, but instead they stepped aside.

Paz urged Rivas to help him with Godoy. Together, they carried him under his shoulders, his heels sliding across the ground.

Amboy searched and grabbed all of the clothes he'd ripped away. Most of them were unsalvageable, but he didn't want to leave them behind. Soon, he was running out the exit of the cave and into a downpour like the one that God had probably started to get rid of his kind if one were to believe Paz.

And that was a question, wasn't it?

How much of what the old man said could be believed?

And why had he been so eager to kill Godoy?

CHAPTER 29

The drive back to the lake was in total silence. Amboy felt the presence of Godoy's body in the back as if it were his own. The weight of it bothered him, not because of the intricacies of the politics, but why Paz had been so quick to pull the trigger. The action seemed so unlikely and an excuse like he was having a bad day wasn't about to fly in the face of redemptive murder.

Godoy had been a father of the church, which meant he was as much a priest as any of them. He'd given sacrament. He'd heard confession. It was more than plausible that he woke up in the morning and imagined himself as one of God's chosen and a good person. So, then why had he turned so quickly on Father Paz?

Like when he'd been a child in the mountains and had gone missing for those months only to return with broken arms, Amboy had a deep belief that things were occurring just below the surface of reality that he didn't ken. Like when you observed a river, you knew beneath it were rocks, substrate, plants, fish, and various water life. But until you immersed yourself into that reality, you really didn't know. You were destined to be an observer and, in that capacity, you would forever be behind in your judgement of what was going on.

And the entire scene with Otiel's nephew and friend was transcendental. Where had they come from and how did his old friend from Vietnam even know what was going on? He wished he could reach out to him. Above everyone in the country, Oteil was the single person he would trust the most. They'd been through too much together. They'd seen the worst of humanity and the best of humanity.

Not for the first time he realized that he didn't have a best friend. That person he could confide his darkest secrets to and who would understand him and accept him regardless of the nature of those secrets. Best friends were a luxury. When you were a kid, you felt that you had a lot of best friends, but with time and distance and maturity, you realize that you never really had one, or if you did, it was only one of the many. A best friend was someone who you could confide in and never worry about the results. He knew many folks who called others best friends, but they really were just the best good friend and not the best friend.

Then it hit him.

If anyone was his best friend it would be Lettie. That strange African-American red-haired girl with a map of Florida on her face had become that which he'd most desired. Someone to count on. So, where was he now when she was hurting? He was sitting in a van during a downpour thinking upon the nature of best friends. They had so much in common and it wasn't just the number of their fingers.

He realized that he wanted to talk to her now. He wanted to ask her what she thought of what Paz had done. He needed her to bounce off his own ideas and to catch his truths. He could almost see her sideways grin and the way she'd snark about everything, then turn awful serious when she learned of Paz's murder. The man had saved her life, just as he'd saved Amboy's.

Still, he couldn't just accept the murder.

He noted the rain had stopped as they pulled back into the village. Lights caused each puddle to glow white in the night and reflected off the surface of the lake. Somewhere out there was Lettie. He'd see her in the morning. He'd save her in the morning.

They exited the van back at the church and carries Godoy's body to the cellar.

Amboy found a bathroom and cleaned himself, wiping vigorously at his hands and neck and face, lest any blood remain.

Paz went to the room that had been supplied for him and changed into clean clothes—but still the same parish pants, shirt, jacket and priest's collar. He went to a sideboard and pulled out a bottle of wine and poured two glasses. He brought one over to where Amboy was sitting and offered it.

He took the glass, drank half, then set it on a side table.

Paz took a seat on the other side.

"You never told me you had connections with the Ahnenerbe," Paz said.

"You never told me you were a murderer."

"Was that what you called it in Vietnam when you shot someone? Murder?"

"But that was war."

"Have no doubt, Amboy Stevens. This is as much a war as Vietnam ever was."

Amboy sipped at his wine. "I don't know anyone from Ahnenerbe."

"You know Oteil Stanislas."

"Of course, I do. We went to 'Nam together."

"Oteil Stanislas is third in command of the Ahnenerbe in

South America. We've had him on our books since he turned eighteen."

Amboy did the math in his head and then shook it. "That can't be. He was twenty-six when he was in the war with me. Then twenty-nine when he left. He didn't have any connection to the Nazis. Trust me. I would have known."

Paz stared solemnly over the top of his glass at Amboy. "Forget the Nazis being tools of Hitler. He, himself, was a tool. Modern Nazis are completely different. They believe in the purity of the German race and the need to gather about them proof of the purity. The Ahnenerbe are one of their groups who go about discovering pieces of God in all forms to be able to demonstrate that purity."

"But the Jews and the camps. I heard stories in 'Nam from some old sergeants who were in World War II. They told me of the atrocities."

"Aryan race theory. Hitler used it to his advantage. It sold well and made the Germans experiencing a heretofore unknown influx of refugees from the Ottoman Empire feel better about themselves. It also allowed for an easy and systematic redistribution of wealth. The Jews had been a target in Europe for centuries and now it was legal to take their homes and fortunes and ship them away."

"How is it different now?" Amboy asked.

"Those who had been subsumed by the Ottomans suddenly found themselves free, but without land. They fled to Europe, many creating a diaspora in Germany. Now, fifty years later, Nazis are now the diaspora. They are spread out across South America and seek a return of a modicum of power. To obtain that, they need powerful artifacts. They've been in search of the Red Unicorn since they arrived and have come close on several occasions."

"Is that why they tracked me and Lettie?" He snapped his fingers. "It had to be. They saw our hands and knew we'd eventually be contacted. Schultz had been watching me all that time."

"That's their solid goal. They want the unicorn."

"You say it as if there's only one," Amboy noted.

Father Paz poured himself another glass of wine, then downed half it in three slow steady sips. "Is that really the question you want to ask?"

And they were back to the eight-hundred-pound gorilla in the room. He might as well ask the question. At this point, unless he approved of the other's motivation, Paz wasn't going to be around to accompany them anymore.

He leaned forward in his chair, elbows on his knees, cradling his wine. "Why?" he asked simply.

Paz leaned back and stared at the ceiling. "As you might have seen, I am not merely an out of work parish priest. I work directly for the Vatican. We have interests in Patagonia we do not want disturbed."

"Then your claim that your mother was disappeared was a lie?"

"No. That's true. She was a member of the *Asociación Madres de Plaza de Mayo*. She was killed and I've been trying to discover who by ever since." He glanced furtively towards Amboy. "You might say that is my driving principle. If I am ever lucky enough to discover who it was, my life might finally have purpose."

"Most priests believe their lives have purpose. You do what you do, right? Save souls, take confession, give communion, and interpret the Bible."

Paz stared deep into his cup. "I'm not most priests."

"No," Amboy said. "You're not." He poured himself more wine. "Somehow, I don't think you're the sort to let the police do their job."

"Not when the police are corrupt."

"As if the church isn't corrupt."

Paz sighed. "We didn't invent the idea. Everyone is corrupt. Not you, it appears. You seem to be incorruptible. But most everyone else. I am also truly a member of *Movimiento de Sacerdotes para el Tercer Mundo*, but I am more of a detective. I try and ascertain where my fellow priests have gone. The Junta here in Argentina has been one of the worst and good people are always going missing."

"So, you're a Vatican Sam Spade."

"As good a definition as any."

"But that doesn't explain why you just killed Godoy," he said.

"No. It doesn't. And I am probably going to Hell for it despite the number of Hail Marys and Our Fathers I will say after confession. But we knew there had been infiltration into the church by Ahnenerbe. We'd been watching for it."

"But killing him?"

"He drew first and if you remember the situation, they outnumbered us. They were seconds away from taking us down. By taking him out, I made things even."

Amboy relived the moment and tactically, Paz's move had been the right one. But Amboy hadn't been thinking tactically. He'd been wondering about a priest with a gun. Of course, there had been two priests with guns. Paz just had been the smarter of the pair.

CHAPTER 30

Amboy was up before anyone else. He cleaned and dressed and found coffee, then left the church and walked to the lake edge. He paced back and forth, staring at the black dot on the horizon where Lettie had been taken.

Eight days he'd been out.

Eight days he'd been away from her.

God knows what she'd been going through.

They said she might be possessed and if it had anything to do with the lilin, then she must be terrified, perhaps curled up into a ball in the corner of her mind, terrified of what was happening to her body. He wanted to punch. He wanted to fight. But how does one strike something unseen?

Fathers Paz and Rivas arrived ten minutes later with everyone's bags. No one said a word. Amboy followed them to a boat that looked like a 1950s Chris Craft—all wood and glistening chrome. It lay low and sleek in the water and looked as if it could hold a dozen people. Probably a commuter boat designed to carry people from one side of the lake to the other.

A driver was already in the boat, warming the engine. He

had the grizzled appearance of a man born in the wild and carved by the wind, his face etched with years much like the inner trunk of a great old tree. His clothes were clean, but worn in the way an old sail might be. He had few teeth and those he had were brown from tobacco, a cheroot ever-present in his mouth.

Paz laid a hand on the older man's back. They exchanged a glance, then the boatmen removed the bumpers and the ropes securing it to the dock. The driver pushed off with a paddle, stowed it, then slid into his seat behind a large round wheel.

Amboy found a seat in the rear and spread out his arms beside him. He closed his eyes and inhaled, the smell of water, algae and fish and the clean scent in the air that could cut through any city pollution. The aroma reminded him of his home in the mountains. They couldn't travel a mile without crossing a stream or a pond or a lake. Water was everywhere, even in the air, the humidity like wearing a frock of liquid. Newcomers felt it clammy and uncomfortable, but he loved the feeling, the damp sassafras scent of the mountains, ferns growing like hairs on the scalp of the earth.

The boat began to rock as it exited the relative calm of the small pocket harbor and into the main lake. He opened his eyes and watched as The Rock came closer and closer. Soon, it was the center of his horizon, rising several hundred feet above the surface of the water. As they came closer still, he noted the beneath it were caves large enough for smaller boats to sail through. Even closer still, the sunlight splattered the insides and reflected in multiple colors.

"Those are the marble caves," Paz said, settling into the seat beside him. "It is also known as the *Catderal de Marmal*, or the Cathedral of Marble. When it was first seen by Jesuit missionaries, they bowed down and prayed to it for a solid week because nothing in nature could have created such a thing without a divine hand at work. Tourists come from all over the world to view the caves.

"What they don't know is that atop the island and out of view of any curious eyes is a hermitage with a small chapel called Virgen del Buen Viaje. Only a few know of it. Brother Benevides of the Alexians runs the retreat."

"Alexians?"

"An order which has its roots in the black plague. It was founded by laymen who felt the need to help those no one else wanted to help. They were recognized by the church several hundred years later. Their name comes from Alexius Chapel in Rome. There are less than eighty of them in existence and of that number, only three are priests."

"This Brother Benevides is a brother, then. Like a monk?"

"As much so. Yes. He hasn't been consecrated, but then they don't believe they have to be. Alexians, much like Franciscans, believe that announcing to God their fealty and obedience is enough for them without the need for any pomp and circumstance."

"The church has a lot of pomp and circumstance. Catholic mass is quite the dramatic presentation."

"It is. We pride ourselves in tradition."

Amboy grinned and waved his hand. "These are not the droids you are looking for."

Paz turned to him. "What's that?"

Amboy turned back to The Rock in front of him.

The closer they got the more colorful the marble became until it was a swirling mass of rocks blending in every color of a children's art box. The swells grew larger and the boat began to sway. White birds dove from the side of the island, some swooping over the water, some diving deep into it. One entire side seemed to be covered in nests, the shrieks of mother and babies carried and blurred by the wind. Barnacles ate at the rock just beneath the swells. The heady smell of algae was heavier here and he couldn't help but inhale, enjoying the connection to the earth.

It took him back to Vietnam, sitting on the edge of a trail, hiding in buffalo grass and ferns, face pressed into the earth, trying to be one with it as NVA slipped by mere ten feet away on a thin trail. Bugs crawled over his face and hands, but he didn't move, he was one with nature, a bipedal extension of the forest, albeit one with a weapon meant to destroy—anathema to the reality of growth and regrowth.

Rivas came up from the inside of the boat and grabbed a rope.

The driver maneuvered the boat to where a great stone ring had been sunk into the rock. The boat gently bumped and Rivas quickly tied the boat secure using a tautline hitch. Then he grabbed several bumpers and threw them over the side so the wooden boat wouldn't batter itself against the solid marble of the thumb-shaped island.

It was then Amboy noted the metal ladder embedded in the wall.

Rivas was first up.

With a sigh and a slump of shoulders, Paz went next, pulling himself from rung to rung, the pain evident with each pull and step.

Although not invited, Amboy knew what he needed to do. He let Paz get ahead of him a way, then began to pull himself upwards. Rather than feeling tired, he embraced the burn in his shoulders and upper arms. He inhaled deeply, filling his lungs, knowing that at the end of the ascent would be Lettie. Just the thought of her made him move quicker. But he had to pace himself, Paz was in the way, moving at a slow and steady pace. Amboy wanted nothing more than to leapfrog him

Finally, he made the top, pulling himself up the last few meters and plopping on the grass that covered the summit.

Small yellow flowers, like buttercups littered the ground giving the entire surface a yellow sheen. He rolled over and plucked one, sniffing it, cradling it in his hand.

As sure as the almost sheer ascent had been hard for him and almost impossible for Father Paz who was still on his knees trying to catch his breath, he wondered at Brother Benevides and how he'd carried Lettie up the ladder without managing to fall. He leaned over the edge and couldn't even see the boat because of the rise and pitch of the island.

Then he turned and surveyed the center of the top of The Rock which was a slight depression. A single-story building with high ceilings had been built from weathered and greyed wood. Part chapel and part home, the front was graced by a blue door while the side presented to him had a row of three windows high up on the wall. Smoke curled from a chimney in the back. No other manmade items were around the edifice. It was as if God himself had dropped the building into place and then backed away.

"Let's see what's going on," Amboy said to Rivas who was helping Paz to his feet.

They both seemed about to argue, but neither had the breath for it.

He strode past them, taking long steps, his head on a swivel, absorbing the landscape. His feet ate the distance and he was soon at the front door, which had two small wooden steps. The door was wider than a single door, but the gap not wide enough to bear two. On it was an idealized cross from the middle ages which had been drawn upon the wood in white paint. Once bright and shining, it was now flaked and dull.

He tried the latch and found it unlocked.

As it should be? Who would think of a home invasion in such a place?"

He glanced back at the two priests who had stopped and were standing side-by-side watching him.

He didn't understand their reticence. After all, Lettie was on the other side of the door.

He opened the door and stepped inside. It took a moment for his eyes to adjust. Like the outside, everything was made of wood. The pews had been pulled to the sides of the room, clearing a space in the middle. In the back of the room sat an old man, huge in size, probably just shy of seven feet. He perched on a stool, making coffee and stirring something in a pot on his wood stove. Candles made from animal fat, by the smell of them, hung in several places around the room, lighting the dark interior, but accentuating the shadows in the corners and the rafters.

The man stood as Amboy entered the chapel and as he did, Amboy noted the thing in the center of the room that he'd somehow missed, probably because his brain refused to process it.

Lettie, levitating above the floor, faced down, her arms and legs out, naked, religious icons drawn all over her body, and beneath her a circle much like the abuela had created in the underground in Buenos Aires.

And then he repeated the observation to himself.

Lettie.

Levitating.

Live without a net.

No strings attached.

Unholy.

And then she turned to stare at him with malevolence in her eyes.

Its eyes.

Because whatever it was, it was no longer Lettie.

CHAPTER 31

The growl was so low it didn't even register at first. Like the tectonic movements of the earth, but localized in the joints and teeth of the woman hanging suspended by invisible strings in the hermitage atop the *Catderal de Marmal*, far out of sight of those who would even presuppose such a thing might exist, the sound was like an ancient stone rubbing against another ancient stone with a backbeat of human suffering. Her arms were stretched out as if they had been nailed to a cross. Her legs were the same, one foot resting atop the other, only the spike missing for authenticity. She was filthy from dirt and dried sweat. Even from the doorway with wind at his back, he smelled he rank stench of the room. Whatever was possessing her had been determined to strip away any piece of her humanity, leaving her nothing more than a guttural creature whose mind had been hijacked by something far more powerful and mean.

"Close the door," the man by the fire—presumably Brother Benevides—said, his voice soft but powerful.

Amboy stepped inside and to the left, momentarily not wanting to get any closer to that which had been Lettie.

Father Rivas came next, genuflecting and crossing himself as he entered.

Father Paz was less pious and wiped at his frock as he sought to recover his breath.

Rivas reached to help him, but Paz waved him impatiently away, so Rivas closed the door behind them.

The effect was instantaneous.

No longer was there light or air from outside.

The shadows from the corners seemed to descend and tug on the edges of the light, smearing it, making it more difficult to see. Now, with the door closed and the only light coming from the candles and the windows set high in the ceiling, the arcane circle beneath the suspended woman glowed with an eerie hue.

Amboy squinted into the face of Lettie and whatever was inside her stared back, feral, tracking, and hungry.

Brother Benevides came around to his left and met Amboy in the corner. Now that he was closer, his size became even more apparent. Easily the girth and width of an NFL lineman, he had a face that had been ravaged by much more than time. His nose and cheeks were misshapen. Several bulges jutted from his forehead. His hair grew sparsely and in tufts, as if sprouting between slabs of concrete. It was his eyes that drew Amboy's gaze, however. Twin orbs of the brightest blue, they seemed like the eyes of a fairy or an elf rather than the human troll they sat in.

"She's close to death," he said, voice even and low. "I've managed to force water into her, but she won't eat. If I had IVs she'd have longer but as you see, we are primitive here."

"Wha—What have you done?" Amboy asked. "Is it lilin?"

He nodded and sighed. "The lilin are old spirits. Like obours, they have been around since the advent of man. Gilgamesh mentions them and how they had to fight against the spirits to survive."

"So, not as simple as a Christian demon," Amboy said, not knowing what else to say.

Benevides gave him a look like a father might an ignorant child. "No. Not as *simple*," he said with a grim smile.

"Have you tried transference?" Paz said limping next to them.

Benevides bowed slightly and touched his hand to his forehead in respect for Paz's clerical rank. "No, your eminence. There's no one to transfer to."

"And the exorcism hasn't worked?"

"If anything, it's made it stronger," Benevides said. "She isn't a believer so she holds no ontological sway over it and my words mean nothing. The more I pull at it, the deeper it grips. I'm afraid if I rip it free, I might rip a part of her as well."

"Rip it free?" Amboy asked. "What is this?" He imagined one of Benevides' immense hands on her skin gripping and ripping.

"Brother Benevides has a particular skill. He can not only identify arcane skeins, but he can also manipulate them, grasping them like a—like a surgeon of the supernatural might."

"What's the problem with the lilin in Lettie, then?" Amboy asked.

"I don't know. It's just too deep. Had I gotten to her sooner then maybe, but I—" He shook his head. "I got to her too late."

"Thank you for bringing her here," Paz said. "It must have been a trial."

Benevides shrugged. "Not so much."

"What is this transference?" Amboy asked.

Benevides eyed Amboy, then glanced at Paz.

The old priest nodded. "Go ahead. Tell him."

"The woman—Lettie, I presume—her body is giving out. The lilin doesn't want to be trapped inside of it when it dies. If she dies, it will be sent back whence it came. It requires another host. An offering. Someone to freely give themselves to the spirit."

Whence it came, not where it came. Amboy thought, as if it came from a different time instead of a different place. Or was it both? The more he interacted with the priests the more he discovered that there was so much out there that he didn't even understand. His world was being expanded and he didn't like it one bit because the expansion was predicated on the ruination of his friend—his lover—his whatever she was.

He stepped forward. "Then let it be me," Amboy said. "I wish nothing more than to protect her and see her alive."

A bell rang from far away. No one seemed to hear it but Amboy. It must have been a trick of the ear because they were so far out over the water there was no way a church bell could be heard.

Paz shook his head slowly. "This isn't up for negotiation. You can't die."

"What do you mean? My life is my choice."

"Do you really think so?" Paz asked tiredly. "Do you really think you have that much control over who you are and what you will become?"

"What I will become?" He laughed hoarsely. "Why not? I'm a grown man."

Paz chuckled. "Spoken like a child."

Amboy straightened his shoulders and lifted his chin. "You think you know me. You have an idea of who I am. But you don't know me. I am at once simple and complex. I can explain the one but not the other. I never claimed to be the smartest man in the room, nor will I ever be the strongest, but when it comes to friendship, I am the best friend a person can ever have."

"Is it because you didn't have those kinds of friends growing up in the mountains?" he asked.

"I had many friends. Most of the mountain was my family."

"You told me that they let you free range. Do you think they cared if you died?"

Amboy was about to reply but then paused. He noted that Benevides and Rivas were staring expectantly at him. Beyond them he saw a baleful eye of Lettie observing him. Whatever the lilin was thinking he had no idea. He wondered if Lettie could see through the evil as if it were the fly-specked screen door of a serial killer. He could respond to the question in a way that would be appropriate, but the truth was, he'd grown up feeling like whether he lived or died were both inconveniences. The children of the mountain were like dandelions and at the end of their lives they'd add themselves to the protein of the mountain. He was but a breath of spring, who somehow managed to survive through summer.

"They cared about us when we lived," Amboy said finally.

"That didn't answer my question," Paz said.

Amboy shifted from one foot to the other. He felt cramped and remembered how wide and beautiful it was outside. So much like his mountains, where one could run free and away from any threats or things that went bump in the light.

"I had many friends. Oteil was one of my best friends—"

"Who turned out to be a German agent," Paz said, interrupting.

"That's yet to be confirmed. He was there for me and I was there for him in 'Nam. What happened after we knew each other had nothing to do with the friendship we had."

"What if he was always that way? What if he was always a German agent?"

"That doesn't make any sense," Amboy said. "Then there's Santiago and his brother Thiago. And of course, Lettie."

Paz looked around as if searching for a cup of wine. He gestured for everyone to follow and then headed to the far end of the chapel. There he found a ceramic jug. He lifted it from the table, shook it, and then sniffed. He blew across the top, then tipped it.

Amboy watched the priest's jugular work as he swallowed, his eyes closed, alone with the wine and whatever it meant for him.

Once he seemed satisfied, he put the jug down. He found a piece of cheese on the table, sniffed it, then set it back down.

"You mention your friends," he said, slowly, his eyes going from the cheese to Amboy. "Tell me what happened to them."

"I don't know what you mean?" Amboy said.

"Santiago. Dead. Thiago. Deformed. Lettie. Possessed. And how is it that you are a good friend?"

Amboy inhaled and felt his chest go hollow.

"And let's not forget Otiel the German agent."

Amboy closed his eyes and then opened them, staring into those of the men around him, avoiding Lettie. He didn't have the emotional energy to deal with her at the moment. He knew the question; he just didn't know the answer.

But that didn't keep Paz from pressing. "I'll ask you again, would they care if you died?"

"I think they would," Amboy said, gathering about him all the good feelings from his memories that he could. "They would die for me."

"Isn't it curious that the people you have been able to curate as the closest of friends have all experienced something terrible, but those who would ignore you are living the life of Reilly?"

"The power of coincidence," Amboy said, eyeing the jug.

"Yet those who should most owe some sort of familial fealty live on without any issues at all."

"You're talking as if I have a say in everyone else's lives," Amboy said.

"Don't you?" Paz asked. "What is your power? To merely breathe? To exist? That's everyone's power. We all have that to start with. But you want to attain something higher. You want to be more special. You want your words to transcend and mean something."

"Why is that so difficult?" Amboy asked.

"It's not. But what are you willing to give up?" Paz asked.

"Give up?"

"What I said."

"So, in order to change who I am, I have to give up what I am, in order to be a better version of what I am, is that what you are saying?" Amboy asked.

Paz nodded and took another pull at the jug.

Amboy shook his head. "That's so much bullshit, I don't even know where to begin."

Rivas's eyes went wide.

Benevides grinned.

"Events occurring as they have no bearing on my relationships," Amboy said.

"A convenient sentiment. To say otherwise would entail admissions and then years' worth of therapy."

"What is it you are getting at, old man? If you want to know, will I sacrifice myself for Lettie, I already said I would. And I meant it. Santiago. Thiago. I'm too late to do anything about them and as far as Oteil goes, I haven't seen him in years."

"You can do whatever you want, but I can't let you die. And this I know. If you allow the lilin to transfer into your body, then you will most assuredly die."

"What's so special about me? Paz. You've spent the last five minutes breaking me down and demonstrating what a terrible friend I am, but I can't die? I'm not allowed to? How does that even make sense?"

Paz passed the jug. "I was too hard on you. The climb tired me more than I believed. What I was trying to get at was despite all of the failures of friendship you've had in your life, you were meant for something greater."

Amboy caught Benevides and Rivas exchanging glances

beside him, but didn't say anything. Instead, he took a draught of the wine only to discover that it was water. Again, what seemed to be one thing was really another.

He turned to the brother. "Let's get that demon out of her. The circle on the floor. It's meant to keep the lilin at bay, right?"

"That's right."

"What happens when we erase it?"

"Lettie gains all the power of the lilin and can exercise it."

"What if she were to die? What would the lilin do?"

"It would try and escape before her death. But that would mean to kill her. I can't allow that to happen."

"If I'm correct, we can ensure that death is a temporary state," Amboy said. "Kill her just long enough to let the lilin escape and then bring her back."

"How will you bring her back?" Paz asked, his face full of speculation.

"Just watch me."

Amboy took a deep breath, then strode past the three clergymen into the center of the chapel. Stepping into the circle was like entering an electric whirlwind. He could feel static encapsulate his entire body. His hair shot straight up on his arms and he could feel the electricity on his head. Looking around, he was no longer in the chapel, but floating above an ocean beneath a crimson sky. Green and yellow lighting crackled in the distance while purple storm clouds boomed back thunder.

The being before him was no longer Lettie, but the lilin instead. Its face was darkness with hints of movement behind it. Faces upon faces, those victims it had consumed, taking their power and leaving them as empty husks. The body was a conglomeration of sticks, as if a beaver in a moment of psychosis had tried to build a dam to keep in the energy of a beast. To look at it hurt Amboy's eyes, but he forced himself to.

"You," said the lilin, the hot whisper of a desert wind.

"Me," Amboy said, then grabbed the lilin by a shoulder. A jolt of electricity went through him, but he hung on somehow and spun the creature until it was facing up. Then, like it was something he'd practiced a thousand times, he swung himself to straddle the body of the monster. He cursed as the lilin began to buck, but locked his heels together. Then, with both hands, he began to strangle.

Strangle.

Such a charged word.

It could mean nothing else than what it said.

To strangle: squeeze or constrict the neck of (a person or animal), especially so as to cause death.

The sky above him raged.

To strangle: hamper or hinder the development or activity of.

Yellow and green lightning crackled across the crimson sky while purple thunderheads slipped free tornadoes to ravage the ocean.

To strangle: suppress (an impulse, action, or sound).

The spray blinded his eyes and the electricity sizzled across his skin. He felt the burn, but still pressed down, gripping with his fingers, digging into what he imagined was Lettie's flesh. He heard screams and knew them to be Paz and Rivas. He also heard Lettie's, her peal ghostly as all the air was pushed out of her.

"Stop it," came the soft words. "Don't kill me, my love."

My love. She said, *my love.*

A surge of tortured joy rose within him and be began to release his grip. Then he felt something stronger atop his hands. He turned and saw Benevides standing next to him, his countenance firm, his eyes to Lettie, and his hands atop Amboy's. The brother understood. He knew what had to be done and wouldn't be dissuaded by any relationship previous to the moment.

Then beneath him, the figure of Lettie evaporated to be replaced by the lilin. It snarled and barked, a feral hyena filled with angry bees. It had eyes that were blizzards of fire. The smell of sulfur grew strong.

"Please, my love. Don't kill me."

Lettie now, her beauty, perfect red hair with her wine-stain map of Florida.

Then growls, preternatural from a beast made before God's name was ever written.

Lightning struck Amboy through the skull, impaling him on the levitating body.

He screamed, his back arching, his head back, but he didn't let go. He couldn't let go. Brother Benevides' monstrous hands were atop his, pressing, limiting, keeping them in place. He turned to stare at the man, whose eyes were closed, as was his mouth, jaw fixed and jutting as if it was taking all of his energy to do what he was doing.

The sky raged for a moment more, then went silent.

Gone was the lightning.

Gone was the crimson sky.

Gone were the purple clouds.

Everything that remained was white—up, down, left, right—nothing but white.

Then he returned to the inside of the chapel. Beneath him was Lettie, all her glorious self. Red hair. Milk-chocolate skin. Wine stain of Florida. And her amazing blue eyes—staring up at him, pupils, fixed and dilated.

Dead.

CHAPTER 32

And beneath him she was dead.

Amboy screamed.

They were no longer floating, but had crashed to the ground.

Around him came a roar as Benevides swung an axe at a creature made of sticks.

Rivas huddled near the stove, a length of iron in his shaking hands.

Paz had a pistol, but Amboy could tell by the way he held it that he knew it would be no use.

Benevides kept hammering at the creature, but each blow rebounded as if it were a spaghetti noodle against a rubber target. His muscles bunched beneath his frock, as he gathered himself, like a lumberjack attempting to fell a mountain.

And beneath him she was dead.

The door flew open and slammed back and forth against the inside of the chapel. Banging and clanging, the sound like the intrusion of an army. A wind rose from outside, as if the very weather sought to help cleanse the earth of the monstrosity before them.

Candles sputtered and died.

The wind found home inside and began to localize as a hurricane of pain as it gathered bits and pieces of broken glass and rocks and dirt.

And beneath him she was dead.

He began CPR.

He slid off of her to relieve her of this body weight, and crossed his palms, locking his thumbs and centered the pressure on her chest. He pumped three times, then breathed into her mouth. He found himself shouting for her to wake up—for her to live.

And beneath him she was dead.

Her eyes continued to stare past him through the Milky Way.

He pressed again, then breathed for her again. Over and over he did this, not allowing her blood to congeal, forcing it through her body to feed her brain. But he knew that with each pump, the blood had less and less oxygen. He could only give her so much, breathing for her as he did.

Because, beneath him, she was still dead.

Yet, he pressed on.

Pumping.

Breathing.

Screaming.

Begging.

Promising.

And then she shot upward, striking him in the face, sending him backwards.

She inhaled deeply, as if her lungs had the capacity of a planet, her eyes returning to normal.

Amboy rolled from her and shot to his feet. He ran to Rivas and grabbed the length of metal he'd been holding and ran to support Brother Benevides. But he was too late.

The brother stood rigid for a moment, then the sticks that comprised the lilin fell, clattering to the wooden floor.

Benevides turned to Amboy and pointed. "You." His face was no longer that of the man, but of something else—something that nature had wrought eons ago, a splinter of the first evil. The lilin was now inside of him.

Lettie began to drag herself away from the battle, but only made it a few feet.

Without even thinking, Amboy shoved the metal rod through the neck of the larger man, pushing him back and back and back, until they fell into the arcane circle on the floor. Amboy rolled away, and scrambled to his feet.

Benevides, or rather, the creature that possessed him, also managed to climb to his feet, but when he came to the edge of the circle, found himself bound within it. Standing with his neck skewered with metal rod, he spun left and right and all around, trying to find a way free, even while the life's blood of the monk poured from the dual wounds. Like a mime caught within an invisible cylinder, he pressed franticly against the invisible barrier. Where the length of metal intersected it, sparks crackled and popped.

He fell to his knees, and then onto his side, his head and shoulders resting awkwardly against the side of the invisible cylinder so that it appeared as if he was half sitting. His chest heaved for several moments, then stopped, the pool of blood surrounding him covering the entire interior of the arcane circle.

Lettie moaned.

Amboy pulled her so that her head was resting on his lap and her body was between his legs.

A creature of smoke and hatred detached from the dead body of Benevides. All sticks and shadow, it rattled against the side of the invisible barrier.

Rivas and Paz pulled themselves over and began to shout a

Latin litany, making signs of the cross and other symbols unknown to Amboy. Neither were in synch, but each of their voices carried power. The lilin was already weak and the onslaught of the two men made it weaker still.

Paz shifted into an Argentinian patois similar to that of the abuela—ritualistic magic that couldn't be sanctioned by the church, but were nonetheless spoken by him. He pulled a piece of chalk from his pants and began to draw esoteric symbols along the edge of the circle. Signs and sigils that made Amboy's eyes hurt.

Amboy tore his gaze away from the scene and attended Lettie.

Her stare was wide and searching, face drawn. Black shadows hugged the pockets of her eyes. The hollows of her cheeks had deepened and her lips were cracked and grey. Sweat soaked her skin in a slippery sheen. She brought her hands up to cover her nakedness, trying awkwardly to do what clothes were best made for.

All the while, Amboy made quiet noises and spoke softly, turning her head away from the scene in the middle of the chapel whenever her eyes strayed that way. He tore away a piece of his own shirt and began to wipe her clean. Eventually he noticed that he was crying and used his own tears to wet the cloth, trying to diminish her pain, her discomfort, but happy for her to be alive.

A moment of panic took her as her chest heaved and she reached out for something invisible.

He pulled her up so that he hugged her tightly from behind, pushing himself into her, giving her his body heat. She began to sob, great chest heaving, and shoulder-racking sobs. He rocked her back and forth as both of them cried. He was just happy she was alive, especially having killed her.

Out of the corner of his eye he caught the figure of the lilin, now half its size, breaking down and rebuilding, the sticks that comprised it turning old and brittle and unable to hold up more than an ounce or two. Then it was as if the circle beneath it opened and both the body of Benevides and the lilin vanished, sucked down the hole, falling forever into the devil's own cesspool.

Lettie leaned forward at that moment to grab her knees so she could better rock herself. And as she did, Amboy noted her back and how the tattoo was no longer there, ripped free finally and gone. How was that possible, unless the creature had lived in the tattoo the entire time—an entity contained in the ink, brought forth by incantation at a later date.

Rivas helped Paz to his feet.

They both ran to the rear of the room and grabbed two pails of water. They returned and sloshed the water over the space where the circle had been, washing away any sign of the arcane, making the wood seem as if it were nothing more than a simple floor in an out of the way chapel on the edge of the world in an all but forgotten Patagonian lake.

All evidence of the exorcism was gone.

Nothing remained to show that a woman had been held, a man had been lost, and a creature had been ruined.

It was as it should be.

Such things shouldn't exist in memory. To remember them was to give them life.

Ten, twenty, thirty minutes later and Lettie was covered in one of Benevides' smocks. It trailed behind her and seemed envelop her, but it covered every inch of her and she hugged it like a blessed second skin. She sat near the fire, facing the middle of the chapel. She'd already drunk three large glasses of water from a jug and now sipped heady wine, her eyes half closed, shaking from the experience.

Rivas strode to the middle of the chapel. Disheveled and his shirt torn, he turned one hundred and eighty degrees, taking in the place, his arms out and his head shaking as if he couldn't believe what had just occurred.

"I thought it would be me, you know," he said, staring at the cleaned space in the center of the place. The floor had been seared, as if from a great heat, steamed to a new condition.

"I thought I would be the one to die," he said.

"Why is that" Paz asked.

Rivas sighed.

Amboy seemed to see him for the first time. He was little more than a kid. He had a goatee and a beard but the dark hair was mere wisps as if they'd just been grown. The young man had been there for them, but Rivas was much younger than Amboy had thought he was.

"I look at you all. Amboy and Ms. Lettie. They are undoubtedly important." He chuckled absently. "They're like two characters from an old story. They are meant to survive to the end. Everyone else who meets them along the way, not so much."

"You feel as if you're replaceable," Paz said.

"Not just that. I'm a stand in. I'm that character in a story that is cannon fodder."

"Not anyone could have done what you did," Paz said.

"Why not?" Rivas asked. "I mean, who am I? I didn't even know Godoy was working for the Germans. How good of a priest can I be?"

"Just because you see the best in people it doesn't make you a bad person," Paz said.

Rivas grinned feebly. "I get that. I just don't feel like this is my story."

"Then whose story is it?" Paz asked.

Rivas gestured to where Amboy held Lettie by the fire. "Theirs of course."

Paz stared at Amboy for a long moment, then asked, "Don't you think that multiple storylines could be going on at once?"

"What?" Rivas asked.

"Why can't you have your story and I have my story and they have their story and so on and so on. We all have our stories and we can't just stop because we feel as if we bumped up against someone else's."

"Then what do I do? My story, whatever it was, has intersected theirs—and what a story it is." He bowed slightly in their direction.

They bowed in return.

"You continue on your track," Paz said. "Benevides is dead. We need someone here until we can find his replacement. The chapel shouldn't be left alone. It is a special place and requires special consideration. Do you think you can do it?" He paused, glancing around the ancient chapel. "Are you up for it?"

Rivas seemed ready to argue, but instead dropped his shoulders. He nodded to himself and walked around the interior of the chapel. "I can do this. I will do what I can. This really is my story now, isn't it?"

Paz grinned and nodded. "It always has been, my son. It's just sometimes stories merge. Now that these two are moving on, you can live your own story yourself."

"And I can do whatever I want," he said.

"It's your story. It always has been. Live it."

Rivas grinned and moved to one of the pews. He tested it for its weight, then began to pull it back in place.

Paz turned back to Amboy.

"We need to be going," he said.

"You're right. We need to go to Rio Gallegos."

Paz backed up a step. "Rio Gallegos? I was thinking back to Buenos Aires."

Amboy shook his head. "Not a chance. We need to find out who put the tattoo on her and why. Until then, we won't have the full picture. And let me tell you—I listened to your conversation with Rivas. It was smart. But I need you to know—I'm going to play my story out even if it ends in tragedy."

CHAPTER 33

The seaplane waited for them in the harbor, a convenience that Amboy felt a little too easy. He thought about voicing his concern to Paz, but he was busy speaking with Lettie in soft terms and she seemed to need the conversation more than he did. The pilot stood in the nose to watch them as they entered below, all three of them battered, disheveled and in need of new clothes. Lettie insisted on waiting until she had some. Neither Amboy or Paz wanted to let her out of their sights, so armed with what he believed to be her size, Amboy hurried into Chile Chico and bought several bags of men's and women's clothes in a whirlwind of spending through several mercados.

Back inside the Ansett Brothers Sandringham, they took turns in the bathroom, cleaning first and dressing, until all three of them were presentable. They were about ready to leave, when the pilot let them know that they had a visitor on the dock outside. One glance out the window, and Amboy was on his feet.

Matias stood in a suit straight off the streets of Buenos Aires, hat in one hand, cigarette in the other. He seemed nervous and kept glancing behind him as if he'd been followed. Amboy wasn't happy at all that his old friend—if that's what you could call him—decided to show. Last he heard, Matias said he was heading for Colombia.

Which is what he said when he met him on the dock.

Matias grinned and stomped out his cigarette, then held out a hand.

"Good to see you too, my friend," Matias said.

"Colombia wasn't your cup of tea?" Amboy asked.

"I never made it that far."

"Clearly," Amboy said, searching the street and parking lot behind Matias. He was looking for anything out of the ordinary. The problem was he didn't know what was ordinary. "Why are you here?"

"You ask it as if I'm doing something wrong." Matias spread his hands. "Is it so bad to want to see an old friend?"

"You never do anything without a purpose, Matias. You operate according to the highest bidder. And since I haven't offered you anything, I have to wonder who it is who has asked you to come to us."

Matias grinned and looked up at the plane. "Beautiful machine, no? I've been inside one before. Quite the luxury. I love the leather and wood. Not exactly something you see in the Air Force."

Amboy remembered the mission they'd had to ESMA which had been sponsored by Nolan and Frank-Just-Frank. He'd ended up killing the target they were trying to get out and it had made him persona non grata. Still, they had access to Wallace Thomson's plane, thanks to Paz, and now came Matias, flashing his smile, indicating he'd been in on the entire thing since the beginning.

"Flying into Rio Gallegos right now is going to be difficult," Matias said. "The air force is on full alert and their jets are still fighting against the Brits. Not the best time to be a tourist there."

"We're not going as tourists. We're going to find out who it was who removed Lettie's port wine stain," he said, leaving out the part about also wanting to find out who put the tattoo of the demon on her back.

"You can tell that to the Argentines. One look at you and this plane and they'll think you're spies for the British."

"That's nonsense."

"War is nonsense, but that never stopped kids from shooting each other with finger pistols." He chuckled. "Then later with real ones. Nolan asked me if I might make your transit easier. I happen to know the general in charge of the base."

"Of course you do."

Matias bowed. "He owes me several favors."

"Of course he does."

"You owe me as well," Matias said.

"I thought we covered that already," Amboy said. "I think saving your life was enough payback."

Matias grinned. "Oh yes. That. Of course."

"Of course."

Matias paused and fiddled with the brim of the hat in his hands. "Aren't you going to invite me on board?" he asked.

Amboy thought of a dozen things to say, but instead rolled his eyes, turned on his heel and went back inside the plane.

Once inside, he announced, "We have company."

Paz's eyebrows raised when he saw the upper-class thug.

Lettie barely paid any attention. She was still stunned from being possessed and the events surrounding it. Amboy wondered if she would ever be the same again.

Matias entered and bowed. He leaned into the cockpit and said a few words to the pilot, then shook first Paz's hand, then Lettie's. Once he'd given his greetings, he found a chair and poured himself a scotch from the Texan's stash.

Finally, the pilot was allowed to take off and after a brief climb towards the Andes, he circled one hundred and eighty degrees and headed south and east for the Pacific Ocean—destination Rio Gallegos.

Paz sat by himself drinking and taking notes.

Matias pulled his hat over his face and slumbered—or at least pretended to do so.

Amboy and Lettie sat side-by-side, holding hands.

Several times he tried to broach the subject of her possession, but every time she pushed him away saying she didn't want to talk about it. He couldn't imagine how she must feel. To rape someone was an act of violence against their body. Then what would you call an act of violence against a soul?

Finally, he settled in and just watched her. About an hour into the flight, she fell asleep, the rise and fall of her chest even and slow. She'd twitch occasionally, but nothing too violent. He could only hope she was dreaming something soothing. Anything really. Anything but what she'd just experienced.

He closed his own eyes and soon found himself in his own dreamscape—part memory and part fantasy, he never knew where one began and the other ended, but he recognized the broad finger-leafed sassafras of his Tennessee youth. A cure-all, he'd loved drinking it as tea with honey. He'd heard it was also used to cure urinary tract disorders, swelling in the nose and throat, syphilis, bronchitis, high blood pressure in older people, gout, arthritis, skin problems, and even cancer. Like aspirin had been to the Indians, sassafras was to the hill people of Eastern Tennessee.

Then he was running, the leaves grabbing at him, each one a hand. He fought against them, flailing, kicking out, but kudzu grabbed his ankles and slipped up his pants until they'd wrapped themselves around his privates, squeezing like they might remove them. He opened his mouth to scream, but instead a bag was thrown over his head and he was dragged free of the brush.

Flash forward to cold. He felt the burlap against his face, but the rest of his body was naked. He shivered and wanted to rub his hands against his skin, but he couldn't. Someone had trapped them and he couldn't move them, much less feel where they were. His shoulders ached and his forearms screamed as if they'd been cut in two.

Cries of other children came from all around him.

Some from girls.

Others from boys.

Where were they and what was happening?

He opened his mouth to speak and simply said, "Help."

The response to his word was quick and violent—a blow to the side of his head that sent him crashing into a hard rough wall. Tears flowed and he fought back sobs of pain. He'd gone from running and being free to trapped with others. Now he could hear their sobs and the occasional cry of pain. So many of them, it was as if all the children from the mountain had been gathered to be cloistered and broken.

He tried again to move his arms, but found it impossible, the pain exquisite.

Then he heard grunts. These weren't from his fellow children. They were from something else entirely. Something not human. Like an ape, but deeper and more raw, echoing, telling him they were in one of the many caves that pitted the hill, or perhaps even a mine.

A girl screamed and took off, the Doppler of her fear causing him to turn in her direction. The rough burlap snatched against his face and scraped it painfully.

The grunts came quick then, followed by a thundering beside him that nearly knocked him down and then silence.

After what seemed like an eternity, he shifted his position.

"Boy, is that you?" whispered a voice he knew too well.

"Billy, is that you?"

"They got us, Boy. They got Tim and you and me."

Someone hissed for them to be quiet.

Amboy scooted closer to the sound of his friend until they were head-to-head, burlap to burlap. "Where are we?" he whispered.

"I don't know. They've done something to my arms."

"Mine too. They hurt so badly."

"What did they do?"

"I don't know. I can't see."

A grunt from far away followed by an inhuman bellow.

"What the heck is that, Boy?"

The smell of urine came strong. Someone had peed themselves. Then he realized it was him. Amboy felt the shame of it, but couldn't get past the terror of the situation. The wet between his legs made him sick and he fought back bile.

"Who was that?"

"Annie, I think." Billy said. "I think that creature got her."

"Did you see it?"

Amboy felt his friend shudder next to him, the shakes coming uncontrollably, rattling the entire childlike frame.

"Its head was wrong. It could—it could see behind itself."

"Behind?"

"Like it was made that way."

Suddenly the beast was upon him, palming his head and screaming at him, breath like rotten meat and sassafras . . .

Amboy let loose a new stream of urine as he too screamed, clawing at the air.

CHAPTER 34

Lettie grabbed his arm and pressed it back down.

His eyes were wild, taking in the interior of the plane.

He'd fallen asleep.

It had been a dream.

But it had seemed so real—like a memory.

Both Paz and Matias were staring at him.

Lettie held out a glass of water.

"What was it?" she asked.

"Nothing." He sat up and checked his pants. Thank god he hadn't peed himself like he had in the dream. "Are you okay?"

She shook her head. "I don't know. I don't remember a lot. One moment, you and I were on the bus and I was in the cave, the next I was in that building with the big man screaming at me."

"That was never me. The bus took off without me. You were talking to yourself all of that time. The tattoo—the lilin—it had you."

"And the man?"

"He was a brother. A monk. A lay priest who fought to save your soul."

"What happened to him?"

Amboy remembered the floor opening up and swallowing both him and the lilin. "I'm not sure," he said. "Whatever . . . he's gone."

"Must everyone die for me?" she asked. "Why am I so special?"

He stared at her thinking of a hundred ways he could answer that. But another part of him reminded this version of him that he barely knew her. They'd only known each other for a matter of days, yet he felt as if he was destined to know her. What had Rivas said? He was worried he was living out a story—meaning the story that was Lettie and Amboy.

"Why are any of us special?" Amboy asked.

He went and grabbed a glass of wine and returned to his seat. They had another two hours before they landed. Half an hour later, the pilot called Matias forward. Amboy heard the man arguing over the radio, explaining that they had to land and that the war had nothing to do with them and them nothing to do with the war.

They eventually landed, but only after circling on Bingo fuel for thirty minutes. The pilot was certain it was the Argentinian Air Force's way of saying fuck you, but they were just happy to land. They found a car waiting for them thanks to Matias.

Amboy thought the whole scenario a bit too contrived. A plane ride and now a car ride? What was going on? What was the pay off?

They motored downtown out of the gate to the airport in a stretch Lincoln.

Overhead, Mirage III and A-4 Skyhawks roared towards the Malvinas.

Outside the gate hundreds of protestors raged, carrying signs and hurling epithets at anyone coming or going. The problem was that the war wasn't working out as they had hoped. The might of Great Britain had come to bear on the small islands and with Argentina's ships already sunk, all they had was a last-ditch air attempt. With the help of the French-built Mirages and the American-built Skyhawks, Argentina hoped to at least get in a few shots at the juggernaut that had once been the world's greatest colonial power.

Amboy knew their chances were slim. Fighting the British was akin to a little kid fighting an adult. A flashback to the cave and the burlap sack and the pain and the monster then back to reality. For all the rage the Argentinians felt, they had to know that they wouldn't win. Yet, even knowing the truth of it, wouldn't he do the same? No one ever told him to roll over and play dead. It wasn't in his DNA and wasn't part of who he was.

Open hands and fists slammed against the doors and windows and for a moment it seemed as if they might break in. Mouths shouting, eyes flaming, races red and souls seething as they tried to bar the way, but the driver kept moving at an inexorable pace until they were free from the pack, who returned their attention to the gate and waited for their next target.

Amboy had all but forgotten there was a war on. Las Malvinas and the British. While he'd been on the bus and on the eastern edge of the country, all the news had been local. What was happening in Buenos Aires and other points east were of little concern to the pastoral peoples occupying the foothills of the Andes.

But now that they were back, it was full-on protest and hopefulness and disappointment. Like the day he'd first heard of Lettie, sitting in a basement surrounded by Matias and his goons. What had seemed ages ago was less than two weeks. So much had happened during that span.

He glanced at Matias staring out the window from his perch in the front passenger seat.

And here he was again.

How deeply was Matias wrapped up in the events surrounding Lettie? And why was the CIA so interested? That was something he still didn't understand. Was it merely because of the number of their fingers? Did that unlock something special? Whatever it was, the Germans wanted her for themselves—for their Ahnenerbe. Were they to be taken and stuffed like animals in a museum? Or were they to be studied? He could tell them right away if they asked that there was nothing special about him, be it six fingers or ten fingers each hand.

Then he remembered. Father Paz had had six fingers but had had the last digits on each hand removed when he'd been a child. He was more like them than not. He'd just chosen to hide his—malformity—deformity—*difference* to the world whereas Lettie and Amboy displayed theirs without fear.

Like Amboy had mentioned earlier, growing up on in Tennessee, a lot of the children of the mountain had six fingers. Tim Whitmire and his brothers had six fingers on each hand. Billy Picket had six fingers as well. They'd all thought it was from a case of inbreeding, their families marrying each other over and over again.

Tim and Billy had been his friends, but they'd also figured out that they were probably cousins as well. What sort of cousin, well, that was for a trained researcher to decipher. All they knew was that no one from the outside ever came to the mountain and yet the families still bred like rabbits. He'd joked about it not mattering if a child went missing every now and then and he hadn't been exaggerating. Kids had gone missing several times while he grew up, which they attributed to bears or caves or sinkholes.

"Where was it you went to get the stain removed?" Father Paz asked.

Lettie shook her head. "I just don't know. I don't even know how I got to Buenos Aires. I remember arriving in Rio Gallegos by coach and having dinner at a particular place, then that's it. My memory of whatever happened next has been scrubbed clean."

"Do you remember which restaurant?" Amboy asked.

"It had a mermaid on the sign and was near the water. Oh. And it had a blue wall, but that's all I remember." She looked out the window and sighed.

Amboy pulled free his pack and inside was hers. He passed it to her.

"I saved this in case you might need to remember."

Her face lit up. "My things. I'd thought them lost."

"They were. I found them in the chapel. You must have been carrying them when Benevides found you."

She flipped through the pages until she found the advertisement that had started it all.

"Here," she said, holding up the pamphlet and passing it to Matias in the front seat. "We need to go here."

The driver made a couple of corrections, then headed into a more industrial part of town.

Amboy didn't know what he anticipated. What kind of place would remove port wine stains? He thought maybe a nail salon or a hair salon with an added specialty. But all of the buildings before them seemed to be warehouses.

Gone were the palms and the plants and brightly-clothed tourists, replaced by bins overflowing with trash and people foraging through them. The road was no longer paved causing the driver to slow, dirt and gravel plinking the underside of the car. They made several turns and then came to a small black single-story building wedged between two three-story gray windowless warehouses.

The sign above the door hung from one side and slid back and forth in the wind.

It read *Louis Icart* on the top line and *Faciales y Masajes* on the second line.

The door was faded red with a single diamond-shaped window at eye level.

Amboy said, "You wait here," and moved to get out of the car.

"The hell I will," Lettie said.

Paz grinned and said, "We're all going. Matias, you want to stay with the car?"

The thug grinned and patted a bulge beneath his left shoulder. "I've got it covered."

Amboy didn't have time to argue. He helped Lettie step out of the car, then was the first to the door, covering the distance in quick angry strides. He tried the door and found it locked. He peeked in the window, but couldn't see anything. He glanced around and didn't see anyone other than his own party. Then he took a step back, then brought his foot up and kicked out against the door. It rattled in place on the first try, but on the second the jamb splintered and the door swung open.

He grinned, glancing back.

Paz had his hand in the pocket of his jacket, probably clutching the pistol.

Lettie chewed on the inside of her lip and tried to see around him.

Amboy stepped inside, smelling the chemicals one might expect in a barber shop or a beauty parlor. The floor was littered with brushes and combs and smashed bottles of some long-forgotten liquid. Inches of dust rested atop everything. He snatched a magazine from the ground and noted after blowing away the dust that it had been published two years before. Several barber's chairs leaned against the far wall, ripped from the floor, the covers gashed in several places revealing springs and metal frames.

Amboy glanced at Lettie who was picking her way carefully over the detritus on the ground. She was shaking her head and looking around. Occasionally, bringing a hand to her face where the wine stain had once been. If Amboy hadn't seen it for himself on her passport, he never would have believed she had one, much less in the shape of Alabama.

"I don't understand."

"This is the address," Amboy said.

"It is. And I'm getting bits and pieces back and remembering the front door and that magazine," she said, pointing at the one in his hand.

He passed it over.

"But when I read it, the magazine was current. This one is two years old. That's—That's just impossible."

"Let me see your passport," Amboy said.

She rifled through her bag and pulled it out, then hand it over.

He looked for the entry date. They'd met about May 4, 1982 the day after the *General Belgrano* was sunk by the British submarine the HMS *Conqueror*. Argentinian air craft had already severely damaged the HMS *Glasgow* destroyer according to the papers. Today was May 19, 1982. He searched for her entry visa and saw it, but didn't believe it. The visa said April 18, 1980. Two years and a month prior to today's date. Which meant she hadn't just been here. If she'd been here at all, it was over two years ago.

He handed back her passport and asked for her notebooks.

She handed them over and he flipped through them until he came to a receipt. One of the notebooks had been purchased at Ministro Pistarini International Airport in Buenos Aires on April 18, 1980, the same day she'd entered the country.

"Lettie. How long have you been in Argentina?" he asked.

"Maybe two months," she said.

"But that's not possible. Look at your passport."

She did and her eyes shot wide. "How? Where—If this is true, where have I been?"

"Where indeed?" He spread his arm encompassing the room. "You remember this?"

"I do. But it was—it was like—"

"Two years ago?" he asked.

She nodded. "Like it was two years ago. Oh, Amboy. What has happened to me? How can someone lose two years?"

He shook his head. Perhaps the only person to know would be Nolan. After all, he seemed to be involved in one shape or another. But why the CIA should even be involved with the life of a young woman with six fingers and toes and a port wine stain of Florida on her face was behind Amboy's ken. He figured they were king makers and country breakers, capable of transforming cultures because of their vast network of resources and technology.

And then Nolan brought Matias into the assemblage. Had either of them known that Lettie had been in the country for two years? Did they even know what was happening? What she was doing? Amboy felt ridiculous standing in the middle of the broken and empty studio where Lettie had conceivably gotten her port wine stain removed and perhaps traded for the tattoo of the lilin.

Paz came later, but was eager to help Lettie. A former six-fingered man, he was more like them than most. Still, his appearance had been convenient, not contrived.

He shook his head and grabbed it with his right hand. How come he was feeling as if he were being manipulated? How come he felt as if everyone else knew what was going on and he was left acting as if he were the odd man out?

He made a hasty decision.

He grabbed Lettie by the hand and said, "Come with me."

He led her out the door to the car.

The driver was leaning against the hood smoking.

Paz stood beside him.

Amboy pulled out his pistol and ordered them to give him the keys.

By the time they were pulling away and Lettie was asking him what was going on, the others had emptied out of the building and stared at his departure. In the rearview Paz looked sad, but Matias fumed, his anger from a place Amboy didn't understand but he felt that he needed to.

CHAPTER 35

"Where are we going?" she asked.

"To chart our own future. We've spent too much time under the influence of others. It's time that we chart our own path."

He took a left, then a right, not knowing where he was going. He glanced in the rearview mirror a couple of times, but saw no one in pursuit. He was tired of not being the agent of his own action. He hated the idea that he was being directed to places. He shared this with Lettie.

"Don't you feel as if we have been manipulated?"

"All the time," she whispered. "Remember. I was the one who was possessed. Do I feel manipulated? Uh . . . yeah."

"I remember. I was the one searching for you. Every second of every day I was able, I was looking."

They drove for another twenty minutes, then found a place on the river. While the jets roared back and forth overhead, they sat down to a lunch on the water, the only couple in the joint, the rest of the people staring at them as if they'd arrived with extra sets of heads.

Amboy relayed to her what had happened after she'd boarded the bus, including stealing the motorcycle and then crashing.

"Eight days?" she said.

"Evidently. I feel it in my muscles. I'm more tired than I should be." He shook his head. "I tried to get to you, Lettie. I really did."

"Why did they do this to me?" she asked. "Why put a demon in me?"

He shook his head. "Since I'm not in the business of possessing someone with demons, I can only guess that it had to do with some sort of control."

"That's why we left the others, isn't it?" she asked.

"It is. I haven't been in control of my life since the day I heard of you."

"Thank you very much," she said, pursing her lips and staring out across the water where a girl was laughing at getting splashed.

"No. It wasn't because if you—I mean, yes it was because of you—but it had more to do with what others wanted me to do."

She took a sip of her beer and stared at a fishing boat rumbling past. Seagulls chased it, drowning out the sound of the motor with their shrieks.

They sat watching the boat depart and Amboy noted that the smell of the water was so much like the smell of the mountains, loamy and full of decaying matter.

"Eight days," she said. "Were you really unconscious for that long?"

"That's what they say?" he said, rubbing the place where the IV had been. "But what is eight days to two years?"

"Yes. Yes." She closed her eyes. "Do you realize that I am two years older than I thought I was? I checked the date. It has been two years. But why didn't I know that? Why wasn't I aware of the passage of time?"

"I wonder if the . . . the procedure to rid you of the . . . the map of Alabama might have taken much longer. Perhaps they had to put you under for a time."

"Two years?" she asked, her eyebrows arched.

He shrugged. "I don't know." He sighed heavily as their food arrived. Shrimp in a green sauce with rice and fruit.

They ate in silence until the food was gone, then she excused herself.

He ordered another beer and stared at the water. Near where they sat, foamy bits of plant matter and trash swirled in a small off-current eddy. Fish picked at it from below while seagulls screeched above. One landed on the railing next to the table, stunning him about the actual size. In the air they didn't seem as large as they were in real life. But wasn't that the truth about so many things. Even memories. They seemed so small and far away, but the events they relived were so large and important.

He glanced around. Lettie was nowhere to be seen. She must still be in the bathroom.

The waitress came and cleared their plates. She left, then returned with a platter of orange slices that had been sprinkled with hot spice. He took one and sucked on it, the salt and the spice in perfect juxtaposition to the sweet and the sour.

If he could come up with the money, they'd get a ticket back to the States. They could get lost in the hills and no one would ever find them. They could also go to the West Coast. He thought about the forests he'd read about with the immense Sequoyah trees. Or even the Pacific Northwest with the Cascades and forests that were as large as some New England states.

Anywhere but here.

He thought about ordering another beer, but decided against it.

Lettie still hadn't left the bathroom.

He hoped she was okay.

He tossed several bills on the table, then used the men's room. When he came out, she was still not around. He asked the waitress and she mentioned that the girl had left half an hour ago.

Amboy stood and stared, stunned at the news.

How could Lettie have just left?

Where had she gone and why had she left him?

He went to the town car and stood beside it, looking up and down the street. He felt panic suffuse him as he struggled with the idea that she'd left on her own. What if someone had come and taken her again? What if the lilin somehow returned and possessed her?

Then he saw her walking down the street towards him.

She had a tortured look on her face and gave him a half-hearted wave.

He was about to go to her when a taxi screeched to a stop beside the car.

Matias, the driver of the town car, and Paz exited the taxi.

The driver walked up to Amboy and punched him in the stomach.

He doubled over, feeling the contents of the lunch and the two beers bubbling up.

He straightened and was punched in the stomach again.

This time his mouth opened and his stomach emptied, spewing everything he eaten onto the street and the shoes of his attacker.

The driver cursed and backed away.

Lettie came running. "You told me you wouldn't hurt him," she said.

"He's not hurt," Matias said, putting a hand on Amboy's back. "He's had worse, haven't you, Amboy Stevens?"

"What the hell?" was all he could say.

Paz stood to the side, a silent observer to it all.

Amboy straightened and wiped at the corner of his mouth with the sleeve of his jacket. "You called them," he said to Lettie.

She frowned and stared at the ground. "Oh, Amboy. I had to."

"You didn't have to do anything."

"Of course I did. You don't want us to be on the run our entire lives, do you?"

That was exactly what he had planned on doing. "Why would that be a bad thing?"

"Always looking over your shoulder? Always worried that the other shoe is going to drop? Always checking to see if the person who says hi to you isn't really hiding something?" She shook her head. "Who could live like that?"

I could have lived like that, he thought. *For you, Lettie, I could have lived any way I could find, as long as we were alone and together.*

But instead, he said, "You tricked me."

"I didn't trick you. I never wanted to run. That was your idea and before we had a chance to talk about it you had a gun to this man's face and were stealing his car."

"Stealing his . . . We were making an escape, Lettie."

"Whose escape? I have nothing to escape from." She grabbed Amboy by the collars. "Don't you get it, lover? I want to be with you, but not on those terms. I want my own terms and I need to see all of this—whatever this is—through before we can figure out what to do next."

He opened his mouth to argue, but she placed a finger on it. "Can you just agree with me for once and not argue?"

He stared into her bluest eyes and then nodded.

She grinned, then grabbed one of his hands.

She turned to Paz and asked, "What's next?"

"Tierra del Fuego," he said flatly.

"To the Land of Fire. That sounds appropriate, doesn't it Amboy?"

He neither nodded nor shook his head. He stood like a statue, knowing that their chance had passed. Whatever was going to happen now was going to happen to them. It would be out of their control and in the control of others.

And he wasn't exactly sure how safe that was going to be or if they would even survive it.

CHAPTER 36

The Land of Fire really wasn't on fire. It was named as such by Magellan's sailors because of how flat it was and how passing the land at night by ship there seemed to be thousands of individual family fires burning. These were from the Fuegian Indians who have since vanished, only to be replaces by oil derricks spewing its own fire. The land itself wasn't on fire, but what lay beneath was certainly on fire.

Just as the plane passed over the invisible boundary, Amboy asked the others, "Do you mind telling us where we are going?"

"The only place we can go, now," Paz explained. "Do you remember the people you met at Nolan's house?"

Amboy flashed back to all the dignitaries, the ambassadors and heads of industry, all seeming with children who had six fingers. He remembered how they'd lined up and the mysterious white stag had chosen not one, but two of the girls. Meagan, the daughter of Wallace Thompson, and the Japanese girl. Everyone had been so happy they'd been chosen and at the same time, the other parents, downcast and upset their daughters hadn't fared the same.

"Sure, I remember them." *And their odd ceremony.*

"And you remember us chatting about the Council of the Cave?"

"I'm not sure if *chatting* is the best word for it, but yes."

"There are actually two councils. If you remember from Chatwin, there's a council in Buenos Aires and another in—"

"Santiago," Lettie said. "They meet on the island of Chiloé. Chatwin mentioned that he was never sure which one was superior, but that they both supposedly answered to a higher authority."

"I know of Chiloé," Amboy said. "I had some miner friends call it the Place of Seagulls. They said Butch Cassidy and the Sundance Kid hid out there before they went to Bolivia and botched their last robbery. Chiloé was also a place for pirates and outlaws to hide because of the deep and forbidding forests."

"Well, the council we spoke of, we're going to meet with them and see if we can't get to the bottom of this," Paz said.

"Then why are we going to Tierra del Fuego? If the council met on the island of Chiloé, shouldn't we be going there?"

Paz sighed heavily. "It's true. That was their traditional meeting place in a cave near the Thraiguen River, just south of Quincavi. But with the publication of *In Patagonia*, those things had to change. In his hubris, Chatwin published too much. The location was never meant to get out, but Chatwin had a way with people and when he heard about the sect of male warlocks—"

"The trail of 1880," Lettie said. "They were from the Righteous Province and had a hierarchy of over all the non-whites—the indigenous peoples. They used a power called *sajadures*, which was the magical affliction of pain or the insinuation of demons." She began speaking more quickly as she riffed through Chatwin's book in her lap. "The cave was supposed to be lit by torches made from human fat. The most treasured artifacts were a book and a bowl of special liquid of an unknown source that would allow the warlock to see every mystery of the world."

She laughed as she glanced up at the others. "But that's crazy, right?"

"Is it?" Paz asked. "You believe everything Chatwin has to say right up until page 107 in the book and suddenly he's not to be believed? Sadly, there were those who did believe so the council was forced to move."

Amboy stood, a little unbalanced because of the plane's movement and stalked over to the bar, poured himself a stiff glass of white liquor, scoured his throat and brain, then turned to the others. "You speak of the council as if you are a part of it."

"A part of it? No. That's not an adequate description." He grinned and stared at Amboy through heavy eyes. "But the church is aware of it. We liked it when they were confined to the island. But they were forced to move which caused no end of friction. Now they've relocated in Tierra del Fuego. Which is fine, really, because the warlocks have been around a lot longer than they've been in Patagonia. Chiloé was but another waystation."

Amboy narrowed his eyes. Was it just him, or did Father Paz seem oddly more comfortable the further south they traveled? Where he'd seemed worn and tired from his interactions with the Germans and the lilin, now he seemed almost rejuvenated. And his turn of phrase—*that's not an adequate description.* He could have easily said that he wasn't involved, but that was not at all what he indicated.

He glanced at Lettie, who was flipping through Chatwin's book.

Matias leaned forward and placed his elbows on his knees. "Is it time to tell him?" he asked Paz.

The old man shook his head quickly, then seeing that Amboy was watching, shook his head slightly.

"What do you want to tell him about?" Paz, asked.

"The invulche, of course."

At the use of the word, Lettie tensed. The book fell from her hand and onto the floor. Her pupils went to the back of her head revealing white eyes. Her entire body jolted straight for a solid ten seconds, then began to shake. She let loose urine, the pungent smell filling the inside of the cabin.

Amboy ran over to her and grabbed her shoulder.

"Lettie. Leticia. Come back. What's wrong?" He shook her and she began to weep. "Lettie, everything is okay. I promise. You'll be fine."

She sobbed harder, her shoulders shaking violently as tears poured forth. "I don't know what's wrong with me. I just . . . I just suddenly hurt all over. My skin feels like it's on fire."

She covered her face with her hands.

"Let me see."

"I can't. It burns."

"Matias. Get some ice," he ordered. When the other man didn't move, Amboy shot him a look filled with hatred and went and grabbed the bucket himself. He returned with the ice and a cloth. He dipped it into the water, wrung it out, then began applying it to the back of Lettie's neck.

"There. There. It's going to be okay. I promise, I will never let anything or anyone hurt you."

As he rubbed her, both of his arms ached when they'd been broken almost thirty years before. The pain was inexplicable, but he ignored it, just as he'd ignored other pains in the past.

The plane banked, showing them fire on the horizon—the setting sun, a great golden ball of heat, haloed by white clouds.

When it re-stabilized, Amboy released his grip on Lettie's seat.

"Come on, girl. Let me see you. I have some ice."

She moved her hands. Tears covered both cheeks. Her eyes

were red and almost the color of her hair. But what made him pause was what he didn't see. He fell back on his haunches and put both hands to the side of his head.

"What is it?" she asked. "What's wrong?"

He grabbed her hands and knelt before her. "Does it still hurt?"

"No, the pain is gone?" She pulled a hand free to touch her cheek. "Why? What's wrong?"

He gulped. "What's wrong? Florida. It's gone."

"What?"

"Your face is as unblemished as anyone's." He pointed to the bathroom in the lee of the aircraft. "Go look in the mirror."

She leaped up and ran to the bathroom, the door open and bouncing against her leg with the pitch of the aircraft ash she stared wondrously into the mirror. Her hand came up and she touched her cheek.

First Alabama.

Now Florida.

Both of her port wine stains had vanished.

She slapped the door open and stood in the doorway of the bathroom, a hand on either side of her to keep her from falling as the plane gently pitched and heeled.

"What just happened?" she breathed.

"It looks like—" He shook his head because he still couldn't believe it was true. "It appears that you just lost the stain."

"But how?"

Amboy shook his head and glanced at Paz and Matias, who were giving each other knowing looks. The oddity of them being friends struck him for the first time. More like, co-conspirators. What was going on?

"It looks like your prayers have been answered, my child," Paz said.

"Have they really?" she asked, spinning to the mirror then back again. The excitement doing backflips across her expressions. "You have no idea how many nights I went to bed praying."

Paz stared at Amboy as he said, "And now here you are. As complete as you ever felt you should have been." He gestured for Lettie to join him and she did, sitting in the empty seat next to him. "You should never give up on prayer. You never know when he might be looking."

She gave him such a look of beatification that Amboy felt she could have been a statue inside a religious monolith somewhere. Her smile was serene and satisfied as if the troubles of the world had ceased to exist. Her eyes sparkled with unspent tears. And her cheeks—her cheeks were a rosy glow beneath her blue eyes, the skin perfect as if she'd just walked out of a cosmetics advertisement.

"Could it have been part of some chemical process that just took a long time?" Amboy asked, trying to include science into the conversation.

"Any rubbing compound needs to be rubbed so that it affects what it's applied to," Matias said. "I didn't see her doing much rubbing."

She turned to Amboy. "He's right. I didn't. I mean, I don't. I don't even like to touch them. They were so ugly."

"And here I thought you'd come to terms with them," Amboy said, uncomfortable with the idea of a miracle.

She scoffed. "Of course, I had. I had no choice. Like a one-armed man, I made do. I pretended it wasn't there and just plowed on through life."

"You were hardly a one-armed man," he said softly.

She stared at him. "What is wrong with you? I thought you'd be happy for me."

"But I am happy for you."

She frowned and turned away. "If this is happy, then I would hate to see what you're sad is, much less you're angry."

He opened his mouth to speak, but realized he didn't have anything to say. He wasn't willing to promulgate the idea that a miracle had just happened despite what he saw with his eyes. Something was going on here and he needed to be clear of such ideas so that he might be aware of alternatives.

He returned to his usual seat.

Matias got a drink and held up the decanter for Amboy, but he shook his head. He needed to be conscious of what was going on. The last thing they needed was for him to be drunk and not knowing what's going on.

CHAPTER 37

She managed to change her clothes and clean herself in the bathroom. She sang all the while, a song they had talked about for what seemed like ages ago, her a capella voice repeating over and over the refrain, *Summertime, when the living is easy.*

Amboy's head began to muffle with the onset of a headache. He would have loved to have had some aspirin, but there was none to be had. So, he sat, eyes closed, listening to the sound of the airplane engines and Lettie's laughter. He remembered the song and the conversation they'd had when they'd first met about *Porgy & Bess.* Sportin' Life had been the drug dealer and a bad influence in her. Crown loved her, but Porgy did to. And then it was Porgy who'd killed Crown and in the end Bess had left with Sportin' Life—something she never should have done. He'd always wondered why she hadn't waited for Porgy to get out of jail and he kept wondering until they finally began to descend.

When they got below the clouds, the view was still dark, with only the occasional light in a sea of blackness. He wondered how the pilot could see his way, but then realized it was probably by instrumentation.

He glanced over at Paz who was awake and staring into space. He looked like a man waiting for an interview. All of his confidence had washed away and instead, he seemed as if he might break down at any moment. Amboy had always been concerned when someone who'd been a rock suddenly showed their cracks. What was going on in the man's mind, he didn't know. A large part of him was afraid to know.

Paz noticed him staring and raised his eyebrows.

"Our destination?" Amboy asked.

"Isla de los Estados."

"Seriously?" Amboy couldn't help but think of the King Kong movie he'd seen. An Island at the End of the World, just like this one. "Is that really what it's called?"

Paz nodded.

Amboy could feel the cold radiating through the walls of the plane despite the internal heaters. "How far south are we?"

"The island is the last land mass before we hit Antarctica," Paz said. "We don't want to go farther. Only penguins and ghosts live there."

"Ghosts?" Amboy grinned. "Seriously?"

"Don't laugh at what you don't understand. The ghosts of Antarctica are especially hungry. For every hundred people who make landfall, one goes missing never to be seen again. The Fuegians talk about the Ghosts who Walk and say it is they who feed so eagerly on visitors."

Amboy found himself shuddering despite himself. He suddenly wished he was back in Buenos Aires drinking a warm beer and arguing politics—the Argentine favorite pastime. Of course, he would have been a target because of how poorly Argentina was doing in the war for Las Malvinas. Still, it would have been away from all of the theatrics that Paz seemed to appreciate, the thuggery Matias couldn't help but emulate, and the helplessness that Lettie owned . . . He corrected himself: Used to own. It appeared as if she was permanently healed—at least on the outside.

He remembered that first black girl he'd seen at the Chattanooga Lookouts game who had flipped him off and her attitude, then remembered how Lettie's had been the same, unwilling to give him slack unless he earned it, her chin up and ready to take whatever right hook the world was about to give her. And now that she had been apparently miraculously healed, her entire demeanor was different. It was as if she were afraid to lose what she had, so she played more the role of someone who accepted what came to her, rather than expecting what she deserved in life.

Despite all of that, he still felt a surge of love for her every time he looked at her. Even now, he wanted to help her, to do anything in his power to protect her. It was a feeling he didn't know he had. Was it her superpower? Was it some sort of energy she broadcast that only he could tune into?

"Prepare for landing," said the pilot. "It's not going to be a soft one either. There's a storm brewing and the waves are high."

The sounds of the engines revving sent Amboy grabbing his straps and belting him in place. The plane rocked and bucked with the wind. He closed his eyes, remembering C130s over Hue Province in Vietnam right before they jumped out. They had the same bucking, the difference being the flak and *ack* sent skyward by the NVA. Black clouds exploding nearby, some even managing to annihilate a jumper with a lucky shot.

He closed his eyes and felt the pilot fighting the wind, the airframe shuddered, even as they skewed sideways at one point. A light skewered the side of the boat for a moment, then moved off. Then they hit. Everyone slammed forward to the limits of their belts, then back against the head rests.

Glasses that hadn't been secured crashed and broke.

A decanter of wine shattered along the side of the plane.

Then they were airborne.

Then crashed back.

Then free of the waves.

Then finally the plane settled and the pilot revved the engines.

"Lighthouse out the port side," the pilot said.

Amboy didn't need to unstrap to see a lighthouse resting on a small rocky island in the bay of the island. White with a red swirl, it seemed classic and still spun as the only light in the darkness at the end of the world.

"Jules Verne wrote a story about it called *The Lighthouse at the End of the World*. If we're lucky, we'll see the *Nautilus* as well," the pilot concluded, referencing the submarine from *20,000 Leagues Under the Sea*.

Amboy remembered the movie where Kirk Douglas was captured by Captain Nemo and a fight with an immense octopus. It was so strange the way memories were triggered from the most common things. To even consider the Ragman's Son in such a place was like imagining himself standing amidst a crew of men in a ship and shouting "I am Amboy," as if he were Spartacus remade.

Even now, Tim Whitmire and Billy Picket, both of them captured for a time when they were kids, loomed large in his memory. They'd died in the mining accident, but between when they'd been grabbed and taken to the cave with the other children and that moment, they'd lived full lives. Of course, they never had talked about what had happened. The creature and the grunts and the violence, pushed down and away as a memory to be forgotten than one to be relived over and over.

He shook his head to clear it. He needed his wits about him. Whatever was going on, he needed to be sure that he was going to be able to protect Lettie and himself when the time came.

The pilot motored the boat around the small island and through several splits of land until it was rumbling in the center of the bay. He pulled to a dock and then let the engines die. Once they'd completely stopped, the silence was unnerving, only interrupted by the ticking of the engine as the heat dissipated and it cooled quickly in the sub-arctic climate.

Paz went with the pilot and they both opened the outside door.

The pilot said, "There was a British warship in the west, so we had to arc around to avoid it. We're not as close to our destination as I would have hoped."

"How far are we away?" Amboy asked.

"Roughly twenty kilometers. On the other side of the mountain."

"I suppose there's massive jungle in the way as well," Matias said.

The pilot shrugged. What did he care? He wasn't going anywhere. "I suspect," he said.

A light shone from outside and Amboy went to a window to see an ancient man, his face with more lines than the center of a hundred-year-old tree, holding up a gas lantern. He and Paz conversed for a moment, then the priest leaned back in.

"The abuela says that another plane landed near the other side of the island. We need to be careful. If it's the Germans, no telling what they might do."

Matias pulled out his pistol and checked the ammunition, then replaced it.

Amboy wished he still had the pistol that the driver had taken from him. He was weaponless. He searched around and all he could find was a small paring knife at the bar used to cut lemons and limes. No pre-made cocktails for Senator

Thompson. He wanted only the best at his disposal. He stuffed the knife into his pocket.

Soon, they'd all gathered their meager belongings and were headed out the door.

The cold hit him first and the dampness second. It was like walking into a wet washcloth. He grabbed Lettie's hand which she eagerly offered. The night beyond the plane was as dark as one could imagine. With the cloud cover and the mist, not a single pinpoint of light was able to break through.

The sound of the surf was mixed with something foreign, like the cries of children far away. Playing games, running back and forth. Cheering. Such an odd sound for such a remote place. The cries came more frequent the further from the plane they walked, the sounds almost becoming a cacophony of fear as the calls piled upon more cries.

"What the hell is that?" Matias asked.

"Seals and cormorants fighting for food. They are all over the place. There's also several families of Magellanic penguins, but those are usually on the southern side of the island."

"They sound like children screaming," Lettie said.

"They act like children," Paz said. "But don't worry about it. There are no predators on this island unless you count yourselves. We are the apex predators of this particular biome."

The old man who'd met them at the plane moved more quickly than Amboy would have guessed. He couldn't really see the terrain, but by the darker silhouette above them, he could tell there was a large mountain in their way. Amboy was less than gratified to know that he was right when they began climbing up a series of switchbacks. The going was tough at first and got worse quickly.

They were all sucking air, much like one of the first ruck marches he had when he was in basic training at Fort Jackson,

South Carolina. They'd meant to complete a simple fifteen-mile ruck march for graduation, but the brand new fresh-off-the-bus and newly-minted lieutenant couldn't read a map so they ended up going twenty-six miles. That was the first time he had sheets of skin slough off his feet. The worst thing about it was the lieutenant got to go home and have a few beers and enjoy a warm shower, where the rest of them had to eat leftover dinner because they'd missed it, and clean weapons until almost midnight. Amboy never really minded the military when it came to war, but he always wondered why they chose the worst people to teach them.

They walked for an hour before they had to stop.

Matias cursed at his shoes which were nothing more than Florsheim knockoffs and certainly not made for the trail. His feet had to be bleeding. If he was smart, he'd leave his shoes on. Once he took them off, his feet would swell and he'd never get them on again.

Paz was almost in as bad a shape, but the shoes he wore as a priest were rubber soled and made to stand on for long hours.

Lettie had on her Chuck Connors which wasn't a big deal.

Amboy wore leather brogans, which were better than the wingtips worn by Matias, but only by a margin. His feet hurt and he knew that he'd pay for it. He already felt the soft pockets of pus from blisters that had formed beneath his socks and he wasn't about to touch them.

What really mystified him was the lack of bugs. With the forest and the ocean and all of the other fresh water running from beneath the mountain, he expected much more insect activity than there was. Whether it was the cold or the climate in general, there were few if any flying insects to worry about.

The trees were stunted and wind-twisted. He didn't recognize their variety, but by the bristly nature of their leaves they had to be some sort of pine. Equally mysterious was that every other tree had been denuded of foliage and stood as a skeletal version of the ones to the left and right. He could only wonder at how powerful the winds had to be to sculpt such a forest. Even as they walked, the trees took on the appearances of people, slumped, burdened, and stunted from the ever-present winds.

They ended up stopping one more time before they reached their destination.

They could hear it first, a chanting from somewhere up ahead, the sounds of human voices insinuating itself beneath the constant thrum of moving air. Then they saw the light, an entire area before them lit, but hidden from view from the ocean. They had to walk down to what turned out to be a small bowl of a valley carved into the side of the mountain. When they broke from the trees, the cauldron was revealed in its full measure, the green and rocky soil running true to the mountain and the bleak and uninviting entrance to a cave. The same trees that had watched them along the way, circled the area.

Paz bent over at the waist, breathed deeply, then straightened.

He gestured and maintained a passable smile. "Welcome to the new home of the Council of the Cave."

CHAPTER 38

Wherever the chanting came from, it stopped when they entered the clearing. With only the far away sounds of the seal mating and the even lower rumble of the surf, Amboy felt as if he were on the precipice of something important. Like the susurration of a crowd before the main event took the floor, a batter about to be pitched to, even nature seemed to be on hold as humanity gathered itself for them to appear and do whatever it was they'd been planning.

Stunted trees surrounded the clearing, each one twisted and gray, leaving the center smooth and void of even the smallest rocks. The wind whistled through their leaves. Moonlight warped between the branches making the trees seem alive as they moved back and forth. But then as they approached the clearing, some of the trees did come alive. They were never trees but people dressed in cloaks the color of a full moon.

First one.

Then another.

Then a dozen, stepped forward, leaving trees behind them to guard their backs.

A single woman lifted her head and stepped forward, speaking in a broken and cracked old Argentine dialect. "Welcome, my child," she said to Lettie. She grabbed her hands and held them between her own.

Lettie glanced back.

Amboy was to her left.

Paz was to her right.

Matias brought up the rear.

The guide who had led them up the mountain was gone.

"We have been waiting for you," the woman added.

Amboy clenched and unclenched his fists as the others closed in on them. He made a decision and moved to stand beside Lettie. The woman, he saw, was a leper, pieces of her face bandaged and missing. Her hands missing half of their fingers.

It was that moment that Lettie noticed the same thing and she tried to pull her hand away. It took two attempts, but she managed it and then looped her arm through Amboy's.

"Who are you?" he asked.

"I am a Unicorn Mother," she said. "We ensure the unicorn lives in peace."

Amboy wished he had a pistol. The woman was giving him the creeps. "Who are these others?" he asked.

"They are also Mothers of the Unicorn. Our lives are dedicated to its survival."

Amboy glanced around the clearing and then into the deep maw of the cave. "Where is the unicorn?"

A roar came from the jungle, almost with enough force to shake the trees. It sounded more like King Kong than anything else. Whatever it was, it was gigantic.

"What the hell was that?" Matias asked, pulling free his pistol. He looked anachronistic standing in the middle of a primordial jungle in a suit and Florsheims with a revolver in his hands. Like a gangster on the far side of the moon, he just wasn't right.

"That," Father Paz said, "was the unicorn."

He approached the women and held out his arms. As they passed, they leaned forward and kissed his hands, fawning and supplicating themselves before him. Soon, he was surrounded by all of them, each one eager to touch him, his face full with a beatific smile.

Amboy narrowed his brows. What the hell was happening? He glanced at Lettie who seemed to be thinking the same.

The roar from the jungle came again, loud enough to make them wince.

"Paz, what's going on?" Amboy said, trying to get ahead of a situation he felt that he was already behind. He stepped forward, but was immediately grabbed by four of the women in cloaks. They weren't about to let him near the older man.

"Enough already, Paz. Tell them to let me alone."

Paz shook his head. "That's not how it's going to be, my friend. I'm afraid things have sorted themselves out the way they needed to."

"'Sorted themselves out'? What is it you mean?" Amboy asked.

"He means that you've been suckered up here for his own reasons," Matias said, slipping to the edge of the jungle. "You really have no idea what he has planned, do you?"

"Planned? Are you in on it?" Amboy asked.

"I cover my bases," Matias said. "Yes. I've been working for Paz since the very first day. We had to get you with Ms. Fennick, after all."

Amboy shook free of the leper women and glanced around the space. It appeared as if there were people inside the cave now, backlit by an orange glow. Did he have any idea what was planned? Hell, no. But he did know that whatever he was going to do was going to include Lettie.

Matias edged closer to the jungle and away from the women. "But then your friend Otiel approached me with another offer."

Paz looked concerned and pushed one of the women away. "Matias, what are you doing?"

"What should have been done years ago. Now, where is the unicorn?" he asked.

As if on cue, another great roar came forth, this one closer than the rest.

"You don't have long to wait," Paz said.

Suddenly, four men stepped from the foliage near where Matias had been standing. Three were young and fit and carried submachine guns. The fourth was taller and older and held a shotgun in his right hand.

"Hello, Boy. How's it going?" he asked in a voice Amboy would have known if a thousand years had passed.

The man used Amboy's nickname, something only a few on the planet knew. One could have struck Amboy with a bat and he wouldn't have been more surprised to see his old friend from Vietnam. "Otiel? My god. What are you doing here?"

"Long time, no see," said the German-American friend of his and co-survivor of many jungle battles.

"Long time, no shit," Amboy said, closing his mouth that had fallen open. Why was he feeling like this was about to be an episode of *This Is Your Life*—that show from the 1950s that had regular people on it with people from their past to surprise them about a particular thing that was about to happen. One, he didn't need anything like that and two, whatever catharsis he might be enjoying was rattled by the constant roaring of the unicorn crashing through the dark primeval forest on the Island at the End of the World.

"What the hell are you doing here, Otiel?"

"Checking on you," he said.

"I met your nephews. Seems to be a nice fellow."

"They take after their mother. Their father's an asshole."

"I take it then the mother is your sister?"

"No. My brother is the father. That's why I know he's an asshole."

"I don't understand how you are involved in this, Otiel."

His friend gave everyone in the grotto a stern look, then handed over his shotgun to one of the men near him. They were all dressed like hunters, complete with vests that probably contained extra ammunition. They also wore Australian outback hats, one side up and the other side down.

"I've been involved since the beginning," Otiel said, walking over to Father Paz. "Weapon please."

"You don't want to be doing this," Paz said.

Several women hissed beside him, claws out.

Otiel ignored him and said, "Matias. Take care of it."

Matias nodded and slid over to a surprised Father Paz, slipped a hand into his jacket, and came away with the pistol.

"Give it to Boy, over there."

Matias glanced left, then right, then passed the gun to Amboy.

He felt better having the weight of a weapon in his hands, even though he wasn't sure what he was going to do with it. "Why are you here?" he asked his old friend once more.

"To conclude something we started years ago."

"What's that mean?"

"It wasn't by accident that we became friends in Vietnam."

Amboy stared but couldn't comprehend the statement.

Otiel continued. "I was assigned to be with you to make sure you survived. Through all three years, I was with you and

ARVN to ensure you left Vietnam on two feet instead of in a body bag."

"You were assigned to me?" Amboy turned to look at Lettie and then Paz, then back. "What does that mean, 'you were assigned'?"

"I was given a picture, your name, and an assignment. The council had a destiny already set in place for you. Let me tell you," he grinned self-consciously, "when I first met you, I didn't like you."

"I was young. I didn't know much."

Otiel nodded.

"I certainly wasn't a man of the world," Amboy added. "All I knew as on that mountain and I couldn't wait to get away from it."

"Which was the problem. You never were supposed to leave," Otiel said.

"Well, I supposed I'm just one long continual disappointment."

"You were destined for this moment," Otiel said. "You had a mission to fulfill. Father Paz here was around to make sure you fulfilled your mission."

"What mission? Paz and I just met a few weeks ago." He shook his head and tried to make sense of what the other man was thinking. "I don't understand any of this."

Otiel nodded. "That was as it was planned. Tell me, how are your arms feeling? Do they hurt? Do they suddenly ache where they were broken when you were a child?"

Amboy rubbed them. "How did you know?"

"You told me about when you were taken as a child back in 'Nam. Then again, I already knew about it. Like I said, you were destined to be here at this moment. When you decided to join the Army, it changed things. No one from the mountain ever joined the Army. It predicated us going into action to protect you. They almost stopped you from going to Vietnam, but you were too slick. Before they knew it, you were in basic training and by then to do anything would have brought too much attention to the mountain."

Amboy grabbed the side of his head where it pulsed madly using the hand with which he held the pistol. He noted how cool the metal felt there and left it for a moment. "You were paid to be my friend?"

"No one paid anyone. I was part of the council. My family has been part of the council for longer than America has been a country. But then you had to go and be an asshole."

"I've been called worse."

Otiel put a hand on Amboy's shoulder. "Not that kind of asshole, my friend. The good kind. You went and saved my life, not once, but twice."

"That's what friends do."

"Evidently." Otiel gave a heavy sigh. "So I had a change of heart. I didn't want to see you hurt the way they wanted to do it. You needed to have the freedom to choose. You'd earned the right."

Amboy felt as if all he was doing was asking questions. He'd lost complete control over reality.

The roar came again, this time almost upon them.

The moon shone full.

From far below came the sounds of seals mating and the dull roar of the surf.

The smell had been lush, but now it was rank from his own fear.

The twisted forms of wood seemed to make their own moving shadows

"Back away, Mr. Stanislas," Paz said.

All eyes turned to the priest He stood amidst a dozen cloaked women, all of whom were staring at Otiel.

"I can see what you are thinking," Paz said, gathering himself once more, suddenly assured and less in fear. "There are twelve of them and one of you, but your friends have machine guns. Can they shoot the women before they can attack? Or, once near you, will they even be able to fire without fear of hitting you?"

"What you are doing to Amboy isn't right," Otiel said.

Paz shrugged. "He's already chosen his destiny. He wants to help Ms. Fennick. He's already pledged his life to her."

"That he might have done, but he didn't know what that meant," Otiel said.

"The fact that he hasn't been paying attention all of this time is on him."

"Wait! Paying attention?" Amboy asked. "What the fuck are you talking about, Paz?"

"The clues have been present all along what you were to become. It's even written in the book she's carrying," he said, pointing at Lettie.

Amboy turned to Lettie. "What am I becoming?"

"What you have always been."

"And what's that? Your stooge?"

Lettie stepped forward and seemed to be of a mind more firm than he'd ever seen her. "No," she said. "You're to be my protector."

Otiel fished a well-worn copy of *Patagonia* from the pocket of his hunting vest. "Turn to page 109 and read."

Amboy caught the book in mid-air and turned to the page. He began to read.

"Out loud, please," Otiel said.

Amboy gave him a look, then shook his head as he began to read. But the more he read, the more he felt a pit inside of him growing and it grew so large, he was afraid he might fall into it and never be seen again.

"Out loud, please," Otiel repeated.

"When the Sect needs a new Invunche, the Council of the Cave orders a Member to steal a boy child from six months to a year old, if possible. The Deformer, a permanent resident of the Cave, starts work at once. He disjoints the arms and legs and the hands and feet. Then begins the delicate task of altering the position of the head. Day after day, and for hours at a stretch, he twists the head with a tourniquet until it has rotated through an angle of 180 degrees until the child can look straight down the line of its own vertebrae. There remains one last operation, for which another specialist is needed. At full moon, the child is laid on a work-bench, lashed down with its head covered in a bag. The specialist cuts a deep incision under the right shoulder blade. Into the hole he inserts the right arm and sews up the wound with thread taken from the neck of an ewe. When it has healed the Invunche is complete."

"And this invunche?" Amboy asked, his voice barely a whisper.

"Is you," Otiel said. "It always has been. Think of it as destiny postponed."

Paz growled. "Or destiny realized."

CHAPTER 39

For the first time the world was completely silent. Not even the seals could be heard, nor the surf. But perhaps that was because of his beating heart. Surely there was sound, but his own internal strife drowned it out. *Invunche*. The word was both alien and familiar. But how could that be? Was that who he was? He remembered Father Rivas now back at the chapel. He'd been afraid that he was part of someone else's story. He'd been so right. This hadn't been about the free will of anyone, but about his own story played to a tragic end.

"Do you remember when you were taken as a child?" Otiel asked. "You told me about it. Your arms were broken. You were taken into a cave."

Amboy nodded numbly. "I remember."

"You were one of three chosen. Tim Whitmire, Billy Picket and you."

To hear his friends' names mentioned made his head spin.

"Billy was killed in the mine. You thought Tim was killed, but he wasn't. He was broken, but okay. He was saved and it was he who became the invunche."

"Tim? The invunche?"

"He's been the invunche since 1967." He pointed to the cave. "He's in there right now, but he's dying. They need a replacement. They also need another voladora. With her comes change and with the change comes a new invunche."

Amboy turned to Lettie. She appeared to be in a trance. Her body was vibrating and her eyes had rolled back into her head.

"What's a voladora?"

"An emissary from the land of the unicorn to the land of the living. Only the voladora can touch the unicorn and survive. All others who touch it perish. She speaks for it. She expresses its needs to the world."

"What if I don't want to be this invunche? What if I don't want Lettie to be the voladora?"

"Then you don't have to be. It's what I've been trying to tell you. Enough is enough. We're going to save you. We've been watching you since you arrived in Argentina." Otiel waved his hand at everything and everyone. "All of this is nonsense. It's something for long ago that doesn't need done anymore. Once I was assigned to watch you. For a time, I thought that was a noble cause. No more. Now, the most noble of causes is to allow you your own destiny."

Amboy thought of tall the Germans he'd encountered—those classified as Ahnenerbe by Paz. From those in Thiago's apartment, to Shultz, to those in the various town cars, they'd been trying to help them all along. He wondered if he'd be in this predicament if he had just stopped to ask a few simple questions.

"Then Schultz? He was with you?"

"Who?"

"A fat German assigned to my apartments. I thought he might have been watching me."

"Herr Himmell. Yes. He was one of ours."

Amboy turned to Matias. "But you shot him?"

Otiel narrowed his eyes. "Who shot him?"

Matias held up his hands as he grinned warily at Otiel. "It had to be done." Then he turned to Amboy. "You needed freedom of movement so we could get you outside the city and involved. This Himmell was wasting all of our time."

"Himmell was my uncle," Otiel said. "Just as the diviners were ours."

Matias shrugged. "Sorry, about that."

"Just as I am," Otiel said, pulling a pistol from a holster at his waist, and pressing it against the side of Matias's face.

Matias seemed about to say something, then Otiel pulled the trigger.

Matias fell to the ground dead.

The sound of the shot echoed in the grotto.

Amboy leaped back to protect Lettie at the suddenness of the violence.

Several men came running out of the cave, each wearing a black uniform and carrying a submachine gun.

Otiel's men leveled their weapons at the newcomers and it seemed as if everyone had drawn down on everyone else. Men screamed for other men to lay down their weapons and then they screamed some more. Someone opened fire and then they all did.

Amboy grabbed Lettie and threw her to the ground, covering her with his body, shielding his own head with his arm.

Both sides exchanged fire for five seconds, but in those five seconds hundreds of rounds traded places, many missing their marks, but enough finding them so that when everything was once again quiet, the ground was covered with bodies and weeping pools of blood.

Amboy creeped to his feet and inventoried the dead.

Matias was already dead.

Two of Otiel's men were dead as well as Otiel.

Six of the women were dead.

Four other men dressed in black were dead.

In the space of five seconds, sixteen people had lost their lives.

And all for what?

The brush parted and a great beast entered the circle, stepping on the bodies, unconcerned.

Amboy recognized it from the picture. It was the size of a large elephant, but with an elongated snout and an immense single horn. It smelled of the earth and something else—a memory from his childhood—sassafras. It could have been a dinosaur, but someone had carved the horn and sharpened it into a deadly spike. A saddle rested on its back, empty, waiting to be filled.

Paz pushed aside the body of one of the women and staggered to his feet. He'd been shot in the shoulder and his face was a guise of pain.

Nolan of all people stood at the entrance to the cave.

He beckoned for Amboy and Lettie to join him.

After helping her to her feet, he asked if she was okay. She nodded quietly, then hand in hand, they both picked their way over the bodies and over to Nolan.

The man wore a Saville Row suit, but his necktie had been loosened as well as his top button. "Looks like things got a little out of hand." He looked them up and down. "We hadn't planned on Mr. Stanislas."

"He was my friend," Amboy said, unwilling to look at the dead.

"You have a lot of friends."

"But few like him," Amboy said.

"You weren't hit, were you?" asked Nolan

Amboy gripped Lettie's hand tighter. "No. We're fine." Then he laughed at the idea of the word.

"Come inside, you have people to meet."

They followed him into the cave and instead of it being rough rock and dirt, someone had installed floors and walls and it looked more like a large room in a home with a few rock accents. Light came from torches on the walls and from hanging sconces. The smell from the torches was of animal fat and noxious.

A little girl ran to him. Meagan. Senator Thompson's daughter, and beside her was the Japanese girl. So young. So filled with energy.

"I remember you," she said, grinning.

"I remember you, as well," he said, holding out a hand. They shook. "Who is your friend?"

"This is Yuki. She doesn't like to talk much."

Amboy bowed to the young Japanese girl which caused her eyes to widen and her hand to rise and cover a smile on her face.

He glanced around. He also saw the Senator sitting and speaking animatedly with the Japanese couple. When the politician from Texas saw Amboy looking, he gave a slight nod of acknowledgement, then dismissed him. Amboy also saw several figures towards the back whom he thought he recognized. Then he realized he did, but only after doing a double take. How they could be here was beyond anything his imagination could supply. They were from the mountain. They were family. One was an uncle and the other was an aunt who had raised him. They'd brought several of his older cousins with them.

"I hate to keep asking this question . . ." Amboy began.

"Then let me ask it for you," Nolan said. "What's going on, right?"

Amboy nodded.

"The ceremony is about to begin and we don't have much

time, but let's just say that we've had a Council of the Cave since the first mention of the Caverns of Socrates and Plato when he developed his cave allegory. There have been those in higher authorities who have shown interest in the idea. You can see why the US Government and the Vatican might want to understand the inner workings of the council. Sadly, they won't let us be a part of it, but we can be observers." He grinned. "Influencers."

"Who are the members?" Amboy asked.

Nolan laughed hoarsely. "No-shit-real-life sorcerers. You should see what they can do."

Amboy took a moment, his gaze continually drifting back to his relatives from the mountain. How they'd arrived at a place called the Island at the End of the World was one thing. How they were involved with such an old conspiracy was another. Part of him begged to run to them to have them tell him their story. But in the end, he knew it didn't matter. Nothing mattered. He finally understood who he was—who he had been the entire time. He was as tired of running from his destiny as Crown was running from his.

"Do you have any questions before we start?" Nolan asked.

"They say I am to be the new invunche."

"How do you feel about that?" He snapped his fingers. "The pain is what makes you balk. Isn't that right."

"Well, yes. Of course."

Nolan shook his head and his perfect private school curls barely moved. "I'd feel the same way. I'm not much for pain. A hangnail can bring me down. But I understand that once you commit, that the pain goes away."

"As in it doesn't hurt?"

"That's what they say."

"Who is they?"

"The council of course. The sorcerers."

"And Lettie is to be this Voladora?"

"She's been groomed since birth to be so. Her job is even harder than yours. Yours is to protect her. Hers is to protect the secret. She must coexist with the unicorn. Did you know that the unicorn is called *camahueto* in Mapodungun? That translates to 'very bad.' And to think that all the special little girls around the world wear pink and play with glitter and love unicorns. If they only knew."

"The picture of the red unicorn," Amboy remembered. "At the house. During the party."

"Camahueto," Nolan said.

"Very bad," Amboy translated.

Chanting began from somewhere deep in the cave.

Nolan handed him a cup and said, "Drink this."

"What is it?"

"Just drink. You want to feel all the pain? Fine, don't drink."

He left Amboy with the glass.

A line of crimson robed figures entered the chamber one after the other, eyes downcast, faces hidden by hoods. Their words were melodious but rough and in a language he couldn't figure. They circled several times, then each brought out a dagger made from stone. They went to the unicorn and made slashes along a flank, gathering fluid along the edge of their weapons. Then each approached Amboy and let drops from their blades add to the concoction in his glass. When the last of them turned and left, he sighed, glancing at the glass, knowing that it was more than any subtle Lewis Carroll *drink me* bottle.

This was something serious.

This was something *forever.*

He turned to Lettie and allowed a waterfall of love to drench him.

He returned his gaze to the glass, then downed it, setting it on a table beside him.

Whatever was in the noxious concoction hit him like a

thousand tons of stone. But this time, instead of inside a mine, he was inside a cave at the end of the word. He staggered and when he opened his eyes again, he felt immensely drained. His eyes struggled to remain open and he found that he had to be held upright by two of the women who had greeted Paz before.

What happened next came in bits and spurts.

The sorcerers came and chanted.

The unicorn roared.

The two girls presented themselves and kneeled.

Their parents looked immensely happy, hands clasped to their chests, faces like cherubs from a biblical painting.

One by one the unicorn bowed its head to the girls.

And one by one it slid the sharp point of its horn through a girl's chest.

First Yuki.

Then Meagan.

No screams.

Just the silence as their blood rolled down the white horn and onto the beast's head until it flicked its head and tossed the dead meat bags to a wall across the chamber. Now it was red, colored from the blood, its tongue licking at the warm heart blood that dripped from his snout.

Then Lettie staggered to the unicorn as if in a trance. She touched it and allowed the blood to coat her skin, then held a red six-fingered hand covered with blood up for everyone to see. A hush fell over those assembled. She turned back to the unicorn and it looked into her eyes. It snorted once, then twice. It pawed at the ground.

Amboy made to rush to her, but found himself held back by an invisible force.

The unicorn stared at him and in that moment it spoke a library of direction. Then it returned its gaze to its voladora. The horn came down fast, but didn't pierce anything, instead stopping mere inches from slamming through her face. Moments passed, the unicorn snorting and her holding up her six-fingered bloody hand. Then the unicorn knelt and Lettie used the knee to climb aboard the great beast, sitting behind the head, her hair a flaming red, her face free of both Alabama and Florida, now containing the joy of everything in the universe.

It was in that moment that Amboy realized that it wasn't the beast. It never had been the beast. Lettie was the Red Unicorn—as rare a sight as one might ever see. She was one of a kind and he would spend his last days protecting her. His heart welled over and he choked back a sob.

The sorcerers took the blood of the girls and mixed it into a vessel which they then took to the parents.

Amboy watched them drink, not caring, not worrying, his only thoughts for Lettie and the unicorn.

When the deformer came for him, he was ready.

As tall as two men, it was a true Patagonian giant and it plucked him from the ground like a child, palming his head in a great hand. Amboy looked into its eyes and knew a creature made for task. This giant had been around for an eternity and its grasp on humanity could be read in the folds beneath its eyes.

The people from the mountain applauded quietly, satisfaction on their faces, a life's mission complete.

And Amboy became something whose love was unconstricting and whose desire to please was never ending, he with his unicorn, and her with her invunche, together, forever, the perfect pairing of black and white, of red and blonde, of male and female, of man and woman—two souls united in a singular arcane bond on a creature whose capacity was to ensure a never-ending life for those who would sacrifice what is most important to them.

EPILOGUE

He who was once human is constantly intrigued about how much pain and love are so much part of the same emotion, the nerve endings firing the same synapses to the brain regardless for whether it is love or pain. Love stories are supposed to end with two people, hand in hand, walking into the sunset, but they also end with deformation, death, and the riding of a Paleolithic unicorn. He vaguely remembers all of the books and movies he'd once known.

Holding hands was what people did.

Kissing was a luxury.

This can't really be a love story then . . . or can it?

Maybe this is a pain story after all. Maybe it's a shared misery that keeps them together, but he feels no misery. When he looks at her his heart leaps. His body vibrates. His stomach empties and it soars with pterodactyls.

Perhaps that's all there is.

Perhaps that's all there was ever was.

Sometimes he believes he was born fully clothed just like he is now. No childhood. No teenagerhood. Just invunche. Now.

A changeling dropped off so his real body with the real memories could be transported to another realm while this one was left behind like an empty placeholder.

The committee and the sorcerers are his masters now. They took him to the *challanco*, a crystal stone where they were able to survey the smallest detail of his life. He was judged and found unwanting, his life of service and attempts to provide hope and friendship the ingredients required for a servant of the red unicorn.

Only men are members of the committee. From the deformer to the invunche to the sorcerers, all are male. The singular female is the only one capable of controlling the unicorn, ever living and never dying. Bruce Chatwin said that no one could recollect the time when the committee did not exist. He further said, some have suggested that the committee was in embryo even before the emergence of man. It is equally plausible, he said, that Man became Man through the fierce opposition to the committee. Chatwin's final words in the chapter from *In Patagonia* are "We know for a fact that the challanco is the Evil Eye. Perhaps the term for the committee is a synonym for Beast."

Whatever the root . . . whatever the source . . . whatever the ultimate price . . . to be invunche is to be love incarnate.

That his bones had been broken before made it so much easier for him to become what he was destined to become.

His head is now twisted so he looks back upon his spine.

No one dare come up behind him.

His arms have been broken and his right arm has been inserted to that it comes through his back.

He is a pushme-pullyou of man, a homunculus of love, a hunchback from another age.

More importantly, he is Amboy Stevens, lover of Lettie Fennick, two people who were once people before fate and a magic older than the continents changed them into something even closer; twenty-four fingers interlocked across mythology and time in a cave in the Island at the End of the World guarding a beast little girls had no idea would happily dance on their ambitions and skewer their eager little hearts if given even half a chance.

He sighs.

He loves.

He is invunche.

And she . . .

She is his red unicorn.

ABOUT THE AUTHOR

The American Library Association calls Weston Ochse "one of the major horror authors of the 21st Century." His work has won the Bram Stoker Award, been nominated for the Pushcart Prize, won four New Mexico-Arizona Book Awards, and been a *USA Today* Bestseller. His military supernatural series SEAL Team 666 has been optioned to be a movie starring Dwayne Johnson. Currently in print are his novels *Bone Chase* and *A Hole in the World*. His shorter work has appeared in DC Comics, IDW Comics, *Soldier of Fortune Magazine*, and *Weird Tales*. His franchise work includes *The X-Files*, *Predator*, *Aliens*, *Hellboy*, *Clive Barker's Midian*, and *V-Wars*. Weston holds a Master of Fine Arts in Creative Writing and teaches at Southern New Hampshire University. Weston is also a veteran of the US military, serving thirty-five years in the Army, special operations, and various agencies.

NOTE ABOUT BRUCE CHATWIN

It's not often an author creates such a travelogue of a region of the world that not only inspires one to travel the land but the imaginary lands of the mind. Chatwin did with *In Patagonia*. Ever since I read it, the idea of the sorcerers and the unicorn was incredible and I needed to figure out a way to tell a tale about it. Little did I know it was going to be the love story between two extraordinary people who came to life beneath my aching fingers. I spent a lot of time finding alternate sources of information. The only section I used verbatim was that about the invunche and I appreciate the agent of Bruce Chatwin's estate for granting permission to use it. Everything else is from my mind and as crazy as it sounds, my heart, because even at the end of the world as a broken and distorted version of a man, I hope Amboy is happy with his red unicorn.